NEW YORK REVIEW BOOKS
CLASSICS

W9-ATJ-677

THE RIM OF MORNING

WILLIAM SLOANE (1906–1974) was born in Plymouth, Massachusetts. After graduating from Princeton University in 1929 he enjoyed modest success writing supernatural and fantasy dramas. By the end of the 1930s he had published his only two novels, *To Walk the Night* (1937) and *The Edge of Running Water* (1939). During the 1950s he edited two science-fiction anthologies, *Space, Space, Space: Stories About the Time When Men Will Be Adventuring to the Stars* (1953) and *Stories for Tomorrow* (1954). Sloane taught at the Bread Loaf Writers' Conference for more than twenty-five years and was responsible for inviting many notable writers, including John Williams and John Ciardi, to join the faculty. In 1983 a collection of his Bread Loaf lectures was published as *The Craft of Writing*. For much of his career Sloane held numerous editorial positions, including a stint at his own publishing house, and from 1955 until his death he was the managing director of Rutgers University Press.

STEPHEN KING is the author of more than fifty novels, hundreds of stories, and several works of nonfiction, including *On Writing: A Memoir of the Craft*. Among his most recent books are *The Bazaar of Bad Dreams*, a collection of stories and novellas, and *Finders Keepers*, the second book in a trilogy of novels featuring retired homicide detective Bill Hodges. Much of his fiction has been adapted for film and television, including *Carrie*, based on his first published novel, *Misery*, *Under the Dome*, and *The Shawshank Redemption*.

THE RIM OF MORNING

WILLIAM SLOANE

Introduction by
STEPHEN KING

NEW YORK REVIEW BOOKS

New York

THIS IS A NEW YORK REVIEW BOOK
PUBLISHED BY THE NEW YORK REVIEW OF BOOKS
435 Hudson Street, New York, NY 10014
www.nyrb.com

To Walk the Night and *The Edge of Running Water* were first published together as
The Rim of Morning in 1964.

Library of Congress Cataloging-in-Publication Data
Sloane, William, 1906–1974.
[Novels. Selections]
The rim of morning : two tales of cosmic horror / William Sloane ; introduction by
Stephen King.
    pages cm. — (New York Review Books classics)
ISBN 978-1-59017-906-2 (paperback)
I. King, Stephen, 1947– II. Sloane, William, 1906–1974. To walk the night. III.
Sloane, William, 1906–1974. Edge of running water. IV. Title.
PS3537.L59A6 2015
813'.54—dc23

                    2015014265

ISBN 978-1-59017-906-2
Available as an electronic book; ISBN 978-1-59017-907-9

Printed in the United States of America on acid-free paper.
10 9 8 7 6 5 4 3 2 1

CONTENTS

INTRODUCTION

[Author's note: Like most introductions, this one necessarily refers to events in the novels, these days commonly called "spoilers." Consequently, you may want to save these few words for last. I want to thank William Sloane's daughter, Julie Sloane, who provided valuable insight into her father's work.]

THE AUTHOR photograph of William Sloane on the back of the 1964 edition of *The Rim of Morning* shows a hawk-eyed gentleman with a pipe clamped in the corner of his mouth and an open book in his hands. He's in a library (perhaps his own); many more books line the shelves behind him. This seems fitting, because books were Sloane's life. He graduated from Princeton (class of 1929), worked for a number of publishing houses, directed the Council on Books during World War II (where books were pronounced "weapons in the war of ideas," which sounds suspiciously like propaganda to me), and went on to serve as managing director of the Rutgers University Press. He also formed his own well-respected publishing company, William Sloane Associates, and served on the faculty of the Bread Loaf Writers' Conference in Vermont. A busy and productive life of books and reading, you would say.

Yet there was more to William Sloane's love of books than editing and publishing. In the 1930s, he also wrote two remarkable novels, *To Walk the Night* (1937) and *The Edge of Running Water* (1939), composing mostly on weekends and during the evenings.* It's interesting to note that in 1937 he met Carl Jung at a luncheon and was amazed to discover that the great psychotherapist had read *To Walk the Night* (in its earlier form, as a play), and felt that the book's central conceit, of a "traveling mind," fit perfectly with his, Jung's, idea of the anima as a free-floating and quasi-supernatural archetype of the unconscious mind. On that same memorable occasion, Sloane met another idol whose ideas are reflected in his novels: J. B. Rhine, inventor of the famous Rhine ESP Cards and pioneer (at Duke University) in the study of extrasensory perception.

Although Sloane was clearly a science fiction fan and conversant with the field—he edited the anthologies *Stories for Tomorrow* and *Space, Space, Space*—neither of his novels are, strictly speaking, science fiction. They are good stories and can be read simply for pleasure, but what makes them fascinating and takes them to a higher level is their complete (and rather blithe) disregard of genre boundaries.

Both books certainly contain *elements* of science fiction. In *The Edge of Running Water*, Julian Blair is trying to get in touch with his dead wife via an electricity-powered machine he has created for just that purpose (although he has a spiritualist medium waiting in the wings, just in case). In *To Walk the Night*, Professor LeNormand and his student, poor damned Jerry Lister, are working on something called "A Fundamental Critique of the Einstein Space-Time Continuum," a study that leads to their deaths.

Both books contain elements of mystery. Much of *Edge* is concerned with just how Mrs. Marcy, the unlucky housekeeper, met her death ... and, of course, whodunit. Much of *To Walk* is a kind of "locked observatory" mystery: what caused LeNormand to burn to death ... and, of course, whodunit. We understand that neither mystery will have a strictly rational explanation, which adds a reso-

---

*Sloane's only other published work—so far as I can determine—was a short story called "Let Nothing You Dismay," which can be found in an anthology titled *Stories for Tomorrow*, which he edited.

nance to these stories that no Agatha Christie novel can match. *To Walk the Night* owes much more to Charles Fort (*The Book of the Damned, Wild Talents, Lo!*) than it does to the mystery or horror writers of the time.

Both books also contain elements of horror. Boy, do they. No one can read *The Edge of Running Water*, the more successful of the two, without a frisson of fear when that awful *blankness* appears in Blair's workshop—a blankness that threatens to suck in not just papers and furniture but perhaps the whole world. And no one can read the story of Luella Jamison's disappearance in *To Walk the Night* without a similar shiver.

Because they ignore genre conventions, Sloane's novels are actual works of literature. Perhaps not great literature; no argument will be made here on that score. If one wants great American literature from the 1930s, one must go to Hemingway, Faulkner, and Steinbeck. But if one compares these novels to what was then being published in SF magazines like *Thrilling Wonder Stories*, or so-called "shudder pulps" such as *Weird Tales*, what a difference in language, diction, theme, and ambition!

Sloane builds his stories in carefully wrought paragraphs, each one clear and direct. Here is a man of the old school, who learned actual grammar in grammar school (complete with the diagramming of sentences, one suspects), and probably Latin at the high school and college levels. It's been my experience that even bad storytellers with a solid grounding in Latin are unable to write bad prose, and Sloane had serious narrative chops to go along with his basic writing skills. The very first sentence of *Edge*—"The man for whom this story is told may or may not be alive"—is as good an opener as I've ever read in my life.

The curtain-raiser of *To Walk the Night* is more businesslike and less enticing, but the writing nonetheless sparkles with witty grace notes: "She led the talk around to the question of the winter styles with all the finesse of a children's photographer arranging a difficult grouping." That's a linkage Raymond Chandler might have made, although Chandler's version would probably have been a bit punchier. Sloane is also allusive in a pleasantly scholarly way that few pulp writers of the day could have matched. In *To Walk*, he writes, "Maybe the Italians can live happily on the slopes of Vesuvius, but I am not that sort of person." It's a nifty insight into the narrator's character, but one has to know what Vesuvius is (and what happened there) to really appreciate it.

Despite the trappings of science fiction (a mere flick of the authorial hand, really), and some of the conventions of the mystery novel (much interrogation of witnesses, and in *Edge*, a fair amount of hugger-mugger about footprints in the mud), I would argue that these are essentially horror novels. In *The Edge of Running Water*, Sloane's subject is nothing less than what may exist after death, an idea I have approached myself in three novels, and never without a sense of awe at the tremendous implications of the subject. In *To Walk the Night*, we discover that a disembodied brain—perhaps an alien from space, perhaps a human intelligence from another time-stream or dimension—has inhabited the body of a mentally retarded girl named Luella Jamison, transforming her vacuity into coldly classical beauty.*

In the hands of his horror contemporaries—H. P. Lovecraft, Clark Ashton Smith, August Derleth—such frightening concepts would have been rendered in thundering, florid prose, complete with words like *cyclopean* and phrases like *the hoary primordial grove*. I'm not knocking Lovecraft—there are plenty of reasons why his contemporaries imitated him—but Sloane is more reasonable in his approach, more rational, and this makes his work both accessible and ultimately more disturbing. Also, Sloane could write snappy dialogue, a talent very few contemporaneous horror writers seemed to possess. "Good God, Julian," *Edge* narrator Richard Sayles exclaims to his old friend at one point, "when you duplicate a seance, you duplicate it. This looks like a Black Mass in a futurist play."

One can't imagine Lovecraft ever writing such a line, especially

---

*No, "mentally retarded" is no longer considered politically correct, but Sloane, writing seventy-five years ago, was even more blunt, referring to Luella as an idiot.

during our first entry into Julian's laboratory, a locked room that drives our curiosity for the first three-quarters of the book. Lovecraft never would have considered highlighting horror with humor. For one thing, it didn't fit his classical concept of the genre; for another, he (like many horror writers then and now) seems to have *had* no sense of humor. Here, though, it works, and works brilliantly. Sloane's writing is drum-tight, but his approach is looser; he pulls the reader in and then begins turning up the heat. He understood that before a pot can boil, it must simmer.

The reissue of these two remarkable novels is long overdue. The general reader will find much here to enthrall and entertain; those who have studied the horror genre but don't know these books will find them a revelation for the way Sloane takes what he needs from multiple genres, an ability only well-read novelists possess, and makes something new and remarkable from them. Put simply, the sum is far greater than the parts. I can think of no other novels exactly like these two, either in style or substance. My only regret is that William Sloane did not continue. Had he done so, he might have become a master of the genre, or created an entirely new one.

Yet we must be grateful for what we have, which is a splendid rediscovery. These two novels are best read after dark, I think, possibly on an autumn night with a strong wind blowing the leaves around outside. They will keep you up, perhaps even until the rim of morning.

—STEPHEN KING

TO WALK THE NIGHT

And mind alone is never whole,
But needs the body for a soul.
        —STRUTHERS BURT, "Pack-Trip: Suite"

To
J. C. S.

FOREWORD

THE FORM in which this narrative is cast must necessarily be an arbitrary one. In the main it follows the story pieced together by Dr. Lister and myself as we sat on the terrace of his Long Island house one night in the summer of 1936. But in retelling it I have not tried to follow exactly the wording of our conversation. To do so would leave many things obscure to readers who did not know Selena, Jerry, and the rest of us. Therefore I have allowed myself the liberties of adding certain descriptions of people and places, and of attempting to suggest now and again the atmosphere of strangeness, even of terror, which was so much a part of my life while these events were in progress.

My belief is that this story is unlikely to attract much attention. Essentially it is concerned with people whose very names, with one exception, are unknown to the general public. One of them is now dead and another is alive merely in the physical sense of the word. The evidence which I can bring forward in support of its truth is almost wholly indirect, and psychological rather than circumstantial.

With some hesitation I submitted galley proofs of this book to Alan Parsons, who worked on the LeNormand case from its beginning. The letter he sent in reply is confidential, and I am not free to print it here. Thanks, however, to valuable suggestions from him the presentation of the facts has been revised in several places, and where my narrative touches upon the evidence in the official records it is at least accurate. Its interpretation, of course, is entirely Dr. Lister's and mine. What Parsons may have thought of it I cannot tell for certain. But some weeks ago, in making a final check on the transcripts of parts of the evidence, I went to his office at New Zion. When his secretary brought me the case folders I observed that she took them out of a file drawer labeled "closed."

I am not sure that it is wise to make this story a matter of public record. Dr. Lister and I have hesitated before doing so. Our ultimate decision is based upon the belief that it is never expedient to suppress the truth. We do not expect it to secure immediate acceptance. There are some experiences which are alien to everyday life; they are "doomed for a certain term to walk the night" before the mind of man either recognizes them for what they are or dismisses their appearance as fantasy.

—BERKELEY M. JONES
Long Island, 1937

1. END OF EVENING

THE DRIVEWAY began to dip to the long pitch of the bluff. The old taxi lumbered around curves and dropped heavily down the slope, its tires making a strong, harsh noise as they rolled over the gravel. The sound told me, without my having to open my eyes, how close we were to the house. Only a minute more to lie back in the refuge of this dilapidated sedan and be carried along without effort and without thought. Then the narcotic of traveling, of surrendering myself to the mere forward motion of train and automobile, would wear off. For twenty-five hundred miles and three days I had tried to imagine what I would do when the wheels under me stopped rolling and I should have to rouse myself to action.

The air coming through the open window was already fresher, with a coolness in it from Long Island Sound. Reluctantly I propped myself upright in a corner of the back seat and looked out. We were within a few hundred yards of the house. There was a glitter of water, darkened to the color of blued steel, shining between the stems of the trees. Fireflies were beginning to show in the laurels on each side of the road, and the birches had taken on a twilight glimmer. Almost there. I wanted to tell the driver to slow down, that I was not ready to have the journey end yet. Instead, I straightened my tie and rubbed some of the dust off my shoes.

We swung round the last bend and left the trees behind us. The familiar outline of the house was black against the sudden sweep of the Sound and there was no light in the windows on the landward side. Even the bulb under the porte-cochere was dark. After all, there was no reason why it should be lighted to receive me. What I had come to tell Jerry's father did not require light or welcome. Always before, when I had come here, there had been radiance in the windows and eagerness in my own thoughts. The impassive face of the building tonight was actually grateful because it did not remind me so much of those other times.

The car ground to a halt in front of the door. Thomas must have been listening on the other side of it. He came out at once. A flood of thin yellow light spilled across the narrow porch, blotched waveringly by his shadow as he came down the two alighting steps. The way he walked, with the stiff carefulness of an old man, startled me; I did not remember him like this. His butler's coat, made for him by Dr. Lister's own tailor, did not fit him any more, and the stoop in his carriage was new too. Seeing him come out to meet me made the whole thing more real and less tolerable. My throat thickened, and I did not trust myself to speak for some seconds while I paid off the driver and hauled my bag out of the car. My muscles, I saw, were almost too weary to obey orders, and I heard myself grunt as I tugged at my suitcase.

"Hello, Thomas," I said, and my voice sounded harsh and rusty.

"Mr. Berkeley, sir," he replied, giving my name the English pronunciation. Even in the shadows of the porch I could see how still and gray his face was, how carefully he had composed the lines at his mouth and eyes to betray no emotion. His appearance shocked me; the picture of Thomas in my mind was of another man entirely. A younger, straighter man with the laughter in his eyes only partly concealed by a professional decorum. Thomas—the Thomas that I had grown up with—was only incidentally a butler. He was a tall, brown man who could handle a jib sheet like a sailor and shoot tin cans in the air with a revolver. He was the companion of Jerry's boyhood and mine, the man from whom we had learned how to ride and fish and swim. The Thomas in my mind seemed to have no connection with this tired old man who was carrying my bag with a perceptible effort. I wondered if my own face was as changed as his. Did I look twenty years older?

As we crossed the porch I could not keep from staggering. There was no sensation at all in my legs, and walking was a laborious, conscious process.

"Steady," I heard Thomas's low voice behind me.

"I'm all right."

"Yes, sir. Of course."

The hall was cool and empty. Most of the rugs had been taken up for summer and the dark oak floor glowed somberly under the wall lights. To the left a broad, heavily banistered stair curved up and away into the dark, but on the right the hall continued clear across the house to a pair of big double doors. Beyond them I had a glimpse of the reach of the Sound and the color of the sunset. As I always did when I entered it, I thought again what a good house this was, full of comfortably large furniture and a sense of space. Women sometimes said that it was like a club, but we never minded that. We liked its dignity and its impersonality, and the absence of any feminine influence—no woman lived in it and there was no reason why it should look as if one did.

Thomas switched on the stair lights. "We have given you your old room, sir," he said, and began slowly to carry up my bag.

"But," I began to object, "doesn't he want to see me right away?"

"The Doctor is on the terrace, Mr. Berkeley. He thought you would prefer to wash and change before—" He left the sentence uncompleted, but I understood what he meant. He had been about to say, "before you go out to tell him about his son's death."

I followed Thomas up the stairs, heavily and without any further protest. Under my hand the banister was smooth and solid. Jerry and I slid down it, I remembered, the first night I had ever come here. Nothing was changed except Thomas. The house maintained its air of stability and peace, and even in the stupor of grief and weariness in which I was I felt again the old sense of belonging to it. We went down the upstairs corridor to the familiar door.

Thomas opened it and switched on the lights in the room beyond. "Home again, sir," he said, and swallowed.

He was right. This low, wide room with its windows looking over the water, its dark-blue leather easy chair, its broad walnut bed, the huge old desk in one corner, and its shelves and shelves of books was my real home, much more so than any of the guest rooms in which I always had to stay when I visited Grace and her husband. Grace is my mother, and she and her second husband, Fred Mallard, have lived for the past fifteen years in a succession of smart, theatrically-furnished apartments which never contained a real place for me. So, when I used to come home from school, and later college, I simply occupied the guest room and was treated almost as a guest too, except for Grace's infrequent attacks of maternal tenderness.

After Jerry and I became such fast friends, Dr. Lister practically adopted me as a second son. I spent more time in the house on Long Island than I did with my mother, and she was visibly relieved to have me off her hands. Grace was grateful to Jerry's father for taking an interest in me, and not in a wholly selfish way. She admitted that she and Fred were not the sort of people who ought to have children dependent on them and she knew that I needed a certain feeling of security and stability that her way of life could never provide.

The room to which I now came had been mine ever since the summer after Jerry's and my third-form year at prep school. We had arrived at the house full of excitement and plans for the summer to find that Dr. Lister had done over two upstairs rooms, put a bath between them, and furnished them specially for us. When he showed me mine he said: "This is your room. You can do anything you like in it provided you keep it neat. When you aren't here, nobody else will be allowed to use it."

I had stammered out some sort of thanks, interrupted by a whoop as Jerry came bursting through the connecting door.

"Hey, Bark! Isn't this somepin?"

But it was more than "somepin" to me—it was what I had always wanted: a place that was securely my own and that would remain so no matter how many times Grace moved from apartment to apartment. I had grown up in this room.

Thomas began to unpack my bag. That was familiar too; he had done the same thing a hundred times before. Even in the stupor which dulled me I saw him give the customary glance of inspection to each shirt and pair of socks before putting it away. A habit he'd got into when he first learned what school laundries do to buttons and fabric. The silence between us contained no unspoken question. I knew that he did not expect me to say anything to him, to tell him the things that had happened. Like myself, he was trying not to think. Slowly and heavily I began to undress.

When I glanced at him next he had stopped taking out my clothes and was holding to the footboard of the bed, looking down into the suitcase and shaking a little. I knew at once what he had come upon and went over and lifted it out myself. It was the silver vase which Jerry and I had found one summer in a Paris antique shop and brought home because we wanted it more than anything else we'd seen abroad. The metal felt cold and heavy in my hand, and the silver curves of the thing reflected the lights and the room in a sliding jumble of distorted images. For a second I hated it. And yet it was a beautiful thing, with a flawless six-inch replica of the Winged Victory on its lid and the long Greek lines of the vase body flowing into the base.

I carried it across the room and set it on the wide window ledge. The goddess strained exultantly forward toward the darkening Sound and the wide spaces of the evening sky. Under her feet, in the hollow breast of the vase, was a double-handful of white crystalline ashes. Thomas must have guessed that I would choose our silver urn to hold Jerry's ashes.

"I'll leave it there until we decide," I said.

"Yes, sir." He went on with his unpacking. "Have you had dinner, Mr. Berkeley?"

"I had something in the station. I'm not hungry."

He nodded, snapped the bag shut, and stowed it in the closet. "I'll start the shower, sir. Will you have it hot?"

"No," I said. "Lukewarm."

"Yes, that's best in hot weather." He disappeared into the bathroom.

I finished my undressing, hardly able to focus my attention on what I was doing. When you haven't slept except in snatches for several days things begin to seem unreal. My memory was flashing disconnected pictures in front of my eyes and some of them were more real than the four walls of the room. They were pictures that I did not want to look at, but they came to me in steady succession in spite of myself. What would it be like, I wondered, if I tried to go to sleep tonight? How many of these images would I have to look at again and again before they faded into blackness? Even on the edge of exhaustion, as I was, I dreaded the thought of shutting my eyes.

The shower felt good. The feel of water running down over my skin was enough physical pleasure to stop me from thinking very much, and it was comfortable to be clean again after three days on the train. The rush and patter of the water began to put tag ends of songs into my mind:

I'll have a rendezvous
With you . . .

No, that was not a good song. There would be no rendezvous again for Jerry and me. Try something else:

Soft o'er the fountain
Lingering falls the southern moon.
Far o'er the mountain—

"Far o'er the mountain!" Far over the looming cliff of Cloud Mesa with the white adobe house in the shadow by the spring! That was something else I did not want to think about. Songs were no good. I turned off the water and dried myself slowly. The more I hurried the sooner I'd be talking to Dr. Lister.

Thomas had laid out flannels. A soft white shirt, and one of the club blazers Jerry and I wore when we sat on the terrace and drank and looked at the water and the summer night. We used to do that often when there wasn't a dance at the club and we didn't feel like going for a drive. I slipped into the clothes, grateful for their cool cleanness, combed my hair, put pipe, tobacco pouch, and matches into my pocket, and started down the hall.

The routine of doing pleasant, familiar things had made the past half hour endurable, but it deserted me part way down the stairs. The worst moment of all was coming now, and I knew it. Jerry's father was waiting for me on the terrace; waiting to hear the story I had to tell him. I had no fear of that; he was equal to anything that could happen to him. I never knew a man who had such mastery over himself as Dr. Lister. Even when I told him that his son had shot himself there would be no crevice in his armor. And because I was almost as much his own son as Jerry had been it would be easier for both of us.

What I was afraid of was something quite different. It was not the telling of the facts about Jerry's death that would be difficult. Somehow I had to give them to him without making him begin to think. I must present my story in such a way as to make it seem natural, and it wasn't natural. It was, on the surface, tragically unreasonable and inexplicable. The idea of suicide did not belong to Jerry's character, and Dr. Lister would know that as well as I did. The first question he would ask would be, why? As I went down the stairs I wondered how I was going to answer that question without telling him at least a part of the things that I had come to know and believe.

There was danger in that. The things he would want to know could not be stated in terms of tangible facts, of events and people shaped into a recognizable pattern. For the first time I admitted to myself that there was a possibility of connection between small, disturbing things in the past and the present fact of Jerry's death. What that common denominator was I did not know, but I was certain that I did not want to find it out. Merely admitting its existence gave me a feeling of tightness inside that was familiar. It was, I realized, fear. And fear of a shapeless, misty thought that was as insubstantial as a ghost.

But Dr. Lister would not believe in ghosts. I did not myself, for that matter. I must tell my story matter-of-factly, as if that shadow in the corner of my mind did not exist. That was all. I must not make him feel, as I did, that something horrible lay behind what I said. It could be dangerous to let him begin to sort and arrange the elements of the past so that he, too, thought he saw a ghost and began to think back, selecting here a fact and there an overtone, weighing one trifle of evidence against another until he had a complete story.

The pieces of the puzzle were all lying in my mind, of so much I was sure. I felt that if I looked at them, thought about them, they would slip together into a picture of the truth, and the feeling frightened me. My conscious mind rejected the idea of knowing or thinking anything more about the events of the past two years. But Dr. Lister would not consent to that, once started. He would want to get down to the bedrock of the truth. Donne's tremendous lines went through my mind:

> Whoever comes to shroud me, do not harm
> Nor question much
> That subtle wreath of hair about mine arm;
> The mystery, the sign you must not touch—

When we shrouded Jerry in our talk tonight we must not question much. He had been unhappy, his marriage had not turned out to be what he had hoped from it, and he had shot himself. Those were the bald facts. If there was anything behind them, it had best stay in the shadows. I would tell my story carefully, as nearly within the bounds of truth as I could, but suppressing some things. It would not be wise, for example, to say that she had been in the room when Jerry picked the gun out of the drawer and ... I was tired too, my own mind not entirely clear. I should have to be very careful.

The double doors at the end of the hall were still open. I stepped out on the terrace. Below the balustrade the land sloped down in a long sweep of grass to the beach and the waves on the sand. Framing the lawn on either side, the trees were heavy clusters of black shadow against the sky. By now the lower air was full of the silent sparks of fireflies. There was no wind at all. Almost in the zenith, the great constellation of Orion sprawled across the sky, and as I saw it I remembered another time when I had stood under it, and another smell quite different from that of the flowers blooming under the balustrade.

Jerry's father was sitting at the white iron garden table to my right. In the middle of it was a candle in a hurricane lamp socket. A tall bottle of sherry, and two glasses. The gleam of the candle picked out the crisp whiteness of his hair and shadowed the sockets of his eyes. I could see no sign of sorrow in his posture; he sat as erect as always with one arm stretched before him across the table top and the brown fingers of his surgeon's hand holding one of the glasses. It was his habit in summer, at the end of evening, to sit out here drinking sherry, and he was doing it tonight. There was something admirable in the fact that he had made no exception of this one evening, and the usualness of it steadied me. I went across the stone flagging and sat down opposite him at the table.

"Hello, Bark," he said, and smiled.

"Hello, Dad." He liked me to call him that.

"Your trip must have been hot and uncomfortable, this time of year," he said, pouring me a glass of sherry. His hand, like his voice, was entirely steady.

I lifted the glass and looked through the wine at the flame of the candle. "Yes." The sherry was noble, neither dry nor sweet and with a fine, full body. "This is good stuff."

"The best. How are you feeling?"

"Tired."

He looked at me. "We can talk about this thing in the morning. Don't feel you have to speak of it now."

"Thanks." He said nothing more but continued to look at my face as if trying to read it. I avoided his eyes and told him. "The ashes are here, in the silver vase. I thought he'd like to have them in it."

"That was good of you."

In the silence that lay between us I heard the bumbling of an insect against the glass of the lamp and the faint slither of water moving on the beach below us. He was expecting me to speak, and I knew that I ought to say something to help him and to lessen the torment of his waiting. But there was nothing to say except "Jerry's dead, and I've brought his ashes back to you in the silver vase." My mind was empty—the least word of thought echoed hollowly in it.

"Don't try to talk, Bark. Sit here with me a few minutes and then we'll go up to bed."

I made an immense effort of will. "It happened the day after I got out there. In the evening. A little earlier than this. I didn't tell you the whole story in my telegram. He . . . he shot himself."

What he said next contained the whole quality of his character. "So. I wondered what sort of accident it was."

"That was it," I said.

He was quiet for a while. When he spoke next his voice was remote, detached. "Tell me how it happened."

This was the danger point, I told myself. What I said now would either satisfy him or set him on the track of the mystery I was resolved he should not think about at all. "He went into the little study. After a few minutes we heard the shot. He was lying across the desk. The gun was on the floor beside him. We couldn't do anything for him."

"We?"

"She and I."

"I see." He took a careful sip of wine. "And there was no letter, no note? He didn't write anything to explain?"

"No." I didn't want him to think about that, so I went on quickly. "I got his body into the car and drove to Los Palos. As soon as I was through with the undertaker and the coroner I caught the train home."

"What about her?"

That was another question I didn't want him to raise. "I don't know."

"Did she drive in to Los Palos with you?"

"No."

"You didn't just leave her in the house?"

I looked squarely into his eyes and said, "When I was ready to leave, she wasn't in the house."

He was puzzled, I could see, and I was aware in some subtle way that he was beginning to doubt something in my story. "You didn't see her again, then?"

"No."

"That is strange. Very strange, and not quite like you, either, Bark." He paused. "Do you know where she is now?"

"No."

"Look here, my boy," he said finally, "I have somehow got the impression..."

"There's no impression to get, Dad. I don't know where she was when I left the house, but I think she had gone up to the top of the mesa. I didn't know when she would come back, and I couldn't wait. She'll be all right. The sheriff's men drove the car back to the house. She can come away any time she wants to."

He was staring out over the water, the clean outline of his profile with its high, thin nose and jutting chin stamped out in dull bronze against the night. I recognized the expression on his face, the sureness of his look, the calm determination in the set of his mouth. It was the way he looked when he performed a difficult operation.

"Bark," he said finally, "are you in love with Selena yourself?"

The question shocked me, it was so wide of the mark. "God, no!"

"But you are afraid of something. I wondered if you were afraid of falling in love with Jerry's wife."

"I've never felt that way about her for a moment."

"Then," he said, "I used to think you might be afraid for Jerry. That you had some intuition it would end like this. Was that it?"

I was grateful for the opening, the chance to give a logical excuse for the feeling he had managed to detect in me. "Yes," I said, "I was afraid of that."

He withdrew his eyes from the dark stretches of the Sound and looked full at me. "Then, why are you still afraid? It has happened, as you feared it might. What else is there still to dread?"

"Nothing," I replied without meeting his eyes.

"You ran away from her. I don't understand that."

"Jerry told me she often went up to the mesa at night, alone. I left her because I thought that was the best way. I think she wanted me to leave her."

He said, "I see," in a tone entirely empty of conviction. Then, after a while, in a low voice and half to himself: "I cannot believe that a son of mine would commit suicide. Even if he was not happy with his wife." For the first time his voice trembled slightly.

"Don't think about it." And then, knowing how his pride and his conviction of Jerry's fineness were being humbled, I said without thinking, "And you've got to understand that what he did was not cowardly."

"Killing yourself is not a brave business." There was nothing I could say to that; it was a part of his own creed, and it was, I could have sworn, no less a part of Jerry's. He went on, slowly, to himself, "I should have expected some word from him—" For one instant the discipline of his face relaxed, and the grief and despair in his heart looked out at me.

"Don't," I cried, "don't! He did think of you. There wasn't time—" and stopped, appalled.

He took me up instantly. "You haven't told me everything!"

"No, not everything."

"Was he killed?" I didn't say anything, and he pressed me relentlessly. "Was he murdered? Did she kill him?" All the violence of his emotions, so sternly repressed up to now, was in the questions.

"No," I told him, "he shot himself. I saw him do it."

"Ah," he said, quietly again. "You were in the room?"

"Yes," I answered.

"And she was there too." It was a statement, not a question.

"Yes." I added nothing more.

He paused and watched me. When he spoke, his voice was gentle. "Will you tell me the whole story, now?"

"It wouldn't do any good, Dad, and it might do a lot of harm. The facts are the only things that matter, and I've told you those. I'm not holding anything really important back. Don't ask me any more questions, for God's sake."

He looked at me quietly, and as happened between us sometimes, I knew what he was thinking. He expected me to remember the fifteen years that the three of us had been together and come to realize that I must share with him whatever knowledge about this thing I had. Relying with such conviction on those years, on the tradition of absolute trust among the three of us, on a thousand inescapable ties, he was sure that I would tell him the rest of it. But he did not know what he had to fight against. No anxiety to spare him or myself was holding me silent. It was, I admitted to myself, fear, and fear of an intangible something too slight to formulate in words. What exactly I was afraid to say I could not tell, but I understood that once I began to talk about it to him it would become more definite and more horrible. Instinct told me that the less shape I gave that shadow the better for both of us. And if, by keeping silent, I had to forfeit his confidence and spoil a relationship that mattered deeply to me, that was nevertheless the smaller evil. I filled my pipe and lighted it, and I did not speak.

The thing that broke my resolve was so trivial and fortuitous that I was not on guard against it. The absolute quiet that surrounded us was broken by the click! click! click! of a dog's nails tapping on the slates of the terrace. Beyond Dr. Lister, in the penumbra of the candle glow was a patch of familiar blackness. It came toward me gravely and joyfully, tail wagging and one crimson triangle of tongue lolling out. Boojum, Jerry's Scotty. With dignified eagerness he crossed the terrace and came to my chair. Sedately he sat up and put one black paw against my thigh; his head was cocked to one side and his eyes were bright. It seemed to me that there was the inevitable question in them, and something hot rose in my throat. I put my hand on the rough hair of his skull and scratched him in the hollows behind his ears. He whined.

I tried to say "Boojum!" and couldn't.

Dr. Lister stirred in his chair. "You can't do it, Bark. I don't know what it is you haven't told me yet, but nothing will be right until you do."

My resolution crumbled. Jerry had been my best friend. To let his father go on believing that he had causelessly, in a moment of insanity, shot himself was utterly unjust to him. And yet, even as I began to speak the sort of quick stab went through me that comes when you realize that you have made an irreparable mistake.

"There's something behind it," I said, "and I don't know what it is, but I know it's there."

"What sort of thing?" he asked me.

"That's what I don't know. But Jerry found out, and once he knew it he killed himself. I've been afraid to think about it, and I still am. It's not an ordinary thing. It's connected with her, and with LeNormand, and with all sorts of things that have happened the last two years."

He said, "If it will explain why my son committed suicide, I want to hear it. And if it's any question of justice—"

"No, it's not a question of justice."

"Or even"—and there was steel in his tone—"of revenge—"

I looked up at the night above us, studded innumerably with stars. "You can't revenge yourself," I told him. "Here's the way it was."

Boojum lay down across my feet as I talked; his body trembled slightly, like a car with an idling motor, as he panted. Dr. Lister listened, leaning forward and twirling the glass with its topaz wine between his long fingers. The night was a vault that shut us in and swallowed my words as I spoke them.

I told him just what had happened when Jerry died. He heard me out with no sign of the agony it must have been for him. Only his face grew stiller, more sharply etched, and the glass in his hands revolved more and more slowly. I left out nothing, from the time I caught the Century out of New York to my return, except one thing that would mean nothing to anyone except me. I even told him my thoughts on the staircase coming down from my room, and of my fear.

"And you haven't defined this thing you are afraid of, even to yourself?" he asked me when I had finished.

"No," I answered.

He took a sip of wine. "Between us we ought to be able to understand it, if we think about it a little."

"I don't want to think about it any more."

"Then it will go on festering in your mind, and in mine as well.

I'll always wonder if you could not have told me something more that would … that would make this thing less intolerable."

I said, "I don't want to die. Jerry thought this thing through, and that's why he's not alive now."

He leaned forward, put his hand on mine for a brief second, and asked me, "Just what do you think living is for?"

For him, perhaps for me, it was a fundamental question. Dr. Lister based his whole life on integrity and he had taught me to do the same thing. Integrity of mind, of will, of loyalty to the people one loved. He believed that the purpose of life was to live it well; unless he could explain to himself why Jerry had committed suicide, there would be, for him, a stain on his honor. I thought of a time when he had turned to me during one of the talks the three of us used to have about life and death and time and humanity and all the incomprehensible generalities and said, gravely, "The one unforgivable fault is weakness."

And now it appeared to him that his only son had done a weak and dishonorable thing. The foundations of his life were attacked by that act—everything he lived by and had taught his son to cherish was smirched by it, put into question. There was nothing in life so important, now, as to probe into the motives behind Jerry's action and find there the honor and courage that his instinct told him must lie behind the immediate fact.

It was not so easy for me. Although I loved Jerry and his father more than any two people on earth, I was not of quite the same breed. It is not necessary for me to know that every action of the people I belong with is founded on honor and courage. I think you have to be born into the aristocratic, Spartan mind, and I was not. There is an easygoing, friendly, perhaps insubstantial strain in my family that is a part of me. But more immediate than my heritage was the memory of two days and two nights under Cloud Mesa. I had told Dr. Lister the story of what happened during them, very much as it is set down in this narrative in a later chapter, but I could not translate to him the odd, tight tone of Jerry's voice—a tone I had never heard before from him in spite of the dangerous moments we had shared—nor the calm, impersonal regret in Selena's eyes. I wondered if she was at that very minute on the flat tabletop of the enormous mesa, looking up at the western stars. And if she was, what was in her heart? As I imagined her there, a curious feeling of alarm went through me. Perhaps she was imagining me here in her mind, putting out the fingers of that damnable intelligence of hers to touch the stuff of my own brain. A prickle went along my spine at the thought. I did not want her to be thinking about me in any way.

Dr. Lister's question was still heavy in the air between us. I had not answered it. If there was any point for me in the process of living, it lay in my relationships with people who were close to me, and if I was to preserve the one most important to me of all I should have to tell him everything I knew, put each separate piece of the puzzle before him. And then the nameless fear in my mind would have a name, and what would happen after that I couldn't even guess.

"All right," I said with despair and fear in my heart. "I'll tell you the rest of it."

He smiled. "Good. I knew you would."

He took out a cigarette, lit it, and poured each of us another glass of the sherry. "Whatever it is you're afraid of, we'll find the answer to it. There's nothing the human intelligence, properly applied, can't cope with."

I tried to put behind my words all the conviction I felt. "Oh, yes, there is. Your intelligence won't be able to do much with this business, if it is what I think. This isn't a detective story or a problem of deduction."

He looked puzzled. "Well, I don't know what you mean. But I think I have an idea—"

"Don't think," I told him. "Thinking won't get you anywhere. Don't refer what I say to any system of logic or to your scientific training. I'm certain of one thing. The answer we are looking for doesn't lie in anything you—or I—know. Maybe it's in what we don't know. And perhaps there isn't any answer."

He said quietly, "We'll see."

"Yes," I answered. "We'll see. But not with logic. We tried before to solve LeNormand's death with our minds, and we failed. know that. Now you want to know why your son killed himself. It the one thing on earth that I never want to know. But I'll help you if I can. Whatever it is, Jerry found it out, and not by thinking."

His look was a question.

"He found out," I said brutally, "by living with it."

"Ah." His fingers tightened on the stem of the glass. "Then it did all start with their marriage?"

"No. Before that."

He nodded. "When they met, then."

"The day before that." I settled myself in my chair and put a fresh match to my pipe. "The day almost two years ago when Jerry and I drove down to the State game."

And as I began to tell him about that a cold finality settled upon my mind. Whatever the end, it was inevitable now.

IN WEEKEND

"THIS looks good enough."

"Sure," I agreed.

Jerry cut the car off the edge of the concrete and into the mouth of a lane that ran back between scrubby thickets of second-growth trees. A few yards in was a battered sign that said:

TO ADATH JESHURUN CEMETERY

"You have a cheerful taste in picnic grounds," I observed.

He grinned. "It'll be quiet." There was a sort of turn-around in a clearing; we swung into it, and he cut the motor and ratched up the emergency. "Is this okay, or do you want to go clear in and look at the monuments?"

Getting out of the car, my legs were stiff. It had been a long drive, and cold. "Do they have monuments?"

"Damned if I know." He handed out the cardboard box of sandwiches.

There were four sandwiches and a couple of hard-boiled eggs in it; I laid them out on the running board. Jerry was rummaging in the compartment back of the seat. In a moment he produced a bottle of Scotch, two or three bottles of White Rock, and a couple of Lily cups. I set them out beside the sandwiches. The whole display looked attractive.

"We ought to photograph that and send it in to *Esquire*," I suggested. "The smart picnic for young graduates returning to their Alma Maters for football games."

"I don't want to photograph it, I want to eat it and drink it, right now." He poured out two stiff ones in the Lily cups, and splashed in a little White Rock. "God, it's cold. This ought to be good for what ails us."

We touched the rims of the cups together. "Well," I said, "here's to 'em."

"And to hell with State."

The Scotch was good, warm all the way down.

We sat on the running board and began on the sandwiches, talking about the team between swallows. A raw November wind was rustling around in the bushes like a rat in a packing case. Even at noon, and with the sun shining, it was cold. After a while we didn't notice it so much, and by the time the Scotch was all gone we felt a whole lot better. We agreed that State was going to be tough, but Mortenson, our right half, would be the best back on the field, and our line was sure to be stronger. Jerry thought we'd win by four touchdowns; I wasn't so sure. Anyway, it was going to be a great game. After a while we stuck the empty bottle and the box and papers into a pile of brush and got back into the car.

"Good-bye, folks," said Jerry, nodding up the road. "Sorry you can't come with us." He swung the big car around with a rush and we headed on toward the game. The Scotch inside us was fine; it was a fine day. Everything was fine. We sang "The Best Old Place of All" at the top of our lungs. The road went away under the tires in a slip-stream of blurred gray.

By and by we saw the towers come up against the sky. Drunk or sober, I love that place, and it always makes a lump in my throat to see those sharp Gothic pinnacles notch up above the trees. Neither of us had been back in the two years since graduation, and I suppose we got sentimental about the fact. Then we were in the midst of traffic, and everything began to feel like a football game. We had to park half a mile from the stadium, and by the time we got to the portal the exercise of walking, and the cold air, had reduced the effects of the Scotch to a pleasant glow.

There was the usual push and jostle around the turnstile. And a classmate whose name neither of us could recall who seemed unwholesomely glad to see us. Once inside the gate, we brushed through a phalanx of freshmen who wanted to sell us programs, cushions, and God knows what. The muffled blare of bands was pouring down the tunnels from the bowl, and outside the door of the Ladies' Room was the inevitable sore-looking gent with a folded blanket over his arm, worrying for fear he was going to miss the kickoff. We shuffled down our tunnel with the roar of seventy thousand people coming at us from the other end, louder and louder. Then the field, amazingly green and mathematically striped with white, and on it the two teams, warming up.

Dr. Lister moved a little in his chair and said, "Don't bother with all these details, Bark, unless you want to."

"I've got to tell the thing this way," I replied. "These things are all part of the picture. You won't find the answer anywhere but in the whole story. Besides, something happened at the game that may have a meaning."

He nodded and drew on his cigarette. I took a sip of sherry and went on.

We were going to kick off. Our boys were strung across the field just behind their own forty-yard line. They looked fine with the sun catching their gold helmets and their light-gray jerseys new and clean. The State eleven, in red and black, weren't so pretty, but they looked like ball players . . . Big Dan Hevutt, our left tackle, was going to kick it; he raised himself on his toes and began to run forward. As his boot met the ball the line of gold and gray was surging forward; the ball arced up into the air.

There's something about a kickoff, something indescribable and thrilling. It's the curtain going up on a new play, it's the little white roulette ball clicking into the compartment, it's waking up Christmas morning when you're ten years old. Underneath the ball as it tumbled end over end through the air the two teams flowed into each other. Men were sprawling out on the grass. The kick was coming down in coffin corner; the State man who caught it never had a chance. Thompson and Ives, for us, hit him like a ton of bricks. And as he went down, the ball squirted out of his arms; one of our gray jerseys fell on it instantly. The noise in the bowl was terrific.

Jerry was pounding my back, and I his, and both of us were yelling. There was a flask in my pocket. We each took a short, quick nip from it.

They lined up. The ball was on the thirteen-yard line. We tried a tackle slant that didn't gain a thing, and then on the next play Mortenson started around right end. He was a beautiful ball-carrier, always driving fast with his knees high. He went over the line standing up; not a State man even touched him. There was so much noise on our side of the field that I could not hear myself yelling.

"Jesus!" Jerry bawled into my ear. "Was that sweet!" Even though he'd made his Phi Bete key junior year, Jerry's language at such moments was always unacademic.

While Hewitt was kicking the goal, I got out the flask again, and we had a stiff one apiece to celebrate. The liquor was warm, but we didn't care. The score was us—7, State—0, and the band was playing "The Best Old Place of All" as the boys drifted down the field and got ready to kick off again.

The State receiver didn't fumble the second time. The red and black jerseys were mad. Their line was charging like bulls, the interfering backs were diving at our boys savagely, and little by little the ball worked its way up the field till the two lines were right below us. Jerry was watching the play like a hawk and silently, except for a few profane and professional comments to me out of the side of his mouth. He'd made his own letter senior year, and perhaps he was too technically intent to notice a thing that began to make a curious impression on me. Something was happening to the crowd.

Yard by yard the ball was moving down the field; our team was roused now and fighting. The two lines were meeting on even terms; the tackling was growing more and more savage. The State side of the bowl had been a torrent of noise during that long advance, everybody over there standing up on every play. It was terrific to watch—the two lines taut against each other, the flash of the ball as the center shot it back, the slog! of the lines as they met, and the wedge of red and black jerseys that disintegrated in the welter of our tacklers. Old-fashioned football, perhaps, but it was tremendous drama, and the crowd knew it.

Now, comparatively, it was growing quieter and quieter in the bowl. Even up in our seats we began to hear the hoarse, panting voice of the quarterback calling out the starting numbers, and the thud of the tackles. There were almost no cheers. Seventy thousand people were sitting silent, leaning forward in their seats, welded into one unit, I began to realize. The back of my neck prickled with awareness of the mass emotion focused on the two teams, the game below us. The whole bowl was filled with human excitement, with hope and fear, with longing for triumph or a desperation of defense. Once I'd noticed it, it seemed to me I could almost taste the damn thing in the air. It was more real than the blue haze of tobacco smoke rising lazily up the slope of the stands. And as I became fully aware of that quality, that intensity, it began to make me somehow uneasy. I wondered if it was like that when there was a lynching, or a war. I had an impression of frightening power without control, of a field of force in some other dimension than our usual three. Perhaps in that fourth dimension of time, for I have no idea how long the whole thing lasted. It may have been only a minute or two, possibly no more than a few seconds. Anyway, it ended when Stanwicz, the State halfback, faded back and arched a long pass dead into the hands of his own right end, who scored right then and there.

At once the feeling of tension broke; the State side of the stadium turned into a riot of color and sound, and around us the gloom was thick. But oddly enough, I felt happier than I had the moment before. It was a relief to have the suspense over with, to know the worst, and to be free of whatever it was that I had just been feeling.

"Let's have a drink," said Jerry. "We're always suckers for forward passes. That end ought to have been covered."

I gave him the flask and took a small one myself after he was through. Just then State missed the try-for-point, and the score was still in our favor, 7 to 6. Jerry grinned. After three years of Bart Wilmuth's coaching he wasn't what the English would call "sporting" about football. In the game, his idea was to win, and win by as big a score as possible. No dirty playing, no cheating of any sort, but fight like hell all the time, be on the long end of the score when the time-keeper fires the final gun, and never mind about giving three cheers for the other side when they score on you.

"If Mortenson can get away once more on that 32 play," he observed, "it'll just be a question of how big a score we can run up. The State boys have about shot the works."

But Mortenson didn't get away. We were crowding them all the rest of the half, and all through the second half as well, but we never quite put the ball across for another touchdown. Up and down the field the two teams surged, and there was a lot of good, hard football played, but it was all an anticlimax after the opening quarter. I kept waiting to feel that sense of crowd unity and mass emotion, but it did not develop again. The game was grand, but it remained a spectacle and nothing more. When the timekeeper's pistol cracked for the end the score was still 7 to 6.

Before the last half was over, the sun had dropped behind Orchard Hill and it was bitter cold in the stadium. My feet were numb, and even finishing off my flask hadn't kept us really warm. We didn't join the snake dance. Neither of us gives a damn for pieces of goal posts, and we felt decidedly let down as we worked our way toward the portal. It hardly seemed to matter that our team had won; there was no exhilaration of victory at all. We were both quiet, and conscious of the fact that the liquor had begun to wear off. I've said a good deal about our drinking, but the truth is that we were not drunk, or anywhere near it. For one thing, we had been out of doors all day, and the not-inconsiderable amount of Scotch we'd consumed had all been drunk in the open air, and the cold. We were simply tired and somewhat cold as we waited for the crowd to empty out of the tunnels, and then drifted along through the outer gate of the stadium.

So Jeremiah Lister and Berkeley M. Jones stood outside the gate of the stadium, whence practically all but them had fled. It was nearly dark; the stars were splattering all except the western sky, and it was cold as Siberia. We began to walk back toward the car in silence. After a while Jerry said something under his breath and stopped short in the road.

"Well?" I asked him.

"I just had an idea."

"No, thanks," I told him firmly. "I've already had all the Scotch I'm having today."

Jerry laughed. "Yeah. Now that your flask is empty."

"What other idea is there?"

"It seems pretty flat, just heading back to New York now. Our first time here in two years."

There was something in that. "We could drop round and see the boys at the Lodge." Its members always referred to our fraternity as "the Lodge."

"No. Let's go see LeNormand."

It seemed inappropriate. I thought of that middle-aged, punctilious, intellectual scholar. "In the shape we're in now?" I asked in surprise.

"Sure. He'll be just the thing after the emotional debauch of a football game." He went on with a grin: "My God, I never realized before how hard the crowd at a game has to work. When you're playing you get pooped, and work up an honest sweat, but when you're watching a game like that one you're absolutely all in at the end of it."

Still I wasn't too interested in the idea. "What about the liquor on our breath?" I suggested.

"He'll never notice it. He's always smoking that smudge-pot of a pipe. Anyway, I haven't seen him since we got out, and he's a decent egg. The perfect antidote to the late lamented orgy." He turned and struck off toward the campus.

I went along. Jerry had always liked LeNormand—he'd been the only man our year to take the course in celestial mechanics—and he and LeNormand used to spend whole nights in the observatory, talking over everything under as well as in the heavens. LeNormand must have been very lonely after he came over to this country. The University had bribed him away from some English college where he'd made a brilliant record. When he got here he found most of us pretty unregenerate, astronomically speaking, and the new equipment he'd been promised somehow never did materialize. So he kept to himself, did what research he could, I suppose, with the inadequate telescope already there, and only let himself go with one or two intimates on the faculty, and with Jerry. He never went out socially, so far as I know, and the rumor was that he hadn't spoken to a woman since his mother. A silent, reserved, intensely intellectual and hard-working man, as I remembered him.

Our senior year he published something entitled, as near as I can recall it, "A Fundamental Critique of the Einstein Space-Time Continuum." Maybe that isn't the exact wording, but it conveys the general idea. I found it unreadable, myself—out of the first fifty words I knew the meaning of only twenty-eight, and it turned out later that I was wrong about one of those. Jerry waded through it, and with the help of his bull sessions with the author, claimed he knew what it was all about. That's not important, perhaps; what matters is that the article brought down a storm of abuse on LeNormand. Apparently the rest of the boys in the astronomy league doubted everything about it from its mathematics to LeNormand's sanity. If he hadn't been such a famous man to begin with, Jerry thought, they'd have asked him to resign from the faculty.

Within a week after the article was published the scientific mudslinging had begun, and Jerry must have been the only supporter LeNormand had. Probably it was nothing but loyalty on his part, but I could never be sure with Jerry. He had a curious facility for picking out the right answer, for cutting through to the truth even without knowing all the facts. And I know LeNormand wanted him to do graduate work in mathematics. Anyway, it was a case of two of them against the rest of the world, at least as Jerry saw it. LeNormand and he would engage in terrific correspondences with rival astronomers all over the world. Some nights Jerry wouldn't get back to the room till three or four in the morning; he did all the typing of those letters for the professor. But that business stopped long before graduation. I remember that one night Jerry came back from the observatory about eleven. I was surprised. I hadn't expected to see him before morning.

"You and LeNormand didn't run out of words to call the other nuts, did you?" I inquired.

He tossed his hat on the window seat and sat down at his desk. "Yes," he said.

"You mean," I asked incredulously, "LeNormand admits he's licked?"

"Hell, no," Jerry was irritated. "He's just not writing any more letters. He told me tonight it would be stupid, and perhaps dangerous."

"Dangerous? Why? He might lose his job?"

Jerry shook his head, puzzled. "I don't think that was it."

"Well, then it must be that he's afraid of the other guys. I suppose they are hellions when roused."

I could see I was annoying him a little. "Don't be a damn fool." He was silent a moment. "It was a good row while it lasted. I used to enjoy those letters he wrote, you know. He's got a knack of saying the nastiest things in the most abstract sort of way. And the funny thing about it all—" he paused.

"Is what?" I prompted him.

"Is that he's just as right as he was originally."

"Maybe they've shaken *his* faith." The shot did not seem to penetrate.

"Maybe so." He was thoughtful. "But I'll tell you this. He had the answer to everything they wrote to him, and they didn't have the answers to his stuff."

I put that down to Jerry's loyalty. "Probably he got sick of the whole argument."

"Perhaps," he said, and began talking about something else. He told me later that LeNormand never brought up the subject of that article again, and he didn't dare mention it to him. But he puzzled about it a long time after. LeNormand's attitude was what he couldn't get over.

The whole episode came back to me as we stumbled up the road to the campus. I turned toward Jerry.

"I suppose you want to find out the latest news in the LeNormand versus Einstein contest," I suggested.

There was an almost imperceptible pause before he spoke, so I knew I had guessed what he was thinking about. "I dunno. I won't bring it up right at first."

"Listen," I said. "If you two savants are going to sit up till all hours talking mathematics, relativity, or whatever the hell, I'm not coming."

"We won't. I just want to say hello to him again. He was damn decent to me, and he's a lonely man."

I was undecided. "Maybe I better not butt in on your call."

"Don't be a damn fool," said Jerry.

But I was, and proved it by walking on up the hill beside him. We were on campus now; splashes of warm and cheerful light were coming out of the windows of the dorms, and more than a suspicion of the sounds of revelry by night. Our breaths were dimly white in the air. Jerry was walking briskly; I could tell he was eager to get there, maybe to get there and get it over with. Our shoes made crisp, far-reaching sound on the slate flagging of the walk.

The Eldridge Observatory is on the highest part of the campus. A cube of a building with a white, bulbous dome at the top. It's one of the simplest structures imaginable, two stories high and with a couple of classrooms on the ground floor. The instrument room, as Jerry called the actual place where the telescope was, occupied the whole of the second floor, and was roofed by the dome. LeNormand used it for his office as well. There was—why do I keep saying "was"?—not everything in this story is in the past tense—there is only one door to the place. We could see it ahead of us at the top of the walk we were on.

"He's there," said Jerry with satisfaction. "The light's on over the door."

We went on up the walk. There's an old saying that every step you take is a step toward your grave.

The door was shut. Jerry rapped on it a couple of times, but nobody answered.

"He's gone home for dinner," I suggested.

"No," said Jerry, "he always turns off the light when he leaves. He must be in there."

He knocked again on the door. It was cold where we stood in the dark, and still except for the faint slither of the wind through the leafless trees. I shivered.

"Let's go. Let's go and find a drink."

Jerry shook his head and put his hand on the knob. "Let's make sure he's not here, first."

The door opened and we went inside quietly. The light in the shallow hall was on. A single raw, yellow globe that left even that small space half dark. The doorways to the classrooms at the right and left were open rectangles of blackness. There wasn't a sound. I felt my guts contract. It was one of those times when some subconscious part of you is afraid for no reason. A deserted house will give me the same feeling.

"Hello, LeNormand," Jerry called. I suppose he wasn't speaking loudly at all, but his voice rang in that little hall.

There was no answer. Or wasn't there? As I think over it now I am not so sure. Perhaps there was a thin sliver of sound above us. I can't quite dredge it up out of my memory, but it was as though someone in the room above us had shifted position ever so slightly. Probably it was nothing.

A couple of steps in front of us was the round iron pillar about which revolved a spiral of steel stairs. That was—is—how you get up to the instrument room. We looked at it.

"It's all dark up there," I said. "Let's go find a drink some place and—"

Jerry took a half step forward, looking up to the place where the stair cut through the ceiling like an auger.

"I think he's up there," he said with a faintly puzzled tone.

"Nuts. He must have heard you and he hasn't answered."

Jerry was obstinate. "Yes, but I think I see a light up there."

I craned past his shoulder. At first I couldn't make out what he meant, but then I did notice something. There was a flicker of light filtering through between the treads of the two top steps. That's just what it was too. A flicker of light, not steady, but wavering from bright to dim and then bright again.

"Hey, LeNormand!" Jerry cried.

Nothing. Not a sound in reply. Only the light kept on flickering.

"Hell," said Jerry. "I'm going up."

I was right at his heels as we climbed the curving iron stair, just far enough behind to keep my nose from getting kicked. Jerry kept going round and up faster and faster with an odd urgency, and beyond him the flickering, wavering light grew stronger and stronger till he was nothing but a silhouette in front of me. He took the last few steps two at a time.

"Come on," he flung at me over his shoulder. "Come on, for God's sake!"

We burst into the instrument room almost side by side. LeNormand was there, all right.

3. THE STARS ARE FIRE

DR. LISTER *interrupted me. "Bark, we've all three talked this over so often—"*

"Yes," I agreed, filling my pipe again slowly. "But always as a mystery. A problem of detection. I have begun to wonder if we've ever discussed it, ever thought about it in another way."

He looked hard at me without a word.

"I mean . . . well, I can't tell you yet just what I do mean. But I want to go over the whole thing just once more, impersonally, narratively. Negative evidence is as important as positive. Listen without thinking of the dozens of theories we've formed and discarded in the past two years. And remember"—I felt my voice grow unsteady—"that Jerry, too, is dead now."

Still he said nothing, though I thought his face had lost a little of its color. Around us and above us the night was black; Orion had swung imperceptibly toward the western horizon. I struck a match and laid it on the tobacco in my pipe bowl; the flame leaped and shrank as I drew on the bit. Its light flickered and wavered, like the light in the instrument room of Eldridge Observatory on that night two years ago when Jerry and I burst into it.

The room was round and perhaps twenty feet in diameter. It was roofed by the observatory dome, an inverted bowl with a great slot cut out of it where the slide was open. I remember that stars were sharply visible through the opening. The walls and the inside of the dome were painted gray, or some light-absorbing color, and the floor was bare. The telescope was mounted on a concrete base in the middle of the room, and its long barrel was aimed up and through the slide in the dome, trained on some star a thousand light years away, I suppose. In the silence of the room there was a single sound, the ticking of the clockwork motor that revolved the dome above us, moving it with the same tremendous precision as the earth itself, spinning on its axis.

Between us and the telescope was LeNormand's plain deal work-table, with a single hooded, gooseneck student's lamp spilling a little circle of light out on its top. Back to us stood a wooden chair, varnished oak, of the sort that universities must buy in carload lots. LeNormand was sitting in that chair, looking at us. His arms hung straight from his shoulders, and his head was so far bent over the top of the chairback that it was completely upside down. His eyes were open, looking right at us, but there was no expression on his face at all. It was like the face of a man asleep. Of course, he must have been dead, even then, but it still seems to me that the eyes moved once, just as we appeared in the doorway.

Fire was growing up his back and around his head like a great vine. Tentacles of it licked the back of the chair and wavered to and fro over his body; there was a great blossom of flame around his head. His face looked out at us between petals of live fire. It was not the kind of fire that a burning log gives. A yellow, lambent glow. It was not like anything I ever saw before. Clear, white, silent, flickering as fast as a snake's tongue, writhing like streamers of kelp in a tide race, it twined over and around and into the body of LeNormand as he sat there. It was a parasite on him, possessing and consuming him, apparently endued with a life of its own and nourished by its host, LeNormand. In the instant we stood, fixed with horror and amazement, in the doorway we began to smell what the fire was doing: the choking fume of burning hair and another smell that was still worse.

Lots of things happened in the next ten seconds. I ordered my legs to take me down the stairs and out of that appalling room; instead, they seemed to be carrying me straight toward LeNormand. As I went, I remember vaguely that I struggled out of my overcoat. Jerry had leaped to the wall near the stair well, and out of the corner of my eye I saw him snatch down the fire extinguisher there. The blast of heat and the stench, as I got nearer, were terrific. With the coat in front of me I flung myself at that incandescent figure on the chair. It and I went over together with a crash.

As we struck the floor, a tongue of flame went across my face.

Then I was kicking the chair away from me and wrapping LeNormand in the folds of my coat. Something cold and wet bit the back of my head, and I began to choke.

"Roll clear," I heard Jerry tell me. His voice was cool and urgent. I flung myself to the side and scrambled to my feet. With the fire blanketed by my coat, the room was almost dark. Jerry was standing with spraddled legs, the fire extinguisher in one hand and the nozzle of its short hose in the other. A jet of hissing liquid probed something black and huddled on the floor; tendrils of smoke were rising. Jerry kicked back a corner of the coat and turned the stream of chemical on whatever was underneath.

That was all I saw. I went down the stairs as fast as I could. My knees were weak as hell. I just about got outside in time. When I was too exhausted to gag any more I went back up. My mouth tasted of bile and Scotch, and yet I could still smell that acrid, sweetish smoke of burning flesh.

When I got back all the lights in the instrument room were on. The place looked impersonal. Jerry had supplemented my coat with his own, but except for that one long, dark blotch on the floor, the overturned chair, and a puddle of stuff from the extinguisher there was no change. I pulled myself up the last two steps by the hand rail and went into the room.

Jerry looked at me. His face was white. He licked his lips, started to say something, and stopped. I couldn't think of anything to say. Most of my mind was busy telling my stomach to stay in the usual place. Finally the silence got to me; I felt that unless I said something I should be sick again.

"Well?" I managed to get out.

"Are you all right?"

I wasn't entirely sure. "Yeah. If I didn't lose any essential part of me down there."

"Jesus, I'm sorry."

"I'm okay now," I told him. "Is he . . . ? Have you . . . ?" I didn't know how to put the question.

Jerry nodded. "I looked at him. He's dead, all right."

"I see you used your overcoat too."

He looked away and said, "His feet were sticking out."

I saw him swallow.

Neither of us said anything for a minute after that. I got to thinking. "What do we do now?"

Jerry took a couple of steps toward the overcoats, and then stopped. "I've been wondering about that myself."

"We ought to tell somebody."

He almost smiled. "Sure. But just who?"

"What do you mean?"

"Well, there's the Dean. And there's Prexy. And we might get a doctor from the infirmary. And the undertaker. And the police, of course."

This last was a new idea to me, but it made sense. There'd have to be some sort of investigation into how LeNormand had come to die. That fire . . .

"I guess we ought to call the police."

Jerry admitted that. But it was a University matter, any way you looked at it. As he pointed out, this would be front-page news tomorrow, and it was important that we do the whole thing carefully. We talked it over and agreed the safest thing to do would be to call Prexy and leave it up to him. He could handle it any way he wanted.

"Listen," said Jerry, when we'd agreed on that. "Suppose you phone him. There's a couple of things here I want to look at."

Probably he saw I was still pretty shaky. "There's nothing here I ever want to see again," I said, and went down the stairs.

At the bottom of the spiral there was a telephone, one of the old-fashioned kind with the brown oak box, fastened to the wall. The University had its own on-campus system. I picked up the receiver. After quite some time a kid's bored voice said in my ear, "University."

"Get me President Murray."

"He's not to be disturbed. There's a trustees' dinner tonight."

I was annoyed. This guy was probably a green kid with a scholarship. "Listen, freshman," I told him. "This is an eccentric old millionaire who wants to leave the U a million dollars. And I want to talk to Murray. Get him."

"Yes, sir." Bells rang, clicks occurred, and eventually Prexy's smooth, careful voice was there in the receiver.

"This is President Murray."

In four years at the University I'd never spoken to Prexy before. I was suddenly nervous. "President Murray, I'm Bark Jones, class of 'thirty-two."

"I'm very sorry, Mr. Jones. I'm extremely busy at the moment. If there is anything I can do for you—"

I cut him short. "This is serious, sir. I'm not drunk or playing a practical joke. I'm at the observatory, and there's been a serious accident. Jerry Lister, a classmate of mine, and I think you had best come up here right away."

His voice changed its quality. Some of the smoothness went out of it. It became alert, suspicious. A trifle peremptory. "What sort of accident?"

I told him Professor LeNormand was dead. He didn't believe me. I told him again.

"Mr. Jones, if this is not absolutely—"

"Absolutely and positively," I affirmed.

"Have you notified anyone else?"

"No," I said. "We considered that this was a University matter. We want you to come at once and take the thing off our hands. Better come alone. It's a nasty business."

His voice still sounded incredulous, but he told me, "Very well. I shall be there in ten minutes."

I hung up and sat down on the bottom step; my legs felt like boiled macaroni, and my mouth still tasted abominably. There was a high, continuous, ringing sound in my ears.

"Hey, Bark!" It was Jerry's voice from the top of the stairs.

"Coming," I told him, and decided on the way up to keep count of the number of times I had to climb those damn stairs. This was the third trip.

Jerry had turned out the lights again and found a couple of chairs some place. He made me sit down, first producing, to my pleased surprise, a flask.

"If you think you can hold this down now, you better have some."

I held it down, all right. It was fine stuff, Irish, and must have come out of the family cellar. Our drinking and our talk, as I reproduce it, sounds callous. Perhaps it was. But after a shock like the one we had just experienced, your emotions retreat to some quiet corner of your brain and you set up, in self-protection, a superficial toughness of mind to keep from going crazy. I was glad to get a drink, and because I could not tolerate too much silence in that room, I accused him of holding out on me.

"Always prepared," he replied. "I used to be a Boy Scout once." His manner changed, and he stared at the floor for some moments without speaking, as though he were trying to decide about something difficult. "I suppose Prexy's on his way?"

"Said he'd be here in ten minutes."

Jerry nodded. "There's a couple of things we better talk over before he comes, Bark."

"My God," I said. "This thing is foul enough already. I don't want to talk about it. Let Prexy shoulder the grief."

He cut me short. "That's all very well. I don't like this any better than you do. Besides, LeNormand was my friend."

"I'm sorry."

"Forget it. We're going to be asked a whole lot of questions, Bark. Prexy first, and then the police, and then, I suppose, the newspapers. Just what are we going to tell them?"

"Why... that we came in here—I suppose it was about six o'clock —and found LeNormand here, burning up in his chair, and..."

Jerry looked hard at me. "Yeah. We came in here and LeNormand was in his chair with his head hanging down over the back of it, and he was burning. Burning like a torch. Suppose somebody told you that story?"

It did sound unconvincing when he put it as baldly as that. The questions I'd been fighting to keep out of my mind began to stampede into it. How did the fire start? How could LeNormand have just sat there while it burned him alive? Had he carelessly jammed a lighted pipe into his pocket and set fire to his clothes that way? Then he must have died soon after, because no man would sit calmly in his chair and be burned to death. Heart failure? Perhaps that was it.

Jerry cut in on my thoughts. "While you were telephoning, I looked round this place. It's going to be pretty hard to explain how it happened, Bark. You saw him just as we came in. Did you think he was dead then?"

"He must have been."

"Did you *think* he was?"

"No," I had to admit. "I thought I saw his eyes move. I thought he was looking at us."

He nodded. "So did I. Maybe it was the flicker of the fire." He paused. "Take a look at that chair, but don't touch it. There may be fingerprints."

I got up slowly and crossed the room to the overturned chair. I had to force one foot deliberately and consciously ahead of the other to get there, and it took every ounce of will power to do it. Leaning over carefully, so as to include nothing else in the room in my field of vision, I looked at the chair. Of course, at the time it was dark in the room, but even the light from one gooseneck lamp was enough to show that the chair was not the way I'd expected it to be. Instead of being blackened with fire and charred clear up the back, it was almost unmarked. There were a few varnish blisters toward the top of the back, but that was all. I thought of that flick of fire that had gone across my face when I tackled LeNormand and couldn't decide whether it had felt hot or not. It must have; all fires are hot, so I must have felt the heat, but I couldn't remember that I had. And apparently the chair hadn't. It simply was not burned. I turned toward Jerry.

"This is the damnedest thing."

He nodded and said carefully, "I looked at him too. His back is burned clear through."

My stomach began to turn on its foundations. "I'll take your word for that."

"You know," he observed calmly, "this thing is going to look like a crime. In fact, murder. A torch murder."

I left the chair and went back to him. "And we'll be the principal witnesses?"

"Witnesses," said Jerry, "or else ..."

"Or else what?"

"Suspects."

"Nuts," I said. "They won't suspect us."

"The only way out of this place is the front door. We had it in view for five minutes before we got here. Did you see anyone come out?"

"It was dark."

Jerry looked at me sadly. "Yes, it was dark, but we'd have seen the motion, at least, if someone had slipped out. Unless the police find some other goat, it looks to me as if we'd be unanimously elected. Somebody did it."

I could see the point. We might be in for a nasty time. "How about saying that we did see somebody—just a shadow—go out the door?"

He didn't think much of that idea. In fact, his opinion was that it wouldn't pay to lie to the police. I thought privately that it might be accident or suicide, or lots of things besides murder, but I could see that Jerry was right about one thing. We were going to be in the limelight for a couple of days. Our final decision was that each of us would tell his own story and stick by it.

All the time we were talking Jerry was wandering round the room, looking at everything. There were some scattered papers and a pencil on top of the worktable, and he spent some time staring at them. As far as I could tell, the papers had equations of some sort on them, and Jerry finally decided to copy them into his notebook, though he kept muttering that they didn't make sense and he couldn't understand them at all. The paper was the sort they sell by the tablet at the University co-op, and the edges of the leaves looked faintly yellow as if the sheets were old.

I began to feel completely shot. My legs ached, my head ached. I felt dirty all over, and tired to death. There was a nasty taste in my mouth.

"What the hell's keeping Prexy?" I said fretfully. "I want to get a shower and some sleep. I feel like the latter end of a misspent life."

Jerry grinned. "You ain't seen nothing yet. Forget about the shower and the sleep. Just impress this place, and the way every thing is in it, on your mind. We'll be questioned till we're liable to forget our own names."

He was obviously right, and I tried to follow his advice. But there were so few things to look at and the whole affair was so conspicuously a nightmare that it all began to seem unreal to me. I wondered if I had d.t.'s. Maybe this was the way they took you. Perhaps if I could get hold of some sleep and a competent doctor I'd be cured of the whole illusion. Just then there was a swish of tires on the gravel.

"Prexy's here," said Jerry. "And now the fun begins."

We crossed to the head of the spiral stairs; there was the slam of a car door, and the brisk click of the latch at the entrance.

"Mr. Jones?" his big voice boomed out in the hall below.

"Right up here, sir," I called down.

He came up the stairs, irritation and purpose in every stamp of his feet on the treads. "Mr. Jones, I trust the extraordinary story you told me over the telephone a few minutes ago—"

And he was in the room, his words abruptly silenced by its quiet austerity. Before he had perfect control of himself, I heard him give a single sniff, as the impact of the smell still lingering in the air took him by surprise. Even though he did not see LeNormand at once, he said nothing, asked no questions, but looked swiftly about him. He had no doubt in the world after that first breath.

Prexy is a fine-looking man, big as a house and built like an athlete, with a granite face and hair as gray as stone. His manner is heavy rather than pompous, and he never appears to be at a loss. My own idea is that his worst enemy has been a terrible temper, and that he has learned to keep it chained up so tight that he gives an impression of being almost devoid of feeling. I always think of him more as a major in the marines than as an educator; sometimes I suspect he does himself. There's no doubt, though, that his iron purpose and executive force have put life into the whole University. That evening he was dressed for a formal dinner—tails and white tie.

Jerry broke the momentary silence. "Over there," he said, with a flash of his eye toward the long, dark bundle on the floor.

"Thank you," said Prexy. "You're Mr. Lister?"

"Yes."

"I'll talk to you both about this in a moment." He went across the room evenly, steadily. Then he was kneeling beside our overcoats. I saw one hand reach out to draw them back, and looked quickly away. The clockwork of the dome ticked steadily on, the pinprick stars burned in the black sky beyond the opening, and I could see my breath, faintly frosty in the cold air of the room. When I looked again, Prexy was just standing up. He came back to us, glancing from Jerry to me without the slightest expression of any sort on his face. But I'd swear it was whiter than it had been, and the lips more firmly pressed together.

"You gentlemen did exactly the right thing in calling me," he said. "It's LeNormand, and he's dead."

Jerry said, "I think you'd better hear our story before doing anything further." And he told the whole thing, quickly and concisely.

When he had finished, Prexy asked: "Have you anything to add to that, Mr. Jones?"

"No, sir."

"Mr. Lister, Mr. Jones, you must surely be aware that your story is almost impossible to believe. Your account of the discovery of Professor LeNormand's body is absolutely incompatible with the nature and extent of the burns." His voice was not quite so decisive. "I have never seen a human body so—" he paused for a word, "so nearly incinerated."

I couldn't think of a thing to say. Neither of us could. We stood there, silent, with our eyes on his face.

Prexy seemed disappointed. "You both came down to the game this afternoon?"

We nodded.

"Unless you are extraordinary young men, you have both taken a few drinks. How many?"

I told him, and he listened, apparently without disapproval. "But we're not drunk, sir," I concluded. "The story Lister and I have told you is true, absolutely, in every detail."

He frowned. "It can't be true. However this thing happened, a man would not sit in his chair and allow himself to be burned to death..." His voice faded.

"Unless he was dead already," Jerry said.

"Heart failure..." Prexy's voice was doubtful.

"On the other hand, what about that fire? Does anything about it strike you?" Jerry's intonation almost demanded an affirmative answer.

"He always used to smoke a pipe," I said. "Perhaps he put it in his pocket before it was entirely out, and then his heart failed, and his clothes caught on fire, and—"

Prexy stopped me with one look. "A wool suit smolders, Mr. Jones. It does not burn like that; it could not have created a fire that must have been as hot as a blowtorch. That is why I wished to make sure that your story is complete. You have left out nothing? You are concealing nothing?"

"No," said Jerry flatly.

Prexy tried again. "It is my duty to report this to the police," he said, "and the moment I do so there will be an investigation. You must both understand that you will be questioned over and over again. The police will be as dissatisfied with your story as I am."

Jerry laughed. A little sharply. "President Murray, we have been over all this together. We debated inventing a more plausible story to tell you and the police. We decided to stick to the truth."

Some idiotic impulse made me add: "'Integer vitae, scelerisque purus,' you know, sir."

Prexy smiled faintly. "How these little tags of learning do stick, Mr. Jones! Let me advise you not to try them on Chief Hanlon. I fear that, like Shakespeare, he has little Latin and less Greek."

Jerry looked pleased with me. I think he imagined I had made a dint in Prexy's court-martial calm. But he brought the conversation back at once to the focal point by asking, "Did you look at the chair, sir?"

"No, I didn't." Prexy's tone was impatient, but at once he went across the room and examined it, just as I had done. As he straightened up he looked at Jerry incredulously and said, "And you are still determined to stick to your evidence that Professor LeNormand was actually sitting in this chair when you found his burning body?"

"What else can we do?"

He didn't seem to have an answer to that. Frowning thoughtfully, he began to inspect the room in detail, staring at its meager furniture and the howitzer barrel of the telescope with puzzled eyes. We watched him apathetically, and when he came back across the room, Jerry said flatly, "Nothing."

"Nothing, as you say, Mr. Lister. Nothing at all."

It seemed to me that this was going on forever, that the events of this night would slow down the hands of time till all creation stopped. Time was not passing—it was stretching like a gigantic rubber band, it had ceased to exist, it was an illusion accomplished with mirrors and beveled gears, and the machinery had ceased to create the illusion. My thoughts were so many and so confused that they canceled each other; every cell in my brain felt as though it were loaded with a different charge.

The thing was becoming intolerable, and I knew Jerry was feeling something the same way; his face was set and the gray of his eyes was darker than I had ever seen it. I knew he was intensely nervous by the way he kept sliding the palms of his hands back and forth against each other.

"You remember that gesture he always had, Dad."

"Yes, I remember it."

"He used to do it just before the kickoff when he was playing football."

"And when he got married, before the ceremony."

I went on with my story, quickly.

Prexy, though, was perfectly self-possessed. He must have been wondering if we were a couple of murderers. He must have been thinking about what all this would mean to the University, about the publicity and the crowds of curiosity seekers that would soon be littering the campus, about the difficulty of keeping his faculty and the student body quiet, and about a thousand and one other things. But he was making his decisions as calmly as though the whole thing was mere routine, like the reading of minutes in a trustees' meeting.

"I wish," he said finally, "that I could spare you two gentlemen something of what lies ahead of you in the next few hours. You can imagine the difficulties in which this places me."

We assured him that we could.

He went on. "The story you have told me is so extraordinary that I believe you are telling the truth. Whether this is a case of accident or murder I cannot decide. Ultimately the police will have to decide it. I must, therefore, telephone them at once and attend to certain other matters as well. I put you both on your honor as University men not to touch anything in this room until I return from the telephone downstairs." And without waiting for any reply he went down the spiral steps and left us alone in the room.

"'I pledge my honor as a gentleman,'" said Jerry in a low voice, "'that during the course of this examination I have neither given nor received assistance.'"

It was the honor pledge we all used to write at the end of every exam paper. I laughed. "So far as he's concerned, we're still undergraduates."

We could hear Prexy's full-throated voice booming in the hall below. He called the police, the Dean's office, the infirmary, and several other places. After a while we stopped listening to him. Perhaps some other sort of person would have been excited at being thrust willy-nilly into the midst of a disaster like the one of that night, but we could find no stimulus in the situation. We were tired. The game had drained us of emotion. The liquor had worn off, and the adventure was not a nice adventure. If I shut my eyes I could still see Le-Normand's body in its strange, horrible position, the great parasite of fire growing out of it, and the flicker of the eyes as we came into the room. It was frightening. The chill in that observatory chamber came from something colder than the night November air. It went in deeper than my bones. It went into my mind.

"This is grim," Jerry observed.

"Oh, I don't know," I said with what must have been a feeble effort at jocularity, "to me this is all in the day's work. I take it in my stride."

"Of course, you do." His face was unsmiling. "Somehow, I'm not quite so much of an iron man. I don't like it."

When Jerry talked that way, it was no use trying to be flippant. I suspected that he saw something more in the situation than I did and that he was alarmed about it. He told me what it was after a while.

"Bark, listen." He lowered his voice. "This is a murder, all right. It's too incredible to think it's an accident, or the result of heart failure, or anything like that. It's a cinch the autopsy will prove I'm right."

"Admitted." He added nothing more, so I went on. "And it's a murder that we didn't commit, though I bet a lot of people are going to think we did."

He shook his head. "I wonder. After all, we haven't any motive. None whatever. And neither of us has any Leopold and Loeb tendencies. And how did we commit it? No, I think the papers will shy clear of accusing us, even indirectly."

"It's the police that worry me, not the papers."

"Don't fool yourself." He was positive. "The police won't be able to find a thing to implicate us, because there isn't anything to find. In a way, I must have been one of the few friends LeNormand had over here. We're in for a nasty siege of questioning, but the police will start looking elsewhere pretty soon."

"How do you figure that?"

"LeNormand had some enemies. And we both know who they are."

I examined my mind and drew a blank. "I don't."

He was impatient. "Don't be thick. How about all that correspondence I used to type? The row he had with Trimble and Pforzman and Stanward, and the rest of them? There's the motive. I'm sure of it."

I looked at him in astonishment. "You mean you think those stargazers and atom-busters would kill each other over the Einstein space-time theory? Nuts!"

Jerry didn't think it was impossible at all. He insisted that the matter was vital, fundamental, that I had no idea of the importance of LeNormand's theory, and that if he was proved right it would reveal a lot of his esteemed contemporaries as scientific jackasses. They wouldn't lose their standing in their own little world without a fight. Jerry thought some one of them might have been desperate enough to kill LeNormand. He pointed out how bitter the letters had been.

To me the idea was unthinkable, and I said so. I asked him if he had any single man in mind.

"No."

"Then," I told him, "forget it. Don't, for God's sake, uncork that idea on the police. Next thing you know they'll have Einstein down at headquarters, going over him with a rubber hose. And the poor guy came over here from Germany to get away from all that."

He laughed. "Okay. I wasn't going to tell them anything except what we saw, anyway. If they find out about that old row, though, I may have to tell them the theory. And there *is* one thing that supports it."

I saw that he really was serious. "What's that?" I asked skeptically.

"The fire."

"What about the fire?"

"It must have been a chemical—maybe thermite or something of that sort. No ordinary substance would burn into flesh and bone as deep and fast as that did. If you get me, it must have been a scientist's kind of fire."

I took a little time to digest that idea. It was plausible, but I simply couldn't believe that any of LeNormand's professional critics and antagonists would want to kill him. Most scientists, in spite of the movies, aren't murderous mad geniuses at all. There were several other things that were against the theory.

"And if I'm right about that," Jerry continued, "the autopsy ought to reveal what the stuff was."

"But what about the chair?" I objected. I felt we weren't getting any place.

He looked thoughtful. "LeNormand must have been knocked out first. The stuff was put on him, and then he was set in the chair. The murderer must have touched it off as we came up the stairs."

"And then he put some more of it on his feet and evaporated himself," I suggested.

Jerry pointed to the open slide in the observatory dome. "He must have gone out that way."

From his tone it was plain that he wasn't satisfied with his own theory. Neither was I, but I had no alternative suggestion. We could think of nothing further to say; each of us was trying to find a theory, however vague, to cover the facts and prove we were not the only ones to visit LeNormand in that cold, round room. After a moment we heard Prexy coming upstairs again. As he entered we stood up; it was astonishing how much he made us feel like undergraduates.

"Sit down, gentlemen. You must both be pretty tired."

Obediently we sat.

"I shall remain here with you until the police arrive. And then," his face altered, but whether to tenderness or pity, or something subtler, I could not make out, "I shall have the melancholy duty of bringing the news of this tragedy to Mrs. LeNormand."

"Mrs. LeNormand!" Jerry's exclamation was one of incredulity and shock.

"Yes," said Prexy, half to himself, "Mrs. LeNormand. You didn't know he was married?"

"No...And he never told me...I saw no announcement...I mean, this is absolutely a..." Jerry was floundering.

"We were all surprised," Prexy admitted. "I don't believe anyone expected it. He wasn't the sort of man who gets married ordinarily."

"For God's sake," I said, "when did it happen?"

Prexy's expression as he looked at us was introspective. He must have been thinking fast with most of his mind and answering us with nothing but the top layer of it. "About three months ago. He appeared at one of Mrs. Murray's summer teas and simply presented her to all of us as his wife. It was quite a sensation."

I could imagine that. The microcosm of University society must have been rocked to its center. LeNormand, of all people! Why, it actually amounted to bigamy, the man was so genuinely wedded to his work. He ate with it, lived with it, slept with it. Many a time Jerry had commented on the fact that LeNormand had utterly no use for women. He wouldn't even employ a secretary, which was one reason Jerry had done so much of his secretarial work for him. He certainly was old enough not to be swept off his feet, and disciplined to the ascetic life he had chosen. I couldn't imagine what he wanted with a wife, and surprised as I was I could see that Jerry was completely thunderstruck. He was staring at Prexy as though he expected to learn it was all a joke.

"President Murray," he said finally, "I wish you'd tell me more than that. Who is she? Where did she come from? Why did LeNormand...?"

Prexy frowned. "I've told you almost all that I, or anyone else so far as I know, can tell you. Not one person in the University had ever seen her before. LeNormand was matter-of-fact about it, at least on the surface, but he's never given us a word of explanation. We couldn't pry anything out of him. We couldn't even—" He checked himself. "This is all really beside the point."

Jerry was urgent. "No, it isn't. If LeNormand got married—and I knew him well, sir, I was his friend—there is something strange about it. I can't think of a thing that would make him want to surrender his...his freedom. Why, even the most beautiful woman in the world—"

With no expression on his face at all, Prexy said slowly, "Some people might say that she is the most beautiful woman in the world."

4. INTERREGNUM

BRAKES squealed on the road outside. We could hear the voices of several men.

"Ah, the police," said President Murray. I thought there was a note of relief in his voice, as though he was glad to have an interruption and a termination to our talk.

Yes, indeed, it was the police. The boys in blue. The guardians of the peace, the representatives of law and order, arriving at the scene of the crime, if crime it was. A little stir of excitement went through me as their steps began to clang on the stairs.

Chief Hanlon was in the van. A white-haired cockerel of a man with sharp eyes and a bit of the brogue still stuck to the knife-edge of his tongue. I hadn't seen him since Founders' night at the Zete house, when a few of us were organizing a little bonfire in honor of the old Lodge. Our mistake was in departing from ancient custom, which dictated the selection of a telephone booth from some farmer's back yard as the pièce de résistance of the pyre. That night we decided to use the town's one and only police booth as a variation; who would have supposed the old boy would hear about it at two in the morning? I saw him grin briefly at Jerry and me when his eyes lit on us.

"Hello, b'ys," was all he said to us.

At his heels was young Pudge Applegate. Pudge is the son, and I presume heir, of Collegeville's former bootlegger, and also Hanlon's son-in-law. He weighs a scant two hundred and twenty-five pounds, practically all of which he carries below the neck. Although his uniform always looked as though he had had it laundered on him quite some time before, he was not so fat as his nickname suggested. If Chief Hanlon was the brains of the force, he was certainly its brawn.

And then there was Old Harry. None of us ever knew his last name; he'd been a University proctor till he got too old and philosophical to bear down hard on the pranks and wanton wiles of Young America on the loose. Then the Collegeville police force secured his services. I don't know that he ever made an arrest.

For a minute or two the three of them, after greeting Prexy respectfully, simply stared about them silent in the presence of that round, cold room, the dark hummock of LeNormand's body stretched out in the shadows on the floor, and the lingering reek in the air. Finally Chief Hanlon made a quick inspection of the body and returned to ask a few questions of Jerry and me. We told our story flatly and briefly, and he did not cross-question us about it. I'll say to his credit that he realized immediately that he was up against something outside his experience, something uncommonly nasty. Almost at once he scrawled a note to Parsons, head of the county detectives, and sent it off to New Zion, the county seat, by Harry, to whom he gave some whispered instructions. I wondered for a moment why he did not telephone, till I remembered that the switchboard girls would promptly broadcast the story. He kept his own hands and Pudge's off everything in the room, and after he had heard our story he sent Pudge outside to watch the building. He verified from Prexy the fact that Doc Nickerson at the infirmary had been summoned. Then he simply sat on a chair and whistled between his teeth. Prexy left after a few minutes, promising to return later, and the three of us were left alone in that vault. The silence was oppressive; the only time it was broken was when Hanlon stopped whistling for a moment, stared at Jerry and me with his cold blue eyes, and said:

"You b'ys seem to be on hand fer the fires."

We didn't know how to take that, so we said nothing. Hanlon grinned after a minute and recommenced his whistling. The machine of the dome kept on ticking. Time went on stretching. I don't know how many minutes elapsed before Doc Nickerson arrived, but his appearance was welcome. He nodded to Jerry, whom I suppose he remembered from football days, and went right to work. His examination didn't take long.

"Don't move him any more than you can help, doc," Hanlon cautioned. "Don't touch nothin' else."

"I haven't moved him at all," the doc said. He turned to his little black bag, took out some cotton and a bottle of something or other. Moistening the cotton with whatever was in the bottle, he swabbed off all his fingers carefully and stood up. "He's dead, of course. Burned to death, apparently. The burns are very severe. The muscles of the upper back and shoulders seem to have been almost entirely consumed. The left scapula is calcined." He closed his bag and came over to us. "How did this happen?" He, too, seemed to feel the same incredulity that had affected Jerry and me and Prexy. "I never saw such burns before."

I started to say something, but Hanlon silenced me with a wave of his hand. "Doc, can ye think of any way that such burns could be caused? The poor fella's half cooked."

Nickerson shook his head. "It seems almost as though a blowtorch had been held at his back."

Hanlon took him up on that. "Thin he must 'a' been dead whin it was used on him?"

But the doctor was being conservative. "I can't tell. Obviously, there will have to be an autopsy."

"Perhaps heart failure . . ." Jerry's voice was tentative.

"It's impossible to tell anything now. But LeNormand came to me a few days ago for a going-over. He did that every year. He was sound as a nut last Tuesday."

"Ye don't tell me." Hanlon's voice sounded a trifle disappointed.

Jerry said, "Doc, could those burns have been made with a chemical?"

"A chemical? What have you got in mind?"

"Something like thermite."

It was a new idea to Nickerson. He paused. "I don't know. I don't know the effect of the stuff at all."

"They use it in welding," Jerry explained. "And the Italian aviators used something like it on the Abyssinians. It's a mixture of powdered aluminum and iron oxide."

Nickerson rubbed his ear thoughtfully. "A chemical analysis of the calcined matter and the edges of the clothing ought to settle the point. But I didn't see any slag. Still, it's an idea."

Hanlon glanced quickly at Jerry. "Ye've a theory, young feller."

"No," said Jerry. "Not even a hunch. Something must have done it, though."

"Isn't it possible," I ventured, "that the thing is an accident? He could have put his pipe, lighted, into his pocket."

Nickerson shook his head. "I don't see it. Even if he had accidentally set fire to his clothes, and even if they had been soaked in gasoline, I don't believe he could have been burned like that." He turned to the Chief. "Do you want me to do anything more?"

Hanlon fidgeted a little in his chair. "Well, maybe you better wait till Parsons gets here. He's head of county detectives. Likely he'll have Doc Merritt with him. The two of yez can maybe put yer heads together and figure the mess out."

"All right," said Nickerson.

We found him a chair, and he sat down with us. Silence descended again. I had expected that Hanlon would keep firing questions at us, try to shake our story, try to "break" the case right away. Instead, he did nothing. For a time I was puzzled, even vaguely uneasy about his inactivity, and then the obvious answer occurred to me. Collegeville is owned, body and soul, by the University. Hanlon was shrewd enough to see that this affair would create tremendous excitement and perhaps a scandal; whoever tackled it would be opening a hornets' nest without gloves. His tiny department was not fitted, any more than he himself, to handle a situation of this sort. He was playing it safe; he was going to turn the case over, untouched and unhandled, to Parsons.

When the county men arrived, they appeared to approve of his decisions. Parsons was a slow, calm, neutral sort of man, but he knew his job. He turned Merritt, the county doctor, loose on the corpse.

He had photographs taken of every inch of the observatory building. He had every surface tested for fingerprints, and took ours, Hanlon's, Nickerson's, and Pudge's. He sent a man over to Prexy's house to ask him if he'd mind coming back at once. After listening once to Jerry's story and mine, separately, he noted down our stadium ticket numbers, and listed the people we'd noticed at the game who might be able to corroborate our presence. He studied the floor, the walls, and every piece of furniture in the room. He took a note of the company that manufactured the fire extinguisher Jerry had used. A man was sent out to examine the ground outside the building under the dome opening. He put us through our stories a second time and a third. He hammered and hammered at us, patiently explaining that our story was not very likely. He suggested that we might care to supplement it. When Prexy appeared, he talked quietly with him for a long time, nodding his head from time to time and glancing over at us or at the place where LeNormand's body had been before his men had taken it away. After Prexy left, he climbed up to the dome slot himself and summoned the fingerprint man after him. He was all over the place, remorselessly, efficiently, and unhurriedly.

It all took a lot of time. Somewhere around midnight he turned to us.

"I don't want to make this any harder for you two than I have to," he said. "I don't want to lock you up. You're the only witnesses I've got, and your story is fishy as hell. But I can't find anything to incriminate either of you so far. By morning we'll have the results of the autopsy, and perhaps some new information. I'll have to go over the whole thing with you again. So you'll have to stay in town tonight. Where are you going to sleep?"

Jerry and I sighed. We had seen this coming. Jerry told him, "We can stay at the Lodge—our fraternity house, the Zeta Kappas."

Hanlon nodded. He knew the Zete house, all right. Parsons seemed not too pleased by the suggestion.

"We can get a bed there, and borrow razors and staff in the morning," I urged. "It's too late to find any place else."

Parsons was still dubious. "Well, I dunno."

Hanlon was on our side. "Sure, Mr. Parsons, the b'ys are roight. They'll be asy to find in the mornin, and it's the sinsible place fer thim to go."

"Oke." Parsons wasted no more thought on us. "I'll send a man around to the Zeta house in the morning, when I want you. Stay there till you hear from me. On your way, now."

We went down the iron stairs numbly. As we left the room we heard him telling Chief Hanlon to arrange an interview in the morning with himself, Prexy, and Mrs. LeNormand, and do it diplomatically. Even the great Parsons was sensible of how much power the President of the University has, and it was plain that he was anxious to offend no one.

Outside, both of us drew in great lungfuls of the icy air. It felt almost like getting out of jail to be walking alone across the campus. Without our coats we felt cold, but something of the oppression that had settled on us back there in Eldridge Observatory began to lift. The ringing in my ears diminished, and my legs felt a little less leaden.

"This is an improvement," Jerry said after a while.

I remarked that the air smelled good. It was not the most felicitous possible observation.

"Poor devil," Jerry muttered. "Hell of a way to die. I hope they get the bastard that did it . . ."

"Amen."

"Married, by God. Married. Bark, what could have got into LeNormand? He had no more use for women than the Sultan's right-hand man. LeNormand was all brain. What do you suppose was in his mind?"

"Prexy said she is the most beautiful woman in the world."

"Not quite. He said some people might think so. And remember the Queen." "The Queen" was campus slang for Mrs. Murray.

We agreed that Prexy might be prejudiced. But neither of us could explain LeNormand's having taken a wife. Jerry thought that if she was half as beautiful as Prexy said she might provide the motive, and the idea seemed to give him a good deal of satisfaction.

"And, Bark," he concluded, "as long as there's this other angle I'm not going to say anything about the row over LeNormand's work. I don't want to stir up that kind of mess, and there's probably nothing in it anyway. The best thing for us to do is to answer all their questions and volunteer nothing at all."

"I'm with you there," I told him. "But it's up to you. You're the one who knows the inside story."

"Let's not talk about it any more," he said, and we walked along in silence through the dark.

By and by we came to the Zete house. The brethren were in good voice by then, and the victory over State was being properly solemnized. We went up the front steps and rang the bell, shivering. A pledge came out, and we identified ourselves. Buzz Clark, the chapter president, came into the hall to greet us. He was magnificently cordial, but he would have welcomed a tax collector in the same effusive way by that time. He told us to hang up our hats and come in and have a drink. We declined, and asked if there were a couple of beds in the house. He asked us gravely where the ladies were. We told him to go to hell. It went on like that for quite a while. Buzz shouted to the pledge to bring us a couple of drinks, but we wouldn't take them.

"My God," he said finally. "You guys lose your grip fast after you get out of this place."

We admitted that we were not the men we used to be in college, but insisted that for a couple of elderly wrecks like ourselves bed was the only place. He took us upstairs finally, and turned us into an empty room. I can't remember undressing or getting into bed.

I stopped speaking and began to sift the sand of my memory once again, hoping and yet half afraid that I had missed telling some small fact, some nuance of word, some impression of eye or mind that might provide the key to the answer. There was nothing.

"*That's how it was,*" *I said slowly.* "*I've told you everything, Dad.*"

Dr. Lister was leaning forward, his forearms on the table, staring at the topaz star that the candlelight kindled in the sherry bottle.

"*Yes,*" *he replied.* "*I think you have. All three of us have considered the matter a hundred times. Parsons, too, is a great detective in his way. There is nothing to go on, no clues, nothing but incredibilities." He repeated the word softly. "Incredibilities."*

"There is an answer," I told him, "but I think the answer itself is an incredibility."

"Why do you say that?"

"I know that Jerry found the answer, and that having found it he killed himself."

He made an impatient gesture. "Why? Because he was afraid to tell it? That's not like Jerry."

"No, I don't think that was it. I have a feeling that he did what he did—(the lifted gun, the flat, hard crack of the report echoing in that Western room)—because he was afraid to have us, or anyone, learn the answer. Afraid that he might tell the truth. A truth he was afraid to have us know."

He poured us each another glass of sherry. "Are you too tired to go on? Shall we wait till morning? It must be almost eleven o'clock now."

"No," I said. "I'm not too tired. I don't want to shut my eyes."

We woke about nine the next morning. I was surprised at how well I felt after a shower, a shave with Buzz Clark's razor, and a good breakfast. Neither of us had a hangover, and though I felt a little lazy and weak in the legs, I found that I was ready for anything the day might bring. Jerry, too, was less grave and preoccupied. We went into the library and read the morning papers. There was nothing in them about LeNormand's death; the story had apparently broken too late, at least, for the out-of-town editions. We read the account of the game the day before. As usual, the papers carried the story as if the game had been a moral victory for State, but they always dislike us, and even bias could not conceal the fact that we'd been on the long end of the score. Bill Bonham's account in the *Record* contained a passage I still remember and which confirmed my feeling about that first quarter:

> State punched out its first-quarter touchdown with an impressive display of power and old-fashioned football. The boys from Brunswick took the ball deep in their own territory, and

in a series of pile-driver bucks and slants drove down to the University twelve-yard line, where Stanwicz heaved the leather dead into the arms of Moroney for the score. The advance had the crowd breathless, and toward the end you could have heard a pin drop in the big bowl . . .

"Toward the end you could have heard a pin drop." He was right, and it recalled to me the odd sense of tension, the surcharge of human emotion and passion I had felt so strongly the afternoon before.

Parsons sent for us as we finished with the papers. Apparently he had shifted his base of operations, for the car drew up in front of the imitation Gothic town hall—in Collegeville everything tries to match the University's style—and we were shown into the police station in the wing at the right.

To my surprise, Prexy was there, and so was Doc Nickerson. Parsons was sitting at a long table with a lot of papers spread out in front of him. He looked gray-faced and deadly tired, but he mustered up a smile for us.

"Sit down, boys. There's nothing formal about this. Just want to ask you a few more questions."

Prexy cleared his threat authoritatively. "I am quite sure, gentlemen, that you will not require the presence of a lawyer at this hearing. Nevertheless, if you wish to have legal advice, you are entitled to demand it."

"That's all right," Jerry said as we took a couple of chairs. "Go ahead, Mr. Parsons."

"When you walked toward the door of the observatory you had it in full view?"

"Yes, though of course it was dark and there was only the one light, and we weren't watching it consciously—"

"But you are both still positive that no one came out of that door during the time you were walking toward it?"

Jerry paused. "Neither of us saw anyone. The odds are that one of us was looking toward the door every second of the way."

"Then, from the time you approached the observatory, you don't believe anyone could have left it without attracting your attention?" Parsons seemed to be aiming the question at me.

"Well," I said, "not through the door. Somebody might have got out through the slot in the dome."

"They didn't," said Parsons grimly. "There's a wide bed of plants on that side of the building, and anybody leaving that way would be sure to leave traces. There aren't any."

Suddenly Jerry stiffened beside me and leaned forward. "There *is* one way that someone could have got out of the building without our knowing it."

Prexy looked surprised, but Parsons smiled. "Aha!" Then, after a pause, "Well, Mr. Lister?"

"Whoever did it might have sneaked down the stairs when he heard us at the door, and gone into one of the classrooms. They were dark and we didn't look in there. Then, when we went up the stairs, he could have slipped out and made his escape."

Parsons looked triumphant. "You've got a head on your shoulders. What do you say, Mr. Jones?"

I was puzzled. "I can't see any reason why it isn't possible," I replied.

"But you don't think it was that way. Why not?"

"Well," I struggled to find words for an intangible impression, "when we entered the hall I glanced at the two dark open doors of those classrooms. There may have been somebody in one of them, but it didn't feel that way. It felt like an empty house." Putting it that way sounded silly to me, but Parsons nodded encouragingly.

"Yes," he said, "I know the feeling you mean. I often rely on it myself. But in this case," he looked at us all thoughtfully, "I think we have to decide that that is how the murderer got out of the building."

"The murderer," Jerry said. "So you're sure it is murder?"

"There wasn't a trace of any organic defect to make it anything else," said Doc Nickerson.

"Did you look for traces of chemical?" Jerry's voice was eager.

"Of course, we can't be positive this early" (the Doc's voice was positive though), "but I couldn't find a trace of any such agency. I tested for thermite—" here he grinned at the two of us "—and I'm almost certain nothing of the sort was used. Of course, we won't be sure until the analyst's report comes in."

"So there goes *your* theory," observed Parsons with a certain satisfaction. "Now, young feller," he went on with a pointed look at Jerry, "from what you said last night and what I've been able to find out, you used to be a friend of the professor's. That right?"

Jerry nodded. "Yes, I suppose so. As much of a friend as he ever had, I think." I noticed Prexy frown a moment at this.

"Then"—Parson's voice seemed to me to contain an entreaty concealed under its brusqueness—"what about any enemies? Did anyone hate him, do you know?"

"Not to the best of my knowledge."

"You don't know of any personal rows he may have had?"

Jerry rubbed his palms together. "Well, he did have an argument with some other astronomers and physicists. But he stopped it of his own accord. In a way, he sort of gave in."

"Ah. What was this row about?"

"Professor LeNormand wrote a paper called 'A Fundamental Critique of the Einstein Space-Time Continuum.' Some of the men in other universities and foundations disagreed with him."

"And the row was over that?" Parsons sounded disappointed.

"It wasn't really a row. It was a scientific argument."

Prexy said smoothly, "That was over two years ago. I am quite sure the whole thing was a closed issue. We all admired LeNormand's work enormously, but the feeling about the paper was that he had left the—er—solid world of scientific fact a bit too far behind him in this work."

Parsons nodded. "It's the kind of murder motive I've never been able to believe in myself." He was silent for several minutes, apparently trying to think of another question to ask us that would make sense. Finally he picked up two folders of typewritten papers. "Here are a couple of statements, one for each of you. Read 'em over and sign 'em." He shoved them across the table at Jerry and me.

We read them carefully. In mine, at least, there was nothing that

I had not said, and that was not, so far as I know, the literal truth. I signed on the last page, and Jerry did the same with his. Parsons gathered them in, inspected the signatures, and jotted down our New York address.

"Well, boys, I guess that's all you can do for us at present. Your stories are consistent, and I can't find a reason for holding you. If you move or anything, keep in touch with us."

We promised to do so.

"And one more thing. If I was you I wouldn't talk about this to anybody. See a lawyer if you want to, but don't talk to the papers."

"For the protection of the University's good name," Prexy said to Parsons but with a weather eye on us, "I am quite sure they will be discreet."

Again we promised to be good boys.

Parsons stood up and shook hands with us. "You can go now. Thanks for helping us out all you could."

My own idea was that he was putting on an act for Prexy's benefit, but it was all to the good so far as we were concerned. The thing could have been much more unpleasant, and certainly we were treated with every consideration. Lightheartedly we left the room and the building. On the sidewalk in front we paused for a moment to discuss our next move, and I felt a hand on my arm. To my surprise it was Prexy.

"Let's walk down the street a little way," he said. "There is something I want to ask of both of you."

A little mystified, we turned and started toward the campus. "If we can do anything more—" Jerry began.

"I know"—Prexy's voice was very careful—"how horrible this has been for both of you. Doubtless you both wish to wash your hands of the whole matter, but I am compelled to ask you to assist me in one more way." He paused. "By the way, you handled yourselves, in your relations with the police, like gentlemen and University men." That was, for Prexy, equivalent to giving us the accolade.

"Thank you," Jerry said. "Of course, if there is anything we can do, we'll be only too glad."

"Good," said Prexy. He swung us right, down Santvoord Street. "Last night, and again this morning, when I talked with Mrs. Le-Normand"—he paused to give us the picture of a strong man noble in the accomplishment of even the most heartbreaking of duties— "she expressed a strong desire to see you. Naturally, she wishes to thank you for your courage and intelligence last night."

Nothing in this world appealed to me less at the moment than the idea of talking to LeNormand's widow. To me it seemed desirable not to bring the full horror of the tragedy home to her in any concrete, immediate way, such as meeting us and talking with us. No good could come of it, and probably there would be a painful scene. Still, there is an obligation to see a thing through, to do anything requested in a time of disaster.

Apparently Prexy guessed what was going on in my mind. He went on: "I urged her not to harrow herself in this way, and assured her that you would both understand it if she did not see you. But she was very insistent that I should bring you. I consented. You will find her a quiet woman, not prone to hysterics."

"All right," said Jerry after a while, "I don't see how we can refuse, in any case."

"Thank you," Prexy said, and the three of us walked along in silence. After a time we turned into Camden Place, and up the walk of the shabby white house where LeNormand had lived. Prexy lifted the brass replica of the Lincoln imp and knocked on the door firmly, three times.

5. BEAUTY FOR ASHES

JERRY told me afterward that LeNormand's living room, into which we were shown by a red-eyed domestic, had not changed in a single detail from his recollection of it. The room was square, with two windows on the street and another on a side yard; you entered it from the central hall through a wide double doorway. There were two Morris chairs with faded upholstery. A lumpy-looking sofa with a cretonne cover, several bridge lamps of the sort sold at the co-op for students' rooms. A small, rather ugly mahogany bookcase with glass doors, and on the walls three or four pictures obviously not selected by the University Art Department. On the center table was a litter of magazines and two untidy ash trays. In short, it was a bachelor's room and plainly the habitation of a man who did not care much how things looked.

What astonished me was the complete absence of the feminine touch. Brides, particularly those of recent standing, generally make an immediate, if superficial, attack upon the bachelor dowdiness of their husbands' quarters. They run to new curtains and vases of flowers, and what they often call "touches of color to brighten the place up a bit." But there was nothing of that nature here. The room was exactly as it must have been before LeNormand married. The air smelled faintly of tobacco smoke, and I noticed in one of the ash trays a black, battered pipe with the marks of his teeth on the bit. The sight of it irritated me; I felt it would have been more decent to put it out of sight.

Prexy, Jerry, and I stood around in the room, not quite knowing what to do with ourselves. I wanted to smoke but wondered if it was the proper thing, and decided not. Jerry's look was fixed almost apprehensively on the open doorway; once he put his hands in his pockets and then took them out again immediately. For no good reason the tune of "Mademoiselle from Armentières" began running in my head. I wanted to whistle it and just caught myself with my lips already puckered. Prexy was studying a mezzotint of an old mill by moonlight as though the thing were the work of a master.

When we heard the sound of steps on the stairs we knew she was coming. It was a slow, uneven tread, with something apathetic in it. Most of all, it seemed to me heavy and slipshod, as though she did not care how clumsily she placed her feet. Then she came into the room.

The human imagination is an odd thing. Prexy had said that some people might consider Mrs. LeNormand the most beautiful woman in the world, and my mind had been busy creating an image of the woman to whom, had I been Paris, I should have awarded the golden apple. She did not look anything like the figure I had constructed in my mind. The first thing I saw about her was that she was atrociously badly dressed. Dowdy was the only word I could think of to describe her appearance.

She had on a dark, rough tweed skirt, badly cut, so that the hem line was uneven. Above it was a neutral-color knitted sweater with unbecoming half-length sleeves. Her stockings were the wrong shade for the skirt and her shoes a pair of new Oxfords, badly scuffed at the toes. The whole effect was precisely what I should have looked for from LeNormand's wife, but I had been waiting to see a beautiful woman. My first sensation was one of relief. I am afraid of beautiful women, and Prexy's characterization of her had thrown me off my mental stride. But it would not be difficult to utter a few banal and sympathetic remarks to this creature and then make a swift, decent exit. She was just a person, nothing more.

As I looked at her a second time I saw with a rush of astonishment that I was wholly wrong. The clothes did not belong to her. It was as impossible to imagine her in modern dress as to think of the Winged Victory in tennis shorts. She was tall, almost six feet, and neither slender nor in any place too full. Her hair, untidily collected at the nape of her neck, was the color of winter sunlight, and her eyes, set wide apart below level eyebrows, were a dark, violet blue. Underneath the incongruity of her clothes was a body perfectly integrated, part with part, so that it had the unity of construction and harmony of relationship that great sculptors have now and again succeeded in capturing. In her body, in her hands with their strong, round fingers, in her face, there was strength, beauty, unity.

So far I have not mentioned her face. At the time, except in one particular, it did not appear to me as beautiful as I learned later, through seeing her often, that it was. Her features were strongly modeled and spaced so superbly from the wide, even forehead to the clean, springing line of the jaw that I had an impression of an abstraction or a conscious work of art which expressed not the beauty of a single woman but the essence of all women's faces. She wore no make-up at all and her skin was so white that it seemed to shine like silver in the shadow of the doorway. Her lips were pale, if anything, but against the clear pallor of her skin they were almost startling. It was almost the face of Pallas Athene, if you like, and yet there was nothing of the goddess about her. Something was missing.

Looking at her as she came toward us, I wondered what it was. I could see no grief or shock in her expression, and not much of anything else. There seemed to be no life in her. As she walked I half expected she would drag her feet with each step. Her face was simply vacant. She hardly looked at us as she came into the living room, and her eyes were withdrawn, as if there was nothing on which it was worth their while to focus. The nearest I can come to a description of her is to say that she was like one of the beggars on a city street whose faces are indifferent to life because they no longer have anything to hope for from it. She was not tragic, or sorrowful, or frightened. She was simply indifferent.

The three of us had unconsciously lined up in an awkward row to meet her. She walked toward us and came to a halt, and I thought for a moment that she was hardly aware of our presence. Her eyes, at any rate, were not fixed on any one of us.

Prexy cleared his throat, bowed, and said, "Mrs. LeNormand, may I present Mr. Lister and Mr. Jones?"

We bowed too, and murmured sounds without meaning under our breaths.

She looked at each of us in turn but did not offer to shake hands or invite us to sit down. Indeed, throughout the whole short, incredible interview—I thought of it as an interview, and not a call or visit—she did nothing that an ordinary woman would do. The glance she gave me when Prexy introduced me was blank, devoid of any expression. I might as well have been a piece of furniture. When she spoke her voice was consistent with the rest of her. It had inflection and beautiful clarity and control, but there was something not in it that I missed. Some color. A small imperfection of tone or accent that would have made it the voice of a person.

She said, "I want to thank you for what you did for my husband." There was no obvious emotion behind those twelve short words.

Even then, the words themselves were something of a surprise to me. I felt they composed a statement, that they were her idea of the proper, appropriate thing to say. And "my husband!" Why had she not said "for what you did for Walter"—surely it was more natural to use the name she must have called him by? There was in the whole speech a quality I definitely did not like. Perhaps the two first-person pronouns. I looked quickly at Jerry to see what he might be thinking about this woman and what she had just said.

He was muttering something like "sorry we could not have come sooner; been of some real use," but his expression, the tone of his voice startled me. I had lived too long with him not to know when he was being natural and when not. Decidedly, this was not any side of his character that I knew. He was on the defensive, and not because of the awkwardness of the situation. And it was more than defensiveness, it was an awareness of danger. At the time I could not have put it so precisely, but he was like a man who, dining with the Borgias, has just felt the harsh rasp of the poison in the wine but seeks to conceal what he is feeling.

She noticed it, I am positive of that, and for an instant she hesitated, looking at him. Then she said, "It is very good of you to come to see me. President Murray has told me of your bravery."

She kept on looking at him until Jerry began to flush. And as I watched her I saw something happen to her face. The vacancy of her look began to disappear. Interest came into her eyes. She seemed to collect herself, to shake off some stupor which had been on her, and to return to the present world. It was astonishing, and I did not entirely like it. There was a dispassionate quality to her inspection of Jerry that was far from complimentary. Whatever it was that was waking in her, it had an unusual effect on me. I wanted to take a step backward, to keep it at more than arm's length until I understood it better. But after all, it was not directed at me. Jerry appeared ill at ease but plainly he did not resent her look as much as I did. He returned it, in fact.

"Yes," she said again, "you were brave. Both of you." The second sentence sounded like an afterthought.

We deprecated her praise, told her it was nothing. There was really no bravery in what we had done, or at least it did not seem so to me at the time. Perhaps I was wrong about that, and she was wise. To her the whole thing may have worn a different aspect.

She turned to me and said directly, "He was dead when you found him?"

The entire interview seemed so strange that her question caught me napping. The picture of LeNormand's eyes moving leaped to my mind, and I must have hesitated a fraction of a second.

"Yes." Jerry spoke swiftly, emphatically. "I want to tell you, Mrs. LeNormand, that when we first saw him his face was very calm. I am sure he suffered no agony at all. The—the details are horrible, I know, but I have the feeling that he must have died without pain."

"It helps to know that," she said carefully. After a moment, still looking at Jerry, she went on. "I cannot understand his death. There is no reason for it."

Prexy said, "You mustn't think about it."

"I know," she replied, "I know. You must not think me strange for asking these questions. The answers to them may help me to stop going over and over it in my mind."

"If there's anything more we can tell you—" Jerry said.

She turned to him again with a curious intensity. "It will seem a foolish woman's question to you, Mr. Lister, but he didn't leave any message, any note, anything to explain what happened to him?"

Jerry shook his head. "There was nothing, Mrs. LeNormand. I am sure he did not know he was going to die."

"No," she said. "Of course not. But sometimes, when he was staying all night with his telescope, working, he sent me notes to say that he would not be home. If there was such a note as that, I should like to know of it."

A little wind had sprung up from the Sound and the trees were whispering in the dark. Under the starshine the water of the bay was moving, the ripples coming faintly toward us and making the Sound seem like a river, flowing out of invisibility and pouring itself on the shore. As I watched it, the illusion of a current was so perfect that I had to remind myself there was no flow, no current there, but only the eternal, unchanging reservoir of the sea.

"Of course," I said to Dr. Lister, "I can repeat the words we said, or something like them, but I cannot reproduce a conversation. Expression, the posture of bodies, the pitch and timbre of voices, the gestures, are all lost in the retelling."

He had been listening to me with the most extraordinary attention. "I understand that, naturally. . . . Neither of you ever told me what was said when you first met her."

"It's odd," I went on, "how quick one is, at moments like that, to take things at their surface value. When she said to Jerry, 'It will seem like a foolish woman's question to you, Mr. Lister,' I think we both accepted her estimate of what she was saying. Now it does not seem at all like a normal question to me. And her story about notes LeNormand used to send to her. Does that sound credible to you?"

"No," he answered.

"You see, these are things that I have been fitting together in my mind. They are all small things, but they add up to something."

He nodded. "You think she knew all along...?" His question did not finish itself; none of the questions I had asked myself over and over ever quite completed themselves.

"When LeNormand died," I reminded him, "she was at home. The cook was still there, washing dishes. She saw her there, sitting in the living room, three times in that half hour. She could not have done it—physically impossible."

For several moments he was silent, thinking. "Perhaps there was a plot. Some accomplice." His voice sounded as if he could think of the answers to that as easily as I.

"She gained nothing by LeNormand's death. What sort of plot could there have been?"

He nodded. He was beginning to lose some of his confidence in his own power of intellectual analysis, I think.

Her question about a note from LeNormand had astonished me. Never once in Jerry's picture to me of the man had I got the idea that he was capable of thinking of anything or anyone else after he once started to work. It was impossible to think of him writing: "Darling—can't make it home for supper. Don't wait up for me; I'll be here late."

"There wasn't any note," I blurted out. "We looked at his papers. They were just some equations."

"Ah," she said quickly, and her tone did not quite convey disappointment. "Equations." And then, after a moment, "You mean, just notes about his work?"

"Yes," Prexy said gently. "Mathematical symbols that he used to express the relationships of things."

"Thank you." Her voice was still perfectly level. "I should like to have the last things he used and wrote." It was a natural sort of request, but somehow it surprised me a little.

"I'm afraid the police will have to keep them, for a time at least." Prexy sounded almost as though he were explaining something to a child.

"Yes. Yes, of course."

Jerry said quietly, "I can't begin to tell you how sorry Bark and I feel about this, Mrs. LeNormand. Your husband and I were friends. If there is anything at all we can do for you, please feel that we'll be only too glad to do it."

She looked gravely at him for several seconds. "Thank you. It is very kind. If there is anything, I shall most surely call upon you."

In the awkward pause that followed, Prexy cleared his throat. "Mrs. LeNormand," he said, "if you would like me to get in touch with any members of your family, or his, make any—er—travel arrangements, I shall be only too happy."

She seemed for the first time at a loss. "I do not know anything about Mr. LeNormand's family.... He never spoke of a family... I don't know what is the right thing to do."

We were all deeply surprised, I think, but Prexy recovered himself quickly. "I understand," he said soothingly. "I shall see what I can find out. Doubtless in England... And what about your own family?"

She shook her head. "I have no one to notify."

"No one?" Prexy's voice was, for all his control, clearly incredulous.

"No one at all," she said with a faint smile.

"I see." But it was plain that Prexy did not see, that she had baffled him, thwarted him in some way not clear to me at the moment.

"When I have had a few days to think this all over," she went on, "I shall consult you, if I may, as to what is best for me to do."

"Certainly. I shall be only too glad." Prexy's voice sounded stiff.

"Please," she said, looking at each of us in turn, "do not be too distressed. Do not worry about me. I shall be all right. And do not think of this dreadful thing which has happened. It will be best for all of us not to think too much about it. We must leave it to the police. Thank you all again for coming." It was an incredible sort of speech for a woman in her situation; without waiting for any reply from us, she turned, left the room, and went up the stairs. I noticed now with what flawless, integrated grace she moved, and how, under her clumsy clothes, her body was a moving statue, incredibly changed into flesh and blood.

For a moment the three of us stood there, staring foolishly after her. The sound of her footsteps died out along the upstairs hall.

"Well!" Prexy's tone was incredulous and for the instant distinctly irritated, but he covered it up smoothly by going on at once. "Since there is nothing more we can do for Mrs. LeNormand—"

We went out at once; I was last through the door, and as I went I felt for an instant as though there was something at my back. The click of the latch behind me was pleasant.

Prexy said good-by to us on the sidewalk in front of the house; he thanked us for coming and promised to keep in touch with us about the progress of the investigation. Again, in a fatherly way, he warned us against talking about what had happened. Then he was off, his broad shoulders square, his step, as Charles Lamb once said, "peremptory and path-keeping." We watched him go in silence.

"And now, what?" I asked.

"Let's see if the car is still there," suggested Jerry, "and if it is, let's get the hell out of this place." He glanced swiftly up and back at the house behind us as we swung off toward the bowl.

It was a cold, clear Sunday. The November sun lighted every twig of tree and detail of building as we crossed the campus. The chapel bell was tolling with bronze insistence as we walked, and our feet scrunched loudly in the gravel.

Without my overcoat, the air had a shrewd bite to it, and I should have been uncomfortable had I not been too busy thinking to notice how I felt. The interview with Mrs. LeNormand, as I went over it in my mind, bothered me more and more. There is no predicting how people will react to tragedy and disaster, and I realized that because Mrs. LeNormand had not behaved or spoken as I expected a grief-stricken widow to do, I yet had no right to see anything queer, or unnatural about it. But there was a flavor to the interview that eluded me, that I could not put a name to, but which I definitely disliked. I thought of her as she came down the stairs, of the way she looked at us and specially at Jerry, when she talked, of the extraordinary quality of her beauty. I tried to imagine her married to LeNormand, their courtship, their sharing a common bed. It was all incredible. She was no more to be imagined in any of those ways than her magnificence was to be confused with the shabby clothes she had been wearing. I thought about those clothes for a while. I felt that if I could understand them I should have learned something about her.

"Jerry," I began tentatively, and stopped.

"What?"

"Those clothes she wore. Did you notice them?"

"No." There was a suggestion of reproof in his voice, but I disregarded it.

"Well," I said, "they were terrible. Dowdy and unbecoming and inappropriate and messy, and everything you can imagine a Bryn Mawr Phi Bete's wearing and no one else."

He glanced at me with a little frown. "I don't see what you're trying to say."

"I was wondering," I said carefully, "why she dressed like that."

"Good God," Jerry replied in amazement, "what do you expect? Paris fashions when her husband's not yet cold—?" He bit off the end of the sentence.

"Easy, easy," I said. "Whatever she wore this morning, it had to be something she already had. I can't believe a woman like that would ever dress herself in that skirt, that sweater, those shoes."

He saw that I was in earnest. "Well, I didn't notice especially what she had on, but I'll take your word that it offended your aesthetic eye." He paused and said, half to himself, "Though if you have an aesthetic eye—well, shoot, what's on your mind?"

"Well," I went on doggedly, feeling foolish, "I just wondered if LeNormand had bought those clothes for her."

"It's possible. What of it?"

"Several things of it. One is that I never got the idea from you or from LeNormand the few times I saw him that he was the sort who would buy any woman clothes, not even his wife."

Jerry grinned. "No, you're right there. But the only thing that proves is he probably didn't buy them after all."

I tried again, another way, "She is a very beautiful woman," I said, "and beautiful women almost always know they are. And they don't dress to conceal the fact."

"She didn't conceal it."

"Damn it," I said, "you don't get the point. Those clothes were too wrong for her even to own them. For one thing, she's too intelligent—"

That was it, of course! Why hadn't I realized it before? She was too intelligent. *Too* intelligent. For all her beauty and her strangeness, it was the quality of mind that had most impressed me about her. The way she had questioned us, the precision and calculation of everything she had said after the first minute or so came back to me in a rush. She had not been speaking from grief or even loneliness. There had been something she wanted to find out from us, something she had found out from us. Perhaps more than one thing. At any rate, she had cross-examined us mercilessly and directly, and I'd been such a dunce I had not even realized she was doing it. I felt my mental pulse begin to quicken. If that was so, what did it mean?

The first conclusion I came to was a disappointing one. Neither her beauty nor any mystery about her was necessary to explain her marriage to LeNormand. He had met someone intellectually equal to himself. She was a woman, and so he had married her. Perhaps she had been as surprised, as glad as he must have been to find, in a world of little people thinking small, imprecise thoughts, a person of the same intellectual size and efficiency. The very fact, I thought, that LeNormand was such a lonely man, so little in need of people, must have made the attraction between them deep and strong. It was natural they should have married, natural even, I had to admit, that she should care nothing at all for clothes. Perhaps it was inevitable that she had reacted to the news of his death in a purely mental, impersonal sort of way. The quality they had in common would make anything more customary for the rank and file of humanity out of place—a psychological absurdity. People with minds as strong and clear as I realized upon reflection hers must be were more likely to be stoical and self-contained. I began to feel I'd been scenting mystery where there was none.

"I don't see," Jerry was saying, "what intelligence has to do with the clothes a woman wears, necessarily."

"All right," I conceded somewhat crossly, "forget it. I had an idea, but on second thought it isn't so hot."

"One thing," said Jerry. "It's no mystery now why LeNormand married her. Prexy was right. She damn well is the most beautiful woman in the world."

"She's certainly one of the most intelligent."

"Maybe." He did not sound particularly interested.

"You needn't try to be that way," I said to him, with a little prickle of annoyance beginning to come into my tongue, "I saw you look at her when she started to cross-examine us."

"What the hell are you talking about?"

"Listen," I said to him patiently, "when she began asking us all those questions, I saw you go on guard. Mentally, I mean. You got something right then that I've only just doped out."

"For Christ's sake, Bark!" His voice was sharp for an instant and he checked himself immediately afterward. Then he looked at me and grinned. "No man can remain a mystery to his roommate, I suppose. Well—" he paused and thought a moment—"you're about half right. Something did go through my mind. I'll admit that. You go on looking into the crystal globe of my character a bit more, and you ought to be able to tell what it was."

He was nice about it, but the snub was there just the same. We walked on in silence, I a good deal annoyed at him and he apparently sunk in some thought that did not include me or my annoyance.

The car was still there, solitary in the parking field and looking like a monument. We got in it and started back to New York without saying anything more. It was bitter cold and we stopped once along the way to have a drink from Jerry's flask.

All the way back there was an emptiness inside me. A Sunday Weltschmerz, due, I suppose, to nervous fatigue. Perhaps a few more drinks or a couple of soda mints would have cured the feeling of foreboding which haunted me, but I don't believe so. Some subliminal part of my mind must have understood that the die of the future was cast, and that Jerry and I were headed toward different lives from any we had known thus far.

6. WHAT SEEMS SO IS TRANSITION

THERE is one thing to be said for Mondays. They take the mind off everything else. When I reached my desk the morning after our return to New York, it was three feet deep in unpleasantly persistent folders from the tickler file. By the time I had worked my way to the bottom of the heap it was six in the evening, and I headed down toward our Greenwich Village apartment with almost nothing in my head but plans for the next day's work and an increasing enthusiasm for a shower and a leisurely pre-supper cocktail.

Although the stories in the papers had been sensational, none of them mentioned Jerry's name or mine, and only one or two referred to the fact that the body had been found by "two graduates of the institution." Most of the reporters seemed to feel that it made a better story to have Prexy discover what had happened to LeNormand, and he had been drawing an infamous quantity of publicity. I was well content to let him have it all, and more than a little grateful to him and Parsons for not giving our names to the press.

Jerry had a fire going in the grate, and the cocktail shaker was already standing on the coffee table in front of the sofa. I took a quick shower, with a drink before and after, and felt fine. Then I went out to the kitchen and fixed supper. It was my week to cook and Jerry's to wash dishes. We ate heartily, but without conversation, and I left him washing the dishes. His only comment was that when I cooked a meal I used every utensil in the kitchen.

Before he came back into the living room I made a discovery that left me distinctly unhappy. The drop leaf of the desk was down, and a partly written letter in Jerry's hand was lying on the blotter. Without meaning—or wanting—to, I read the salutation. It was:

My dear Mrs. LeNormand—

It gave me an odd start to see her name, and although my first thought was that perhaps I, too, ought to write her some sort of note of condolence, the more I considered it the more out of place a letter from us—either of us—seemed to me to be. Perhaps Jerry had thought of something else that he wanted to tell her, but I doubted it. The only other idea that occurred to me was that he wanted to write to her, and the implications of that were not entirely plain to me.

After a while he came in from the kitchen and sat down at the desk; he never even glanced in my direction, but began to go on with the letter. I tried to read. The scratch of his pen across the paper distracted me.

"If you're writing to Dad," I said, "tell him from me that his Irish whisky saved my life."

He didn't look up. "Oke," he said, and his pen went on steadily.

I turned on the radio, feeling pretty cheap as I did it.

"For God's sake," said Jerry, "shut the damn thing off. I can't think with all that noise."

I flipped the switch and sat down in another chair, feeling restless. There is something irritating about having a person write a letter in the room where you are; I always want to interrupt them, and in this case I wanted to more than usual. After a few moments Jerry got up and took a book out of the bookcase, glanced at it, and carried it over to the desk. Some insane impulse prompted me to say

"I did but see her passing by.
Yet will I love her—"

"Damn you!" Jerry whirled round in his chair. "Did you see this letter?"

"I don't have to," I told him. "Remember sophomore year? You used up half Palgrave's *Golden Treasury* on that babe from Pough-keepsie. I know the symptoms."

His face was white. He stared at me for a minute, and I wondered if he was counting ten before he spoke. "And you don't approve?" he asked politely.

Then I had a choice to make. Either I could provoke him to a point where we'd have a row—and it was really less painful and in-jurious to go through a mangle head first than row with Jerry when he was angry—or I could turn the whole thing off with a decent re-mark, in which case the tension would subside. The trouble with the second method was that sometimes it left a rankling sore, and be-sides, I wasn't sure but what it would be better to have Jerry mussing up my back hair with his customary athletic thoroughness, unpleas-ant though the process would be for me. It might snap him out of the whole thing.

"As a matter of fact," I said as cuttingly as I could, "I did acciden-tally see the salutation of your letter. You shouldn't have left it out. And I don't approve." The look on his face, the slight narrowing of his eyes, told me that he was getting ready to take positive action, and suddenly the impression came over me that this would not be like the other swift-brewed, swift-forgotten rows we had had in the past. "But I've acted pretty stinking about it," I told him, "and I'm sorry for that."

He put his pen down slowly and went over to the sofa. I couldn't tell what he was thinking about.

"It doesn't really matter whether you approve or not," he said, but his tone was almost questioning.

I admitted the truth of that.

For a while he lay on the sofa and looked up at the ceiling. "I know what you're thinking," he said. "We could have a row about it if you—if we—liked. Brothers always have the nastiest sort of fights, because they're really civil wars."

I couldn't refuse that olive branch. "Hell," I told him, "I don't want to fight." I searched my mind to make what I felt clear enough for words. "I'm more worried, I guess, than anything. Mondays are always foul."

He nodded and then looked across at me. "Why does my writing to her worry you?"

I couldn't put it specifically. "It's just that she's . . . I don't know how to phrase it. She's not your type."

He lay back on the sofa and laughed until I began to get mad at him. "My God, Bark! I suppose if the Old Man sends me down to City Hall tomorrow, and you hear about it, you'll think I've gone down for a marriage license!"

"Nuts!"

"Only one nut, and you're it." He stopped grinning, and went on sadly. "I want to ask her when the funeral is going to be. I think it would be decent for me to go, don't you?"

My face began to feel hot. "Will you excuse it, please?" I said to him, and then, less flippantly, "I forgot about that. I'm an ass."

"Okay, forget it." He went back to the desk, finished the letter in a minute or two, and took it out to the mailbox right away. When he came back he had an evening paper with him and we read over the account of the case in it. Nobody seemed to have found out anything, nobody was giving any interviews, and the only new item in the whole story was a picture of Mrs. LeNormand. Even in that inferior reproduction the extraordinary, sculptural quality of her face came out strongly.

We went to bed early because we were tired and neither of us wanted to run the risk of further talk. But as I was dropping off to sleep, something slipped back into my mind, and I spoke into the darkness of the room.

"Hey, Jerry."

"What?"

"Just why in hell did you need a book of poems to ask her when the funeral was going to be?"

"You go to hell."

Instead, I went to sleep.

He lit another cigarette and said, "You never told me about that episode."

"It isn't one I'm very proud of."

"Then you are telling it to me for a purpose."

"Yes," I said, and paused. The night was luminous around us. Starshine is the lovely word for the light that is faintly implicit in the dark of a clear and moonless night. But it is not the greater part of it. A radiance from the stars. Jerry once told me that most of it was caused by the fact that the gravitational field of the earth bends the rays of energy from the sun around the curve of the earth and causes the whole upper air of the night to glow dimly from the molecules which those rays strike and excite.

The tip of his cigarette turned red-white for a moment. "And your purpose is . . ."

"To explain how he felt, even then. Except when it was a question of her, Jerry was never . . . devious . . . like that. From the very first, you see, he was different about her. He must have felt that there was something not quite right . . . I'm not being very clear."

"I understand you," he said, and turned to look out across the Sound.

The funeral was that Thursday. Jerry took the whole day off to go to it, but I sent some flowers and stayed in the city. I knew he did not want me to go with him, and there was no real reason why I should. Several times during the day I had a momentary feeling of uneasiness, though when I stopped to think about it I was not just sure why I should feel that way. Once I detected myself wishing flatly that I had gone along.

When I got back to the apartment, Jerry was already home. He looked tired, and quiet, and somber in his dark suit and black tie. After a few tentative remarks I discovered that he did not want to talk, and silence suited me just as well. When you have roomed together as long as Jerry and I had, it is almost like a marriage. There are plenty of times when it is more comfortable simply not to talk, and our silence was a friendly one.

After supper Jerry poured himself a drink and looked across at me. "They buried him out at the Clear Brook cemetery."

"Oh," I said.

He twirled his glass in his fingers. "I arranged for the stone. She asked me to." He paused and stared into the amber of the whisky. "She asked me what to put on the stone."

I couldn't think what to say to him about that. It was all of a piece, I thought, with her behavior when we called at her house that Sunday morning.

He said slowly, "I told her just his name, and his dates and S.T.T.L."

I was startled. "Why that?" I asked him.

"LeNormand wasn't a Christian exactly... He was a scientist. And I remembered your telling me that the Romans always put that on their tombstones."

The whole idea was astonishing to me. Why should Mrs. LeNormand have asked Jerry about the details of her memorial to her husband? A moment ago it had seemed natural to me, because it was consistent with her behavior at that strange interview with her last Sunday. Now, it seemed to me that the only rational element in the two episodes was their common denominator of strangeness. Neither of them was to be understood in common, human terms. "S.T.T.L.!" I thought of the inscription on a grave far out along the Via Appia outside Rome. A stone that an ancient Roman matron had erected for her husband, T. Sulpicius Arva. That, like so many of the others, had borne those initials, and I remembered my telling Jerry about it and what it meant—*Sit tibi terra levis*.

"May the earth lie light upon thee," I murmured half to myself.

"Yes," Jerry said, and then, after a moment, "He wasn't really a Christian, and I don't think she is."

"I know," I said curiously, "but he wasn't a pagan, either; and even if she does look like a living Praxiteles, I doubt if she is."

He looked a little embarrassed. "Well, maybe it wasn't the right thing, but she was so proud, so steady, so in command of herself that

I thought of her as one of those Roman matrons, and the whole thing just came into my mind. It seemed appropriate, somehow."

"Oh," I said. Then what I had taken for an intellectual coldness that came from the mind because heart was not involved in Mrs. LeNormand's reaction to her husband's horrible death had seemed to Jerry a stoic, Roman suppression of emotion. Well, maybe he was right. I began to see her in a new light, even to discard some of the hostility that my one encounter with her had aroused. Perhaps I had not been entirely fair.

"Hell," I said to Jerry, "it was a swell idea. It just surprised me at the moment. I see the reason for it now." Another thought came into in mind. "Who else was there?"

He stared into his glass and finally said, "Just she and I and Prexy and old Doc Lassiter from the Math Department." There was pain in his voice. "Hardly any flowers, even. It was rotten. I felt sorry for her."

"What's she going to do now, I wonder?" And I found suddenly that I was intensely curious; what new niche could such a woman as Mrs. LeNormand find in life? She had told Prexy and Parsons that she had no family. Apparently, then, she had no home to which she could go back. Life in Collegeville, surely, would prove almost intolerable to her under the circumstances, even if her strange beauty—I cut that thought off right there.

Jerry did not look at me as he replied. "I told her that she ought to get away. She can't stay on there, Bark, it would be plain hell. She needs to get away someplace where the life would be different, and take her mind off what's happened. Someplace where she could disappear from sight, find new friends and a new interest in life. Don't you think that's the dope?" The entreaty in his voice was plain. He looked at me half defiantly, half pleadingly.

Naturally, I knew then what else he had said to her. He had told her to come to New York. I faced the issue squarely; subconsciously I must have known all along what sort of effect she could have on Jerry, and no matter what I thought of her there was no possibility of evading the ultimate issue. And just as you know at the very outset of a Greek tragedy that the gods have willed a full carload of grief for the protagonists, so now I felt certain that if Jerry and Mrs. LeNormand were to fall in love with each other there could be no happy ending to it. It was not my affair beyond a certain point, and I felt instinctively certain that that point had already been passed. Tragic though the outcome might be, there was nothing for me to do now.

"Well," I observed as casually as I could, "the obvious place is New York."

He nodded and gave me a grateful look. "That's what I told her."

"And what, Mr. Bones, did she say to that?"

"I think she agreed. She told me she hadn't made any plans as yet, but she's going to let me know if she comes to the city." He was silent for a moment, and his eyes were withdrawn. I guessed that he, too, was looking ahead and weighing things in his mind. Then he smiled, as though he had thought of something pleasant. "When she does come, we'll have to rally round and give her a good time."

"Sure," I said, making the mental reservation that it probably wasn't in me to give that woman a good time but that she'd never miss me so long as Jerry was on hand.

For a while, then, the conversation came to a full stop. Neither of us could think of a way of getting it going again, though I could see that Jerry had something else he wanted to say if he could find the right formula. He took one or two thoughtful pulls on his highball.

"Listen," he said finally, "I know you think this whole thing is crazy. Probably it is. But to tell you the honest truth, I was wondering if Grace . . ." He stopped and looked at me.

I couldn't imagine why he should mention her at this juncture. My mother is one of the most delightful women in the world from one point of view. From more than one point of view. In fact, Grace is a wonderful woman who was simply not designed by God to be a mother. She is gay and charming, still looks only about thirty, dances superbly, dresses in the most flawless taste, has a notable flair for interior decoration, reads a lot more books than you'd suspect, and lives the ideal life for her with Fred Mallard. He inherited about a million dollars at the age of twenty-one and they retired from life's more strenuous battles. The two of them travel over Europe and America together, dance, drink, make love to each other—they're a disgustingly devoted couple—move into a different apartment every year just to have the fun of fixing up a new place, collect various minor sorts of objets d'art, and are generally as delightfully ornamental additions to the theory of the leisure class as you could hope to find. They have a vitality about everything they do that is practically indistinguishable from youth, but it is never obtrusive.

But Jerry's half-finished question about Grace startled me. He and she had always got on superbly together—partly because she was so grateful to Jerry's father for virtually adopting me and hence removing the problem of little Berkeley Jones from the bright lexicon of her life with Fred. Jerry, I knew, had always liked her, and recently, as he had got old enough to appreciate her, I think she had begun to delight him. After all, of her sort she is perfect, and irresistible, and Jerry, to whom she was indirectly indebted and for whom she was not in any way responsible, was really a protégé of hers. She used to labor over his taste, give him subtle little presents of a bit of chinoiserie, or a rather over-ornamental dressing gown for Christmas, in what I feel sure was a campaign to feminize his solidly masculine taste.

But where, I asked myself, did Grace fit into the idea that Jerry was trying to convey to me? I could not believe that he had any notion of chaperonage. I decided to be blunt. "Where does Grace come in? I can't see what—"

"I know," he said quickly. "But she—Mrs. LeNormand—doesn't know a soul in town and I thought maybe Grace could—"

The idea struck me as supremely funny. I laughed long and loud, perhaps a little too long and loud. "Jerry, for God's sake!" I finally managed to get out. "Grace is not the person. Not now, for Lord's sake!" I could see Grace trying to organize sober little dinner parties of intellectuals and the kind of social start that would be possible for the recent widow of a college professor.

He looked pained at my laughter, and a little embarrassed. "Sometimes, Bark, I think you don't appreciate your mother."

"Of course, I appreciate Grace, but what could she do?"

Jerry hesitated. "She could talk to her and, well," his voice a bit defiant, "she could sort of tell her things."

"Tell her things?" I couldn't see at what he was driving. "What sort of things?"

He got red and looked away. "Things like how to fix your hair right and where you get clothes, and all that woman's stuff."

My first temptation was to laugh again, but I stifled it. This was the kind of conversation that seems silly and pointless on top, but underneath I knew that we were working out something, and that it would be easy to say one really wrong thing and thereby close a door that we might need to keep open. I began to see, too, that Jerry was a man with a fixed idea, and that he had gone far enough with it to map out a plan of campaign. I was still wondering just what he was trying to prove when he stood up and started toward the kitchen with his empty glass in his hand.

"You see," he said, with his receding back toward me so that I could neither see his face nor have time for a reply, "I got to thinking about all that stuff you said last Sunday, and she does wear pretty terrible clothes." The kitchen doorway swallowed him.

I filled my pipe slowly and tried to figure just where we were at this point. One thing stood out plainly: there was nothing hypothetical about Mrs. LeNormand's coming to town. It must be pretty well understood or Jerry would not have begun counting on Grace to make Mrs. LeNormand over into the well-dressed woman. But that presented me with another thought, one that on closer inspection I did not care so much for. It meant that Mrs. LeNormand had been easy to persuade about coming to New York. Either she had been planning it ahead of time, or Jerry had had little difficulty in selling the idea to her. There was no reason why she should not come to the city, that I could see, and certainly no special reason why she should. Unless ... unless the only reason she had to go anyplace was the slight one of Jerry and her slender contact with him. Perhaps that reason was more compelling than I liked to think about.

The whole situation appeared to me strange and made me uneasy, with a feeling of anxious uncertainty that was not related to the past. By that I mean I was not now thinking about the death of Le-Normand, and the horror of his body burning in that chair under the round, gray dome of the observatory. Instead, it seemed to me that whatever it was I dreaded lay in the future. There was something less than final about LeNormand's death anyhow. Even then I was sure that it would not be solved by the police, at least until they discovered the motive for it. I wondered if Mrs. LeNormand knew the motive. If she did, apparently she had not confided it to the police, for they, to judge by the papers, were making no headway at all.

Well, it was plain that she was coming to New York, for unless that was so, I knew that Jerry wouldn't have brought up the matter of Grace, and her function as a civilizing influence on Mrs. LeNormand. For an instant I let my mind play with the probable progress of that experiment, and the ultimate complete annihilation of poor Grace's lightly gay efforts (most of her efforts were lightly gay, but generally they were effective) to make a silk purse out of... out of what? Out of the most beautiful woman in the world. Grace, I considered, would be definitely fighting out of her class and would not be able to accomplish anything. How wrong my imagination was in this respect I was not to find out till later.

Jerry came in from the kitchen.

"Listen," I said to him, "let's quit this beating around the bush. There's no point in it. When is Mrs. LeNormand coming to New York?"

"Tomorrow."

I started to say "Jesus!" in surprise, and then choked it off. The surprise lasted only a fraction of a second, but the cold inner conviction of alarm stayed with me all night. It was too soon. It was too swift. It had passed out of the realm of things that are odd and unpleasant into a sphere where they are so odd that their cumulative effect is terrifying.

7. TRIFLES MAKE THE SUM

ALWAYS before, when I have thought back to the weeks between Selena LeNormand's coming to New York and Jerry's marriage to her, it has seemed to me that nothing important happened in them. And yet the small things might have added up to much more than I made of them at the time. I think now that my psychological state blinded me to a good deal that a more sensible man would have noticed and added together.

Jerry was a man in love. He was certain that Selena was the only woman in the world, and looking at her magnificent beauty it was not hard to understand why he thought so. There are undoubtedly a number of more valid reasons for loving a woman than her beauty, but I have never heard of a beautiful woman who went through life unloved by any man. If I had not formed a deep dislike of her, tinged somehow with fear, at that first meeting, I am sure I should have been in love with Selena myself. As it was there were times, particularly after Grace had taken the clothes question in hand, when it stopped my breath to look at her.

From the very start it was obvious that she was attracted by Jerry. When I saw them together I could never be sure that she loved him, but remembering the change that came into her face when she first saw him, in LeNormand's house in Collegeville, I never doubted his power to affect her deeply in some way that was not at all clear to me. I don't believe there was a single minute from the beginning when she did not intend to marry him.

One of my reasons was that she never paid the slightest attention to any other man. Judging her by other women, as I used to do in those days, I considered she must be in love with him. Now I think that she intended to marry Jerry for two reasons. The first was that he could give her something that no other living man could. When they were together she depended on him as though she were an alien and Jerry a fellow countryman of hers. That was natural enough when you remember that Jerry had been almost the only friend of LeNormand. Though it sounds absurd to put it so melodramatically, her second reason must have been that she was afraid not to marry him. He was the best alternative which presented itself to her, and he gave her, I now believe, more understanding than anyone else could have. And in that fact lay her chief danger and his.

Of course, I am being clearer and more definite about the relationship between them now than I was at the time. The weeks when their romance, if you could call it that, was developing were miserable ones for me. It was impossible for me to like Selena, and Jerry knew that. The fact made relations between us awkward and uncomfortable. Yet it was not a fact that either of us could refer to openly. I had to put up some appearance of pleasure in his happiness, and it was a strain. Part of the time I felt like a hypocrite. Our two immediate families were the only people, I thought, who guessed what was going on, and I could not talk to them because I would seem selfish and ungracious if I confided my misgivings about Selena. Many times I decided to go and talk the whole thing over with Grace, but there was the question of my loyalty to Jerry.

My solution to the quandary I was in was not the wisest one in the world. I spent all the time I could eating, drinking (a good deal of that), working, and sleeping. In every way I could I tried to conceal how unhappy I was and put up a presentable front. Inwardly, my solution was to think as little as possible. The result was that between alcohol and a self-induced obtuseness to events I managed to overlook the actual meaning of several episodes.

The first of them happened a few days after Selena LeNormand came to town. As Jerry requested, I had explained the problem to Grace. Grace is an acute person, in her way, and when I talked to her beforehand about the situation and what she was supposed to do, I think she fathomed my feelings, and I know she was prepared for something out of the ordinary.

Jerry and I had gone round to the latest decorator's delight in which Grace and Fred were living. The walls of the living room were some of them leaf green, and others a dull, twilight sort of blue. The furniture was upholstered in dull silver-colored cloth, and there was one of those Brancusi streamline things in an alcove at one end of the room, indirectly lighted, so that it gave you the feeling of an evening star. The place was magnificent, and exactly like a stage set. We both goggled at it; they'd only moved in a month or so before, and though we were used to Grace's apartments, this one was a stronger dose than usual.

"Well, darling," I said to her, "this is positively one of your nobler efforts."

She smiled at me, and said, "Yes, isn't it rather sweet? I've always loved these colors and meant to have a room in them someday."

Jerry was surveying the place with a look of amused interest; his eye lit on the Brancusi thing and he smiled briefly, then sat down tentatively at one end of the big sofa. Grace saw his glance.

"I do hope you approve, Jeremiah," she said in the tone of a woman who is talking at the bridge table to cover up a finesse she intends to try.

He nodded at the wall niche. "That thing there is good. I like it."

Grace was taken aback. I could see that she had hoped to be able to tease him with it. To find him approving the most extreme item of a décor carried to the far edge of extremity puzzled her. But she rallied nobly. "I knew you would, my precious."

Jerry dismissed it with his highest praise. "It's almost pure mathematics."

Grace sat down somewhat abruptly at the other end of the sofa, lit a cigarette—mercifully not one of her special, imported ones—and said, "Your friend telephoned a few minutes ago. She has a lovely voice."

Jerry said, "Hasn't she?" in a noncommittal tone.

Grace gave him her quick smile and crossed her legs. "Poor Fred had to go out tonight. They're doing something or other at the Brook Club."

"Probably drinking again," I suggested. Grace and Jerry let the remark go.

"Anyway," she went on, "I think we can get along without him for one night."

I saw that she did not mean to let Jerry off easily. She had deliberately got Fred out of the way for the occasion, but she meant him to know it and appreciate the fact.

Jerry landed one of his rare quick lefts to the chin. "Thank you," he said.

I laughed, and Grace gave me a little snoot of mock irritation.

"She said she was on her way," Grace went on.

Jerry said, nervously, "This is very good of you."

"Nonsense," said Grace. "I'm complimented, my pet, really. Two tributes to my taste, from you, in the same week!" She waved her cigarette toward the Brancusi. "But, of course—" and she grew quite serious, for her—"I am not altogether comfortable about this, Jerry my lad."

He looked at her calmly. "I know," he said. "You have scruples. You think maybe you ought to tell Dad."

Grace looked genuinely shocked: "Heavens, no. Not that. But"— and she sighed delicately and so perfectly that I couldn't tell whether she meant it or no—"I don't approve of getting serious about life, and matrimony, and the opposite sex, at your tender age. I did, and I know now that I should have waited and played around a few more years."

Jerry said doggedly, "I've thought about all that."

"And you're determined to be unreasonable?" Grace cocked an eyebrow at him.

"Yes," he said firmly.

"Very well," she told him. "Very well. I shall do my part—that is, if it's possible. Now tell me something about your young woman, Jerry. Bark's so hopeless at describing people."

I had been at pains to give Grace a detailed picture of Selena, but not an altogether flattering one. Something of my personal bias had shone through, and Grace, like a conscientious workman, wanted to get the specifications direct from the drafting room.

The doorbell rang exactly then, and Grace got up at once to answer it. Jerry, sitting on the sofa, began to rub his hands together and stare at the pearl-gray carpet. I got up, uncertainly, and put my hands in my pockets. After a moment Jerry rose too, and moved toward the foyer. We could hear Grace's light, gay voice saying things like "My dear, it's so nice to meet you," and the quiet, perfect modulation of Selena's voice answering.

They came into the room, and as I saw Selena again, the prickle went down my spine. She was tall—a whole head taller than Grace, and she moved down the room toward us with the long, free stride of an Italian hill-village woman. I looked at her face, wondering why I could not like her and if there would be anything in her expression that I could get hold of and put a name to in my own mind. There was nothing, or almost nothing. It seemed to me that her mouth was deliberately curved into a smile and that her eyes were wary. At any rate, she took in the room with one instant glance, but it had no visible effect on her.

This time she was wearing a black evening dress, and the white-silver of her arms and shoulders and throat was unforgettable. But the dress itself was hopeless. I saw Grace purse up her lips momentarily when she looked at it. For one thing it was cheap, and a little too short for her. Then, more than anything else, it was vulgar. Glittering black sequins which were too large, and all wrong anyway. The line in front was too extreme, and at no place did the thing really fit her. Worst of all, there was a sort of girdle around the waist made to imitate braided gold and fastened in front with a large buckle containing a sizable fragment of ruby glass, which, if it had been what it pretended to be, would have been worth a young fortune.

This time I noticed something about her hands. The fingers were long, and round, and gave the impression of tremendous force and strength. They were lovely, but aside from being scrupulously clean, they were quite uncared for. The nails were untinted, and short—not even polished.

We sat down, and Grace smiled at all of us, reassuringly. Jerry and I were covertly staring at Selena, though I suspect with very different expressions, and Grace was looking at Jerry almost as though she did not trust herself to join us in an inspection of Selena.

"This is a very interesting room," Selena said. Her tone conveyed to me that she meant the words literally. The room interested her.

"I'm so glad you like it."

"Grace," I said, somewhat heavy-footedly, "is a good bit of an interior decorator. She takes a fresh apartment every year, just for the fun of trying a new stunt with it." I can remember still how inane my own voice sounded as I delivered myself of that conversational gem.

To my surprise, Selena turned to me and said, "New things are always an adventure."

Grace started, and looked pleasantly surprised, but Selena's next comment aborted whatever hope she may have been feeling.

She had turned and was looking at the Brancusi. A good twenty feet from where we were sitting. It glowed there in its niche. A cylinder of perfectly symmetrical polished brass, tapered at each end to a point. "Ah!" Selena's voice was coolly regretful. "What a pity it isn't perfect."

Jerry and Grace were floundering. "Why—" said Grace, and "What is—" said Jerry, simultaneously.

I thought this was the best chance I was likely to have, and I leapt at it. "If it were perfect," I said to her quickly, "it would not be beautiful." The thing looked flawlessly symmetrical to me, I'll admit, but I had to find out what she would do when attacked.

Jerry scowled a little and looked as if he did not like what I had said, but Selena turned to me with something that I thought was real interest.

"Then you think it is beautiful," she said in the tone of someone making an incontrovertible observation.

Grace laughed easily, and probably sincerely, stood up, and beckoned to me. "Bark and I will go fix some drinks. I need him to get the ice out of the Frigidaire; this one is a very stubborn case." It was flat, not at all up to Grace's standard, but it had to serve. We left the room to Selena and Jerry.

Once in the pantry, Grace leaned against the dish cupboard, stared at me, and said, "How old is that woman?"

It was something that had not occurred to me before. I ran over her image in my mind. She was obviously young. How old were the Greek girls in the frieze of the Parthenon? "Oh," I hazarded a guess, "around twenty, I suppose."

"You think so?" I could see that I had surprised her. "You don't like her enough to be charitable," she said with a grin, "but I should have guessed she was at least thirty-five."

Thirty-five! I couldn't believe it for a minute, but Grace was damnably shrewd about other women. While I melted the cubes out of a couple of trays of ice I reviewed Selena, again, mentally. Grace was watching me with an expression of bright interest on her face.

"You can't be right," I said finally. "There isn't a line on her face."

Grace nodded. "No, my lamb. But the eyes."

"What about her eyes?"

"Well," said Grace slowly, "they aren't the eyes of a girl who's just lost her husband in a dreadful sort of—accident. They aren't the eyes of a girl at all, really."

"All right," I conceded. "They aren't the eyes of a girl."

"There you go again," said Grace. "I can't imagine how I came to have such a stuffy child. Your father was rather sweet, you know."

The ice finally and reluctantly separated itself from the last tray. As I tossed the cubes into the bucket with what I hoped was an air of indifference, I said, "You still haven't told me how her eyes tell you she is thirty-five."

Grace shrugged. "You need to have everything so literal. Look into them the next time. They are wise eyes, cool and wise." She said nothing for a minute, then she laid her arm on my shoulder. "She is not my sort, Bark my angel, but I think she is lovely. I'll do my best with her, for Jerry's sake and yours."

She always made me cross when she talked like that; it was as much a pose with her, and as little as everything else she said and did. I looked at her hard, and said, "Look here, Grace," and stopped.

"I know," she said lightly, "don't be difficult. I don't like her any more than you do, but"—and she looked me in the eye firmly and with a certain twinkle—"we both owe a lot to Jerry, my pet, and I'm going to give him just what he wants. He's made up his mind anyway." And she slid through the pantry door with the tray of glasses, leaving me to follow with the ice bucket.

The rest of the evening passed somehow. I tried to decide whether Selena was as old as Grace thought she was, and couldn't. The conversation was jerky and unreal; Grace did her best to get it started, but somehow every subject was stillborn. She mentioned Noel Coward's latest play, but apparently Selena had never heard of it or him. I tried football and books, but neither of them was a subject that Selena appeared to care about in the slightest. If Jerry could have appeared ill at ease, he would have that evening; I knew him well enough to know that he was desperately uncomfortable. He eagerly seconded all Grace's attempts at small talk, and all three of us drank a good deal in an inconspicuous sort of way. As for Selena, I had wondered what liquor would do to her. She tasted her highball almost curiously at first, without any expression of either pleasure or distaste. Later, after we had had a couple of rounds, she drank about half her first glass. A moment later she set it down on the table and looked at it with a fleeting expression that seemed to me at the time to have been surprise or wonder, and never touched her drink again for the entire evening.

Grace was really superb. She led the talk around to the question of the winter styles with all the finesse of a children's photographer arranging a difficult grouping. She asked Selena what she thought, of the new something-or-other hats.

Selena thought a moment. "I don't think," she said finally, "that I have noticed them."

"But, my dear," said Grace instantly, "You simply must. They're so absolutely *right* for you. Do let me take you round to my man. He makes all my hats for me. Designs them individually."

Jerry struck in quickly. "You know, I think Grace is right. They'd be stunning on you."

Selena looked at him quickly, and there was something in her look that was, if not warm, at least eager. Then she turned to Grace. "That is very kind of you, Mrs. Mallard. I'd like to have you help me, if you would. I am afraid I've not been paying the proper attention to clothes."

There was nothing to say in the face of a remark like that. Jerry colored a little around the collar, and I looked hard across the room and tried to keep my face impassive. Grace was not apparently affected by it, but what she said next was, I think, designed to draw a little blood.

"Of course not," she said sympathetically; "you haven't any reason to. But when you're my age, my dear—"

Selena studied her for a moment; I half expected her to ask Grace just what her age *was,* and began metaphorically reaching for my hat. Instead, she smiled, and said, "You must excuse me. I am afraid I am not accustomed—" and then stopped suddenly. It was the first time I had heard her utter an incomplete sentence, and the effect was somehow pleasing. I felt a little less appalled by her than ever before.

Grace softened instantly, and made immediate talk about trifles, and the evening wore along. Before we left, the women arranged to meet next day, and I realized that Selena was as good as made over. Once Grace got started on her, she would never stop till the job was finished. Jerry, I could see, was pleased that the covert purpose of the evening was advancing so satisfactorily, and he shot a glance of gratitude at Grace. But he was obviously anxious, once the appointment had been made, to leave, and we went before ten o'clock.

The three of us came to a halt at the front door of Grace's apartment house.

"I'll take Selena home," he said to me. "You don't need to bother, and thanks a lot, Bark. Grace is one of my favorites, and I wanted Selena to meet her."

"That's all right," I said awkwardly, and then, "I'll leave the light on in the living room, and the door unlocked." I turned to Selena;

she was standing at the curb in the electric twilight of a New York street at night, straight, tall, and beautiful, so that it made my throat ache to look at her, and I hated her and was afraid of her,

"Good night, Mrs. LeNormand," I said.

I meant to add that I'd be seeing her, or something to take the curse off the moment, but I couldn't say anything more. She looked at me, and I felt that everything I was thinking and feeling must show in headlines on my face.

She gave me her hand. It was cool and very strong. "Good night, Mr. Jones. We'll see each other again soon. Your mother is very kind; I'm sure that she will be able to help me a great deal."

A taxi swooped in to the curb, and she and Jerry got into it. The red taillight dwindled down the empty street. I stood on the curb and thought about her last remark. She had certainly gone right to the heart of the evening's purpose with a directness that was disconcerting.

"You see," I told Dr. Lister, "these are little things. Perhaps they have no meaning."

He poured us each another glass of sherry, the bottle was beginning to look empty, but neither of us felt any reaction to the wine. Drinking it was a formality. A thing that gentlemen did together. Perhaps it blunted the strangeness of our talk together and made it easier to go on. I raised my glass and sipped slowly.

"What you are telling me," he answered thoughtfully, "includes many things that I have always wanted to know. Neither of us can be sure just what is important."

"We have talked all the big things over so often—LeNormand's death, and Jerry's marriage, and Selena. The answer must lie, if we can find it at all, in the small incidents, the overtones."

"Yes," he said. "You're right. Go ahead, if you are not too tired."

I wasn't tired. I was long past that point. But I was afraid. Already some dim idea of the sort of story I had to tell was taking shape in my mind, and what I could distinguish of it was beyond the edge of reason.

The transformation in Selena during the next two weeks was astonishing. It was plain that she was thrusting the past resolutely behind her, that she did not intend to wear mourning either literally or figuratively. The fact that she was willing to go everywhere with Jerry so soon after LeNormand's death surprised me, though I was more embarrassed on Jerry's account than critical of her for it. As for Grace, she made no comments, at least to me, but she remade Selena from the skin out, and it was amazing to watch that beauty come to light day by day; always before, I had been violently conscious of Selena's clothes, but now you never noticed what she had on. Just looking at what she was took all your eyes. Grace's innovations had another curious effect. She had taken Selena to her own hairdresser, and he had done something to her hair which was masterly in its way. Lipstick and a manicure, too, subtly changed her. There were other things. I have mentioned the long, free stride with which she walked. Gradually it shortened, and though it lost no grace, her walk became less conspicuously different from other women's. At first she had never used a gesture when she spoke, but imperceptibly she began to accompany some of the things she said with a motion of the hand or a turn of her superb head. Watching her, one evening, I realized that there was something familiar about her new gestures, and in a moment it came to me that they were Grace's, flawlessly imitated and employed at just the same moments. Even the way she walked...

My original feeling that Selena was a statue come to life gradually dissolved. I no longer thought about her as some disturbing sort of Galatea, and though my deep distrust of her never disappeared I found myself talking to her more, and more as I would to any other woman, and thinking about her indeed, not as a woman, but as the girl Jerry was going to marry.

By that time there was no pretense about it between the two of us. He never made a formal announcement to me; the nearest he ever came to it was once when we discussed what would be the earliest advisable date. When, as sometimes happened, I went out with them of an evening, I fell into the easy habit of making joking, more or less concealed, references to their getting married. Doing so made me feel, to myself, a pretty good sport about the whole thing, and while Jerry took all my remarks at their face value, there was at least one time when Selena, after one of them, looked at me gravely and said, "You are a generous person, Bark." I had the grace to feel ashamed of myself.

One night, early in December, the three of us were to go to the theater. It was one of those occasional balmy days at the outset of the New York winter when the weather is more like May than December, and it is almost too warm to wear a coat. We had two or three cocktails at the apartment—that is, Jerry and I did while Selena ate some of the canapés. After that first highball at Grace's I never saw her take another drink.

When we went down to the street we decided to walk a few blocks before taking a cab. The night was bland, and we sauntered along, talking, past the brownstone and brick fronts of the houses. I felt quite happy. All at once a girl came down the stoop of a house as we were passing, and turned up the street ahead of us. What followed was trivial, but somehow it disturbed me deeply and, as well as any one thing, it illustrates the quality in Selena that froze my occasional efforts to like her.

The girl was sixteen or so, I suppose, and she had on a party dress and high-heeled slippers, and an evening cape that was obviously new. Jerry and I watched her, idly, and the same observation must have reached us almost simultaneously. Plainly, our predecessor had on her first "grown-up" party dress and slippers. She walked along with the most careful dignity, looking neither to right nor to left. Everything in the carriage of her head, the formality of her walk, the care with which she put one silver slipper down in front of the other proclaimed that she was feeling not only thoroughly mature; but a lady, or more likely, a movie queen. As we came to a darker stretch of the sidewalk, her promenade suddenly stopped. She skipped over to the curbing and began to walk along it, balancing herself with her arms and almost running along the edge in quick, uneven steps. Then she crossed the sidewalk, half running, and darted up the step of another house. We could hear the radio playing dance music inside.

Jerry's grin of amusement met my own, and we began to laugh. Both of us were delighted; there was no need to comment at all. All Jerry said was "Swell!"

Selena looked at each of us in turn for a moment. We were still chuckling. "Why are you laughing?" she asked us.

I looked at her, but she seemed serious. "That girl," I explained.

"Oh," she said, and then, "but what was there to laugh at? Do you know her?"

"No, no. But she had on her first party dress, and she was so grown up, and then she simply had to go and try walking the curbstone."

"But how do you know that was her first party dress?" she asked me.

"Good heavens," said Jerry, "You were a girl yourself once, weren't you?"

That was the night I got the letter from Parsons. For once, Jerry and I came home together after leaving Selena at her hotel. The night elevator man handed it to me as we went up, and as soon as I saw the Collegeville postmark I stuck it in my pocket. I didn't know who was writing to me from there, but I had a sudden, cold feeling that it was going to be something I wouldn't like, and the fact that it was a special delivery proved it must be important.

I put it on the bureau and waited till I got into my pajamas. Jerry eyed it once or twice, but said nothing. Finally I was ready for bed, and there was nothing left to do but open it and read. The typewritten address didn't tell me a thing. I tore the envelope open.

My dear Mr. Jones:

No doubt you will be surprised to hear from me in this way, but as the matter is not strictly official, I prefer to write you. I want to ask a favor of you. Will it be possible for you to come down to Collegeville sometime this week? I am still working on the case, as you probably know, and am anxious to have some help from you if you can give it to me.

The question is one which I think only you can answer for

me satisfactorily, and as I would like to keep it confidential, I hope you will come down alone. Unless I hear from you I shall expect you on the ninth, by the eleven o'clock train. Please meet me at Police Headquarters.

Very truly yours,
Alan L. Parsons, *Chief, County Detectives*

Jerry had been watching me as I read. When I finished he said, "Somebody die and leave you a million dollars?"

"No," I said, trying to sound impersonal, "Just something I have to attend to later in the week."

But I lay awake a long time, wondering. It hurt to lie, to conceal something from Jerry, but worse than that was my conclusion that Parsons must have found something, some clue, and wanted to confront me with it. And if he wanted me to come alone, it meant that whatever he had found must implicate Jerry. Or perhaps it implicated me. Maybe he had come upon the story of LeNormand's using Jerry to type the letters to the other astronomers, and wanted to ask me about it separately. But that didn't seem entirely logical. I revolved every possibility I could think of in my mind. I even considered waking Jerry up and telling him, but then I felt I had no right to do that.

"Say, Bark," his voice came to me through the dark from the other side of the room. "You asleep?"

"No. What?"

"I just thought I'd tell you. Selena and I are getting married next month. We plan on the twelfth."

"Gosh, that's swell. You're a lucky guy." I hoped my voice sounded convincing.

"I'll have to ask Dad to be best man, of course, and it'll be just a very small ceremony."

"Sure," I said.

"You'll be there, of course."

"Absolutely."

8. QUESTIONS, NO ANSWERS

THE ELEVEN-o'clock is a good train. It makes the run to College-ville in under two hours. I sat in the smoking car, watched the miles pour past the window, and tried to figure out something that had happened the night before.

After I'd got Parsons' letter I'd asked my employers if I could have leave of absence for the ninth. They gave it without any questions. Then the idea came to me that since I wouldn't have to work on the ninth, the evening of the eighth would be a good time for a party. So I asked Jerry and Selena and Grace if they wanted to go out on a binge. I owed Grace something, in an indirect way, and I wanted to show Jerry that there were no hard feelings and be the first to celebrate his and Selena's setting a date for their marriage. All three of them liked the idea, and we arranged to meet at the apartment at seven.

While dressing, Jerry and I had one or two cocktails just to make sure there was no poison in them. After a while Grace came in, wear-ing a dull-red dress with swirling skirts and gold sandals. She had her hair done a new way and looked entrancing. As soon as I saw her I knew she'd firmly decided to look like nobody's mother. Competi-tion with Selena may have been in her mind too; and if it was, she'd struck just the right note to get away with it: They were so utterly different that no one would think of comparing them.

I was suddenly delighted with her and glad to see her and felt very unfilial indeed. When I kissed her I noticed that she had on a new perfume.

"Well, darling," I said. "You're enough to start an Oedipus com-plex!"

She laughed and remarked, "Fred thinks you're mean not to have invited him."

"This is his night for the club, isn't it?"

"Yes, but tonight he didn't want to go especially."

"I bet that was after he saw you in this outfit."

She went over to the tray and picked up a cocktail, tossing me an impudent grin over her shoulder. "What an imagination you have!"

I told her it didn't take any imagination, and we had a quick cocktail together. It was Jerry's week in the kitchen and he was out there fixing a few hors d'oeuvres. What with my previous drinks and Grace looking so attractive and the conviction that in throwing this party I was doing something really nice for a change I began to feel extremely good.

"By the way," I asked her, "what's that perfume you're wearing? I like it."

"Gracious but you're gallant tonight, my pet. It's called *Adieu Sagesse*."

"You ought to give a bottle to Selena."

She stuck out the tip of her tongue and said "Miaouw" at me and we both laughed.

Jerry came with a plate of stuff that he'd made to go with the cocktails, and told Grace she looked stunning. We all had another drink. Then he told her that he and Selena were to be married the twelfth of January.

Grace shook her head at him in admiration. "As a child, Jeremiah, I remember you were the shyest little boy I ever knew. And here you are, positively bursting into matrimony. Are you going to marry her in the ordinary way or come riding up on a big white horse and sweep her into your arms and dash off?"

He blushed. "Grace, it's not so bad as that, surely."

"No," she said, "I know it. I'm really delighted, of course. Selena's the most beautiful person I've ever seen, and you're lucky. And so is she."

He blushed again. "Please. Spare my blushes."

"You do it so nicely."

He laughed and said, "You're hopeless, Grace."

"Not entirely, my lamb. But pretty old to change. You must allow an old woman her peculiarities." Then her manner changed, and she stopped smiling. "I'm just foolish enough to rush in where angels would fear to tread, Jerry. Have you told your father?"

He nodded. "Yes. I called him up last night."

"And what did he say?"

Jerry looked a little uncomfortable. "He said he'd talk to us both about it when we go out there this weekend."

Grace laughed. "The famous Lister reticence extending to the telephone, I see. Well, as for that, don't worry. Just let Selena handle him."

The doorbell rang, and she came in. A pleased smile came over Grace's face, and I suspected she was complimenting herself on Selena's dress. And well she might; it was a masterpiece. Silver green, the color of aspen leaves, and cut so simply and severely as to be very nearly ostentatious. Jerry's heart went into his eyes, and I could not blame him.

After the greetings were over I proposed a toast to the wedding and the three of us drank it. Selena, as usual, drank nothing, and watched the rest of us with a faint smile as we clinked our glasses together. But it was all very gay—gayer than any time I spent with Selena either before or afterward.

She was wearing a ring. A square-cut emerald with a deep, burning green heart to it that was the sort of thing you see displayed in Tiffany's window all by itself. We exclaimed over it.

"Goodness, darling," said Grace. "If any of my men had ever offered me an engagement ring like that, I'd have insisted on marrying him right then and there for fear he might escape me."

Selena looked pleased. "Jerry must have been extravagant," she said.

"Yes," he told her, "and gosh how I loved it!"

But I stared at the emerald without being able to think of a word to say. It struck a note of finality that took some of the bloom off the evening for me.

After one more cocktail apiece we sallied forth to do the town. Walking toward the avenue and a taxi, Selena and I dropped a few steps behind Grace and Jerry. After a few yards she turned to me and said, without preamble:

"You are unhappy about Jerry and me."

"No, I'm not."

"Please, Bark. Tell me the truth."

"Well, then, I think you're rushing things a little."

"You mean that we ought not to be married so soon?"

"Exactly."

"Jerry said some people might think that. But why do they?"

I turned to look at her in the dusk of the street. Perhaps she was making fun of me. But apparently she was serious. Her lips were level and her eyes direct.

"Well," I told her, "it's customary to wait a little longer."

She was insistent. "Yes. I know that. But why?"

I referred her to *Hamlet,* Act 1, but she did not know, or pretended she didn't, what I meant. In desperation I explained that the popular view was that it took more than a month or two to forget a first husband and turn to a second love.

"Oh," she said. "I wondered. Sometimes it is hard to understand just what is behind your ideas."

It was an extraordinary remark, and I did not know how to take it. Before I could ask her, she went on. "But I think it is all right for Jerry and me to be married, even so soon. You see, I never loved Le-Normand."

This was getting beyond me. I told her that whatever she and Jerry did was their affair.

"Yes," she said, "but I want you to understand it. You are Jerry's best friend."

"And as such," I told her, "the only thing I want is to see him happy."

Mercifully a cab drew up at the curb beside us before this insane conversation could continue. I was angry at Selena for simply tramping into the middle of a complicated situation and talking bluntly about it. I resented the fact that she had put me so thoroughly on the defensive, and concluded finally that the less I had to do with her direct interrogations, the better the evening would go for me.

It was after a good dinner over which we sat until past ten o'clock that the incredible part of the performance took place. The three of us, at least, had drunk enough not to want to end the evening there and then. It was too late for the theater, and we decided that the thing to do was to dance. After a lot of argument between Grace and me we took a cab to Barney's. It's a small place, east, in the middle Fifties, but the thing I liked about it was that the music was never too loud and somewhere Barney had picked up the idea that people can be amused in other ways than by bawdy jokes and undressing girls. Not that I have any objection to either of those forms of entertainment. But some instinct in me rejected the notion of celebrating our particular occasion in other than the nicest way I could think of. And I counted on Barney to provide as much niceness as was consistent with having a good time.

The music was really good. I had not danced with Selena before, and the moment I began I knew it was going to be an experience. My expectation had been that we'd have a difficult time together on a dance floor. There was too much constraint between us and an antagonism of character we both recognized. In addition, she was very tall. And yet, she danced as no woman I have ever met. I forgot myself completely, and I could not think of her any longer as a woman. Instead, it seemed to me that my arm was around the moving shape of the music itself. The low, insistent beat of the rhythm was in every muscle of her body and she was completely weightless. We moved round the floor like a part of the melody. I remember thinking that this was the first time dancing had ever seemed to me an art. The people sitting at tables on the edge of the floor followed us with their eyes. I am not an exceptional dancer—scarcely even average—yet when the music stopped there were scattering hand claps from the spectators and I discovered that we had been left almost alone on the floor. Also, it occurred to me with surprise that we had not exchanged a word in the entire dance. I took her back to the table. Jerry and Grace were sitting there talking together.

"Fella," I told him, "this girl of yours can dance."

He was pleased. "It's an experience, isn't it?"

Selena smiled and said, "This is easy music."

I sat down at the table and picked up my highball. The way Selena had danced did not at the time seem to me to belong in her character. I thought of her awkward clothes when I had first seen her, of the stiffness and coldness of most of the things she said. The contrast with the fluid rhythm of her body in my arms a moment ago was puzzling. I told Grace about it later, when Jerry and Selena were on the floor. She watched them awhile with her eyes partly closed, smiling to herself.

"You never know," she said.

After Grace and I had trod a couple of measures it was midnight. Most of the lights went out and Barney himself pattered out into the middle of the dance floor and held up his hand. He had a spotlight trained on the bald spot at the back of his head, and with his round, pink face he looked like an Old Testament cherub.

"Ladies, gentlemen, and visitors from out of town," he began, and went on to tell us that he had a special attraction to offer this evening. It turned out to be an Egyptian "Prestidigitator *and* magician," who, at least for business purposes, called himself Galli-Galli. After some inevitable puns on the fellow's name, Barney announced that following his performance Galli-Galli would circulate among us and perform sleight-of-hand tricks at the tables. We were welcome to figure out how he did it if we could.

Barney retired and was followed by a long roll on the orchestra drums and a flood of light from the spots. Into the middle of the noise and brightness leaped a little brown man with a wizened face. He wore a turban and a green-and-white striped robe with long, flowing sleeves.

His first concern was to bow elaborately in all directions and look us over with a pair of large, melancholy black eyes. Then he exclaimed "Galli-Galli!" in a high, pleased voice and began throwing colored balls into the air. There was an astonishing number of them, taken, I suppose, from his sleeves, and his juggling was beautiful to watch. He wove patterns and figures with the arcs of the balls in the air, and at the end made them disappear as surprisingly as he had produced them. There was a burst of applause, and he smiled delightedly at us. His own skill, in the acts which followed, seemed to delight him, and he was constantly saying "Galli-Galli!" with a sort of childlike enthusiasm.

Selena was watching him without expression. Once or twice, at some particularly dexterous or mystifying bit of business, she smiled slightly, but that was all. After the first few tricks, she seemed bored and paid no further attention to him. Grace, on the other hand, was fascinated. She had her mouth open in an "oh!" of surprise most of the time. When the lights came up, Jerry and I clapped loudly and shouted "Encore!" The little man bowed to us several times and finally made his way directly to our table.

On closer inspection he was even older than he had looked under the spotlight, and I don't think there was much doubt that he was an Egyptian. I liked him at once.

"Galli-Galli do card tricks," he said, producing a deck. "You like?"

We told him we would and he asked us to inspect the cards, which were in a sealed deck. We broke the paper and looked carefully at them, front and back. There were the conventional fifty-two and everything seemed to be in order, so we told him to go ahead.

He made cards appear and disappear in one way and another, but most of the tricks I had seen before. Perhaps he knew others even better, but we never got a chance to see them because the most inexplicable of the things Selena ever did in my presence intervened. It happened in the middle of one of his tricks. He had handed the deck to me and told me to shuffle it. I did so, thoroughly. Then he told me to pick out a card, in my mind, but not to separate it from the pack. Mentally I selected the four of clubs.

Still following instructions, I asked Grace to cut the pack, which she did, and handed the cards to Jerry. He spread them out in a fan across the tablecloth, back up.

"Now," said Galli-Galli to me, his black eyes smiling, "you know which card is yours?"

I hadn't the faintest idea. "No."

"You know?" he asked Grace.

"My dear man . . ." said Grace.

"And you?" Selena was apparently startled at the question.

"Certainly," she said, reached out one white hand, and turned over the four of clubs.

For one instant a look of incredulous surprise stamped itself on Galli-Galli's face. My own jaw must have been sagging. Then the little Egyptian rallied himself.

"That right?" he said to me.

"It certainly is," I told him.

He bowed very low, more to Selena, I thought, than to the rest of us, scooped up the cards, bowed again, and left the table. The three of us watched him go and then turned with one accord upon Selena.

She was looking distressed.

"Darling," said Jerry, "would you mind telling us how you did that?"

"Goodness, Selena," said Grace, "we ought to form a bridge partnership at once, my dear."

She shook her head.

"Listen," I said. "You can't just do a thing like that and leave us all in the dark. How is it done?"

But she wouldn't tell. At first she refused to say anything about the trick and then she insisted that it had been simply luck.

At the time I didn't wholly believe her, and sitting in the Collegeville train the next day the thing seemed fantastic. Not once had she touched the cards, and I had told no one which card I had picked. I went over and over the scene at Barney's in my mind, and the answer eluded me. If it was luck, it was one chance in fifty-two, and there had been nothing uncertain about the way she turned that card over. More than anything else, her calm, almost disinterested manner had impressed me. She seemed to view it as a trick to amuse children.

Familiar landscapes and towns began to flash past the window. I saw that we were only a few miles out of Collegeville, and my thoughts turned to Parsons and his reason for sending for me. Perhaps he had made some progress on the LeNormand business, though there was nothing in the papers to suggest it. In any case, it must be more or less unofficial, or his summons to me would have been of a different sort. On the whole, I decided, the indications were that he had discovered nothing definite.

My anxiety about Jerry's marriage, my instinct that it was in some way wrong and undesirable, had preoccupied my mind. For a week I had hardly thought about the murder of LeNormand except casually. I was convinced that it was insoluble, and my memories of it were so appalling that I had walled it off in a corner of my mind and tried to forget about it. And yet it was a part of the fiber of every day I lived and of most things I did. Only last night I had been sitting in a night club with LeNormand's widow, almost without realizing how short a time had elapsed since her husband's death. So much had happened in the intervening weeks, that the night when we had found his burning body seemed a year, instead of a month ago.

Jerry, I reflected, had not put the thing out of his mind to the same extent that I had. Several times I had come home to find him at the desk, surrounded with crumpled sheets of paper on which were marks that looked to me like the figures and symbols on LeNormand's observatory table. Once I had found in the wastebasket a floor plan of the observatory, apparently drawn from memory, and he had even used the University Directory for some purpose, for I found it on the table one morning. I wondered why he was so eager to get to the bottom of the thing. The obvious suggestion was that because it concerned Selena it was important to him. But I rejected that idea. Psychologically, I should have said the normal thing for him to do was to think as little of the past as possible, to seek to put as much distance, mentally, between it and his present as possible.

The sight of Armitage Tower coming up above the trees ahead of the train heightened the feeling of tension that had been growing in me. Whatever was to happen in the next few hours, I was afraid of them. As the train pulled into the station and I started down the car steps I was aware of a dryness in my mouth and an uncertainty in my knees that were symptoms of a nervousness that was first cousin to fear.

9. INTERROGATION

I TOOK a taxi to the town hall and went up its steps with my heart hammering at my ribs. Parsons was in the police-station room where he had talked to us before, sitting at the same long table. In front of him was a large black entry book of some sort and a pile of papers. He was chewing on the stub of a cigar and jotting down notes on a block of scratch paper with quick, decisive stabs of his pencil. There was an air of effectiveness about him.

He looked up for a second as I came in, waved a hand in a gesture of welcome, and remarked, past the cigar, "Sit down. With you in a second."

He was genuinely busy, all right. I thought for a moment that he was putting me off to let my nervousness and anxiety come to a head, but as I watched his broad, blunt fingers scrambling through the papers in front of him and the quick way he glanced from them to his notations on the pad I realized that he was tremendously concentrated, perhaps even excited. He had something, or thought he did. I filled a pipe and lit it, trying hard to keep the match from trembling in my fingers, and leaned back in my chair.

Finally he straightened up, pulled a couple of fresh cigars from his pocket, thrust one of them toward me, and then, seeing my pipe, retracted it. After he had his own smoke going well, he blew two or three rings at the ceiling, shoved his chair back, put his feet on the table, and looked at me.

"One thing, Mr. Jones," he said. "There's nothing to worry over. This is just a talk between the two of us. Nothing official about it."

"I'm not worried," I told him.

"Good." He was silent for a moment. "I suppose you and Mr. Lister have done a lot of thinking about this thing the last few weeks."

"Well," I said, "some, of course."

"Tell me. Have you got any new ideas since I saw you?"

I was a little surprised at this question, and wondered what he was trying to get at. "No," I told him. "At least I haven't."

"You haven't," he repeated. "What about Mr. Lister?"

"I don't think he has, either." He was silent, so I added, "We don't talk about it very much."

"I can understand that," he said, and looked at me thoughtfully. "Mr. Jones," he said finally, "I'm going to be frank with you. This is just between us two."

"I won't repeat a word of it."

"All right." And then, with emphasis he added, "Not even to Mr. Lister—or Mrs. LeNormand."

I nodded.

"The fact is, I haven't got to first base with this case. I don't know any more than I did four weeks ago, except that everybody's story seems to be straight. I can't find a single clue or a single fact to go on. I haven't even been able to find a single person who saw a stranger on the campus that night." He paused and smiled. "And when the police begin looking for mysterious strangers, it's a sign the case is not going so well."

His manner was certainly disarming. He had me on his side, whatever it was, already.

"Now," he went on, "when I get stuck like this on what I'll call the physical side of a case—what you'd say were clues—I try to figure on the thing from another angle. And that's the characters of the people in it. Psychology, you'd call it, and motive." He looked at me pretty sharply, but though I'd likely have given away any thought I had, I didn't have one. My mind was a blank, so I suppose my face didn't help him much.

"Motive," he continued, "is usually a pretty easy thing to spot. Money first, by a long shot, and then women. There are a couple of others, like hate and revenge, but you hardly ever run into them unless there's a maniac somewhere."

I thought about that. "Well," I said, "none of those seems very useful in this case."

He nodded. "Money, certainly not. He had nothing besides his salary and a five thousand dollar life insurance policy. And apparently he had no professional jealousy to deal with in his work. So I figured out it must be that the motive revolved around some woman."

I began to see where he was headed, and the palms of my hands started to sweat.

"And the only woman," he went on inexorably, "is Mrs. LeNormand." I didn't say anything, so after a time he asked, "What do you think about her?"

I took a moment to frame an answer to that one. "It's hard to tell. She's not like anyone else. She's intelligent, and quiet, and she knows her own mind..." I floundered and stopped.

Parsons took a long pull at his cigar. "Mr. Jones, you've used some funny words for a young man talking about a pretty woman. 'Intelligent,' 'quiet,' 'knows her own mind.' I'd say you didn't like Mrs. LeNormand much. Right?"

"Yes," I admitted.

He took his feet off the table and leaned forward earnestly. "What I want to ask you next is something that could be misunderstood. Before I say it I want to tell you that I think you're okay. I mean, I like you and maybe I understand a little something of the spot you're in. And you strike me as—well—as regular. So don't go thinking I mean what I don't mean."

"All right," I said. "Go ahead and ask."

"You don't like her, and you admit it. Are you sure you aren't jealous?"

I got red and then laughed. "That's a hell of a way to put it," I said. "I guess it might be fair to say this: Jerry and I grew up together. We've been a close corporation for ten years or so. Now the corporation—" I realized that I was saying too much and stopped suddenly.

He paid no attention. "Now the corporation looks as though it might be dissolved, and by someone you don't like. That about it?"

"Just about," I admitted.

"Well," he said, "you've been honest with me. And don't think I wouldn't have known if you'd been lying." He tapped the pile of papers in front of him. "I've got a complete file here on what all three of you have been doing ever since you left town." He gave me a sharp glance. "I'm a policeman. I've got to know things like that. Don't get sore."

"I'm not sore." But it did make me angry to realize that we'd been spied on all the weeks since LeNormand had died.

"That's good," he said, and I could see he didn't believe my denial a bit. "Now then, the point is this: You aren't jealous of Mrs. LeNormand, but you don't like her. You resent her. Mr. Lister, on the other hand, is in love with her."

I simply stared at him. The man was as calm, as unconcerned, as sure of himself as God Almighty. I began to get really angry. "What the hell business of yours is it—" I began.

"Don't be silly, Mr. Jones. You know what business it is of mine. I'm paid by this state to find out who killed Professor LeNormand, and by God I'm going to do it if I have to injure every single one of your delicate feelings."

He was right, of course. I began to calm myself down a bit. "I'm sorry," I said. "It is true that Jerry is in love with her, and I suppose if you know what we've been doing you couldn't help finding it out."

Something I said must have amused him, for he grinned to himself an instant and went on. "What I'm after is why you don't like Mrs. LeNormand. That interests me a lot more, frankly, than why Mr. Lister is in love with her. I'm hoping that you can tell me why you don't like Mrs. LeNormand."

"Well," I began, "I'm not sure that I can." I could, of course, have answered instantly, "I don't like Selena because I am afraid of her," but that wouldn't have made sense to him. It didn't make sense even to me. So I said, "I think, as near as I can put it, I don't trust her."

My answer seemed to excite him. He studied me carefully a

moment and said quietly, "You don't trust her. Can you tell me why, or tell me at what times you don't trust her, or what she does that gives you the feeling of distrust?"

That was the question I'd been asking myself for weeks. If I could explain to my own satisfaction what was the basis of my distrust of Selena, life would become a whole lot easier. The very fact that I did not know what it was about her that I hated—or feared—was at the bottom of much of my recent unhappiness. Perhaps Parsons' questions would clear up some of the confusion in my mind.

"You've asked me a hard question," I told him. "I've been thinking about it for weeks and I can't decide. It's no special time and no special thing. She asks the damnedest things, sometimes. And if she has a sense of humor, it's not like other people's. She strikes me as cold-blooded." He was watching me intently and nodding his head at each statement. "I tell you what she's like," I went on. "She's like a foreigner, like some of the Germans over here during the war, I imagine. She doesn't want to let on that she isn't an American." This suddenly struck me as carrying coals to Newcastle. "You must have interviewed her. You know the quality I mean."

"Yes," he said, "I know the quality, but I don't know how to describe it. I thought maybe you could help me."

"That's as close as I can come to it."

He was silent a moment, rolling the dead cigar in the corner of his mouth and looking out the window. "You said she was like a foreigner." I didn't add anything to that, so he went on. "Well, Mr. Jones, *is* she a foreigner?"

The question took me by surprise. "I don't know. You must have the answer to that. Don't you always take down everything about a person in a case like this? Where they came from and how old they are and whether there was any insanity in the family and all the rest of it?"

He continued to gaze out the window. "Usually. Usually. Not this time."

"You mean to say you didn't ask her all those things? Jerry and I practically had to list the fillings in our teeth."

"Of course, we asked her." He was frowning. "We asked her a dozen times. All she would tell us was that she didn't have a family or any relatives any place. She wouldn't even trust us with her maiden name."

I made my tone as sarcastic as I could. "And naturally you wouldn't take advantage of her in her bereavement."

"Listen," he said, and from his hard stare at me I saw my remark had not pleased him, "this case is dynamite. I can go so far, and then the whole University will be down on my neck. What do you want me to do? Take her to the station house and try persuasion? The whole force would be out of a job in a week."

"All right. I spoke out of turn."

"You did. Anyway, forget it. Maybe you can tell us poor ignorant policemen what we want to know. Who is she and where did she come from?"

"I don't know."

He sighed. "Then I'll have to ask you another question that's liable to make you mad. Can you find out?"

"If she wouldn't tell you she probably won't tell me."

"That's not what I mean. You've admitted that Mr. Lister is in love with her. If anybody will know, he's the fella."

"For God's sake," I asked him, "do you want me to play stool pigeon on my best friend?"

He grunted. "I thought that's the way you'd take it. Use your head, Mr. Jones. I've got to have that information, and how I get it won't make any difference if she's not mixed up in this thing. If she is, do you want your friend going around with her?"

"No," I admitted. "But all the same I can't get it for you. I doubt if Jerry himself knows, as a matter of fact. At least, he's never said anything to me."

"So he doesn't know either." Parsons' tone was not surprised. "Well, well, well!"

"Surely," I suggested, "even if she wouldn't answer your questions you could find out about it in other ways."

"Surely." His voice was deceptively gentle. "I suppose your idea would be to work back from clues, eh? Labels on her lonjeray and so forth?"

That was more or less what I had been thinking.

"Well," he said, "if it's any comfort to you, we did trace her clothes."

"And what did you find?"

He held up his thumb and forefinger in the traditional symbol of zero. "We're not as dumb as cops are supposed to be, Mr. Jones. We've traced a lot of things. Maybe later I'll have to tell you a little about that. Right now I want to see if we can get at this thing from another angle."

"If I can help you—" I said humbly.

"Right." His tone was brisker. "About this strangeness of Mrs. LeNormand's. This feeling you have that she's a foreigner. Assuming for a minute that she isn't, would you say that she came from a definite social class?"

"What have you been doing," I asked him, "reading Karl Marx?"

He smiled. "Well, I have read some of it at that . . . we got a lot of God-damned reds in this country. Some of them right here at the University." He looked down at one of his notes. "I see here where a fella named Berkeley M. Jones used to belong to the University Socialist Club. That was two years ago, of course. You outgrown it?"

"Some of it," I admitted.

"Takes time, Takes time." He was relishing the point he had scored. "But this isn't pitching any hay. What I'm getting at is, do you think Mrs. LeNormand came from a family that was, say, of the proletariat, or—er—the bourgeois, or is she an out-and-out blood-sucking capitalist?"

"I never thought about it." The question puzzled me, like everything else connected with Selena. Nothing about her seemed to fit into conventional pigeonholes. "She has a good mind. My guess is that her family was probably professional. Her father might have been a lawyer or a doctor or maybe a professor." The minute I'd mentioned the professor idea I felt sorry. Suppose it started him off on that whole business of LeNormand's row with his fellow scientists?

Jerry would be dragged back into it, and there would be a whole hell of a mess. But Parsons was apparently talking about something else.

"—and when I told you I was stumped on this case, Mr. Jones, I meant it. I don't know what the next step is. Everything we find out leads us up a blind alley, and the only light I can see . . . I guess I'll have to tell you all about that and then ask you some of the same questions over again. Maybe when you understand what's in the back of my mind you'll be able to help me more." He was arranging papers and folders in front of him into precise piles. Then he lit another cigar and leaned across the table in my direction. There was uncertainty in his manner, as if he doubted the wisdom of telling me what was on his mind. And well he might. In the months afterward, when I had to live with his story and its implications, I wished a thousand times that he had thought better of it, kept it to himself. And yet, even if he had never spoken, there would have been no difference in the outcome. Thwarted as he was by the case at every turn, he had no choice, I suppose.

"Quite a while ago," he began, "I mentioned that we'd even gone so far as to look for some outsider, some mysterious stranger, as I put it, on the night of the crime. When we couldn't find one I figured we better check back on a few other things. Local gossip naturally was one. But there wasn't any gossip about LeNormand and his wife, outside of a lot of old hens brooding around about her and who she was and why he married her and why she married him, and all like that. Now in my experience, Mr. Jones, a murder is a thing that doesn't just happen out of a clear sky. By that I mean, if you look close enough you'll discover a whole lot of little things, straws in the wind, you might say, coming ahead of it. Usually you can uncover some of these things by keeping your ears open. But like I said there wasn't any real gossip. Nobody even thought there was any bad blood between them. It's hard to believe with a woman like her and a husband like he was that there was never any trouble, but I couldn't even find a single old cat who claimed that Mrs. LeNormand had been playing around with another man. So the gossip angle petered out. Sometimes, too, in my experience, some of these things that come ahead of a murder go so far as to get into the police records." He opened the big black ledger in front of him. "So Cap Hanlon and I went through the blotter book for a long ways back." He sighed. "It seems to be fairly restful, being a policeman in this town. We didn't find a possibility till we hit August. And then we came on something that probably doesn't mean a thing. Except that it's an open case, and it has a woman in it."

For the life of me I couldn't decide what this was leading up to. But I could see that we were coming to something that excited him.

"Early in August"—he looked at the book—"on the seventh, to be exact, there was a disappearance in this town. And the person that disappeared was a woman." He stopped speaking and began to fiddle with his pencil. There was something uncertain about him then, as though he were trying to decide a point that was vital to him without letting me in on the story. Finally he jabbed the pencil at the scratch paper and said, "I'm going to tell you the whole story because it's the only way I can get the information I need. But I want you not to interrupt me, and I want you to give me your word of honor as a gentleman that what I have to say will go no further. You're not to speak a word of it to anyone. Okay?"

I gave him my word of honor. Keeping it turned out to be the hardest job I ever tackled in my life.

Parsons was looking grave and a little doubtful, but he went on finally. "About eight o'clock in the evening, August seventh like I said. A tourist named Jamison, Stewart Jamison, stopped up here by the Sunoco station to get some gas. He was driving an old Ford. A model A. In the car with him was his wife and their daughter. It was their daughter that disappeared."

He paused and licked down a flap of tobacco on his cigar. "I want to tell you about the daughter. Her name was Luella—Luella Jamison. The Jamisons live in a little town in South Carolina, and if you don't mind I won't tell you the name of it. They've got a farm down there, and they're dirt poor. Cap says the car was a wreck on wheels, and when he talked to them he noticed that their clothes were old and mended. But he says they seemed kind of a high type, for all that. They were clean and nice-spoken. Both of them, he says, were tall and fairly good-looking, but it struck him that they were pretty old to have a daughter only twenty. The man must have been about seventy, and the woman, his wife, not much younger. That's about all I can tell you about them—I've got some pictures that I want to show you later. All except for one thing. The daughter was an idiot."

That hit me. I had not known what to think about Parsons' story except to wonder what connection it had with the LeNormands and with Jerry and me. I could see still less connection after he spoke these last five words, but something went through me almost instantly after I heard them. The only way to describe the feeling is to say it was like the click of the latch on a door closing behind you. But even as I felt it I lost the reason for the feeling; for one fleeting second things had made sense, and then it was all a jumble again.

"The way it happened," Parsons continued, "was like this. Mrs. Jamison got out of the car, and got her daughter out to go to the rest room. Mr. Jamison was checking the air pressure on the tires at the moment. You know how those filling-station rest rooms are. You get to them around a couple of angles of pretty close latticework. The ladies' room at the Sunoco place is very small—just big enough for one person at a time. So Mrs. Jamison fixed up Luella first, and then she led her out and put her hands on one of the uprights of the latticework and told her to hold on to it. Then she went in herself, and when she came out, the girl was gone. There wasn't a trace of her, and nobody saw her go. It was just the end of dusk, and the girl had on a dark cloth coat. Mr. Jamison and Jack, the guy at the station, were stooped over, working on the tires, and Cap couldn't find anyone who saw the girl.

"I better tell you a little of what Cap and I found out about Luella. She'd been an idiot from birth. She was nearly six before they could teach her how to walk, and she never did learn how to dress herself, or feed herself. And furthermore, she couldn't even speak. 'She used just to make a few little noises sometimes,' her mother told me. None of the doctors in their part of the world could do a thing for her, and naturally it was pretty tough on the Jamisons, she being the child of their old age and all, and an only child at that. They hadn't got married till Mrs. Jamison was way over forty, and they hadn't expected to have any children at all. When Luella came, they were tickled to death, at first. Then, when they saw how it was, they decided it was God's will and did everything they could for the kid. Being poor, it wasn't much, but they always kept her neat and clean, and never gave up hope that sometime they'd find a doctor who could do something for Luella. She wasn't so much of a burden on them as you might think. At least that's the impression I got after talking to them. She wasn't subject to any kind of violent fits, or anything like that, and always did what they told her to if she understood it. Things like hanging on to that lattice post, I mean. They never used to worry about leaving her by herself at the farm; if they both had to be away for a while, they'd latch the door to her room and leave her sitting in her chair. Mealtimes they would have her at the table, and Mrs. Jamison would feed her. Every way they could they tried to bring her out, and there's no doubt about their both loving her. There's a big photograph of her in the living room of their house now...

"I'm telling you all this so you'll get the picture of these people. I must say I like them. Both good Anglo-Saxon stock from away back. His people were English and he's proud of them in a quiet sort of way. He told me his great-grandfather was a famous scientist, or mathematician, or some such thing. He had a couple of books the old boy wrote more than a hundred years ago." Parsons smiled apologetically. "They were so glad to have a visitor, they showed me everything in the house. Maybe I'm getting softheaded, but I'm positive those two would never cook up a disappearance act even if they didn't love their kid, which I'll bet my last dollar they did."

He looked out the window again. "It was pathetic the way she cried when she talked about Luella.

"Well, came the New Deal. The Jamisons were cut in for a slice of the AAA money that was going round, and they decided to use it on Luella. They wrote a lot of famous doctors up north about her case.

Most of them answered that it didn't sound as if there was anything that could be done, but one man wrote and said if they could get her up to him he'd make an examination and charge them just his minimum fee. Then, if he thought he could do anything, he would make some sort of arrangement about later payments. It was a good man, too," said Parsons. "I looked into that."

He picked up a folder from among his papers and glanced into it thoughtfully. There seemed to be half a dozen photographs in it. A sudden anxiety to look at them came over me. I reached out my hand.

"In a minute," he said. "The rest of the story is short so far as facts are concerned. The girl never turned up. It's pretty hard to see what could have become of her. Even if she'd fallen into the lake, her body would have come up. Cap and the boys dragged most of it, anyway. I thought for a while she might have got picked up by some other car, maybe, but there's no evidence of it, and that idea raises a whole lot of others. I won't go into them all with you now, but I'm pretty well satisfied, myself, that that didn't happen. For one thing, the state troopers were having a driving license checkup a mile or two down the road, and they'd have been apt to notice anything as out of the way as a car with some guy in it who'd just got hold of a feeble-minded girl by mistake. Now I want you to look at the girl in this picture."

He handed me what turned out to be an enlarged snapshot of the front of a farmhouse. There was a section of path in the foreground, edged with white-painted stones. Then the house. A small, clapboarded one with a veranda across its whole front length. Even if the boards were obviously in need of paint and the whole place looked as pinched and poor as you could well imagine, it was neat and clean, and not in bad repair. I couldn't see any broken boards in the veranda, and the curtains at the windows were trimly and evenly looped.

Two people were sitting in rocking chairs on the front porch. One was a spare, almost gaunt woman in her sixties, with the thin hair pulled up from her ears and piled in an old-fashioned coiffure on the top of her head. She wore a bleached-looking Mother Hubbard and old, high-button shoes. There was a basket of what seemed to be sewing in her lap. The other figure took my eye at once; I was hardly aware of the rest of the picture at first. It was a girl—Luella, of course. She was sitting in a rocking chair next to her mother. But where Mrs. Jamison was clearly looking at the person who had held the camera, the girl's eyes were not focused on anything. She was simply staring into the distance. Her mouth was partly open, and her whole body was slumped into the chair. Her arms were lying out along the sides of the chair, and in one hand she held something which I could not make out at first. Then I saw it was a rag doll. It was dangling from her fingers. She wasn't paying the slightest attention to it. Even if no one had told me she was an idiot, I could have guessed it after one glance. Everything about her was mindless, vacant, not human. I looked at her face a long time. It seemed to have regular features. The eyes were the same distance apart as Selena's. The hair was apparently darker, but the porch was in shadow.

I pointed that out to Parsons. He merely observed that the color of hair was one of the least permanent things in this world.

He showed me other pictures, several of them. Even one blurred enlargement of the face of Luella Jamison. I dislike remembering that enlargement even to this day. I looked at all of them for a long time. I remember my heart beat so sickeningly in my throat that I could scarcely breathe.

Parsons finally broke the silence. "What do you think, leaving the hair color out of it for the moment?"

"God," I told him, "I don't know. It's inconceivable that it could be Selena. In a general way, I suppose this girl does look something like her. But I can't tell what that face would be like with a mind behind it.... Can you?"

He seemed disappointed. "No, you're right about that. But in general, Mr. Jones, would you say that it was impossible for her to be Mrs. LeNormand?"

"I can't say that it would be impossible. But her hair would probably have to be bleached—and I know damn well Mrs. LeNormand's hair isn't bleached—and she'd have to have more than the ordinary amount of intelligence before she'd be even close."

"Yes," he said, and then after several seconds, "yes" again.

"I don't get it," I said finally. "There must be something more up your sleeve than this. What about fingerprints?"

He grinned at me. "You might make a detective someday. I've got Mrs. LeNormand's, of course. But I haven't got Luella Jamison's and I can't get them. Mrs. Jamison is too good a housekeeper. She washed Luella's room, cleaned all her things, once a week. And when she went back home, brokenhearted, she got the room all ready again for the girl. There may be some of her prints down there, but none that could be identified positively. I couldn't find any at all except ones made by Mr. and Mrs. Jamison. A girl like that," he added, "touches mighty few things, when you come to think about it."

"Listen," I said to him. "I don't see your point at all. You seem to have gone down there, and spent a lot of time on this Luella Jamison. From what you say, you must think she has some connection with Mrs. LeNormand, or even could be Mrs. LeNormand, and yet you know her. You know she is intelligent. You know how she speaks and handles herself. You even know, or ought to know," I added thinking of his reports on our New York activities, "that she dances."

"Oh, yes." He was quite calm. "I know she dances, all right. She dances a month after her husband is murdered." He must have seen me wince. "I don't blame Mr. Lister. He thinks he's got to get her mind off it, and he loves her anyway and wants to dance with her, so it's a good idea to take her dancing." He waved his hand again. A large chunk of cigar ash fell off onto the table. "Damn. And I know she talks too. Not a trace of a Southern accent, either. But there are some things about the way she talks that puzzle me. It's what she doesn't say."

I asked him what he meant by that.

"I seem to be giving you a lot of lectures this afternoon," he replied. "Being a college man, maybe you're used to them. I'll tell you, Mr. Jones. Even professors talk like human beings. What I mean is that when they're not dishing it out to their students, they talk in a way that tells you a lot about their past lives, if you listen close. Little words, expressions they use. Gestures too, and facial expressions. You know what I mean. Individual ways of saying things that have been built up over years of talking. It's like a style in writing, I guess. And it's never quite the same in any two people."

Certainly I knew what he meant, and I knew that it was the absence of this quality in what Selena said, particularly when I first knew her, that bothered me. It was unnatural.

"I see what you mean," I told him.

"Mrs. LeNormand talks as if she was reading it out of a grammar book," he said.

That had been Walter LeNormand's way too, I suddenly remembered. And the thought gave me a twinge of uneasiness.

"LeNormand talked that way too, generally," I told him. "At least, he did when I spoke to him the few times we ever met. And he was precise about everything connected with words and figures."

"Unh hunh." He didn't seem specially interested.

Neither of us said anything for a minute or two. I was thinking hard, and Parsons' idea seemed completely fantastic when I got through considering it. How could this Luella Jamison have run away from her parents and turned herself into the sort of person Selena LeNormand was? I put this to Parsons after a while.

"I know," he said. "Its almost impossible. If her insanity was due to a piece of bone pressing on the brain, and it got knocked back into place and made her normal again...sort of an unlikely thing, though, and I can't find a doctor that will admit the possibility."

"Naturally not," I said virtuously.

The remark appeared to nettle him. He looked at me a moment then and said, "All right, put this in your pipe and smoke it. Luella Jamison disappeared the evening of August seventh. On August ninth, at ten-thirty in the morning, Joe Peters over at the county building in New Zion issued a marriage license to one Walter R. LeNormand of England, and a certain Selena Smith. Smith!" There was contemptuous suspicion in the way he said it. "Selena Smith, of Lafayette, Oklahoma. Aged twenty-one. And there isn't any Lafayette, Oklahoma."

10. CRAS AMET QUI NUMQUAM AMAVIT

"You can see what sort of a case it is, Mr. Jones." Parsons' voice was harassed, and he chewed irritably at his cigar. "There isn't a damn thing I can go to work on. Nothing but a half-baked idea, and every time I think of that I wonder if I'm getting too old for this sort of work."

He was right, of course. He knew practically everything I knew, except one thing. One thing that I hardly liked to admit even to myself: that Jerry was going to marry this woman, whoever she was, in a little over a month. As soon as I thought about that I realized something else, something that instantly destroyed my whole peace of mind. I knew this possibility about Selena, and I had promised Parsons not to tell anyone, not even Jerry, about it. It was frightening to know I'd have to live with the story of Luella Jamison, and think about it every time I looked at Selena, and never be entirely sure it wasn't true.

"Of course," Parsons was saying, "I've tried to trace LeNormand's ever being seen with Mrs. LeNormand before August seventh. And no one that I can find ever saw her until the ninth. LeNormand didn't even leave town except once, and that was on the tenth. He took his car out of the garage about seven, and drove north along Route 72. I don't know where he went or what he did, and I can't find out. He got back to town in the evening."

"Did they get married in New Zion?" I asked him.

"No. A man named Willetts, a justice of the peace, married them. He lives on the Collegeville turnpike about five miles this side of

Zion." He paused to grunt and then went on. "Sometimes I wonder how some of these birds learn enough to be justices of the peace. They've got to know how to read and write. That's about all this Willetts does know, and he writes awful slow. But his story agrees with Joe's, over at the county building, in one respect. It was raining on the ninth, and both of them remember that Mrs. LeNormand was wearing an old trench coat that was too long in the sleeves for her. Joe said it was a man's coat. She didn't have a hat. And there was a trench coat in LeNormand's closet when we went through his things."

"What about their cook?" I asked him.

He grinned. "Bessie! God, what a time I had with that woman! She talked more than all the rest of the people in this case put together. The trouble was, she was up in Hampton till the fifteenth, visiting her cousins. LeNormand gave her the first two weeks in the month for her annual vacation. When she got back, she says, Mrs. LeNormand was already there, and she rambled on and on about how messy the house was. If that means anything."

There was a long silence while he looked at me with a smile on his face and waited for me to say something. I looked back at him and tried to imagine some explanation for what he had told me. I couldn't find any. There seemed to be no proved connection between one set of facts and another.

"Mr. Parsons," I said finally, "I never knew that detectives would talk so frankly. I wish I could, but I don't quite see how I can help you, or what all this proves."

"Hell," he said without losing his smile. "There aren't any secrets in this case, and you're doing all you can. I don't suspect anybody because I can prove that nobody I know of at the present time was anywhere near that observatory when LeNormand was killed. You two were the closest, and I can't find a reason in the world why either of you should want to do a thing like that. I'm taking President Murray's word for it that neither of you knew about Mrs. LeNormand before that night."

"We didn't," I assured him.

His smile changed a little. "Of course, if I could trace her and prove that you or young Lister knew her before she married LeNormand—"

"Well," I said, "I can't *prove* we didn't, of course, but the psychological evidence, at least, is all against it."

He nodded. "Yes. I grant you that. Now I want you to think carefully once again: do you remember anything Mrs. LeNormand ever said that would give a clue to her past? Where she came from?"

"No," I told him. "I've begun to notice that she never talks about anything that happened before . . . before last month."

He was disappointed. "Hasn't she even mentioned any names, people or places, that she knows?"

"None that I can recall."

"Well, be on the lookout for things like that, will you, and let me know if you come on anything?"

I didn't like that idea much. "After all," I started to say, "I can't very well—"

"Get this straight," Parsons said, taking the cigar out of his mouth and looking at me with no smile at all. "I don't suspect her, personally, for a moment. There's no evidence of any row between her and LeNormand. She was in the house when it happened, according to Bessie's own testimony, and nobody on the streets saw her between her house and the observatory. No, she couldn't possibly have done it. But there's a mystery about her, and I can't clear it up. If I could, I'd damn well know who killed Professor LeNormand. And I want to point out to you, my friend, that if she turns out to have a past, and the kind of past that breeds a murder, the quicker Mr. Jeremiah Lister finds out about it the better. If he doesn't, there's always the chance he'll find himself burned to death one of these days. That's one reason why I want your cooperation."

Of course, he was right. I agreed to let him know anything I found out. He thanked me and stood up. I gathered that was my cue to leave, but I had one more question I had to ask him.

"Mr. Parsons," I said, "you've told me a lot of things bearing on why Professor LeNormand was killed—"

"Proving," he said quickly, "that I can't figure out why he was killed. Or who killed him."

"Yes," I said. "But do you know *how* he was killed?"

He scowled. "Yes and no. Half the faculty here has been working on that. The consensus of opinion is that he was burned to death—"

"No kidding!" I exclaimed.

"—that the burns were not made by fire or by chemicals, but by some sort of rays."

"Rays?" I said.

"Yes," he said. "They tell me they can produce burns like that, only very small ones, down in the physics laboratory. I don't know. They aren't going to try it on me. None of them claims he could do it, but they all say maybe the fellows in their field someplace else are ahead of them. Germany, perhaps. They wouldn't know of it, of course, because it would be a military secret over there."

"For God's sake," I said, "I pity you. Even an international angle!"

He shrugged. "Like everything else in this case, there's no proof one way or another. Whatever the stuff was, it didn't leave anything to analyze or work with. I'm not smart enough in the scientific field to work down that angle. About all the good it does me is to tell me the sort of person the murderer is likely to be."

"Maybe," I shrugged, "he's a mad inventor someplace in South Carolina who knew the Jamisons and—"

He shook me warmly by the hand. "Good-by, Mr. Jones. You were very kind to come down here." He was pushing me gently but firmly across the room. "I'll keep in touch with you. Let me know if you find out anything. And for God's sake"—by this time he'd backed me through the door—"don't try to think up any theories like the mad inventor"—I was halfway down the front steps—"because you won't get anywhere with them. I've thought of them all myself, already."

I shouted back a good-by to him through the swinging door and turned toward the station, chuckling. You couldn't help liking the man. Thinking back over the discussion, I realized he'd handled me skillfully. But he hadn't extracted the fact that Jerry and Selena were going to be married in a month. And as I thought of that, I felt a sense of despair.

A shooting star plummeted down like a tear of light and vanished in the dark above the Sound.

Dr. Lister's face was set into lines that were strange to me; he looked cold and watchful, like a man waiting for the sun to rise on his execution day. His gaze was fixed on the yellow shape of the candle flame— odd how much it looked like that Brancusi Grace had in her apartment.

"You see," I said, "I am breaking my promise to Parsons. I am telling you something that he told to me in secrecy, but I think he would want me to speak now, if he were here."

His lips moved slowly. "Yes. Yes, of course he would. I see what you have been living with. I'm sorry that there were those weeks . . . when we did not understand each other."

"That doesn't matter."

"It matters to me," he said heavily. "I was not as wise as I should have been."

"You didn't have any way of knowing. Let's not speak of it again."

He nodded his head quietly, and after an instant said, "Have you found out yet whether she was—is—Luella Jamison?"

The question seemed to echo at me from the night that held us suspended like two motes in a drop of dark water. I wet my lips with my tongue. "Yes, I think I have."

Life in New York for the next month was pure and unadulterated hell for Berkeley Jones. I could not work—fortunately the holidays gave us a slack season and I got by on that score—and I could not eat, and I scarcely slept. Most of the time I was more or less drunk, and doubtless I was thoroughly unattractive to those who loved me. Grace, after a bad evening at her apartment in the course of which I cried maudlinly and stupidly about Jerry's approaching marriage, told me that I was disgusting and ought to see a doctor she knew. She had him call on me and he turned out to be a psychoanalyst. Dr. Lister was more intelligent—after watching me put down three highballs in about fifteen minutes he told me that my enthusiasm was admirable but I'd be having quite a hangover one of these days if

I didn't taper off. He spoke of what happens to the insides of permanent alcoholics and predicted he might be operating on me one of these days. Then he asked me if I was sleeping well, and I told him that I'd given the process up as a waste of time. He wrote me out a prescription, and in a lucid moment I had it filled. I got several nights of real sleep out of those powders, but then the prescription ran out, and I was ashamed to ask for another.

Jerry did his best to keep things from getting too bad. He knew me so well that he understood it wasn't the fact of my not liking Selena, or the regret that we were breaking up our partnership that was making me act as I was. But he couldn't understand why I didn't want to go out with the two of them once in a while—why I refused even to go to dinner at Grace's when Selena was going to be there. (He didn't have a mental picture of the face of Luella Jamison, idiotically empty, and sickeningly half familiar, to tempt him into comparisons every time he saw Selena.) He was patient with me, and kind, and put me to bed several times, and swore at me, and kept plenty of liquor in the house so I wouldn't go out and get boiled where he couldn't keep his eye on me. But there were times when his patience wore thin, and once he said, "For Christ's sake, Bark, either tell me what's eating you and get it over with or quit making a damned exhibition of yourself every night like this!"

But I didn't tell him, or anyone else. Liquor doesn't make me talkative, so I gave nothing away. I told Jerry that even if he didn't understand what the hell was wrong with me, not to worry about it. I promised to snap out of it sometime soon.

"God," he said. "I hope so. I've never seen you like this."

"Live and learn."

He bit his lip, and for an instant I wondered if we were going to have a fight. I should have welcomed it. Instead, he shook his head. "Something's got into you. I don't know what it is and I wish you'd tell me. We'd both be happier."

"Forget it. I'm all right. It's nothing to do with you, anyway."

"You're not all right. And since you won't tell me, I have a good idea it's something about Selena."

"You're crazy."

"No, I'm not. Listen, you ape. Don't worry about hurting my feelings. Go ahead, tell me what it is. I promise not to get mad."

I was tempted. It would be so easy to blurt out the whole story. In a way, he had a right to know it, in spite of my promise to Parsons. Jerry was the one who was marrying Selena, and if there was something wrong with her, something dreadful in her past, he was entitled to fair warning. It was on the tip of my tongue to begin telling him about Luella Jamison. But what good would I accomplish? He was in love with her. Nothing I could say would keep him from marrying her. To put that ugly story into his mind would simply poison some of his happiness without altering his course in the slightest. Jerry was not the man to change his mind once it was made up. So I held my tongue, and merely said, "You're making a mountain out of a molehill. The trouble with me is that I've been piling up hangovers, one on top of the other."

"You don't like Selena, Bark. I know it and I can't help it. But you didn't like her before, and it didn't take you this way. You were swell the night we went to Barney's. What's happened recently that makes so much difference?"

"Nothing."

"You and Selena haven't had a row, have you?"

"God, no," I said. "Listen. Quit worrying about me."

"Damn it, she doesn't feel this way about you. She thinks you're swell. Did you know that?"

I thought, oh, she thinks I'm swell, does she? Like hell. She knows what I think about her. If she can turn over the four of clubs out of fifty-two cards without batting an eye she can damn well read my mind and learn what I think of her. All I said was "That's nice."

He turned on his heel and went out of the room. "Sometimes you make me sick."

I felt rottener than ever and went out to have a drink. It tasted sour on my tongue, but then so did everything in those weeks. I hated myself and ordered another drink while I reflected on what a louse I was and how much like Luella Jamison Selena looked sometimes.

That was the day I went out and bought them a wedding present. I must have been no soberer than my average for the month because what I got was a library edition of the Encyclopaedia Britannica. At the time there seemed to me something ironically humorous about that. 'Jerry and Selena,' I thought to myself, 'two such fine minds, can sit in front of the fire. He can read volume EXTR-GAMB and she can have JERE-LIBE, and it will be a lovely domestic evening."

Then I grew ashamed of myself and bought them a watercolor by Marin that I'd always wanted, and was so broke I had to borrow money from Grace. She made me promise not to use it on liquor.

Jerry was finding this a trying period too. His family were united in their opposition to his marriage and did little to make his life tolerable. They grumbled and pleaded with him in groups and severally. The worst of the lot was his Uncle Horatio Delavan. A little dried-up gospel shouter of a man who walked in on us unannounced one night. Jerry met him at the door.

"Hello, Uncle Horry."

"Good evening, Jeremiah. I should like to have a word with you."

I could see that Jerry didn't expect it to be a matter of one word, but he swallowed something that was on the tip of his tongue and asked the old boy to sit down. I retired to the bedroom but I didn't close the door.

"Jeremiah," said Uncle Horry's voice in the tone of a bank vice-president calling up a small depositor to tell him he has overdrawn his account, "I won't beat about the bush, my boy. I want to talk to you about your—er—abrupt marriage to this woman."

"My marriage to Mrs. LeNormand, Uncle Horry. Please remember her name. It'll help."

"Very good. This Mrs. LeNormand. Your aunt Mabel and I are very much distressed, my boy, very distressed indeed."

Jerry's voice was ominously calm. "I'm sorry about that, Uncle Horry. I don't believe there is anything to be distressed about."

"Possibly not. But your aunt Mabel and I feel strongly that you are not acting with proper circumspection." He cleared his throat and inserted a note of unction into his voice. "After all, there is generally a good reason for most customs. And it is customary to allow more time to elapse between the—er—end of one marriage and the beginning of the next."

"There is no good reason I can think of why we should not get married next month."

"Convention, Jeremiah. And this murder case. Your are both implicated, innocently, I grant. But people will talk."

"Let them talk all they want. I don't give a damn."

Uncle Horatio sounded pained. "Tut, my boy, there is no occasion for strong language. Let us discuss this matter like gentlemen."

"There's nothing to discuss. It seems to me wholly my own affair, uncle. Dad and I understand each other, and that seems to be all that matters."

"Of course, if your father—"

"Dad's having the wedding in the Long Island house. Is that evidence enough for you of his attitude?"

Jerry was becoming quieter and lower-voiced with each answer, an invariable sign in him of mounting rage. He answered the next few questions, which had to do with Selena's religion, in a tone that ought to have warned his uncle. But sensitivity to the moods of others was never Uncle Horry's chief claim to fame. When he learned that Selena was not a communicant of any church he began opening up the vials of wrath, quoting liberally from Old Testament sources. The gist of what he had to say was that any member of the family who married a heathen would need no blowtorches in his afterlife. How long he might have gone on I don't know. But after one particularly perfervid sentence, Jerry stopped him.

"Careful, Uncle Horry. Don't say anything you'll be sorry for later." I heard his chair scrape across the floor as he rose. Nothing came out of Uncle Horry after that but a splutter. In a few seconds Jerry said with cool impersonality, "It is better to marry than to burn."

That was the end of this particular episode. Uncle Horry took an indignant leave. When the front door slammed shut I came out of hiding.

"Well," I told him, "apparently Uncle Horry is on the side of the angels, anyway."

He glared at me and then began to smile. "He's harmless, of course. Only he does get under my skin."

"Listen, fella," I told him. "Why don't you shut him and all the rest of them up? Postpone the marriage. A few months and they'll come round."

"You too?" he said. "Damn it, Bark, I don't get any peace from the lot of you. Even Grace. Last night she called me her 'impetuous young Lochinvar' and a lot more stuff. What do they think I'm going to do? Sit around and let Selena go on living alone in a hotel, with no friends and nothing to do, and be miserable? With that nightmare of his death to haunt her day and night? Even if she never did love him, it's a horrible thing to have to remember." He looked at me pleadingly. "Can't you see how it is? I don't even know how much money she has. Maybe right now she's worrying about not having enough. Damn it, Bark, I want to look after her. I love her and she loves me, and why the hell should we wait months and months just because it's customary?" He began pacing up and down. "Listen, Bark. I think you have the idea that this is all in my mind. Well, it isn't. I don't want to wait for her, but I would if she wanted me to."

The implication of that took a second to reach me. "So she wants the wedding for next month?"

"Yes," he said. "And I see why too. I've told you. She's not the kind of person who makes friends with every Tom, Dick and Harry. She hasn't any real friends except you and Grace, besides me."

That, I considered, was putting down the best possible total for Selena's friends. Grace had introduced her, I knew, to some of her own crowd, but with Selena such a recent widow, and not speaking the same language that they did, I suspected that she had many lonely hours sitting in her hotel room, waiting for the evening and the time when she could be with Jerry. The thought awakened no sympathy in me because she never impressed me as a person who needed friends.

Of course," I said cautiously, "it must be a rotten way of life, the one she has now. And I see that she couldn't have stayed in Collegeville."

He looked at me directly, and said, "When we got engaged, Bark—and I wouldn't tell another soul in the world this—she said, 'Marry me soon, Jerry. I need you.' So we decided on January. I told her it would be like this with most of the family, but she doesn't care and neither do I."

Yes, I admitted to myself, she did need him in some obscure way I could not understand. From the very first time they had met, there in LeNormand's house in Collegeville, I realized that she had been attracted to Jerry. And if that was so, and if she asked him to marry her soon, I had to admit that he was doing the right thing, although I felt it would have been decent of her to think about him as well as herself.

"Hell," I said, "don't let them upset you. You're probably right, and if Dad approves, that's all that matters."

"Yes," he said thoughtfully, "Dad doesn't mind." I said nothing, and he seemed to be thinking to himself for a minute. "Selena handled him marvelously. We went out there that weekend after your party, you know. Someway or other, she got round him that first night. I thought there'd be a row, but there wasn't. They went into the library and talked awhile, after I told him our plan, and he just came out and gave me his blessing, so to speak."

He stirred in his chair, took out a cigarette and lit it. In the glare of the match his face was composed.

"Yes," he said in the impartial tone of a man who neither defends nor praises himself, "I told Jerry to go ahead. I could not have prevented their marriage, and I wanted to have him feel that I was behind him in whatever course he chose for his life. Let me tell you what happened in the library:

"We went in," *he began*, "after dinner. I told her that I wanted to talk a little with her before anything was settled too finally. We sat down beside the fire, and I tried to choose my words carefully. Aside from her beauty I realized that I knew very little about her. So I began by telling her something about Jerry, and what he meant to me.

I mentioned the fact that I had had to bring him up myself, and that if there were faults in his character which she discovered later on, she must not think too harshly of me.

"'Of course, he has faults, Dr. Lister,' she told me, 'but so does every human being. I do not mind that. I expect that.'

"That struck me as rather cool, and I felt that I hadn't created the atmosphere in which I wanted to talk to her. So I told her that she must understand that Jerry did not need my consent for anything he chose to do, but that I loved him and wanted to see him happy. I told her something, too, about our family, and that we are proud of it because we have held ourselves to a code of personal conduct that is not altogether the ordinary one. I explained that even though she felt she was marrying Jerry, it was not a case of Jerry alone. That we are, on the Lister side at least, a united family of which Jerry was a part.

"My expectation was that she would tell me something of herself, but she made no reply to me at all, so I asked her finally, as tactfully as I could, if she would mind telling me who she was and where she came from."

He drew deeply on his cigarette and looked reflectively along the terrace. I felt that he was trying to make clearer something that was still puzzling to him.

"She did not answer me at once. As I waited for her to speak, Bark, I had a feeling that I had said something that offended her, but I paid no attention to it because it seemed to me I had asked nothing that was not proper for me to know.

"At last she sighed and said, 'You are entitled to ask me that question, Dr. Lister. But it is easier for you to ask it than for me to answer.'

"I had the feeling that she was putting me off. My next remark was some sort of apology if I had said anything to disturb her.

"'No,' she said, 'it's not that. Perhaps, if I explain what I mean, you will understand why I cannot tell you more.' She gave me the definite feeling then that what she was going to tell me was all the information I would get out of her. 'Walter LeNormand once rescued me, Dr. Lister. He was a man I think you would have liked.

Your son liked him. I ought to tell you that I did not love him. But I liked him and I admired him. He took me into his house, he married me, when I was alone and in need of protection. He is dead now, and nobody knows how or for what reason. But when we were married my past ended. It was a new life for me. A life that he gave me and made for me. There was nothing in my background that you need to think about or worry over. Jerry loves me for what I am, not what I have been. I want you to do the same thing. I shall be good to your son and try to make him a good wife.'

"Then she said nothing more for a while. 'In a way Jerry, too, rescued me. After my husband's death I did not know what to do. I was alone again, and in a world of unfriendly people. Jerry has changed all that for me without having to question me. Please think of me as Selena LeNormand and no more than that. I want you to like me or not like me for what I am, not for what I have been.' She stopped and looked at me a long time. 'I give you my assurance that there is nothing dishonorable, by your own standards, in my past, and that my people, too, are the equal of yours.'

"When she finished speaking, Bark, I did not know what to say. I felt that she would tell me no more even if I questioned her further. As I repeat it to you, all that she said constituted nothing more than a polite and devious way of telling me that she would not tell me anything about herself. But as she spoke to me in the library, I felt a great respect for her. There was character in her words and the way she said them.

"I debated the wisdom of trying her again. If there was a mystery in her past, I felt that I had to know of it. Yet it was essential to me not to maneuver myself into the position of opposing the marriage. You see that, don't you?"

"Yes," I answered, "I see how difficult it was for you." His story interested me, but I had known all along that he knew no more than I did. And yet, had he only realized it, he had had in that library the only opportunity any of us ever had to save Jerry's life. There was no blame in that. If he had known what the stakes were, he would have played his cards differently.

"It seemed wisest to me," *he went on,* "not to insist. I simply asked her if she felt there was any danger that her past, whatever it was, might sometime confront her and Jerry when it was too late.

"She leaned forward in her chair and replied, 'No. No. I promise you that will never happen.'

"We went on talking for a while about other things. I began to feel a great admiration for her as a person. She gave me the impression of tremendous inner strength. And I could not doubt her intelligence. Jerry, I felt, had chosen wisely. It would be an experience to live with a woman like Selena. I thought of their future together without fear. She was his equal, I believed, in the things that really matter. If I had to choose between an ordinary girl, no matter how much I might approve of her background, and this woman to whom I was talking I should not have hesitated.

"Only once did I wonder if my judgment was wise. We had been talking about the future, and without meaning to pry into any understanding there might be between her and Jerry I mentioned my pleasure at the thought that he was getting married and said something about my hope that they would have children.

"'No,' she said again, urgently. 'You must not expect that.' My face must have showed some surprise or disappointment, for she went on, after a moment, 'at least, not for a while.'

"My first feeling was one of embarrassment. Evidently I had blundered into something. I told her that I did not want to make her unhappy, but that I hoped there was nothing to prevent their having a family when they got ready.

"She smiled at me, the warmest, most sympathetic smile I think she ever gave me. 'Oh, no,' she said, and there was a note of something like hope in her voice. 'I want to have children someday.'"

He was silent, and I knew that he could add no more to the problem that concerned us both. Time was passing, and I went on with my story immediately. Nothing he had said gave any further substance to the shape without shadow that was haunting my mind. And yet, neither did what he had told me seem to conflict with the growing clearness of its outline.

Jerry and I went out to the Long Island house several days before the wedding. Grace was there too, and a couple of Jerry's aunts and uncles. Everything was very quiet, of course, and though all of us had our reservations, probably I was the only one who felt really serious about possible objections to Selena.

She behaved, I must say, beautifully. The first evening she was there, Dr. Lister showed her all his prize books—the Sir Thomas Browne that he found in a little shop in Tokyo and bought for a few yen because the Japanese proprietor thought it was only an English book, the special Melvilles he was so fond of, the association copy of *Endymion,* and his collection of Arabic treatises on mathematics. She spent about ten minutes looking at one of those, I remember, although she confessed that she did not know a word of Arabic. Just the same she gave it back to him with a smile and said it was interesting. He laughed and said she was the first woman who ever thought *that* about it, and she was welcome to come in and read it any time she liked.

Of course, her beauty was like a candle in the house. Wherever she moved she seemed to bring a light with her, and it was pathetic to watch Jerry follow her with his eyes. Yet I never saw them exchange any very passionate intimacies. Once, coming into the room we always called the extra room—a sort of little box that opened off the library and had originally been intended for a secretary's workroom —I found him sitting beside her on the old, battered leather sofa in there. He wasn't holding her at all, but was bent over her hand, kissing it. She was looking at his head with a clear, almost wondering gaze, and, there was, I thought, a little smile on her lips like the ones children have when they are not quite sure of themselves.

I excused myself hastily, of course, and went away, but I felt good about it. They made a swell couple, and perhaps she did have a heart. Later I found her in the library, alone, looking at some of Dr. Lister's books again. She had on a heavy, dark-cream knitted sweater and a dull green woolen skirt, and no ornaments at all except the big, square-cut emerald ring Jerry had given her. I asked her if I could come in.

"Certainly, Bark," she said, and put down her book.

I settled myself in the big chair that I liked, over by the hearth. Looking at her, meeting those extraordinary eyes of hers gazing steadily across at me, I felt suddenly sheepish. "Selena," I said.

"Yes."

"I just wanted to tell you that I am sorry for the things that have happened this last month. I haven't acted very decently, I'm afraid."

"You mustn't feel that way."

"I know, but I'm sorry about it. Listen, Jerry is a swell guy, see? The best is none too good. Treat him well."

She kept on looking at me. "I want to," she said finally. And then, "What do you wish me to do?"

I couldn't meet her eyes. "Oh, you know. Give him a break."

"No," she said, "I do not know. Am I not being the way I ought to be?"

The conversation, I felt, was getting out of hand, and I began to feel silly. "Yes," I told her, "I suppose you are. Don't mind me. Maybe I have a hangover." Then I began to get stupidly intense. "If you don't know what I mean, it's a compliment to you, but all I want to say is, remember Jerry is the finest man you'll ever meet. There's only one way to be with him, and that's completely honest." It was on the end of my tongue to add, "And if you are Luella Jamison for God's sake tell him so," but I did not risk that.

She listened to me without moving and without changing her expression. Then she got up and crossed over to my chair. As she stood there, looking down at me, I began to feel sorry that I'd said as much as I had. Maybe it was the impersonal calm of her expression, but I felt again the touch of dread, brushing the fringe of my consciousness, which she seemed capable of imparting to me. She put one hand on my shoulder as I sat there.

"Bark," she said, "I am going to try to do what you want me to do. And I shall try as wisely and as hard as I can. Does that satisfy you?"

"'Yes," I told her.

"You hope," she went on calmly, "that I shall make Jerry happy.

You do not hope it a fraction as much as I do. But, you must stop thinking about me as you have been doing."

"I haven't been thinking about you in any special way."

"You have been resenting me. I do not object to that because it is natural, I believe. But you distrust me. You must not do that. You must forget anything that may be in your mind about me. Jerry and I have more things in common than you think. We shall be all right if no one interferes with us."

Without looking back once she went out of the room. For a long time I sat there, staring out the bay window at the snow swirling and eddying in the air outside. Maybe it was watching the storm that made me feel so cold. But I think it was my passive realization that whatever it was I did not like about Selena—and I still could not put a definite name to it—nothing in me was strong enough to resist her. There was a profound force of some sort in her.

What she had actually said to me was not a snub, which I had richly deserved, but a warning, and so assured a one that it frightened me. Yet, looking back at the scene, listening to her repeat those words in my mind's ear, I realize that there was something else in them which I did not perceive at the time.

After a time I persuaded Thomas to bring me a drink, and went on sitting beside the fire. Grace came in, looking charming and full of enthusiasm. She disapproved of my attitude and occupation.

"What are you doing, my lamb, sitting here and moping and drinking?"

"Yes," I said.

"Cheer up," she said brightly; "tomorrow's the great day. You'll feel better once it's over."

"Sure."

She settled herself in Selena's chair. "You're still not reconciled, I see."

I got up and kissed her. "Come on, darling. Give me a break. I'm a damn fool, I know, but I hate the fact as much as everybody else tells me they do."

She said soberly, "I think you're spoiling things a little for Jerry. It's your manners I criticize."

"And not my motives?"

"Get me a cigarette, will you, my angel? Thanks." She projected a cloud of smoke large enough to conceal her expression. "No. I think your motives are of the purest."

I felt a rush of gratitude toward her. There was one person who did not believe I was a complete fool, then. "You take some of the weight off my mind. I was wondering if I was going nuts."

She spread her hands in a gesture of humorous resignation. "Selena is a beautiful woman, but . . ." She said no more.

"But what?" I asked her.

She got up, came over, and pulled me out of my chair. "But I still don't know how old she is." She tucked her arm under mine and we went away together. Grace had her moments, all right.

The morning of the twelfth it stopped snowing and the sun came out. The decorators were busy in the house, so Jerry and Selena and I went sliding on the drive. There's a long run down the bluff and on past the house to the very edge of the Sound. A couple of the pitches are pretty steep; Jerry and I had been going down them for years, but I'd never got entirely accustomed to the drop just below the terrace, where the sled shoots out into the air and you feel yourself in a free fall the second before the crash as the runners bit the slope below.

Our big sled just held the three of us, and I must say for Selena that she never turned a hair. Once when I turned and looked at her sitting behind me there was a look of exultation on her face.

After a while we went inside and Thomas brought us hot buttered rum in front of the fire. We sat there talking and laughing, and Jerry and Selena held hands. Then it was time for lunch, and then it was after lunch. In no time at all we went upstairs to get dressed. The ceiling of my room was white with the reflected sun off the snow. I had a drink, while I dressed. Happy is the bride the sun shines on and God damn that collar button. Time to go downstairs and pin a smile on your face as you go out the door. Thank heaven, it was not a large wedding. The fewer people present the better. The music playing Lohengrin, because Jerry insisted that only the most conventional and sentimental of weddings would do for his girl after a first marriage presided over by a justice of the peace named Willetts.

"Here comes the bride"...walking by herself and looking so beautiful in Grace's dress I felt almost sick. Silver-gray cloth, like metal and as soft as velvet, and a narrow fillet of flowers around her head. Lilies of the valley from the hothouse, probably...Her eyes, shining and cool, remote as the stars and with a light in them. Her face was still and she looked more than ever like a statue come to life.

"Where is the groom?"...Jerry in a cutaway, standing beside the hall table made into an altar, and looking white and thin-faced and dangerous, the way he used to look when he lined up on the field before the kickoff and tightened the chin strap under his helmet...The quick smile when he glanced at his bride while the minister was praying. The responses, firm and low from both of them..."And if any person know just cause"...I knew what might pass for a just cause..."or forever hold his peace."...All right, forever hold my peace. Jerry kissing Selena, kissing his wife. Everybody kissing the bride...Your lips are cold, Selena...Yes, such a lovely ceremony...I'll have another glass of champagne when you get to it, Thomas...Yes, doesn't time pass quickly. It does seem like only yesterday that we were...The two of them going upstairs to change. Plenty of time. The boat doesn't sail for hours....No, I don't think it's any secret. They're going to Bermuda...Thanks, Thomas. This is swell champagne...Here they come now. Whack him on the back as he goes out the door.

"So long, fella."

"So long, Bark. See you in six weeks."

"Right."

The sound of a loose strand on the chains, flailing away methodically under the left rear fender. Damn, I meant to fix that before they left...champagne...No, Dad, I'm all right. This stuff is harmless ...talk...champagne...now what did I say?...more champagne... (and suppose I should tell you, my dear lady, that my best friend just married a woman who was probably an idiot less than a year ago?

How would you react to that, I wonder?)...just one more, Thomas. I can take care of myself....Sure, I'm going up right now...just a little drunk, that's all...hold still, Thomas, and we'll get into these pajamas okay...God, what a night outside! Moon on the snow... Happy the groom the moon shines on...My God, that stuff makes the room go round. That's Orion, that big constellation...I remember...damn all memories....

11. EVENTS LEADING UP TO A TELEGRAM

I DEVOTED the next couple of weeks to pulling myself together. It was high time. I'd been drinking so much that my hand trembled every time I picked up a glass, and several mornings I had to go to a barbershop rather than risk shaving myself. Work was beginning to pile up at the office, and somehow or other I got through it. Actually I was glad to be busy because it kept me from thinking or feeling lonely, and I did so well in a couple of cases that they gave me a raise in salary. In some respects, life was very satisfactory.

On the other side of the ledger was the fact that there was at this time what amounted to an estrangement between Dr. Lister and me. The way I had behaved before and after the wedding (and I was very drunk indeed—Thomas informed me afterward I said things that all present would remember for years) was unpardonable. Dr. Lister told me frankly that he was ashamed of me and that he found it hard to forgive my conduct.

The result was that I found myself more alone than ever before in my life and for ten days I could not get adjusted to it. Coming home each evening to an empty apartment with the prospect of long hours by myself had a depressing effect on my morale, and there was the constant struggle to stay away from the Scotch.

Often I wondered if I had acquired some sort of obsession about Selena and her marrying Jerry. There seemed something unbalanced about the distrust of her that I felt whenever I thought about her. After all, there was little cause for my feeling except that LeNormand's death was an ugly thing, and it was out of that horror that she and Jerry had met and not-so-ultimately married. The fate that had overtaken LeNormand, whatever its cause, was not a thing I could contemplate quietly as a possibility for Jerry, and there were too many unresolved mysteries about Selena and her first husband's death to please me. Maybe the Italians can live happily on the slopes of Vesuvius, but I am not that sort of person.

While Jerry and Selena were still away on their wedding trip I rented a two-room apartment for myself farther uptown. For a time, at least, they planned to live in our old place, and I spent a good deal of time down there getting it ready for their return. I resolved that it would be in impeccable order when they got back to it, and believe me, it was. New paper on every closet shelf, everything put away in the proper place, wedding presents all unpacked and arranged, even the pictures hung for them. I put my Marin over the fireplace, where it looked very well indeed. Uncle Horatio's lithograph of the Good Shepherd—a grisly sort of thing—hung in the foyer where it would, if necessary, soften up bill collectors and help speed the parting guest.

I must admit that there was an element of selfishness in all this. I wanted Selena, in particular, to be in my debt; it gave me a sensation of nobility to bury my personal feelings and think of her and Jerry's pleasure and comfort. The whole performance was a piece of self-dramatization, but they got the benefit of it and it was harmless.

So far I haven't mentioned the letter I had from Jerry. It was as reserved and noncommittal as all his letters, but I could read between the lines that he was happy: "The weather here has been warm and sunny almost all the time. You ought to see the moonlight nights we have." And more of the same. He mentioned Selena only once. "I know you are going to like her when you know her better. She says to send you her regards." Well, that was as might be. At any rate, it was rather a pointless letter except for a postscript: "P.S. Have you heard anything more from Parsons? I suppose he hasn't made any progress? There's not much American news in the paper down here."

So far as I knew he hadn't reached any solution. I hadn't seen him again myself, but Dr. Lister went down one day to New Zion. On the way home he dropped in at my new apartment—one cold February evening it was—and we had a drink together. He told me where he had been.

"Did Parsons have anything new to contribute?" I asked him.

He shook his head. "No. I don't believe he knows any more now than when he started on the case."

I wasn't so sure of that. Offhand I could think of one discovery of his, Luella Jamison. Of course, that had nothing to do with the case. But the coincidences were curious.

I decided to fish around. I wanted to find out whether Parsons had mentioned anything about Luella to Dr. Lister. "What is he working on now?" I asked.

"That I don't know." He went on, a little embarrassedly, I thought. "When this engagement of Jerry's first came up, I wrote Parsons."

"Oh," I said. "I didn't know that."

"Of course, I did. I had to make sure that the authorities didn't believe she was implicated."

I nodded.

"Parsons told me then that he could guess why I was writing to him. He assured me that so far they were fairly positive that Mrs. LeNormand was not implicated. He said that she had a perfect alibi personally, and there was no evidence to show she was an accessory before the fact." He smiled grimly. "He also remarked that there was no evidence that she was not."

"That was just official caution."

"Yes," he agreed. "So I thought. But I went down to see him today to find out whether anything new had come up that concerned us. I'm pretty well satisfied that it hasn't."

"Thank God for that."

He put his fingertips together and stared at them. "I don't believe the police will solve the LeNormand business."

"No," I agreed.

"It's unfortunate, in a way. I think we'd all be happier if it were cleared up."

Personally I wasn't so sure about that. It depended on what the truth was. "I guess so," I replied.

"You and Jerry haven't suppressed anything that might come out later?" He sounded apologetic as he asked the question.

"We haven't suppressed anything."

"Good. I think the wisest thing we can all do is to forget the whole matter until the police have something more to report."

"Absolutely."

He talked on about small affairs for a while and then he left. I felt unhappy. We had talked together like chance acquaintances.

The *Empress* docked on a Wednesday afternoon, and I went down to see her come in and meet the two of them. Dr. Lister had planned to be there too, of course, but an emergency operation came up at the last minute and he could not make it.

Jerry was looking magnificent, radiating a quiet happiness, and conspicuously proud of his beautiful wife. Selena did not seem much changed to me, and certainly she had lost none of her beauty. People, even in the irritating confusion of the customs, stopped to stare at her, and once a couple of schoolgirls sidled up to ask for her autograph. Apparently they thought anyone as gorgeous as Selena must surely be in the movies. They were plainly disappointed when I told them she was just my friend's wife and nobody they'd ever heard of. Though after I'd assured them of that I wondered if it was strictly accurate. In fact, one of them did say, "We're sorry, mister, but my friend and me thought sure we'd seen her in the movies or the papers or someplace."

In the taxi going uptown, Jerry presented me with a pipe he'd bought in Bermuda, and I was glad to have it. They made me sit between them, and were so cordial and generally sweet, particularly Jerry, that I had a suspicion they'd decided I was a problem child and would have to have special, careful treatment. But all in all, things passed on pleasantly and I left them at the door of their place feeling glad that I had arranged it so perfectly for them. All they had to do was walk in and begin living in it. I'd even started the milkman to coming again.

The months that followed were good ones. Jerry must have told his family how decent I had been about the apartment. They began to look at me again as if I was human, and best of all, Dad and I returned to the old intimacy that meant so much to both of us. I went out to Long Island many times, and often when Jerry and Selena were not there. On such occasions Dad and I did not discuss them. We had an unspoken agreement about that.

I had hoped to grow to like Selena as I came to know her better. But it just didn't happen, though I learned to admire her in certain ways. She had a quiet self-control that made any open break impossible, and an almost unbelievable modesty about her beauty. A very rare quality in my experience. As time went on, I found it easier to be with her because I finally discarded Parsons' thought that she might be Luella Jamison. She knew too much, her mind was too clear and logical, she was too full of information about the most abstract subjects ever to have been an idiot. Watching her, I came to the conclusion that she had had a long and exceedingly thorough education. That alone could account for the way she could talk to Jerry and Dr. Lister about astronomy, or mathematics, or archaeology. It might, too, account for her almost gauche insensitivity to the prejudices and peculiarities of the people around her. Wherever she came from, she had been educated in an atmosphere of objective intellectuality, and her interests molded in ways unlike those of most other women. Then I would remember the way she danced, and not be so sure.

When she was out at the house, she spent a lot of time in the library, reading every conceivable sort of book. Jerry and I would urge her to go driving with us, or play ping-pong in the basement, or occasionally, on a fair day, go out on the Sound in our sloop. She seldom came along, but when she did she was equal to the occasion. I remember one blustery March morning when we were out on the water and she was taking her turn at the tiller. A cold, shouting wind was coming down the Sound, and the sloop keeled under it till the cockpit coaming was all but awash. Selena sat there with the wind blowing her hair and whipping color into her face, calmly watching the level of the water racing along the lee deck. At the instant when I'd decided that we'd be wet the next second, she eased off the helm and the wash retreated from the coaming. She never batted an eye.

That proved to me that she had courage and steady nerves. But I was glad to take my turn at the tiller. I like to play things with a margin of safety.

That side of her was, if anything, admirable, but beyond admiring her, there was nothing else you could do with Selena. She had somehow never learned the little easy give-and-take that lubricates every agreeable human relationship. She could talk well on many subjects, but she never seemed able to converse, and it is conversation liberally sprinkled with badinage that I enjoy. When she spoke she never made an allusion; she never reminisced, she never said anything silly. Every sentence was a statement or a question. She seldom laughed, but she did have a silent sense of humor of some sort. At intervals she would give a silent, almost secret smile that told me she was relishing something to herself. I find it hard to recall examples of the quality I am trying to suggest, but I remember one night when we had all been sitting in the library.

After a time we fell to playing bridge in a desultory sort of way. Grace was out at the house that weekend, and Jerry and I had been playing against Selena and her. Incidentally, Selena was the most astonishing bridge player I ever met. She never seemed to lose an unnecessary trick, and though occasionally a finesse of hers would go wrong, I noticed that when it did she always smiled in that little private way of hers. After an hour or two we got bored, and decided to stop. Grace, who had been keeping score, had no trouble adding up Jerry's and my side of the ledger, but the entries in the female column were staggering. Grace puckered up her fore head and wrestled with her pencil, muttering to herself, while Jerry and I laughed and told her we conceded the match.

Suddenly Selena leaned forward, picked the score pad out from under Grace's nose, glanced at it casually for a moment, and remarked, "Seventeen thousand eight hundred and sixty."

Jerry took up the pad after her while Grace simply sat looking astounded and relieved. After a minute or so he said, "That's right," with a note of puzzled admiration in his voice. Jerry was exceptionally quick with figures himself, which was why he was such an asset to his firm of statisticians. I think he was piqued by Selena's speed. "You're quite a lightning calculator," he observed. She simply went on smiling lightly and impersonally.

It was that summer, a few months after the bridge game, that Selena showed me a new side of her character, and one that I was to think of often later on.

One day, in August if I remember rightly, Jerry was playing in the club tennis tournament. He'd put me out the day before, to my relief, and it was really too hot to do anything. I suggested to Selena, on some impulse or other, that we drive out to Montauk. She agreed readily enough, though I felt that the idea didn't specially appeal to her.

For an hour or so we rode in silence. From time to time I glanced at her, sitting coolly and easily in the corner of the seat opposite me. She was immaculate, in a dull blue, severely simple frock and a wide, plain straw hat with a white ribbon around it. Just looking at her made me feel cool, and in a way rested. I felt that there was a truce between us, and resolved firmly to do nothing to violate it.

After a while, without apparently speaking at me directly, she said, "I think Jerry is very happy."

"Yes," I told her. "Why shouldn't he be?" It was meant to be gallant, of course, but she did not take it that way.

"You didn't expect him to be happy after he was married to me."

"Nonsense," I said, but I thought to myself that it was going to be hard to keep civil if she went on this way. She was an infuriatingly direct woman.

"On the contrary," she said, "You are thinking that I am being annoying. I want merely to know whether you have any suggestions."

"Suggestions?" I said blankly.

"You remember how once, before Jerry and I were married, you told me to be good to him?"

The recollection made me squirm a little, but I had to admit it.

"So," she said, "I have tried. Do you think I have succeeded?"

"Yes," I told her.

She looked at me through those disturbing violet eyes of hers and said, "You know, I am not accustomed to people like you and Dr. Lister and Jerry. Perhaps sometimes I make mistakes with you."

"Yes," I said, feeling that this was getting curiouser and curiouser, "from my point of view, you do. I think you ought to relax a little more."

She sighed. "I don't quite know how to do that." Her tone of voice suggested that she would look into it in the near future and learn the technique of relaxing.

"Anyway," I said, "let's not talk personalities. You're you and I'm me, and I guess that's about all there is to it."

"Yes," she said, and smiled that odd smile of hers.

"Tell me," I said, after a pause, "do you like this part of the world?"

She looked at me in surprise. "Why do you ask me that?"

When I had asked the question, I had been merely making casual conversation, but her reply put a sudden scheme into my head. "Oh, I was just wondering. Some people think California is God's gift to geography. And I have a cousin who thinks highly of the state of Maine. Everybody has his favorite part of the country."

"Long Island is a satisfactory place, don't you think?"

"Yes," I admitted. "The north shore, anyway. I like parts of the South, too—the Carolinas and Georgia. Ever been down there?"

"No," she said. "I don't believe I should like it. The Southern girls that Jerry knows always seem to me unintelligent, and they have double names like Mary Lou and Sue Ellen. They seem silly to me."

"Well, there's something in that," I said, adding mentally that she could add a little Southern charm to her own character without loss, and feeling distinctly irritated that I hadn't trapped her into some sort of admission about her past life and where she came from.

She looked at me and smiled. "You're strange, Bark. You ask one question and really want to find out the answer to another one, don't you?"

I felt annoyed at her for calling the turn so exactly. "How do you always know what I'm thinking?"

"You give it away," she answered.

"How?" I asked her.

"Why," she said, and paused. "I suppose you'd say that if a person went into a room and shouted something loudly, even if he was all alone in the room, he wouldn't be keeping what he was saying entirely to himself?"

"Yes, but—"

"That's what you do with your mind, Bark."

"You mean you can read my mind?" The idea terrified me and embarrassed me simultaneously.

She smiled. "Not the way you mean it. But everybody gets some thoughts from the people round them. You know that."

"Well," I began hesitantly.

"You all talk incompletely," she went on. "Listen to what people say to each other sometime. The real conversation isn't wholly in the words. The words are clues to what the person speaking is trying to convey. The rest of it goes direct from one mind to another. You must have noticed that."

"This is odd," I thought to myself. "But I suppose she is partly right." Aloud I said, "And I give out clues to what I don't say as well as to what I do?"

"Of course."

"Hmm." I decided to try her out. "Suppose you tell me, then," I said, mentally deciding that her theory was ridiculous, "what I'm thinking now?"

She laughed. "Stop the car. I'll give you a demonstration."

I pulled up along the edge of the road.

"Now," she said, "you don't believe I'm right. Just sit back a moment and listen."

I leaned back in the seat and waited. Selena was not smiling any more, but I did not feel that she was wholly serious, either. I felt suddenly and uncomfortably that she was amusing herself at my expense. Gradually I felt that she wanted me to do something. What, I did not know at first, and I looked at her puzzledly. She never smoked, of course, but I thought I might offer her a cigarette. The silence between us was getting uncomfortable. I pulled my case out of my pocket and extended it to her. "Have a cigarette," I said.

The tension between us snapped at once. "Drive ahead," she said. "You know I never smoke, Bark."

"Listen," I said. "What the hell was all that about?"

She said composedly, "I just asked you for a cigarette without speaking. And you offered me one."

That was that. I thought about it as we drove along, but I didn't come to any conclusion. "It's a good stunt," I said once.

"Yes," she said.

"I hope you don't pull that sort of thing on your poor defenseless husband."

"Oh," she said, lightly, "Jerry isn't a bit like you."

And with that I had to be content.

We had a picnic lunch out by the lighthouse, and watched the waves come in, and it was all very agreeable except for a few minutes in which Selena undertook to explain to me the theory of neap and flood tides, all in response to some idle remark of mine about how far above the water the high-tide mark seemed to be that day. I was too sleepy and full of sandwiches and iced beer to care much. But it annoyed me mildly that she should know everything like that. A certain amount of ingenuous ignorance, I decided, was a great factor in feminine charm.

Riding home that afternoon, I thought to myself that I had never before spent a day alone with a person and learned so little about them. Inevitably it is an irritating thing to have a person—man or woman—refuse to let you see a single inch into his or her character. My stock of small talk had run out, and I was simply driving along the turnpike, watching the road and the other cars and thinking of little, when a curious thing happened. Selena reached forward suddenly and ratched up the emergency. Instantly the car began to skid; the tires screamed on the asphalt, and I had the devil of a time keeping us from turning turtle.

In the middle of my struggle with the wheel a bright yellow roadster full of prep school kids shot out of a narrow drive in front of us and swerved roaring off down the highway. They must have missed our front bumper by inches. I unlocked the emergency and we rolled on; sweat was running off me in rivulets. It was the closest call I ever had in my life; undoubtedly Selena's quick yank on the brake had saved us from an ugly smash. As I thought of it I realized that the road down which the yellow car had come was entirely hidden from the highway by a stone wall and a belt of trees. There was no way I could have known that that car was coming.

"God!" I said to Selena, who was sitting perfectly quietly beside me. "Thanks! That was too close. I can still hear the angels singing."

She nodded quietly. "There was no way you could see that road."

"No," I agreed. "Damn kids like that. Their parents oughtn't to give them cars." She was silent, and a belated question came into my mind. "How did you know they were coming?"

"I—what is it Jerry says?—I had a hunch." And she smiled.

"Well," I told her, "keep on having them!" But it seemed to me that she acted with amazing speed and directness for a woman with nothing but a hunch.

I ought to have felt grateful to her, and in a way I did. In another, the incident had in it one of the seeds of the irritation and uneasiness that Selena always seemed able to evoke in me. How had she known that car was coming? I went back a day or so later and looked at the place; there was absolutely no way of seeing past the wall and the trees. The only explanation was a sort of clairvoyance. Hunches as good as that one of hers simply couldn't be due to chance.

The months that followed flowed into one another without anything of importance to this story. I was getting on well in my work, and devoting more and more time to it in consequence. I saw less of Jerry and Selena that winter than I had expected to, and I could see, when we did meet, that Jerry was delighted with my progress and puzzled by it. He himself was not deeply interested in the statistical work he was doing, though I understand he did it brilliantly. On several occasions he told me that most of it bored him. He admitted he put in a little time at his office as he could, and I wondered if he was growing lazy, which would have been unlike him, or just what he was doing that occupied the rest of his time. One evening I found out.

He and Selena and Dad and Grace were to come round to my apartment for a buffet supper on a Sunday night. I liked to give a sort of informal meal once or twice a month that way and ask just the people I really was fond of. I suppose partly because I was making some money and wanted to spend it on entertaining the people who'd done so much for me, especially Dad. Sunday was the best night for my schedule, and Grace was glad to come because Fred was playing in a golf tournament somewhere in Florida.

This particular time Jerry and Selena came early. The cocktails were not even ready and I was in my shirt sleeves, but Jerry was so plainly excited and enthusiastic over something that details like that didn't matter. He had something under his arm, and as soon as the greetings were over he presented it to me with a flourish.

"Here, Bark. With the compliments of the author." And he grinned.

It was a thin, gray-covered little magazine with a three-deck title, some sort of journal of mathematics. I ran my eye down the table of contents, and sure enough, there was the name of Jeremiah Lister.

"I'll be damned!" I said, turning over the leaves to his article. "What hath God wrought!"

"You may well say that," he told me exultantly. "That obscure and droopy-looking little publication is more exclusive than the Racquet Club. And I have crashed its austere gates."

"Well," I said, sparring for time and looking at the article, "this is a surprise. And my novel only half done. You've beaten me to publication, all right."

Jerry's piece occupied only two pages and it might as well have been a Sanskrit inscription for all the sense I could make out of it. There was a short editorial foreword by the brain that conducted the magazine in which Jerry's work was spoken of as "brilliant," "original," and "highly suggestive." After looking helplessly at the text for a few seconds, I said, "I bet Selena helped you with this."

"No," she said, apparently taking my jest seriously, "I didn't help him."

"I should say not," he added. "She was opposed to the thing from the start. She told me it was a waste of time, but even in the face of discouragement I persevered. I like doing stuff in that field."

"As that immortal opus we had in school, Fraser and Squair's French grammar, would say, 'chacun à son goût.'" I was really pleased about the article. Jerry was a bright lad, all right.

"What does that mean?" asked Selena.

"Every man to his own brand of folly," I told her.

She looked surprised. "But this isn't foolish. Jerry's article is absolutely correct."

"I was being flippant. The real translation is, 'every man to his own taste.'"

"Oh."

Jerry said, "Don't try to read the thing, Bark. Just put it away on your shelf of first editions. It'll be a collector's item someday."

"Nuts," I told him. "I'm intellectual as hell. Everybody knows that. I'm going to leave this lying round on the living room table to impress people."

He laughed. "It'll be all over rings from highball glasses in a week, then."

I took it across to the bookcase. "In that case, I'll put it beside the Gertrude Stein book Grace gave me for Christmas. The two of them will serve to remind me that there are plenty of things I'll never be able to understand."

Selena followed me. "Who is Gertrude Stein?" she asked me, with interest. "A woman mathematician?"

"Not exactly," I informed her. "Here. Take a look," and I handed her the volume.

She opened it and looked at the first few pages. "Are there people who understand this?" she asked me.

"Well, there are people who say they do."

She went over to the sofa and sat down with the book. I hung up their coats and began mixing a cocktail. In a few minutes Selena got up and put the Gertrude Stein back on the shelf.

"It doesn't mean anything," she said. "You ought not to put Jerry's article next to it."

"I'm just teasing him," I told her.

"Don't pay any attention to him, darling," said Jerry, lolling back in my best chair. "He's trying to keep me from getting a swelled head."

I poured the cocktails. They were good. Grace came in and we had another round. I showed her Jerry's piece.

She wrinkled her forehead over it for a minute. "Goodness, Jeremiah my sweet, I don't see how you have time for such things with a wife who looks like Selena."

Jerry blushed and laughed. "What I haven't got time for," he said, "is my job at Howard and Neurath, Statisticians. I'm quitting the end of next week."

"You are?" I was surprised, though I knew he was not tremendously keen about working in an office.

"Yes," he said, "I've about decided that what I really want to do is teach."

It seemed right to me, and I told him so.

"First, though, I've got to get a Ph.D. That means writing a thesis."

"Swell," I told him. "I can think of nothing more repulsive than writing a thesis, but you're the type to enjoy it."

"Thanks. It'll be a year's work, anyway. Selena and I are thinking of going to that place of Dad's out west."

I remembered then that the Listers owned some sort of house in Arizona or New Mexico that neither Dad nor Jerry, I think, had ever been to. An artist or somebody left it to them, but they'd never made any use of it.

"Isn't it way the hell and gone in a desert?" I asked him.

"Yes. But it'll be quiet and give me a good chance to work. We won't be lonely." He looked fondly at Selena.

Grace turned to Selena. "Are you going to let this entirely mad young man make a female anchorite out of you, Selena? I wouldn't tolerate it for a moment!"

"She doesn't mind," said Jerry.

"No," Selena admitted. "I don't see any reason why we should not go. Only I wish Jerry didn't have to write this thesis he has in mind." She turned to me. "Can't he teach without writing anything?"

"Well," I told her, "you can't get a job these days in any good college without a Ph.D. And that means a thesis, as Jerry says."

"I see," she said, and her voice sounded thin and curiously disappointed. I did not understand why, but she was an incomprehensible woman.

They left within a few weeks, and we all went down to see them off. When the train had pulled out into the cavernous gloom of the Grand Central cave and left us standing on the platform, I felt an obscure feeling of sadness and foreboding. Jerry and I had been growing apart, of course, as our lives diverged, but this time, as we separated, it felt like the end of something.

We wrote, of course, from time to time. Jerry's letters were postmarked "Los Palos," and at first they came about once a week. Gradually they grew more infrequent, and so did mine. I gathered that he and Selena were enjoying their lonely life out there, but in the last one or two of his scrawls there was an unfamiliar note that I could not quite analyze:

"Selena seems to like the country out here [he wrote me in June] and it certainly is big and impressive after you get over the bareness. I'm working hard and making real progress; the only trouble is that there are so many things I'd like to be working on at once. My study window looks right out over fifty miles of desert—it would be as easy as hell to get lost out there and nobody would ever find you. Selena walks a lot and sometimes I get worried for fear she won't get back before dark, but I guess she can take care of herself. You'd get a kick out of this place, Bark; why don't you come out here sometime later?"

I wrote him and said that I'd like to come sometime, but that I was hellish busy and doubted if I'd find much time even for a week's vacation. His letter left an uncomfortable impression in my mind, though. I felt that he wanted me to come and was too proud to ask me. Then, when I thought it over, I realized that he was just lonely, and I stopped worrying about him.

A month later my doorbell rang at nine o'clock in the evening. It was a Western Union messenger. The telegram said:

CAN YOU COME AT ONCE MEETING LIMITED TUESDAY
MORNING LOS PALOS HOPE TO SEE YOU

JERRY

I cursed, got leave of absence from my office, and caught the Century the next day. Dad came down to the train with me.

"You'll let me know at once," he said, "if it's anything serious."

"Sure," I told him.

Both of us were wondering why Jerry had wired only to me, and what had happened, but there was no certainty of reaching him in time with a telegram from us. They had no telephone at Cloud Mesa, and Dr. Lister thought it was too far from Los Palos for Jerry to come in every day.

As the train pulled out, I saw his anxious face watching me through the glass of the Pullman window. I gave him a grin that I hoped was reassuring, and settled back in my seat. Something told me that what was ahead was all of a piece with the strangeness of the last year and a half. The switch points clattered under the wheels, and the train began to rush northward, through the tunnel under Park Avenue.

12. CONVERSATION PIECE

LOS PALOS lies along one side of the railroad tracks. In the sharp light of early morning it had an almost surrealist clarity of outline. I stumbled down the Pullman steps, half awake, and looked it over without pleasure.

Only one building in the ragged row that faced me beyond the highway was of brick. The rest were wood, cracked and bleached with sun and want of paint. A shambling rogues' gallery of stores, saloons, garages, and restaurants. There seemed to be no reason for the town's existence. Beyond the highway and the tracks the bare, gigantic sweep of brown valley fell away for mile upon mile without a single spot of green or the solitary cube of a house. There was not even the interruption of a fence. It was far from cold, but I shivered as I looked into that immense emptiness of desert and turned back to Los Palos.

On my right the scrubby façade of Main Street terminated in a blazing red-and-white service station, and to the left, at the other end of town, was another, equally garish in yellow and scarlet, to mark where the town ended and the desert began. The station itself was a drab frame building without even the dubious distinction of the jigsaw scrollwork that belonged with its period. Beyond it, towering over the whole town, stood the water tower.

Los Palos, in short, was simply one of those desert towns, born when the railroad was building, maintained in a precarious, stunted life while desert-pastured cattle were still worth shipping to market, and dying slowly ever since the profits had gone out of ranching. As I looked it over, it seemed already half swallowed in the immeasurable miles around it, like an old, battered tramp steamer foundering slowly out of sight of land on a calm sea. It depressed me. If this was Jerry's contact with the rest of the world, certainly Cloud Mesa must be a solitary place. I stretched my eyes across the valley to the westward, and though there was a rampart of naked mountains far, very far away, I could see nothing that corresponded with his descriptions.

There was no one on the platform but a thin old man in a shiny blue serge suit whom I took to be the station agent. He looked at me for a few minutes, idly, and went inside the building. Main Street was deserted, and none of the stores seemed to be open. Certainly nothing in Los Palos was worth waking up for as early as quarter of six in the morning. I put my two suitcases down where Jerry was sure to see them if he drove up before I came back, and strolled across the highway—Main Street—to look for breakfast.

After some wandering up and down I discovered the Sanitary Lunch, where one unshaven counterman collected a breakfast of sorts with maddening deliberation. My impatience proved pointless. The coffee tasted like the lees of the water tower, the baked apple had been there a long time, and the bacon would have disgraced a camping trip the first morning out.

"Ain't come in yet." And then, after a silence of several minutes, "That'll be four bits."

I paid him and got out. Main Street had waked up while I had been eating; I noticed a man sweeping the sidewalk in front of the Tres Hermanos saloon, and a small dog several doors away was smelling at the base of a telephone pole. And just before I crossed the street a dusty Hudson sedan, moving at better than sixty miles an hour roared through Los Palos in about fifteen seconds. I looked after it enviously and went back to the station. There was nothing there, of course, but I sat down on the baggage truck and lit a pipe.

The country was something to look at. If you are used to the little landscapes of Long Island, of New Jersey, even of upstate New York, it takes quite a while to realize the real size of Western scenery. The southernmost peak of the range across the valley was probably as far from where I sat as New York is from Philadelphia. And there was scarcely a thing to catch the eye between me and it. I sat there and let my gaze range over the wide floor of the valley and pretended that time was passing. After a while I consulted my watch and it was five minutes after six. I had been in Los Palos less than half an hour; it occurred to me that anyone who could stand fifty years of the place would have lived five ordinary lives anywhere else.

All this is trivial, in a way, but it gave me a queer, lost feeling to be sitting there on the station platform gazing out over several hundred square miles of desert with the death-in-life of Los Palos at my back. I was nervous. My pipe tasted bitter and strong in my mouth and my heart felt as though it were beating faster than was necessary. There was no use speculating on why Jerry had sent for me, but the fact that he had done so bothered me. I had expected when we said good-by to each other in New York that we would meet again rarely and casually. There had been an atmosphere of finality about that parting. Jerry, I had felt, now was a part of my past, but hardly of my present. And suddenly he had sent for me, begged me to come at any cost. All the way out on the Limited I had wondered whether he needed me because of Selena, and some quarrel he had had with her. Or perhaps the loneliness out here ... But Jerry was not that sort of person. He knew how I felt about his wife, and he was proud, much too proud to admit that he was lonely with her, or that I, who of all people had been most opposed to his marrying her, could do anything to help him. Jerry never needed help.

And yet, what else could he want? He knew that it was inconvenient for me to come ... I gave the whole thing up, but there was something disquieting about it just the same.

My own thoughts annoyed me. They were born of nothing more than irritation, perhaps, at being kept waiting in a dismal little town with nothing to do and a bad breakfast in my stomach. Los Palos was not my kind of place; I was incongruous in it. Even my clothes were ridiculously good and wholly inappropriate for such a town. I started to call myself a fish out of water until I looked again at the leagues of desert. They made the phrase a ludicrous understatement ... *Litotes,* the Greek word for it was ... There was no water out there, no water and even no moisture except perhaps, in the center of some cactus plant or the veins of a rattlesnake. There was nothing at all out there. Except one remote, minute, crawling pennant of dust with a dark speck at the head of it.

For three-quarters of an hour I watched that plume of dust come nearer. It grew with agonizing slowness, but long before I could make out the details of the car I felt sure it must be Jerry. Now and again the sun caught the windshield and flashed brightly back at me, sometimes car and dust cloud were hidden behind a brown swale in the valley floor, but as I was finishing my second pipe it swung up over a last rise down beyond the water tower, crossed the tracks, and roared up to the station.

My first thought was that Jerry looked marvelously well. He was wearing a white shirt, open at the neck and with the sleeves rolled up; his face, his neck, his forearms were burnt dark with sun, and his hair was bleached to a pale gold color. He jumped up on the platform and ran toward me. Again I had a moment of uneasy surprise. Never that I could remember did Jerry run except when he was playing some game. He sauntered toward you, usually. But now there was an eagerness in him; I knew at once that he was more than ordinarily glad to see me, and that, too, surprised me. But he gave me no time to think or to be surprised.

"Hi, Bark!"

"Hello, Jerry."

"Sorry to be so damn late. Got a flat halfway here and lost a lot of time."

"That's okay," I told him. "I've been giving Los Palos the once-over."

He grinned swiftly. "Swell place, isn't it? You ought to see it Saturday nights. Some of the stores stay open till half past eight or nine at night." He looked at my bags. "These your things?"

"Well," I said, "the rest of the crowd has gone and left these, so I better take them."

"Hell," he said, "it's swell to see you."

We got into the car. "By the way, want to pick up anything before we pull out? Last chance."

"Listen," I told him, "if you know a quick way out of this place, for God's sake, take it."

"Hold on," he said and put the accelerator down on the floorboards. We went out of Los Palos like a bat out of a belfry, and I didn't look back. When we cut across the tracks and hit the desert road we were doing all of fifty, and in spite of the one-track, sandy cart trail we seemed to be on, we kept going like that. The big Packard swallowed the countless turns and dips and pitches of that road with a sort of dizzy recklessness, and after half an hour or so I began to feel uneasy at our unrelenting pace. After all, if anything happened, we were already a thirsty day's walk from the nearest town, and the mountain range ahead of us appeared to be no nearer, I looked tentatively at Jerry. He was sitting easily behind the wheel, wrenching the car around the curves and meeting the savage roughness of the road with a sort of negligent carefulness that partly restored my confidence.

"Don't spare the horses, you hard-riding Westerners," I suggested.

He looked at me fleetingly. "It gets hot out here after eight o'clock in the morning," he observed and went on driving.

And it was beginning to get hot. I took off my coat, vest, and tie, and stowed them in the rear seat, nearly getting pitched out in the process. Then I lit another pipe and tried to relax while we burrowed down one slope and up on the opposite side without slowing for an instant. From the station platform the country over which we were driving had looked fairly level, but I now saw that there was no flat stretch in it. And no end, either, though after a while we began to go up more often than down and I deduced that we were headed up the far side of the valley. The range ahead of us began to look less naked; I could make out trees in some of the canyons and we commenced to run quarteringly across a series of draws in which there were a few small, dry bushes.

I looked back. Los Palos was small and clear in the desert air, shrunk to the size of a Chinese ivory carving. Now and then its image wavered as I looked at it; the heat was beginning to rise from the baked sand and bare rock of the earth between. The ridges, the sharp, unweathered angles of the rocks, the wild, jumbled rise and fall of the land gave me a sense of isolation. Man was a stranger to this sort of country; it belonged on some airless planet circling sunward of the earth. I looked again at Jerry, glad that I was not alone, and saw in his face something that I had overlooked at the station. For all the brown of his skin, it was tighter over the bones of his face. There were wrinkles at the corners of his eyes that I had not seen before, and his lips were thinner and set together with a nervous firmness. He had to watch that devil's road with all the concentration in him, of course; at the speed we were traveling, but even that failed to account wholly for the tension in his face. And I had the feeling that though he was glad I was with him, he wasn't thinking about me much. Something else was occupying the part of his mind behind his driving reflexes. And I did not have the faintest idea what it was.

Sometime after eight o'clock in the morning our road turned gradually left and southward, and after a while we were running parallel to the mountains west of us. The motion up and down the barrancas began to be almost as regular as a long ground swell. After several miles we came to a deeper draw with a steep face to one side, and along its base a patch of shade. Jerry pulled the car into it and turned to me. In the sudden silence I could hear the bubble, bubble of the water boiling in the radiator.

"We'll stop here a little and cool off," he said and got out of the car.

We walked around some, and I told him it was lonely country.

"Yes," he said. "It takes time to get used to it. Then you love it."

"I suppose so."

Suddenly he looked at me and grinned. "Hell, I forgot. We have breakfast." He rummaged in the back of the car and brought out a thermos of coffee and several bacon sandwiches. I thought of another picnic meal—how long ago?—that we had eaten together on the running board of a car. I hoped this time . . . and then shut my thoughts off. The coffee was hot and exceptionally good.

"Selena seems to make better coffee than most brides," I said to him.

He pushed at a pebble with his foot. "I made this," he said. "Selena doesn't cook."

"None of the old biscuit jokes need apply?"

"No. She doesn't really care much for food, one way or the other." His voice implied he hadn't said everything that was in his mind.

I wondered if this was his way of getting at something he wanted to tell me. "Well," I observed, "at any rate, you certainly have it all over the Sanitary Lunch so far as coffee is concerned."

"God, don't tell me you had breakfast there!"

"Four bits' worth."

"I'm sorry. We should have stopped before. I just kept on driving without thinking, I guess."

I finished my second bacon sandwich. "It's okay. This makes up for it."

"Too bad we haven't any Scotch."

So I knew he was thinking back too, but I made up my mind not to let him know. "Oh, hell, I've signed the pledge, or practically so. Abstemious is the word for me these days."

He was silent a long time. "I'm glad you're doing so well at the job."

"I wouldn't say that. But it's an improvement over my performance awhile back. Hell, Jerry, I owe you an apology for a lot of things. I acted like a fool."

He didn't look at me. "You had reasons. In a lot of ways they were good ones."

"I didn't even have an excuse, really."

He got on his feet and began walking up and down in front of me, looking at the ground. "Listen, Bark. Before we get there, I want to talk to you a little while. So you'll know what you're getting into and why I wired you."

"All right."

"First of all, don't get the idea there's anything wrong between me and Selena. I—well, I'm more in love with her now than I was when we got married."

"Sure," I said. "You're a couple of swell people."

"Thanks. And I'm going to sound like an ass when I tell you what's on my mind. In one way, I'm happier than I've ever been before, and in another—well, everything's just enough wrong so I'm worried." He wet his lips and went on. "You aren't married, so I don't know quite how I can explain it to you. It's just that everything goes so far, between us, and then it stops."

I started to say something and stopped, embarrassed.

"No, It's not that ... We—I mean, the sex part of it is all right. It's something I can't put into words, exactly. But when you're in love, you want to give everything to the person you love. Sex is only one aspect of it. Does this make any sense to you?"

"Of course, it does."

"And you don't only want to give everything to the person you love, but you want to be given everything in return. It's a two-way proposition for each person."

I quoted:

"My true-love hath my heart, and I have his.
By just exchange, one for another given."

"Yes," he said. "It's got to be a just exchange. That's the point."

"And it's not that way?" I asked him.

He stopped walking and faced me. "I feel all the time as though she was holding something back. Sometimes it's almost as though she felt I wasn't old enough to know something. And I can't find out what it is. What it is she knows that I don't. There's something in between us, that's all. And yet, she loves me, Bark."

There wasn't anything in this that I couldn't give him a comforting answer to without having to open my memory to that fantastic story Parsons had told me, that story of Luella Jamison. There was, thank God, a more plausible explanation.

"After all," I said, "you make her sound as if she had a sort of mother complex. And that's natural enough, in a way. Don't forget this is your first marriage, but it's her second."

He began to pace back and forth again, kicking at stones. "No, that's not it."

"Of course, it is."

He shook his head, "Don't forget, she wasn't married long. And to LeNormand. That first marriage doesn't count."

A premonition of something unpleasant went through me; I don't know what I expected him to say next, but what he did say shocked me for a moment.

"You see," he said in a low voice and without looking at me, "when we got married she was a virgin."

After I rallied from that sudden statement it did not appear so surprising after all, and I felt glad for him in an inexplicable way. And then I saw what he was getting at. It made it all the harder to explain something that he felt was missing between them.

At this moment a sense of loneliness so acute that it was almost like fear came over me. I remembered the bleached sterility of Los Palos with nostalgia. Here in the middle of an enormous and lifeless desert I was talking to the man who had been, who still was, my best friend, and yet if I could in any way have escaped from him I would have done so at once. No reason for my sudden gust of feeling presented itself, but I knew that I ought not to be there, that already the whole horrible web of circumstance that had caught us both and changed us, and from which I thought I had escaped, was closing in on me again. I looked at Jerry, and the tightness of his face began to make me feel afraid. He had changed, and there was a long gap of unshared time between us. A time when we had been growing and altering in different directions. I was afraid not of him, but of what he wanted with me.

"So you see," he was saying, "it isn't the ordinary thing at all. We're not unhappily married. Don't get that idea."

"Hell," I said, "I haven't got any idea at all."

He looked straight at me. "I've got to try to tell you what's bothering me and then I want you to tell me something. Something that I'm sure you know. You've got to know it."

"All right," I said. "Anything I can tell you I will."

"Selena and I got married pretty quickly after LeNormand's death," he said, and there was a perfectly objective tone in his voice; I could not tell whether he regretted the fact or not. "The rest of you didn't approve of that. One of the things you and Dad both said, at various times, was that we ought to know each other better. You remember that?"

"Yes," I told him.

"Why did you tell me that?"

It was a question I did not want to answer, so I parried it as smoothly as I could. "I guess both of us felt it was a little too rapid for, well, for being entirely sure of your happiness."

He looked disappointed. "I imagined that was Dad's idea, but I thought maybe you had something more definite in your mind."

"No," I said at once.

"Well," he went on after a pause, "it wouldn't have made any difference." He stopped as if he wanted me to agree with him, or disagree. I couldn't be sure which.

"I don't see what you're driving at."

"Damn it!" he said harshly. "I don't know any more about Selena than I did the day I married her."

His voice seemed to ring in the trench of the barranca where we were. The sound of his words seemed to expand, to go into the ground and penetrate the rock wall under which we were standing. It echoed in the air, in the heat, in the sun that encompassed us. A year and a half had passed since Jerry had married Selena. In all that time she had not told him who she was or where she came from, then. The only possible explanation was the story Parsons had told me, the terrible theory that Selena was Luella Jamison.

He was watching me closely.

After a while he went on. "I don't know if I can explain it to you. You know how, in stories, some little habit of the wife's or the husband's grows and grows out of all proportion in the mind of the other until finally there is an explosion? Well, that's the way it is with me. And I'm afraid of the explosion. Bark, do you know that everything Selena ever says to me is based on nothing but the present or the future?" He stopped a moment and looked down the ravine and out across the desert. "You don't notice how many things people say that go back to their childhood, or to their past. People they refer to, things they remember, familiarities with this and that. Everybody is like that and doesn't know it. Everybody but Selena."

"Listen," I said to him. "She had a shock, don't forget. Naturally she doesn't want to think back of that."

He sighed. "No, Bark. She's talked to me often enough about Le-Normand, in a funny sort of way, and quite a good bit more about Collegeville. Faculty wives and all sorts of things. But never anything at all before that."

I was afraid to ask what was in my mind, but I knew that it was then or never. "Doesn't she ever talk about her family, even?"

He stared at me with dry eyes and a set mouth. "No. Never. That is—" and he stopped suddenly.

"You see," I said, "you're holding something back. It isn't so bad as you make out."

"Once," he said, and his voice was tighter than before. "Once she said something about her family. At least, I suppose it was her family." Then he was silent for quite a while. "It was when we were on our honeymoon in Bermuda. We had a little house to ourselves, you know. One night I woke up. Our bed was by the window and the full moon was coming through it in a perfect flood of light. She was lying there in it, in the moonshine, asleep." He licked his lips and went on. "I saw her lying there, lovely, perfect, asleep, with the moon full on her face. You know how beautiful she is?"

I nodded.

"Well, I can't tell you exactly what just looking at her did to me. It somehow made me a bigger person after a while. I stopped being myself or knowing anything except how much I loved her. And I leaned over finally and kissed her, and she woke up. She looked at me a minute and I could see she wondered why I had waked her. And then she smiled a little as if she knew how much I was loving her, and moved over closer to me. We lay there and looked out the window at the moonlight on the lawn and the trees and the distant ocean, and didn't speak. Finally she sighed a little, or I thought she did, and said something in a low voice. It was meant to be to herself, I reckon, but I overheard it." He stopped again.

I didn't speak.

"She said—" Jerry's voice was low and wondering—"she said, 'This is the thing my people do not know.'"

"Jesus!" I said before I could stop myself. I had expected anything but that puzzling remark; it did not fit in with the things Parsons and I had discussed; it made no sense for Luella Jamison to have made that remark.

Jerry took careful aim and kicked a bit of rock out into the hard sunshine on the other side of the ravine. "That's the only reference she's ever made. Oh, I've asked her, but she never tells me. Sometimes she just laughs and says I've got to forget she had any past at all. Several times I've tried to press her into telling me."

"What happened then?"

"It sounds silly to say it, but she got so angry I was afraid to go on."

"Do you think she has a guilty conscience or anything?"

"God," he said impatiently, "I don't know. I'd swear she had nothing in her whole mind that she was ashamed of. But it's the not-knowing that torments me. It's the noticing that she never goes back of that time in Collegeville. It's the feeling that there's something she won't share with me, some part of her that she won't give. And it's begun to scare me. Suppose it is something pretty horrible—that wouldn't make any difference to me, and she knows it. Suppose this damned thing—this reason she has for not telling me who she is—comes out sometime and I'm not ready for it. It got so that I was afraid to have her meet strangers for fear they were a part of that past of hers, whatever it was. That's one of the reasons we came out here."

I could think of nothing to say to him.

"'This is the thing my people do not know,'" he quoted slowly and half to himself. Then he turned to me and said, "Bark, I have a hunch that you know something about Selena that I don't. You've got to tell me what it is."

"Don't be silly," I said quickly. "How could I? You've been with me practically every time I've seen her, and all through the LeNormand business."

"No," he said. "You're not being honest with me. I know you pretty well, Bark, and I've been thinking back over everything. After that time you came back from Collegeville, you were different, in lots of ways. You drank more. You avoided being with us. There was something on your mind, something that you knew. And it's either something you found out by yourself when you went back there, or it's something Parsons told you. And it's something that I've got to know. Maybe you think I'm hysterical or foolish or completely nuts, but I tell you I've got to know what it is." He looked at me steadily and with an eagerness that made me feel almost sick.

Yet, there was my promise to Parsons. I could break that and tell him the story of Luella Jamison, but there was no way in which I could see that doing so would help him. Instead, it would simply add another uncertain horror to revolve in his mind. After living with the story of that incredible disappearance and the possibilities it contained, I knew what it could do to a mind that fastened upon it. No, certainly I would never tell him anything about that.

"Parsons," I answered carefully, "was stuck. He told me we were being followed; he knew all about what we had been doing. Knowing that, got me sort of nervous. That was why I was funny about things then."

He disregarded my words. "So you won't tell me."

"Listen," I said. "The only thing I know that you don't has nothing to do with you or Selena, except indirectly. It's nothing that will help you in the least, and I gave my word to Parsons that I wouldn't tell anyone about it. He told me because he wanted me to tell him whether it had any connection with the LeNormand case, and it didn't and I told him so. That's all there is to that."

He shook his head. "All right. You're a stubborn guy when you make up your mind. But I want you to promise me one thing."

"What is it?"

"After you've been out here awhile, I want you to think whether you'll tell me what that thing was, and whether you notice anything else that could help me."

I nodded. "All right," I said, "but I'd have told you long ago if I'd thought it was a good idea."

We climbed into the car again without saying anything more. As he put the car in gear, Jerry said, "And Parsons never found out who killed LeNormand."

"No," I said. And then I wondered if somehow he had the idea that Selena had anything to do with it. "Anyway, he told me he was positive that Selena and you and I didn't do it. He said he could prove that much."

Jerry said nothing for a moment as he swung the car back into the miserable road. "Parsons is a smart man. I thought he would solve it."

"Well," I said, "he didn't have anything to go on. No clues, and no motive, and no witnesses."

Jerry drove intently and without looking away from the road. "There were those equations.... Remember the sheets of old notepaper on the table?"

"Yes." But I couldn't see what they proved. "After all, figures don't lie, let alone murder."

Jerry smiled fleetingly. "I've been playing around with those equations. Selena came in the other day and found me at it. Like a fool I told her what I was doing. She didn't like it."

"Oh," I said. "Why not?"

"I dunno, exactly. I suppose it's a piece with the rest—not wanting to have anything to do with the past."

"Well," I observed, "I remember she was interested in those Arabian books of Dad's."

"Yes," he said, frowning a little, "she knows a lot of math. I can't figure out where she picked it up. From LeNormand maybe."

After that it grew too hot to talk. The car rolled steadily along, about west by south, on the long road to Cloud Mesa. Just before eleven o'clock we reached it.

13. CLOUD MESA

Around and above us the night was growing old. The stars were points of smaller light, the shadow masses of the trees had denser, less distinguishable shape against the sky, and the water of the Sound glinted seldom and faintly..."The darkest hour"... That hackneyed tag of speech went through my mind as I turned to Dr. Lister.

"It will be dawn soon," I said. "But this is the part of the story that matters most."

"Of course," he said. "Are you too tired to go on?"

"I'm too tired to stop."

"You mustn't be afraid to call a halt if you wish."

He did not seem weary at all. Erect as ever, quiet, with his eyes fixed upon me steadily, it gave me strength to look at him.

"We could never go back to this," I said. "It is better to finish now."

"Yes." His voice was calm, but I noticed that one of his fingers was tapping against the edge of the table.

The last few miles of our ride, the road went uphill steadily. We must have climbed nearly a thousand feet. Then we swung round a shoulder of the mountains and saw Cloud Mesa.

It was something of a geological puzzle to me. In shape it resembled the ordinary mesa of the Southwest, with the usual steeply sloping sides, covered with rocky detritus and ending toward the top in sharp cliffs of naked rock. The level expanse of its summit was as sharply marked as the edge of a table, and on the valley side it rose sheer from the floor of the desert. But its western edge seemed only partly separate from the wall of mountains behind and the northern, narrower end slid down to the floor of a mountain ravine into which our car began to dip. Sharp and clear I could see the cube of the house about halfway up the mesa's northern slope and shining white in the sun.

The place had been built by an artist named Eberhardt whom Dad had once befriended. He had come out to the West to paint and to recover from the effects of a dose of gas in Belleau Wood. Before he died he did some strange, harsh-colored pictures of the desert country which I never liked because there was a brutality in them that you couldn't ignore. He left most of them and the house as well to Dr. Lister—out of gratitude, I suppose. It had remained empty until Jerry and Selena came there, and my heart sank a little as I looked across the ravine. If there was ever a lonelier place, or one more dwarfed by its setting, I never saw it.

Jerry pulled the car up in front of the weather-beaten sort of shack that was apparently used for a garage, and we got out stiffly. He hauled forth my bags and we went toward the house. Seen at close hand, it was not quite so forbidding; the walls were a white-washed cream in color, and there were the conventional blue shutters. It was larger than it had looked from where I had first seen it. Apparently there was a spring just behind the house; at any rate, there was a patch of green which must have meant water in this thirsty country.

Selena was standing in the doorway to greet us; she was wearing a yellow linen dress and sandals. Her beauty was unchanged, so far as I could see; the sun did not appear to have tanned her bare legs and arms, and her face and hair were as I had remembered them, sculptural and perfect. Later, when she moved, I saw that she was walking once again with the same long, swift stride that she had when we first knew her and before she began to imitate Grace.

"Hello, Bark," she said, and held out her hand.

I took it and told her I was glad to see her, which was a lie. I think she knew it.

"Well, Bark," said Jerry. "Welcome to our humble home." His voice didn't sound quite natural to me.

I told them both I was glad to be there, and we went into the house. Inside it was dark and cool; the floor was tiled, and the heavy adobe walls seemed to hold the freshness of the night all through the heat of the day. The room we entered was clearly the living room, with a big fireplace to the left, at the eastern end. It did not have much furniture aside from several Navajo rugs on the floor. A long settle in front of the fireplace. A large table of unpainted wood, and three straight chairs.

Jerry opened the door on the far side of the room. "This is your place," he said, and carried my bags in. The room was scarcely more than a cubicle, with a bed, a washstand, and a single window opening to the east. "I think you'll find everything you want."

"Sure," I said, "this is palatial." But actually I found myself thinking of it with an obscure sense of relief as a sort of refuge.

After I'd washed and got into some old clothes, Jerry showed me the rest of the house. Next to my room was a sort of small study, well lined with books, which he told me was where he worked. Behind the study was a large bedroom where Jerry and Selena slept, with a door opening out of its west wall. The kitchen was in a lean-to shed at the southwest corner of the house.

I wondered what there was about the place that bothered me. It was pleasant enough inside, and done with a simplicity and directness that were agreeable. Even the half dozen or so of Eberhardt's pictures on the walls could not explain why I felt uneasy. But as soon as I stepped out of doors again I saw the reason. The great bulk of the mesa loomed towering and imminent above the house; incalculable tons of rock and earth seemed almost suspended above its roof; the very scale of that slope above you made you feel like an ant. I don't know how better to give the effect than to say that I felt always as if a giant were about to step on the house and all of us in it.

Jerry showed me over the place with much pride, and I began to feel that I had been a fool about my first reaction to it. But behind his enthusiasm and the steady flow of talk which he kept up I felt his relief at my coming. How long had the silences been when just the two of them were there alone? And later, in the afternoon, when the blue shadow of the mesa poured down and over the house and left us in a sort of twilight my uneasiness returned to me. We watched that shadow swoop down the slope above us, and after it had swept over the house I turned to go indoors.

"Wait a minute, Bark," said Jerry. "I want to show you something else."

He led me a few yards up the slope and pointed to what looked like the remains of an uneven rock stairway that began behind the spring and clambered up the wall of the mesa above us.

"Cliff dwellers. God knows how long ago, but you can still climb their stairs. Want to go up?"

I saw that he did, so I agreed. It was not a really hard or dangerous ascent; the stairs were steep but in pretty good shape. Although we stopped to breathe and look back and down several times, it was only a quarter of an hour or less until we were at the top.

Below us spread the gigantic sweep of the desert, tarnished gold where the sun still lay, and purple blue where the shadows from the western mountains were racing across it as the sun sank behind us. Watching that great tidal wave of darkness pouring across the valley, I suddenly realized how truly the earth was a ball, hung in gulfs of space and spinning around its axis with majestic precision and power. I almost thought I could feel the eastward surge of the mesa under my feet.

After a moment we turned and walked across the level top. It was very bare, with a few bushes, and here and there a low mound that Jerry said he suspected was the remains of ancient houses. Ahead of us was a slight rise in the ground; as we drew near it I saw that on it stood an oblong of rock.

We halted and looked at that single piece of weathered stone, massive, rough-hewn by the chisels of men who were dust a thousand years ago. Unmistakably it was an altar.

"'To the unknown God,'" I said.

Jerry stared down at it a long time. "Yes," he said finally. "'To the unknown God,' only I suppose they had a name for him. The people who lived up here."

Certainly this was one of the "high places" that men of the very ancient world had felt to be holy, whether in Palestine or in the American desert. Even when houses had stood on the mesa top, this must have been a still place, aloof and plainly not a part of the business of human living at all. So they had hewed a stone and put it where it could lie for century upon century, here on this height, under the sky and swept clean forever by the great winds. An altar, yes, and in a place where they had felt that the immensity of the universe touched the immediacies of the earth on which they lived. This stone was their ebenezer; it marked their recognition of the something more than they could put a name to. A memorial to the tremendous force or will that had created the earth and the stars.

I turned away from it reluctantly, and yet eager to leave the height and the wind that blew by us. Such vastnesses lay around us that I was suddenly hungry for a roof and a fire and four close walls. Jerry seemed more than willing to go at once; we scrambled down the shadowy stairs with cautious haste, and as we went we saw that Selena must have lighted a fire, for flickers of orange radiance spilled out of the windows below us.

Jerry and I got the supper ready. Selena sat in the living room and read; I remembered that Jerry had said she did not cook, but I felt a little annoyed at her just the same. When we finally got it assembled, it was a workingman's supper; the climb and the air had given me a tremendous appetite. The two of us ate heartily, but I noticed that Selena moved the food around on her plate but swallowed hardly more than one or two bites. It was a quiet meal, perhaps because we—Jerry and I—were wolfing our food, yet as I ate I thought how seldom they spoke to each other. But the food was good, and I didn't much mind the silence.

After it was finished, we pushed back our chairs and I lit a pipe. A feeling almost of peace came over me; for the first time I felt at home, not strange in any way. I smiled at Selena and said, "This is very pleasant, Selena. I'm glad I came."

She smiled back at me almost automatically. "It is a beautiful place, isn't it?"

Jerry seemed determined to keep the conversation going; he

began to explain that the life grew on you, and that you never got tired of watching the desert and the mountains, and that we should have to take some tramps as soon as I got used to the climate.

After a while Selena asked me if I thought I had everything I needed in my room.

I said I thought I had.

She told me, "You'll be sleepy early tonight, I think. The desert makes you sleepy, and the air at night."

Jerry added quickly that, while I could turn in any time I wanted to, he hoped I'd sit up and talk for a while. He began to stack the dishes and carry them out to the kitchen, firmly declining my efforts to help him. Selena went back to the settle in front of the fire and picked up her book again. Once, as Jerry was cleaning the crumbs from the table, she turned and looked over her shoulder at him.

"Are you going to work tonight, Jerry?"

"Well," he said, and there was a faint flavor of apology in his tone, "I'm almost through, you know, and I thought I'd do a bit more. I think I'm getting somewhere."

"Darling, it's no use, you know. I wish you would give up the whole idea."

His face set a trifle stubbornly. "Ah, you must allow for an old man's crotchets. I get a kick out of it." And then, turning to me, he said swiftly, "I'm doing a bit of mathematical research for my thesis. It's really based on that dope of LeNormand's, but I think I see a way to present it so the boys will swallow it. If I do, it'll be worth publishing."

So that was what he was working at. I wondered why Selena did not like it. Plainly it annoyed her very much, but she contented herself with saying, "You are wasting your time."

Jerry laughed. "Don't worry your handsome head over my math, my sweet. It's harmless."

She made no answer, but I thought in the uncertain light of the fire that an expression had gone over her face of a sort I could not quite define. Still her face was shaded by the lamp behind her, and I was not sure.

We could hear Jerry, back in the kitchen, whistling to himself and splashing the water in the dishpan, but she read on in her book without lifting her head, and I sat smoking my pipe and watching her. Suddenly I saw a curious thing. She was crying. There weren't any tears, and she didn't make a sound, but her face was contorted with grief and the hand lying beside her on the settle was clenched till the knuckles were white.

Any woman, by crying, can make me entirely miserable, but with Selena it was doubly unbearable. I did not associate that sort of weakness with her, for one thing, and, for another, because I did not like her it made it impossible for me to notice that she was crying at all. So I got up and stood by the mantel and smoked my pipe and looked at the fire and pretended that I did not know what she was doing.

Some fragment of sound made me look up. She had risen, and without looking at me or making the slightest sign she went down the room and out the front door. It closed behind her, but in the instant when she opened it I had seen beyond her the black, star-sprinkled sky of the Western night, and the distant shouldering silhouette of the mountains to the west. A gust of cold air went through the room and the fire flickered. Jerry stuck his head into the room for a moment when he heard the door close, but returned at once to the kitchen without saying anything. The water went on splashing in the dishpan, but he had stopped whistling.

Nothing in life, I think, ordinarily happens in great, thunderous episodes of obvious and dramatic force. Life is a series of small things, and most of them mean much or little depending on how the observer thinks of them. I, for instance, didn't pay any real attention to the things that happened in that room that night. And yet, if I had I would have seen a pattern in them, the pattern of the fifth act of a tragedy, when the play is all played out and only the final words, the ultimate destruction of the protagonist, await fulfillment. I see these things now for what they were worth, the last small events before an unthinkable horror of a thing was to happen. But at the time I thought merely that Selena had gone outside to get control of herself, that she would be back soon, and that it was embarrassing to be stuck into the middle of a mess like this. And I couldn't quite get over a feeling of surprise at Selena's crying. There didn't seem to have been enough cause for tears, even for a woman with much less fortitude than Selena had. Thinking back, I couldn't believe there was any real reason for her crying at all; she had been annoyed with Jerry, not hurt by him.

After a moment I went over to the settle and sat down. Selena's book was in my way, and as I moved it to one end of the seat, I saw it was an old copy of Hans Christian Andersen's fairy tales. A book that I felt sure came from the bookcase in Jerry's room in the Long Island house. I picked it up idly—she had left it face down and began to read at her own place:

"...and as evening grew darker hundreds of variegated lamps were lit...The sailors danced on the deck, and when the young Prince came out there, more than a hundred rockets shot up into the sky."

"Hey, Bark!" It was Jerry's voice from the kitchen.

"What?"

"Will you have Scotch or rye?"

"Scotch."

He appeared with a tray, a bottle, a pitcher of water, and two glasses. "Even if you have practically signed the pledge, as you claim, a nightcap or two won't hurt us."

"Hell, no," I agreed. "I'm all for an occasional renewal of youthful folly anyway."

"You always were a philosophical so-and-so," he said. "Personally, I just drink without thinking out a formal reason for it."

He poured us a couple of stiff ones. They tasted good there in front of the fire, and I took a long pull. "This is the McCoy, Jerry."

"Yeah. It's good to see you again."

"Here's to it."

"Down the hatch."

He poured out another apiece, and we took it slower. Jerry stared into the fire for a while and then turned to me, almost impulsively. "You see how it is."

"Damn it," I said, "I don't see anything."

He looked at me thoughtfully as if to find out whether I meant it. "She's gone up there, you know."

"Up where?"

"Up to the top of the mesa."

"My God," I said. "In the dark? She'll fall and kill herself!"

His answer came after quite a while. "She never has."

I let that sink in for a minute. "You mean," I asked him incredulously, "she goes up there often?"

"Almost every night."

"Are you serious?"

"Yes, I'm serious as hell."

"But, Jerry," I argued, "it doesn't make sense. What does she do it for?"

He swirled the whisky and water in his glass round and round and stared at it. "I wish I knew. I wish to God I knew."

"Listen," I said. "There must be some reason. Maybe she likes to be alone and look at the stars and moon up there." Even while I was speaking, it sounded foolish.

"Maybe." He added nothing to that one word for a time, and then took another drink. "I followed her once. It took me a hell of a while, even in the moonlight, to get up there. When I did, I couldn't see her anywhere. The moon was bright too. But, of course, it's a big place. After a while I called, but she didn't answer." He put his glass down between his feet and fished out a cigarette. "She must have heard me, though, because the next morning she bawled hell out of me for going up. Told me it was too dangerous, and I mustn't do it again."

"For Christ's sake!"

He was groping in his pockets. "Got a match?"

I found a solitary paper packet in my own pocket. There were only a few matches left in it. "Here."

He lit his cigarette, blew out a long funnel of smoke, and observed, "I've got so I don't mind any more."

We had a few more drinks and felt fine and talked over the old days, and it was pleasant. Twice, I remember, Jerry put more wood on the fire before we went off to our respective beds. And when I blew out the lamp in my room, I had neither seen nor heard Selena come back to the house. But I thought to myself, she must have come in by the door into their bedroom.

The next day was much cooler. A sharp wind was coming down off the mountains, and I was surprised to see a gray scud of cloud across the sky. Jerry and I set out, after breakfast, for a walk up toward the peak beyond and behind the mesa.

Selena must have come home, for she was at breakfast, looking very still and without any morning small talk. She said she didn't want to walk, and that it was not a nice day, but she hoped we'd have a good time.

There was nothing really worth telling about the walk. We climbed pretty far up one shoulder of the peak and sat down to eat our sandwiches in the lee of a rock pinnacle. After we finished, I filled my pipe and Jerry put a cigarette in his mouth. Then, for a few minutes, we thought we didn't have any matches. Finally he found the paper I'd given him the night before, and by the mercy of God I got my pipe going with the last one. He lit his cigarette from the pipe, and I sailed the empty match paper out into the wind. We watched it fall, idly and without attention. If I had known what was to happen, I might have paid a good deal more heed to its long, curving drop out of sight. As it was, though, we sat and smoked contentedly for a while, and looked down across the desert.

"Bark," said Jerry, keeping his eyes on the view, "would you be willing to tell me now what it is you know?"

"I can't," I told him honestly. "It wouldn't do you any good and it wouldn't prove a thing."

"Would it prove anything about who killed LeNormand?"

"No," I said. "I'm positive it wouldn't."

"Okay." He was quiet, as though planning what to say next. "I've got something I want to tell you, and get your reaction to. Do you mind my talking about it?"

"Of course not."

He leaned back against the rock, "I've come to the conclusion that if I could find out who killed LeNormand and why, I'd know about this thing that's between Selena and me. I've been thinking over the whole business for a long time now. And I'm reasonably sure I've figured out what the only clue is."

"Pretty long-range work, wasn't it?" But I was worried; I didn't want to reopen that whole murder case. I most emphatically did not want to remember that night in Eldridge Observatory.

"No," he said calmly. "It wasn't long-range work at all. I had the clue with me. Those equations that were on LeNormand's table. He was working at them when he died, I'm sure of that."

"Even if he was," I told him impatiently, "a few pencil scratches on a piece of paper are seldom fatal."

"That depends. They are if they're an order to a firing squad. Listen, Bark, you don't know what a big thing LeNormand was on to. The biggest thing in the world, by God!" He was silent for a second. "Do you remember any of your college math?"

"Not much."

"Well, I'll try to explain it to you in words, then. Only it's hard to put into words. LeNormand's work followed the stuff of a guy named Minkowski. Ever hear of him?"

"He sounds sort of Polish."

"Damned if I know what he was, except that he was a great mathematician. LeNormand always spoke of him as if Minkowski was the only man who would have understood his own ideas. But LeNormand was way beyond Minkowski."

This didn't interest me much. "Minkowski! Why do these mathematicians have such cockeyed names?"

"Nuts," said Jerry. "There have been jokes about your own name, if it comes to that, and mine sounds like part of a mouthwash. Let me try to get this across to you. Minkowski worked on the problem of time, among other things. Lots of people talk about time as if it were a fourth dimension. In a way it is; everything tangible has length and breadth and thickness and also it exists in time. It lasts. It has duration. If it didn't, you wouldn't be able to grasp its existence any more than you could figure out something that lacked one of the other three dimensions."

"All right," I said. "I agree to all that."

"But," he went on, very earnestly, "in another way time isn't like the other dimensions. You can't see the time dimension of anything. You can even forget about it the way Euclid did, and do lots of things to geometrical figures, at least on paper, without taking it into account at all. This fellow Minkowski discovered that time is not any ordinary spatial quality of anything, but his idea was that it would become so if it was multiplied by the square root of minus one."

"My old friend," I remarked, "the square root of minus one! I haven't thought of it in years. It's in the same class with that other thing, the nth power. And wasn't there a funny-looking symbol that represented infinity?"

"There is." He looked at me curiously. "The inside of your mind must be a queer place."

"It's cozy," I told him.

"Yes. Well, LeNormand figured out a set of equations that proved the serial nature of time."

"Hunh?"

"Sure. There isn't just one time. There are lots of times. Why, everybody believes in that, if you stop to think about it. You've heard people say, 'time passes slowly,' or 'the time went by like lightning.' Well, it's sort of like the old song about who takes care of the caretaker's daughter? If you talk about time passing, you're actually measuring it against something, and that something is a sort of second time."

I felt distinctly confused, but I knew that once Jerry started to explain something all hell would not deflect him, so I sat and waited for the rest of it to roll over me.

"The nearest way I can give you an idea of LeNormand's work is to say that he applied this theorem of Minkowski's to the conception of a serial time, or a bunch of times running on up into infinity. I know you don't get it, and it's not a thing you can explain even with diagrams, but I guess you can see that everyone, from Einstein to little old Bill Feldman in the Math Department, was on his neck for it."

"My God," I said, "I don't see how they even understood it."

"They didn't. Well, that's about all I can tell you about LeNormand's theories, because it's all I'm sure I understand. There's one last equation. I'm working on it now. If I can decipher what he was putting down in that…" Jerry's voice trailed off for a moment. "Anyhow, you see why I think LeNormand had hold of something big. He used to tell me some things you could do with his stuff, just for fun. I remember he said once that if you could control your mind after you were dead and outside your body, you could make it travel through time. He used to tell me that it would do a lot of Christians good to go back and take a look at the Crucifixion before settling down to an eternity of bliss."

"Nice," I said, "a very nice, pleasant thought to take home with you."

"Hell," said Jerry. "I don't suppose he meant that stuff. Or most of it, anyway."

We sat there for several moments without any more words. Perhaps Jerry was thinking. For my part, I knew that I could never understand what he had been talking about, so there was no use my trying any thought. I just sat.

After a while he went on, and his voice was lower and graver, somehow. "LeNormand was killed by some kind of chemical, or else a ray of some sort. More likely a ray, though God knows where it came from. And it must have been because of his work. There was no other reason to kill him."

"There was Selena."

"Yes," he said. "Selena. Selena who won't tell me who she was before we met her. Bark, can you, for God's sake, tell me why she should be so silent about her past unless it would connect her, or someone she is sheltering, with that murder?" His voice was suddenly strained and urgent.

"Listen," I said quickly, "there's nothing to that idea. And if it's any comfort to you, it wasn't what Parsons and I talked about, either."

"Thanks for that much." He stopped a moment and wet his lips. "You don't know, I suppose, whether he ever investigated to find out who Selena is?"

"Yes," I told him, "he did."

"And did he find out?"

"No."

"You see what I have to think, don't you, Bark? I know it was a scientist's murder. I am certain Selena knows who did it. That's why she's keeping such a careful watch against giving anything away about her past."

"And she married LeNormand just to keep an eye on him?"

He nodded grimly. "Yes. Damn it! Do you think I like this? Do you think I enjoy suspecting my wife of being implicated in a murder—a horrible murder, at that, and of a man I liked damned well?"

"I think you're building a lot on a pretty slender foundation."

"Yes," he admitted, "I know that. But there's another thing. She hates my working on that stuff of LeNormand's. She doesn't like it and she tries to stop me. Remember last night how she told me it was useless? That's the word she uses when she wants to say a thing is altogether bad. Suppose she has the idea that if I go on with what I'm doing, the same thing will happen to me that happened to LeNormand?"

It came over me at last in what torment he had been living; there was nothing I could say without putting another and equally horrible alternative in his mind, the alternative that Selena was Luella Jamison. And yet, I wish now that I had told him Parsons' story.

"Bark, don't you see how much of it fits? Think how intelligent Selena is. Half the time I believe she knows more about LeNormand's work than I do. Just from little things she lets drop once in a while. Where else could she get that intelligence from but a scientist's family, that intelligence and her knowledge?"

"You're born with intelligence. You don't acquire it."

"Maybe."

"Anyway, your whole idea is crazy. It's as thin as tissue paper, and as improbable as a movie scenario. What scientist do you suspect?"

"I don't suspect any of them. There are fifty men whose careers would have been ruined by LeNormand's work."

"Are any of them missing a daughter or a wife?"

He looked at me, hard. "I don't know yet. I'm getting reports on all of them from an agency."

"Good God!"

"You see, Bark," he said quietly, "if I can't eliminate this horrible idea I have in my mind, I'll have to live with it for the rest of my life."

14. SOMETIME IS NOW

WE GOT up, after that, and started down the mountain. The wind was cold at our backs, and we hurried. Several times I should have liked to smoke another pipe, but the matches were all gone. I muttered about that annoying fact to Jerry, and was surprised to find that he was very much bothered about it. He was certain that the matches we had used there on the mountain were the last ones in the house. I couldn't believe it, but he was really worried. He insisted that since he was the one that did the housekeeping, he would know whether there were any more matches, and most assuredly there were not. Neither of us liked the idea of a fireless evening, a cold supper, and a long drive into town the next day. Suddenly he stopped and turned back to me with a grin.

"Say, I know what we can do! We'll get a fire with a spark from the car battery. Why didn't I think of that before?"

And we went slogging on down the slope with lighter hearts. Jerry was worried about Selena's being pretty well frozen by the time we got there, and we hurried as fast as my legs and shortness of wind would permit.

Our path brought us round the shoulder of a ridge and into sight of the house about a quarter of a mile ahead of us. The moment we saw it, both of us stopped. The window at our end, a living room window, was glowing with light. From the orange warmth of it in the shadow of the wall, from the way it flickered, even at that distance we knew the light could come only from the fireplace. Instantly I was disappointed. Probably some primitive survival in the back of my brain, or possibly nothing but a hangover from Boy

Scouting, had made me look forward to our fire making experiment with a perverse sort of anticipation. Now it would not be necessary. Selena had a fire.

The effect on Jerry was different. He looked at the light a while without speaking or moving. For a minute or two his expression was incredulous, and then it changed, tightened, altered, in a way that I could not analyze.

"Well," I said, "we won't have to try our luck with a couple of dry sticks or a pair of battery cables, after all."

"No," he said. "She's lit a fire. She's lit a fire." He seemed puzzled and perhaps slightly uneasy.

"Maybe she thought of the battery stunt before we did, or maybe she found a match," I suggested.

"No," he said, "the car's still in the shed and there wasn't a match in the house . . ." His voice trailed off slowly, reluctantly, I thought.

"Oh, well," I told him, "any fire is better than none. 'Take the gifts the gods provide.'"

He looked at me. "What's that? Oh, yes, sure." But he wasn't thinking at all about what I had said.

He kept the lead as we went on to the house, but he was no longer hurrying. In fact, it seemed to me that he was hardly moving with any purpose at all. If it hadn't been the end of a fairly long tramp, I'd have thought him merely strolling. Several times he lifted his head and looked toward the house; each time I noticed how tense his face was, and how remote the expression around his eyes.

Sure enough, when we entered the living room there was a big, crackling fire on the hearth, dried desert wood that burned intensely and was gone to ash in an hour. Selena was sitting on the settle, looking into the flames. There were filaments of fire glowing in her pale, bright hair, and a faint flush on her cheeks from the heat.

"Hello," she said. "Have an interesting walk?"

"Sure," I said, "only keeping up with a long-legged mountain goat like your husband is no job for one who hath been long in city pent."

"He does walk fast, doesn't he?"

I went over and stood with my back to the fire; the heat soaked into my legs and took some of the tiredness out of them. Jerry was standing behind the settle, behind Selena; he took out his package of cigarettes and put one between his lips. His voice was perfectly casual.

"Gimme a match, will you, honey?"

That woman could think, and think fast. Only the smallest trace of some expression went over her face; then she stooped and pulled out from the flames a long twig of mesquite.

"Here," she said, and held it to his cigarette.

He drew in a long drag of smoke and looked at her across the flame without saying anything except "Thanks."

She tossed the twig back into the flames and sat down again.

"We were worried," I remarked. "Jerry was positive there wasn't a match in the house, and we used our last up on the mountain. But I see you found one."

Jerry came round the end of the settle and stood at the opposite side of the fireplace, looking down at his wife. "Yes," he said, with an unsuccessful attempt at lightness in his tone, "where did you find the match?"

She looked up at him and there was a sort of stillness in her face that I shall never forget. "Does it matter?"

"No," he said, "it doesn't matter at all where you found it. It matters if you found it."

The remark made no sense to me at all, and I still don't understand it, but Selena did. She stood up.

"You shouldn't have said that." There was no anger, no sharpness in her tone, only weariness and what sounded to me at the time like despair.

Jerry was staring at her; the look on his face was so thinly sharp, so direct, so full of horror that I was instantly aware that this conversation, which was meaningless to me, possessed some sort of positive and dreadful implication for him. "So," he said, "so that's it. I've wondered for a long time."

She looked at him calmly. "I tried to stop you."

"Yes," he said. "You tried to stop me. That was kind of you."

He threw his head back and laughed. A short, nervous laugh that had the timbre of fear in it. "That was condescending of you—Selena."

"No," she said in a very low voice, "no, Jerry, it wasn't condescension."

He was watching her, I noticed. His eyes never moved from her face. I saw, too, that he was trembling, that his hands, at his sides, were twitching, and that his lips, which had suddenly become thin and gray, were quivering slightly. He licked them. "I would have found out sometime," he said to her at last. She made no reply. "But sometime is now."

"Yes," she said, and her voice was impersonal.

Suddenly he was in complete command of himself. "Do you know what I am thinking?"

"Of course," she said.

"Am I right?"

She nodded her head gravely. "You know that too."

"All right," he said, as though agreeing to something, and turned to me. "Bark, you don't know what this is all about, do you?"

"No," I told him.

"That's good," he said, and there was affection in his voice. "I want you to do me a favor."

"Sure," I told him.

He left the fire. "I want you to take something to Dad from me when you go. I'll write it out now . . . before I forget it." He went into the study, and I followed him somewhat uncertainly. The whole thing was confusing, and for some obscure reason I felt frightened. Selena followed me, but she stopped in the doorway.

Jerry was sitting at the desk in there. The last gray light from the east came through the window behind him and lighted the room with a dull, unlovely color. He was writing by the time I reached the room, with a swift, racing drive of his pen as though to finish before the light faded entirely. I watched him a minute, conscious of Selena white and glimmering in the dusk of the door behind me. All at once, with a quick, impatient gesture he crumpled the note and flung it into a corner.

"Hell," he said, with a swift, tight grin at me. "It's not so important, after all."

The rest happened before I knew it. The gun must have been there in the desk drawer, ready to his hand. He simply put it up to his head and pulled the trigger.

The crash of the shot in that small room made my eardrums ring. The revolver clattered to the floor beside his chair; his arms went out across the desktop, and his head sank forward between them. It seemed to me that for an instant after the shot his eyes were looking at me. Then I couldn't see them any more.

For a long time, an unmeasured sequence of nothingness, I stood there in the room and stared at him. There is no way to explain how I felt, for I don't suppose I felt at all. My only sensation was one of having ceased to live, and a horrible tightness in my throat.

I was aware that Selena was moving past me. She walked to the desk slowly but without uncertainty, and her face was perfectly quiet, the face of an angel who knows neither sorrow nor loss nor death nor anything else that quickens the pulse of living men and women. She placed her hands, palm down, on the surface of the wood and leaned forward a little, looking down at him silently. Then she put her hand, her long hand with the strong white fingers, on his hair, so lightly that she scarcely touched his head. The next instant she was across the room and stooping to pick up the crumpled note in the corner. I watched her take it up and go out of the room. A moment later, I heard the front door open and close again.

Of course, I did all the things that you think of to do. He was dead, but I felt his heart to make sure. He was still warm inside his shirt. Some cheaply melodramatic instinct made me wrap up the gun in my handkerchief; afterwards I was glad I'd done so. I saved a lot of trouble with the sheriff. I carried his body into my own room, and laid it out on my bed; I could not imagine taking it into the room he had shared with Selena. Closing his eyes was the hardest part. Then I went into the living room and built a very big fire and lit all the lamps. The whisky bottle was in the kitchen; I found it easily enough, but I did not drink much. It seemed to stick in my throat. There was nothing else to do till morning; that long and twisted road into Los Palos would be indecipherable in the dark.

As I sat there I began to wonder if Selena was coming back. I kept listening for the sound of her step outside the door. But there was silence except for the strong rush of the wind past the house and the steady crackle of my fire on the hearth.

Nothing that I thought or felt through that long night is of the least consequence. In reality I was simply waiting, in a chaos of loneliness and sorrow and fear, for one of two things: Selena's return or the first light of morning. After a long time the eastern window began to show gray; I went at once to start the car. In the dusk outside, the great loom of the mesa over my head made me shudder in spite of myself. I looked up where I knew the line of steps to be, wondering if she was coming back to the house. But there was no one there.

The car started easily enough, and I got it round to the front door, as close as I could. When I went inside again, I left the engine running. I liked the sound it made. Getting him into the tonneau was horrible enough, but I was past the ability to feel any more. Before I left, I put out the lamps and the fire, and left the door open, in case she came back. Then I blew the horn, over and over again. Its harsh, deep yell went echoing up and down the valley and came back flatly from the face of the mesa behind and above me. She did not come. I put the car in gear and rolled slowly down the road toward the desert and Los Palos, seventy miles away.

The rest of it isn't important, though it was tedious enough, and long before the formalities with the sheriff and the undertaker were over the numbness that had got me as far as Los Palos without agony had worn off. I don't know why they all took my story so readily at its face value, but, of course, there was the gun and the powder burn on his forehead. The sheriff went back with some of his men to try to find Selena, but she wasn't there, and he told me the house was just as I had left it. He managed to make me admit that Jerry hadn't been entirely happy with his wife, and that seemed to satisfy him and the coroner's jury. They let me go quickly, and it was just three days until I caught the morning train out of Los Palos. The only stop I made was at my apartment. I wanted to put Jerry's ashes in the silver urn.

15. EARLY LIGHT

WHEN I had finished speaking I felt tired and empty of all emotion. For better or worse, the story was told. As I looked back over it I wondered whether there was in it anything more than the record of personal obsession, springing out of the shock of finding LeNormand and a subconscious jealousy of Jerry that an analyst might put an ugly name to. The episodes that seemed strange to me might appear natural or coincidental to a calm, clear mind like Dr. Lister's. Nowhere in the course of my narration had I produced any tangible proof of my instinctive belief that Selena was different from all the rest of us, and that in some way not clear to me she was responsible for the deaths of two men.

And yet, sitting there tired and miserable, I had a swift feeling that something was yet to be said or done. It seemed to me there was an immanence in the air and that we were not at the end of the story. I could not guess what the end would be, but I dreaded it.

Dr. Lister did not speak for a long time. His hands were clasped in front of him on the table and he was staring at them as if the shape of his own knuckles was strange to him. Neither of us moved. Above and around us the night was undergoing a change; the great constellation of Orion was low on the western sky and the darkness was turning to a tarnished, misty silver. Again, as on Cloud Mesa, I thought of the eastward spin of the earth, rolling through space. The minute area of its surface which the two of us occupied was being turned toward the sun—the house, the trees, the wide reaches of the Sound, the whole eastern edge of the continent borne along inexorably into the light of a new day. Miles away a train whistled once. A thin, lingering insertion of sound in the silence around us.

He unclasped his hands at last and looked at me thoughtfully. "That is all you have to tell me?"

"Yes."

He put his palms down flat on the table, stood up, and blew out the stump of the candle. "It does not seem to prove anything," he said, and sat down again. "Do you believe there is some connection between all the things you have told me?"

I studied for a minute, trying to find a way to give him the feeling that I had. "Yes, I'm sure there is. I know there is something behind the whole business because I know that Jerry found out what it is. That's why he shot himself."

"And you don't know what this thing is?"

"No," I said slowly, "I don't. Except that it is connected with Selena. Everything goes back to her."

He nodded. "She is a strange person. I grant you that. But except for her character—which I don't wholly understand, I'll admit—I can't see anything definite to give you this impression you seem to have."

"What about LeNormand's death? No one's been able to explain that, but it happened. And what about Galli-Galli and the cards? That seems to me something more than just chance or coincidence. How about the things that happened on that trip to Montauk? And the fire she lighted out at Cloud Mesa. How did she light that?"

Even as I asked the questions I could imagine the answers he would make. LeNormand's death was an unsolved mystery. The police had never been able to find the murderer, but they don't find every murderer anyway. Galli-Galli and his cards was a trick, in a night club where I was none too sober and probably easy to fool. Most mind reading of the sort I'd accused Selena of on the Montauk road was a matter of close observation of the small gestures and expressions of the other person, and Selena was a highly intelligent woman. She had pulled on the brake because some scrap of sound or a flash of sun reflected from the approaching car had warned her.

And as for the fire at Cloud Mesa, she had simply found a match. There was no part of my story which did not have a rational explanation.

"All those things," he said quietly, "are out of the ordinary. But I don't see any mystery in them. I can think of an explanation for every single one. Except LeNormand's death, of course."

"And Jerry's," I said brutally.

"Yes," he replied in a low voice. "That is the hardest of all for me to accept."

"Please, Dad," I said, "before you make up your mind that I'm suffering from some sort of delusion, try thinking about what's happened from the other point of view. If you can show me that there's nothing in it, you'll be doing me a profound service."

"All right," he agreed, and lit a cigarette. He looked across at me with sympathetic toleration. "Let's skip the minor things for the moment. Begin with Jerry and LeNormand."

"There are some common factors there," I said.

"Yes. What are they?"

"The most important of all," I said, "is that there's no explanation in either case. The presence of Selena, and Jerry, and me too, I suppose, in the immediate vicinity both times."

"Anything else?"

"One more thing," I told him. "The equations. LeNormand's equations. They were part of the setting."

"All right," he conceded.

"And there was a fire, both times."

He nodded.

"You can eliminate some of those factors. Jerry had nothing to do with either fire. And I didn't. That leaves Selena. Selena and the equations. Jerry was working on them out at Cloud Mesa. Don't forget that."

He leaned forward. "Go on."

The pieces were slowly fitting themselves together in my mind, but nothing was wholly clear yet, and the picture which was forming was not translatable into ordinary words. "The only other thing I'm sure of," I said lamely, "is that when Jerry realized Selena had managed to light that fire, he thought at once of something else. But I'm not entirely sure what it was, and I can't put it into words."

"Well," he observed after an uncomfortable pause, "most of what you've said tonight has been about Selena. That's true, isn't it?"

"Yes."

"And that means, or suggests, that if you are right the answer must lie in her."

"I know it does." There was no shadow of doubt in my mind on that point. "It's got to. If we knew who she is and where she came from—" I could not complete the sentence.

"Luella Jamison?"

"What do you think?"

He shook his head. "I don't see how she could be. Even if the idiocy were the result of some mechanical factor, and not congenital, it could not have cleared up so fast." Then he looked out over the Sound and said in a low voice, "Though I see what you've had to live with. It's no wonder—" He stopped suddenly.

"It's no wonder I have a fixation about her, you were going to say. If I have one. I'm still not sure. Tell me honestly what you think of Selena. You could look at her without thinking the things that have been tormenting me."

When he finally spoke he chose his words slowly and carefully. "Selena is the most intelligent and the most beautiful woman I've ever met." He paused again, and went on in an altered voice. "I was not entirely happy about Jerry's marrying her. She seemed hard to me, not merely on the surface but all the way through. I kept watching her, hoping to see her tender or openly in love with Jerry, and I never did. She was cold and reasonable; impersonal is perhaps the word, and I never knew whether she was different to Jerry. I worried about it. I didn't believe, till tonight, that she had another side at all."

I was puzzled. What, I wondered, had I told him to make him revise his estimate of Selena? "I still think all that about her," I told him. "She frightens me. She's all mind and no heart. She simply stood there, knowing what he was going to do, while Jerry—"

"Yes," he admitted, "I know everything you can say. But there are two little things. You said she touched his hair after... after..."

"Hell," I said, "she's seen movies and plays. She learned that gesture somewhere, the same way she imitated Grace. And it wasn't much."

"No, not much. But the other thing she couldn't have learned. You told me that the first evening you were out there, she was reading one of Jerry's old books. Do you remember saying that? One of his old books of fairy stories."

He had put his finger on the one thing that seemed really out of keeping with the rest of her. Her other actions and moods—if you could call them that—seemed to me wholly consistent with some rigorous private standard of her own. A standard that came from the mind. But I could not understand why she should be reading Hans Christian Andersen. And as she read, she had been crying, silently, to herself. Why? It was incredible.

"Yes," I admitted, "that was strange. I can't explain that."

"I think I can," he said, and his tone was gentle. "I am glad you told me about it. To me it proves that she was fond of him." My look must have informed him that I didn't understand what he meant, for he smiled and went on in the voice he reserved for his rare personal confidences. "You've never been married, so you may not understand. But to some women—Jerry's mother was one of them—the thought of their husbands as children, as small boys, is extremely touching. I suppose very likely it's the maternal part of their sex instinct dominating all the rest for the time being. That's why Selena was crying when she read Jerry's book, one that belonged to him when he was a boy."

Of course, it was possible. Neither Grace nor any other woman has ever yearned over me as a child or as a husband, so I didn't know. But my immediate feeling was that Dr. Lister was wrong. If Selena was moved to tenderness and even tears by something, I felt sure it was not because she was thinking of Jerry as a boy. There had been an intensity and a bitterness in her face then, as I remembered it, which did not fit in with such a theory.

It was hard to believe, indeed, that anything Selena read would stir her deeply, especially a fairy story. She was not the sort of little girl, I was willing to bet, who cared much for fairy stories, and to suppose that now, when she was so appallingly mature and with a mind like hers, she should deliberately invite tears...No, it didn't fit. She read anything and everything that came under her hand, but none of it affected her. And if this story had moved her, it had done so by sheer chance.

Anyway, what I'd seen on the page to which the book was open hadn't seemed sad. What was it? Something about lanterns being lighted and sailors dancing. I couldn't quite bring it back into my conscious memory.

"I was trying to remember what story she was reading," I told him finally, to explain my silence. "I only looked at the few words I told you about—sailors lighting lanterns on a boat or something."

He nodded. "Yes, that was a favorite of Jerry's when he was eight or so. I used to read it aloud to him while he ate his supper. It's the one called 'The Little Mermaid.'"

I didn't remember it. "Oh," I said vaguely. "Well, I don't suppose it matters."

"'The Little Mermaid,'" he went on, "is the saddest and the best of all Andersen's stories. You must have read it. Don't you remember the little mermaid princess who lived at the bottom of the sea? One day she came up to the top of the water and saw a ship with a prince in it. She saved him from drowning and brought him to land. And she fell in love with him."

It came back to me with a rush. "Yes," I said with a sense of inner excitement that I did not stop to analyze, "that's it. And didn't she go to some witch to be made into a human being?"

"The witch transformed her fish's tail into legs and feet, but whenever she walked she felt as if she were treading on sharp knives. She gave her tongue to the witch, so she could not speak. And she agreed that if she didn't win the prince's love, she had to die without an immortal, human soul." He looked away. "Jerry always used to cry about that part of it."

The rest of the story was flashing through my mind as he spoke. How the little mermaid, after devoting herself to the prince, found that he was going to marry someone else, and how, on his wedding night, she slipped over the rail of the ship on which the wedding party was sailing, and dissolved into the sea foam. I remembered it all, now, and the hot feeling of tears in my eyes when I had first read it. Perhaps it had moved even Selena.

Perhaps. But in the instant when the memory of the story completed itself in my mind, another explanation for Selena's reaction to it occurred to me. She might have cried because the story was moving and beautiful—or because it was true.

It was a fantastic, horrible notion, and I wanted immediately to stop thinking it. I remembered Jerry's face as he looked at Selena there on the settle before the fire she had somehow managed to light. Certainly there had been horror and incredulity in his eyes. It was possible that he had been thinking, then, the same thought that was beginning to crystallize in my own mind. I felt an intense acceleration of every image, feeling, operation of my consciousness. My thoughts were not under my control; they flickered back over the whole of the story I had just told. And nowhere did they find positive proof that the thing which was growing, expanding into unwelcome life in my brain was impossible.

The panic fear that swept over me as I realized that I might have discovered the answer was indescribable. I felt no sense of triumph at having found out the secret of Selena and her life with Jerry and the rest of us. Instead, I was sinking into icy, black water, being suffocated by its pressure, drowning in arctic night and winter. Layer after layer of cold and blackness was piling up above me and the fright of death itself was pounding in my pulse. Fear like that, real fear, is an invasion. A physical thing full of ice and death that enters into every fiber of the body and possesses the mind. The worst of it was that there was no tangible thing with which I could deal. There was nothing to run away from and nothing to confront. This terror sprung from a nebulous idea. A half-perceived theory...

My face must have given Dr. Lister a suggestion of what was in my mind. He was staring at me with alarm. "What's the matter, Bark? What's happened to you?"

His voice came from a distance. I tried to answer, but my lips were stiff. I licked them. "Something just occurred to me. Something that might explain her, or part of her."

"What is it?"

I wanted to tell him, but I knew that he would think I was out of my mind. There was no way of expressing it that would not sound incredible. "I can't put it into words, yet," I said. "But it's about Selena. I don't think she's—well—normal."

Incomprehension was stamped on his face. "I don't see what you mean. Do you think she's insane?"

"No," I said, "not insane. There's nothing wrong with her mind at all."

"What is abnormal about her, then?"

"Her self," I told him, separating the two words deliberately. "There's something entirely different about her. She isn't like most people. She has a better mind and a better body, but the quality I mean hasn't anything to do with comparatives."

"You think she's unique, in some way. Nobody else in the world is like her?"

"Well," I answered, "I don't know about that. Maybe there are others of her kind. If there are, they're cleverer. They don't show it." The thought that I might be right about that made me pause. Even the possibility of encountering again someone like Selena, or of living in a world where another like her existed, was appalling to me. I went on quickly. "Anyway, I hope she's the only one. Can't you see how utterly different Selena is from you and me and Grace and everyone else we know? It's a difference that's much worse than if she'd lost an arm or a leg, or had her face smashed in an accident. Those things are just on the outside. This is something that goes clear through her."

He shook his head. "I haven't the remotest notion what you are trying to say."

"Well," I replied, "I'll have to phrase it differently. Don't you feel that there's a lack in her? Don't you see that she is incomplete, somehow?"

"No. No, I don't believe I do."

"You said yourself that she was cold. I'd put it another way. She hasn't any soul."

He made an impatient gesture with his hand. "This isn't getting us anywhere. Let's stick to facts."

"Facts!" My voice sounded harsh in my ears. "There are all kinds of facts. Do you admit it's a fact that Selena is different from every other person you've ever known?"

"Yes, I'll admit that."

"And what sort of difference is it?"

"No two human personalities are ever identical."

"You're evading the question."

"No," he said. "I'm not evading anything. Selena is not like you or me or anyone else. But the same could be said for you, or for me, or for anybody."

"Good God," I said in desperation, "can't you see that she is more different than anyone you've ever known? Can't you understand that the reason for it isn't the normal variation between one person and the next? She's never been a part of the rest of us. She's been a visitor in every thing and every place I've ever observed her."

"A visitor?"

"Yes," I said, shivering with a cold that did not come from the air around us. "She's never been anything else."

He looked thoughtful. "That is a good description of her attitude . . . I never thought of it in just that way. There is something alien about her, perhaps."

"And another thing. Her mind. You admit that she's intelligent. She's more than that. She's so intelligent that she's either a genius or else—" I did not dare complete the sentence.

He caught me up on it at once. "Or else what, Bark?"

"Or else," I went on, with every word sticking in my throat, "she isn't human at all." He stared at me. "Her mind, I mean. Not her body."

"I don't know that I understand you."

"I don't understand it myself. I don't know what it means, either. But I think that Selena's intelligence isn't human. It isn't akin to anything in the rest of us. Her mind wasn't part of a baby and then of a child and then of a girl. It didn't grow up and go through the experiences that are common to every human life. It wasn't given to her by heredity, the ways yours and mine were given to us, with traits of our parents and maybe our ancestors blended into it. And I don't believe it was shaped by environment, either. According to your own science, Dad, every living minute of every person is recorded on their brains. Each thing that ever happened to you or to me is a part of us, written into some page of our minds. I don't believe the writing on the pages of Selena's mind is in any language you or I know. At least, not till recently. The first entry we could read, I think, would be dated August seventh, two years ago."

"That was when Luella Jamison disappeared in Collegeville?"

"Yes."

He was looking at me as if he couldn't believe that he had understood me at all. "Then your idea is that Selena's mind suddenly began to function on that day?"

"No," I told him. "My idea is that her mind appeared on that date."

His voice was incredulous. "Appeared? Appeared from where?"

The question was one that I had known he would ask. If I knew the answer—and I was afraid to think whether I did or not—I did not want to speak it. There would be finality about uttering it, and I did not want anything final. "I don't know from where. From some other place. That's as near as I can come to it."

"You can't believe that. There's no conceivable... Unless you think she's possessed?"

I nodded. "Yes, something like that."

"Impossible. I'm not even sure there is such a thing as possession. Split personality, perhaps. But Selena isn't a split personality."

There was no argument about that, of course. "No," I assented, "she's all of a piece throughout."

"Well, then," he said, and I could see that he was impatient, "I don't see how you can say—"

I cut into his sentence. "Her mind is all of a piece. It doesn't belong with her body. It's just living in it, if you like to put it that way."

"This is a terrible idea," he said slowly, and shook himself as if to get rid of it. "I don't believe you're right about it. It's not scientific."

I shrugged. What difference did it make whether every truth was a scientific truth?

"What," he went on carefully, "is your theory of the cause or purpose of this . . . this mind visitation in Selena?"

"I'm not sure. But there's the Hans Andersen story to go back to. The little mermaid wanted a soul. I think that's what Selena wants too."

He struck his hand down on the table. "Let's be sensible. I don't like these vague words. Exactly what do you mean by 'soul'?"

"Everybody means the same thing by it," I retorted. "Soul is the part of you that isn't your body and isn't your mind either. It's what ties you together inside. It's the essence of what you are."

He shook his head. "Emotions—which appear to be about what you mean by 'soul'—are effects of certain glandular imbalances arising from sensory stimuli."

"Stop being a doctor, Dad. You know better than that."

"Sorry." He looked at me gently, excusing me because of my fatigue and what I had been through.

"No," I said sharply. "I don't want you making allowances for me. Do you honestly believe that all that scientific rigmarole you just recited really means anything? Does it explain anything to you? What about art and religion and love? What about sorrow, Dad? Are all those things nothing but the product of some glandular imbalances as you put it?"

"I don't know," he said, and his voice was so low I could scarcely hear it.

"Yes, you do. They aren't. They can't be. Ask Selena. She'll tell you they can't."

He answered quietly. "You're not very coherent. Perhaps if you explained this whole idea of yours in simple words, I'd be able to understand it."

I was ashamed of my outburst. "I wasn't attacking you, Dad. But I know I'm right. Let's put it this way: Selena cried when she read the story of the little mermaid. She cried because she saw in it the elements of some experience of her own. She is an alien too. And so that story moved her deeply."

"Naturally," he said thoughtfully, "if you are right, it would do so." He was silent for some time, staring at the tabletop. "I cannot accept your assumption. It is too full of mystery. I have a scientific mind, perhaps. I can't believe that Selena is anything but an extraordinary woman—an adventuress perhaps and possibly a foreigner."

I had expected he would say that. "I hope you're right," I answered. "My theory is—Well, I wish to God I'd never thought of it. But it does explain a lot of things that you can't."

"Go ahead," he said. "It will be better for you to get this off your chest."

"It all begins," I said, "on the evening when Luella Jamison was standing outside the rest room of the Sunoco station in Collegeville with her hands on the lattice. Think of her there. A body with no mind, no intelligence at all. Probably the brain cells were inside her skull all the time, but they weren't connected to anything. Within three or four minutes Luella Jamison vanishes. It took intelligence to do that one thing and do it as fast and efficiently as Luella did it. Ten times more intelligence than Luella ever displayed before. You'll grant that."

"Yes," he said reluctantly, "I'll admit that, I suppose."

"Luella's body suddenly acquired a mind. I don't know yet where it came from, though I have a guess. But anyway, it went straight to one certain place in all Collegeville, like steel to a magnet. It went straight to Walter LeNormand. He must have been in the observatory at the time, getting ready for his night's work. Luella Jamison walked in on him. What happened between them I don't know, but in two days he married her. And Luella Jamison, who did not know her own name, probably, became Selena LeNormand."

"You're theorizing," he interrupted. "How do you know she went to LeNormand?"

"Because there is no other place she could have gone, and no other likely place Selena could have come from. Because Selena has to have an intelligence near her powerful enough, like LeNormand's, to give her some point of contact with human existence. When we met her first, after his death, she was dull and stupid, almost in a trance, till she met Jerry. His mind was the same kind as hers. It made her come to life again. Jerry and LeNormand had the same sort of intelligence. They were mathematicians. For that matter," I added, "there were mathematicians in Luella's own ancestry, if you'll recall."

"Yes. Parsons said that."

All the time I was talking to him, the certainty that I was right kept growing and expanding inside me. With every word I spoke, the truth came to life in my brain like a winter-torpid snake in the spring sun. I no longer fought against the fear of it, because there was no room left in which to fight. Revulsion and terror were in every corner inch of my consciousness. My face must have reflected some of it, for Dr. Lister watched me with concern and a professional suspicion. But I was indifferent to that. All I wanted was to complete the story, as if, by communicating it to him I could siphon off some of the cold dread I was experiencing.

When Luella Jamison walked into Eldridge Observatory, she went there because she knew that LeNormand was there. At least, she knew his intelligence was there. With the force that was in her mind that was a part of her, it would be easy to get him to marry her. Hadn't she made me offer her a cigarette when I knew she never smoked? That was a small thing, but she could have done anything with me, and even with a man like LeNormand. So she lived with him, learning the ways of people, adapting herself to an unfamiliar life, just as the little mermaid lived among mortals when she first came up out of the sea.

"Surely you don't think Selena's mind came out of the ocean?" he asked me when I reached this point in my exposition.

"No," I said. "It wasn't the sea."

So things had gone for several months. And then LeNormand, who must have been living by that time in a strange world of surmise and perhaps of fear, went back to his work, his great paper on space and time, and began to go over his equations. He must have made his final discovery the afternoon of the State football game.

And when he made that last stop which put the whole thing clear before him, a demonstrated truth, he must have sat there thinking about it. Certainly then she knew what he was doing, even though she was not in the room with him. I remembered how she had read my mind so often in the past, in unobtrusive ways that I had overlooked because I did not see their implications. How much more easily could she have known what LeNormand had found, what intense and mathematical symbols were forming in his brain as he worked and thought! She sat there, in his house, and understood what he had found. To her it seemed so clear, so true, so irrefutable, that she decided he had to die.

Dr. Lister cleared his throat. "Why should LeNormand have been a menace to her because he'd made some sort of mathematical discovery?" His tone suggested that the question ought to reveal my own folly to me.

"I can't tell you that. But remember what Jerry said about its importance? 'The biggest thing in the world, by God!' All I can guess is that somehow LeNormand's discovery was connected with Selena."

"His mathematics, you mean?"

"Yes," I answered him slowly, "his proof of what Jerry called the serial nature of time. It had something to do with her."

"But what?" he said impatiently. "Do you think she was jealous of it, or what?"

"No. I think LeNormand believed he'd found a way to test his theory."

"The only way he could do that would be to travel through time, physically, or at least mentally."

"Yes," I admitted.

"But that's absurd."

"Selena didn't think so. She killed him to keep him from trying it."

"This is all mad," he asserted. "Why should she care?"

I looked at him and tried to make him feel the conviction that was in me. "Because she didn't want him to find out where she came from."

"So," he said, and his tone was pure amazement. "You think she—or her mind—came through time."

"Yes."

"From the past or the future?"

"I don't know. Maybe there isn't any difference."

Dr. Lister looked at me with pity openly in his eyes. "This is all delusion, Bark. Your mind is playing tricks on you. There's no sense to this notion of yours, and no evidence for it."

"Yes, there is," I told him. "There's one piece of evidence. That is what she said to Jerry in Bermuda, lying beside him in the moonlight. She said, 'This is what my people do not know.' You see, she was beginning to find out what she had missed with LeNormand. Her mind was learning from her body. It takes mind and body both to make a soul. Living with Jerry taught her something of what it means to be a human being."

"Then why should she have let him kill himself?"

"You must see that now. Jerry never stopped wondering about LeNormand's death. His love for Selena made him all the more anxious to find the solution to it. He believed that those equations were the important clue. He had tremendous mathematical ability, and he studied them until he understood what they meant. After that, when he saw the fire that Selena had lighted, he thought of the fire that killed LeNormand. And then he knew why LeNormand died, and how."

"Selena was responsible for both the fires, then?"

"Yes."

"How did she create them?"

I was very tired, and I could see that he did not believe me. I had not convinced him. The dark thought that obsessed me, the fear that was almost overwhelming me had no existence for him. There was no use going on. "It doesn't matter how she created them. I don't know. You're just asking the question to humor me. I haven't convinced you."

He spread his hands in a gesture of apology. "You're tired to the point of collapse, Bark. People's brains get queer kinks in them when they're as exhausted as you are." He was quiet for a while. "In a way, I wish I could believe you. Any explanation would be better than none at all."

"Not this explanation," I told him. "I've never been so afraid in my life as I am this minute."

He tried to smile. "You'll feel differently after a good sleep. I'll give you something that will relax you."

"I hope so," I replied. "I hope you have the chance to do that."

"Of course, I will."

"Yes," I said, "you will if I'm wrong. But not if I'm right."

"Why not?"

"Think back," I told him. "Remember what happened to the other two people that found out."

"And if you're right, you think the same thing will happen to us?"

I steadied my voice as much as I could. "She will know that we have found out. And she will come here. After all, it's been almost a week since Jerry… She could have been here days ago." The very certainty in my voice alarmed me. "She'll come, all right. Whether she'll kill us or not, I can't tell you."

"No," he said, "you mustn't let thoughts like that get the upper hand. Selena is just a woman. A strange woman. This nightmare you've built up in your mind will pass in a few days. You've had a shock, and you are tired. That's all there is to it. We'll go upstairs now and have some sleep."

"All right," I said. "I don't want to argue with you. I want you to be right. I'll take your sleeping powder, or whatever it is, and wake up sane again. But, first, I'm going to sit here for five or ten minutes. That'll be time enough to demonstrate to me that she isn't coming. It was quick, the two times before."

We sat waiting. The dawn was absolutely still around us. Nothing moved. Dr. Lister looked at my face quietly with his hands folded. I think he was planning the details of his treatment to restore me to myself. I hoped that the first thing he would do would be to exorcise the cold, irrepressible fear that went through me in steady, pulsing waves with every beat of my heart.

The pause seemed never-ending. Gradually I saw resolution begin to shape his mouth. He was on the point of saying something. At that very instant there was a stir at my feet. It was Boojum. He walked out from under the table, stiffly, and turned to look down the terrace toward the corner of the house behind Dr. Lister. He did not growl, nor wag his tail. He simply looked. After a few seconds his ears went up stiffly into two triangles. Both of us were watching him; out of the corner of my eye I saw something like hesitation come into Dr. Lister's face.

There was a sound of footsteps beyond the corner of the building.

The color went out of his face, then, in one swift wash of gray that left him looking old and broken, but not afraid. The lines around his mouth tightened; he lifted his head and half turned in his chair.

She came toward us walking with that same long, swinging stride. Even when I knew, as I did then, that she was not a person, not human, not of my own sort at all, there was something so magnificent about her that no fright or revulsion could cancel the effect of it. The fear inside me was swallowed up by a passive expectation. This was the inevitable end of the story, and whatever was to happen, it was out of my power to influence it in any fashion.

She came to the table and stood beside it, with the tips of her fingers resting on its top, looking down quietly at both of us.

"So," she said, after a while, "you found out." Her eyes rested on me with no expression in them that I could read.

"Yes." My voice sounded perfectly calm.

She gave me a half smile. "You are a strange person, Bark. I should never understand you. I suppose you hate me."

"I am afraid of you," I told her.

"There is no need for that," she said, and her voice was cool and impersonal. "Nothing will happen to you or to Dr. Lister. I do not intend to kill you. What little knowledge you have is of no danger to me. You cannot prove any of it, and the rest of the world will not pay any attention to your story if you tell it."

Her calm, complete assumption of superiority stung me, even in the lethargy of will that possessed my mind. "That isn't what I mean."

She studied me thoughtfully. "You are afraid of me for some other reason, then."

"Yes," I said. "For what you are."

It seemed to me that a look of pain came into her eyes. "Oh. To you that makes a difference. And yet you do not know what you are yourself. You do not know what any other human being is. You know as much about me as about anyone. More, perhaps. We have seen each other often. Once, I even saved your life. But you are afraid of me because I am not like you."

"Yes," I said again. "Go back where you came from." She moved her hand, almost irresolutely, across the top of the table. "That is not so easy... Living here has changed me. Why should you hate me when you do not know, all of you, where you came from yourselves?"

"Leave us," I told her. "Even if you know the answers to all our questions, leave us. You don't belong here."

Her voice was quiet. "I have found that out. I shall go back."

Dr. Lister turned his chair and stared at her. "Before you go," he said, and his voice was hard and bitter, "I want to ask you something."

She lifted her hand in assent.

The expression on his face as he spoke was a mingling of loathing and incomprehension. "You seem to know what Bark has said about you. Is he right?"

She met his look squarely, and in the way she stood and answered it in silence for a moment I could feel the power of her anger. "Did you suppose," she said finally, "that you were alone in the enormous spaces of the universe? Do you believe that you are the ultimate product of creation? There is nothing unique about you." Her tone was so level, so coldly insistent that even Dr. Lister averted his head and seemed to shrink in upon himself. "Is there any reason why I must leave you alone? You do not own me and you have no power over me. Why," she said, and there was an edge of bitter amusement in her tone, "when the earth has traveled around the sun a few more times, you will be dead."

He lifted his head and there was defiance on his face. "Yes," he said, "and you do not seem much concerned with death. You have lived here two years and in that time you have brought about the deaths of two men. You talk as if that were nothing."

She dropped her eyes. "I know how important that seems to you. Believe me, I did not mean to kill either of them."

Dr. Lister said coldly, "I don't believe you."

"Walter LeNormand's death was sheer accident. I had no intention of killing him. I wanted nothing but to stop him from thinking, prevent him from going on with his work. I knew what he had discovered, what more he would find if he went on thinking. I was determined to stop him. There aren't any words to tell you what I did; there is a way of using the force of the mind, and I used it. I turned it on him, I willed him to stop thinking, to lose consciousness. My plan was to go, then, to the observatory, and destroy his work. But I forgot one thing."

"What was that?" said Dr. Lister, as if he were humoring her.

"The football game. Thousands of people sitting at it, excited, emotional, pouring out a force a thousand times more powerful than a bolt of lightning. It was that force that killed him. It magnified, if you like, the force of the impulses I was sending until they were so powerful they consumed him."

"I see." There was nothing in his voice to give me a hint of what was in his mind, but when he spoke next there was a level deadliness in his tone that I had never heard in it before. "You also killed my son," he said.

She turned toward him so that I could no longer see her face. "Jerry," she said, as though the sound of his name hurt her intolerably, "yes. Jerry had to die too, and because of me. But what else could have happened? He realized the truth. Do you think he could have lived with it?" There was no answer, and she turned to me. "Do you, Bark?"

"No," I said.

She turned back to Dr. Lister. "Bark's answer is the only one. I tried to stop him. I didn't want him to find out. But he did. And he was too intelligent for the rest of you. In time he would have found a way to make people listen to him. I could not let that happen."

He dropped his eyes from her face and looked at the table. "Damn you," he said.

"Before I go," she went on without paying any attention to his words, "I want to tell you one thing more. If I could stay, if there were anything here left to stay for, I should do so." She turned and looked full at me. "The little mermaid had to go too, because there was no longer any possibility of love." I saw that there were tears in her eyes. "Good-by, Bark. I loved your friend." Turning to Dr. Lister, she half lifted her hand as if to touch him, in the same gesture I remembered from Cloud Mesa, and then withdrew it. "And I loved your son," she said. "Remember that."

With a single quick motion she stripped her finger of the two rings, the one with the great square emerald in it, and the narrow band of gold with which Jerry had married her, and put them on the table between us. They lay there, bright and beautiful, on the painted iron, and we looked at them. I did not see her go, but the sound of her feet died along the terrace and around the corner of the house.

When I picked up the emerald ring, it was still warm from her finger.

"Whoever she is," said Dr. Lister after a long time, "she knows how to make an exit." He said nothing more for a full minute. "There is no proof. It is all fantastic. She talked like a madwoman, and yet... The only real fact is that Jerry is dead."

He stood up, and we went into the house together.

There are two things to add to this story.

When the place at Cloud Mesa was closed and its contents shipped east to us, I went through Jerry's papers with care. The notebooks for his thesis alone were missing. What became of them I have never found out, but the inference is obvious.

Luella Jamison has been found. I heard about that from Parsons. It appears that her father, getting up early one morning to go to town, found her standing at the front gate. She was holding on to the pickets of the fence beside it. He led her into the house and she slipped at once into the routine by which she had always lived. According to Parsons, the Jamisons are happy because she is home again.

THE EDGE OF RUNNING WATER

1.

THE MAN for whom this story is told may or may not be alive. If he is, I do not know his name, where he lives, or anything at all about him, except that there is something which it is vital for me to tell him. It is a strange, clumsy method of communication, this expedient of writing an entire book without even the certainty that it will come into his hands, and yet I can see no other way of warning him. There is, I think, a good chance that it will succeed. Someday, perhaps in a bookstore, perhaps in a library, he may come on a copy of this narrative. Or someone he knows will innocently mention it in his hearing, and he will be impelled to seek the book out and read it. People somehow manage to learn of the things that are supremely important to their lives or their work. What troubles me is not so much the possibility that he will never come on this message as that it may already be too late.

A great deal of what happened to Julian Blair, Mrs. Walters, Anne, and the rest of us there in the house on Setauket Point is purely personal. I suspect that the man whose attention I must catch will be impatient with all that; he will wonder why I have wasted so much of his time with irrelevancies of thought and feeling. Julian himself would disapprove of my presenting the facts in the form of a narrative. And yet, that is the only way I can see to bring home the actual meaning of his project, the significance it will hold for living men and women and the human effect it must inevitably have.

It would be comfortable to believe that there is no danger. That Julian's research was an isolated, aberrant thing that could not conceivably be repeated. But that is not the history of discovery. It is a curious fact that men who know nothing of each other tend to work in the same direction at the same time. Darwin and Wallace, Mendel and de Vries. Blair and . . . ? It is that unknown name that I have got somehow to reach.

If this man for whom I am writing exists, if he has already begun to ravel out the same thread that Julian Blair followed—I think to the very end—the chances are that no one else will know what he is doing. He will go quietly about his business, taking nobody into his confidence until his apparatus is complete. At least that is the way Julian did it. Then, unless what I have to say here deters him, he will test the thing he has created. The moment he does so he will learn something that even I do not know. He will find out where Julian Blair is now.

That question must never be answered. A year ago it would have seemed to me ridiculous to assume that there are some facts it is better not to know, and even today I do not believe in the bliss of ignorance or the folly of knowledge. But this one thing is best left untouched. It rips the fabric of human existence from throat to hem and leaves us naked to a wind as cold as the space between the stars.

The fringe of that cold touched me once. I know what I am talking about.

2.

THE PORTER woke me at six that morning. My mind came back from wherever it goes during sleep and reluctantly took up the business of apprehending the outside world. It began to listen to the roaring clamor of wheels on rails and observe through a gray-green Pullman twilight the steel curve of the car roof, close over my head. But beyond being aware of these things I had no part in them. As always when I wake, this was that interval of physical paralysis when bodily motion is out of the question, and this time it was evidently going to be harder than usual to emerge from it. The muscles of my legs and back were stiff from offsetting the irregular lurching drive of the train's northward flight. Consciousness and body lay together in my berth, not yet articulated with each other and accepting their particular discomforts passively. Then they flowed together in one sharp synthesis and I remembered who and where I was.

There is something stupefying about the noise and motion of a running train; I felt drugged, reluctant to face the prospect of a new day, and more tired than when I had finally managed to fall asleep in the small hours of the night before. But the porter's hand was thumping insistently against the green curtain:

"Barsham Harbor in twenty minutes, boss. Better be gettin' up."

"All right. Thanks." My whisper must have suggested how thankful I was because he chuckled as he moved away down the aisle.

I began to wrestle my way into my clothes. The process of getting dressed in an upper berth is degrading, especially for a man of my height. It took me so long that by the time I got to the washroom there was no time to shave. The place smelled stalely of last night's cigars and the water was lukewarm. I cursed myself, the hour, the railroad company, and everything else I could think of, including the necessity for hurry. The whole trip was probably unnecessary anyway. Even before the last strap on my bag was tugged and buckled the brakes were beginning to grind heavily under the floor.

The sleep I hadn't had was heavy behind my eyes and there was a flat taste in my mouth. I stumbled down the Pullman steps and onto the rickety boards of the station platform at Barsham Harbor completely unprepared for the impact of a Maine morning in September. Its sharp brightness struck me like a physical blow and suddenly I was wide-awake.

The sun must have been up for a good hour before I landed on that platform, but a night coldness was still in the air. I shivered as I drew in my first breaths of it. Behind me in the sleeping car *Western Lake* the atmosphere was part of the New York I had left seven hours ago. It had been warm, heavy with the exhalations of people and machinery. This stuff I was taking into my lungs now was different—thin, cold, and reporting the open sweep of fields, hills, and the river. I felt bewildered and out of place. This entry into an unfamiliar air and landscape was too abrupt.

The porter took my tip with a sleepy mumble of acknowledgment and slung his metal stepping stool back into the car. When he heaved himself up after it, there was a sudden wrench in my mind as if I were losing a friend. He was my last contact with the familiar things I had abandoned to come up to this Godforsaken place and I didn't want him to leave me behind. For one instant I had an impulse to toss my bag up into the vestibule after him, swing aboard, and go on with the train. It would be returning to New York that night, I thought, and I wanted to be on it when it did. The prompting not to be left was so strong that I stooped and actually caught hold of the suitcase handle.

Given two more seconds of grace, I might really have got back aboard. I don't know. It was a strong impulse, and as I think over the steps by which I became involved in the mystery and the disappearance of Julian Blair it is easy to believe that there was something prophetic about it. There's no great difficulty about being wise after the event. Anyhow, as I lifted the bag the train hissed, clanked, and began to move. The opportunity was gone.

Not that I knew it was an opportunity. At the moment I was surprised at myself. A psychologist, particularly one with enough confidence in his science to spend his life teaching its rudiments to the youth and flower of a reputable university, had no business giving in to such infantile whimsies as that half effort of mine to return to the train. So I reminded myself, but instead of turning away at once I stood there with my bag in my hand, watching the steel walls of the Pullmans moving past my eyes in a crescendo of speed and irrevocability. One part of my mind, the professional part, informed me that I was acting like a fool. But there was a less articulate something that reproached me for not being on it. "Why?" I demanded impatiently, but there was no answer. Not then, at any rate.

With a dwindling roar the train shrank down the track and I turned to confront Barsham Harbor and whatever the day was to produce. The most immediate fact was that Julian had not come to the station to meet me. Of course I knew him too well to suppose it would even occur to him to come, but when I saw he wasn't on hand I damned him under my breath all the same. Anne was not there either, and I discovered that I was disappointed about that. Five years ago she would have insisted on welcoming me, would, as a matter of fact, have driven the car down herself and let the policemen who didn't approve of fifteen-year-old girls driving lump it. No doubt she had changed. She was twenty now, of course, and even at twenty most women have developed a reluctance to getting up with the sun. For that matter, I admitted to myself, so have most men.

None of which went far toward deciding what I was supposed to do next. Hire a car, presumably, and go on out to the house, wherever it was. On that point Julian's letter, to my city mind, had not seemed very helpful. I hauled it out of my pocket and looked at it again to make sure.

Barsham Harbor, Me.
September second.

Dear Richard:

I have been extremely busy since we saw each other last. My work has now reached the point where I am in need of your friendly advice and counsel. The problem is one on which I should be willing to consult only such an old friend as yourself. If you possibly can, please come up for a few days before the academic year begins. I beg you not to fail me, if only for the sake of auld lang syne. Anne is with me, of course, and anxious to see "Uncle Dick" again. Come as soon as you can, the sooner the better. I think I can promise you that this is profoundly important.

Sincerely,
Julian Blair

Characteristically, there was a postscript added with a blunt pencil at the end:

P.S. We are living in a house they call the Talcott place. I had much rather you regarded this address and letter as confidential.

Looking it over, I had to smile. That phrase "since we saw each other last" covered a matter of well over four years. But time never meant much to Julian. It had come as a shock, even to me, to realize just how long it had been since we had forgathered, and when his letter reached me I had, in a burst of self-reproach, canceled a number of engagements and caught the first train. Apparently my wire asking him to meet me at the station had failed to penetrate his usual absentminded absorption.

Two nondescript sedans were parked along the far edge of the platform, and a faded sticker on the windshield of the one on the left said "Taxi." The driver was sitting behind his wheel staring at the station and paying no attention to me in spite of the fact that I was the only passenger on the train who had been fool enough to get off at Barsham Harbor. The man's indifference puzzled me. Without being insulting, there was something contemptuous about it. I didn't want to lug my suitcase across the platform and ask him if he would be so kind as to drive me away in his car, and yet that was just about what I should have to do if I didn't want to spend the morning standing right where I was. In New York, the cab drivers are actually eager to have you ride in their hacks, but not this man.

Before I approached him, I took a minute to survey the town, this place to which Julian Blair had seen fit to come for some obscure reason of his own. My heart sank as I stared toward it. There was something malapropos about the idea of Julian's living in this village. It didn't even look as if the local power plant would be able to supply enough electricity for his ordinary laboratory requirements, assuming that he had built a laboratory. He certainly wouldn't find one ready-made in this fly-in-amber of a colonial town. The thought of a great electrophysicist in a place that looked as if it must still be using whale-oil lamps was incongruous. An uneasiness crept into my mind. Quaint, even beautiful as this town was, it was no place for Julian Blair unless . . . I disliked putting the thought clearly, even to myself, but what it amounted to was, unless he wanted to be secret, unless what he was doing was something as unbalanced and pitiful as the obsession that had led to his leaving the university almost five years ago.

Barsham Harbor is built on the rising land along the right bank of the Kennebec. Its main street runs diagonally away from the station, where I was standing, toward the water, and it is no level city avenue but a dirt-surfaced town road that dips and rises to the modeling of the land itself. The huge old trees on each side of the way were solid fountains of green that morning, jetting superbly up against a thin blue sky. Between their boles I could see the white fronts of the houses, square, solid, three stories high. Most of them seemed to have porticoed fronts that expressed inescapably what the people who originally built these houses had thought of themselves. Above the trees one sudden, narrow spire leaped up into the morning sun and glittered like hammered metal.

Beyond the trees and the houses I saw that the road dipped again, and the distant buildings there looked gray and weathered. Stores, probably. In the notch between the last of them was a fleck of blue water, like a tile in a mosaic, and past that again a distant row of hills on the other side of the valley, checkered minutely with farms and wood lots. The whole air of the landscape was glowing with the early sun and the reflected light from the broad surface of the Kennebec.

Yes, impossible as it would be for me to return to it, there is no denying the fact that Barsham Harbor is beautiful. A hundred years and more ago, when it was alive, when it had some meaning and significance of its own, it must have been comparable to any town of its size in the world. Those were the days when Kennebec men were building and sailing the fast ships that had gone down this river before me and away to the four corners of the world. In the sweltering ports of Bombay, Madras, and Calcutta they had sold their cargoes and even their ballast—great chunks of ice sawed in blocks from the frozen river itself and worth a fortune in the heat of the tropics. They had come home again with gold clinking in their strongboxes and their holds full of rum, silks, spices, tea—all the wealth of Ormus and of Ind for Yankee merchants in Boston, Portland, and Bath. Their captains and owners had built those pillared houses in the days when Barsham Harbor was closer to India than to Illinois.

On that bright morning their town was as clear and unchanging as the profile on a Roman cameo. Dead for a century though it had been, its aspect was still beautiful and proud. In all the future decades and centuries through which the town might manage to preserve its shell, I could not imagine that anything of importance would ever happen here again. As I looked at those white houses they seemed as truly mausoleums as if they had stood in a cemetery. The past was buried in them, not to stir again until the day of resurrection. Barsham Harbor was through with life and with the only phase of time which matters to living beings—the duration of change.

I was wrong about that. One thing more was to happen in Barsham Harbor, a thing both violent and terrible, which its citizens have surely not understood to this day. It is incredible that with even an inkling of the truth behind the events to which they were all witnesses, those people could go on living in their village; it is hard enough even for me to sleep without dreaming of it. How can they look down their own streets and across the river to the point where Julian's house once stood without feeling the hairs lift on the backs of their necks?

I wonder that they can walk the streets of their town and not know that every shadow is haunted. There must be something that is more than night darkness in their lanes after the sun has set. What do they think when they turn their eyes toward Setauket Point, black against the water? Even in the calmest weather the villagers along the lower Mississippi look now and again toward the levee that rises above their roofs. Where the river in flood has once broken through there can be no absolute security and peace again.

Hysterical words. Perhaps I don't mean them too literally. After all, no further danger exists for those townsmen. Lightning does not strike twice in the same place, and if the thing I mean continues to exist at all it does so only in the brain of some man who, like Julian Blair, sets out to travel one certain, dreadful roadway of the mind. It is the people around that man who are in danger without knowing it, not the folk of Barsham Harbor. They are as safe as any of the rest of us. Cut as they are from the remnants of a greater cloth than they can weave for themselves, they are unlikely to produce a man or woman who will duplicate Julian's experiment. Even while he was there among them they did not know what he was about, really. They simply resented him with the blindly obstinate dislike of the countryman for the "foreigner." Now that he is never coming back, they will have forgotten him in a year or two more.

3.

FOR THE second time I stooped to the handle of my suitcase. However unlikely Barsham Harbor might look, it was Julian's address and my destination. I was impatient to finish my journey. Also, there was a hollow under my belt where no breakfast rested as yet and I wanted to fill that. I crossed the platform and halted beside the sedan.

"Good morning," I said. No reply; the driver went on looking into space. "Is this a taxicab?"

He turned his head deliberately, then, and looked me over from head to foot without speaking. There was no expression on his narrow face or around the pale flatness of his eyes. When his inspection was completed he nodded once and said, "Ayuh."

The man was disconcerting and, when I spoke again, it annoyed me to hear that my tone sounded apologetic. "I was expecting a friend to meet me, but he doesn't seem to have showed up. I suppose I better go out to his place. It's Mr. Blair. He lives in the old Talcott house."

Something happened behind the flat eyes that were watching me, but I couldn't tell what it was. After a minute he looked away and said indifferently, "Reckon I know where it is." He thrust back a thin, brown arm and opened the tonneau door beside me. I slung in my bag and started to follow it. "It'll be a dollar," he said.

"That's all right. Do you want me to pay you now?"

"Please yerself."

I took a bill out of my pocket at once. Something in his manner made me want to put him in my debt. "Here," I told him, "and if you're not sure about the place, we can ask in town."

He was putting the bill into a battered wallet with meticulous care and thoroughness. "I said I knew where it was." After buttoning his wallet into a hip pocket he added, "Don't have much occasion to go out that way lately."

"I suppose not," I said. "To tell you the truth I didn't expect to find anyone who would know the way so easily. Mr. Blair's letter wasn't very clear on directions. I wasn't sure anybody would know where he lived."

He smiled temporarily, and his teeth were the yellow-brown of a tobacco chewer's. Later I understood that smile. It was for my city man's assumption that anyone could live in Barsham Harbor for more than a few days without being known to every living inhabitant. When he was through being amused, the same indifference, tinged with something stronger this time, returned to his manner. "Ever'body round here knows the Talcott place," he remarked briefly and swung the car down the station drive.

I settled back in my seat with a grunt. "Oh," I remembered suddenly, "I haven't had any breakfast yet. Is there a place in town where I can get something?"

"Ee-lite'll be open, I reckon," he said and cut the car into the street. We went unhurriedly down along its rolling length with the high white houses on either side of us. Most of their windows were still shuttered but the chimneys were smoking. Except for that there was scarcely an indication of life. Our car was the only moving object in sight; everything else seemed transfixed by the brightness of the morning.

The driver cleared his throat. "That'll be extra," he observed.

I reassured him. "All right, but I won't keep you waiting long. How much of a trip out there is it, anyway?" For all I knew the house might be right in the town. If it was then his charge of a dollar was robbery. When he said, "'Bout six miles," I felt better.

The four business blocks, when we reached them, were a seedy contrast to the stately places we had been passing. Most of the stores were cheaply constructed frame buildings in need of paint, and their show windows were not quite clean. The merchandise behind them looked as if it had been there a long time. More than anything else, this part of the town was without any character of its own. It might as well have been a piece of Gary, Indiana, or Gallup, New Mexico. The Elite Lunch turned out to be an epitome of the meager standardization of the rest. Its nickel coffee urn was not tarnished, but neither was it bright. The stools along the counter were upholstered in a sleazy, imitation red leather, and there was a perceptible film of grease on the surface of the white table where I ate my breakfast.

That meal was far from elite. The coffee was hot enough, but thin and bitter, the egg hinted at cold storage, and the toast was abominable. But I downed all three and the emptiness under my belt disappeared. Some of the uncomfortableness with which the day had begun faded from my mind, but not all of it. The more I saw of the town the less I could understand Julian's being here. It had gone to seed too obviously. The street beyond my window was rutted and lined on its opposite side with haggard ice houses and frowsy garages. There was litter around them all. The clean sweep of the river, which I could glimpse between them, was a pleasant contrast.

It was inconceivable that there was a decent laboratory within a hundred miles of this place. It takes apparatus and a complex set of facilities to work in the field of electrophysics today, and usually a staff of research assistants. Surely Julian didn't have money enough to build and equip a complete place of his own? Even if he had, why locate it here? What had his letter meant by "advice"? The only advice that occurred to me then was to tell him to get out of this place and back into the world where he belonged.

There was just one answer. He was still living in that tragic dream, born of despair and grief, that had taken possession of him the day of Helen's funeral. He had come here to work on it in secret because there was enough of the old Julian left, somewhere, to realize what his colleagues would think of him if they got wind of it. He had not been able to reconcile himself to the fact of her death and now, after years of inevitably wasted time and effort, he wanted help of some sort from me. How could I help him? What I suspected him of needing was a psychiatrist, not a psychologist.

None of us at the university had heard from Julian for so long that if we had not forgotten him, we had pretty well stopped talking about him. The offer of his old chair in the physics department was still open, of course, and Arthur Wallace and I had occasionally talked over ways and means of persuading him to come back to it, until one day we realized that we no longer even knew where he was. That had been Julian's fault, too, for he had never answered our letters. For a time I had felt that I ought to keep in touch with him merely in order to be sure that Anne was all right. But after her note telling me that she was going abroad to study, even that motive disappeared. The memory of Julian had retreated into the background of my mind.

In saying that I seldom thought of him I don't mean to imply that I had forgotten him. There were too many ties between us for that. The earliest went back to the years when I had been struggling to earn my way through college, tending lawns, firing furnaces, even washing dishes for the education that I was so determined to get. Julian had somehow picked me from his entire sophomore physics course for special attention and, when he found out my circumstances, he made me give up all my outside jobs and work for him as a laboratory assistant. He did it without sentiment, merely as though he were arranging the apparatus for an experiment, but I think he saw something in me that pleased him. Our relationship was a curious one—utterly impersonal and yet intensely close by the very nature of the work together. He had a driving scientific passion for discovery and the apprehension of truth that stimulated me. I learned from him then that the universe was larger than man. I came, in time, to be fond of him, as well as grateful.

There was that past between us, and another. About it I shall have more to say later, but the fact that we had both loved the same woman kept us together even when I had gone into a different field of work and begun to teach. I thought of Helen often enough, and that meant thinking of Julian, too, at least indirectly. He and I had shared work, love, and grief in a curious pattern. I found myself half afraid to see him; the things that we had in common were strong and deep, and I did not know what they would do to me if they were to rise up again after the truce of years.

Well, there was no use speculating or opening up old unhappinesses. I paid for my breakfast and went out to the car. As I came through the door I saw that my driver was still sitting behind the wheel. Beside the car, with one foot on the running board, was a thin, sharp-faced man in blue jeans and a white shirt open at the neck. My driver and this fellow were two of a kind, I thought, a kind that I did not understand and felt ill at ease about, without knowing exactly why. When I came out of the Elite Lunch neither of them was talking, but I had a suspicion that they had been, a moment before, and about me.

Why it should be so disquieting to think that strangers have been discussing you I don't exactly know, but it is. I crossed the sidewalk swiftly and got into the back of the car again. The stranger, with one foot on the running board, bent his body just enough to let me get in without my having actually to shoulder him out of the way.

"All set," I informed the driver.

The thin man nodded to him and moved off down the street without a word. His gait was loose and bent-kneed. The way a man places his feet reveals whether he is accustomed to pavements or the ridges and furrows of ploughed fields.

At the end of the street we swung left and began to go north along a tree-lined road that followed the level of the river and sometimes ran along the very edge of the water. Within five minutes the houses of the town were behind us. In another five the farms at our left had given way to marshy pasture land. All at once we left this river road, angled abruptly right, and rattled across an unrailed wooden bridge spanning a sluggish creek. The Kennebec appeared to have swung to the east of us and I realized that for the last mile or two we had been skirting a bay in the lee of a promontory. Our new road bent constantly further to the right until I saw that we were running almost due south.

"This here's the Point," my driver remarked.

"I see," I replied, wondering why he had suddenly decided to volunteer something for nothing.

"Talcott place's down at the end."

It was a lonely spot, I thought, about as far out of the world as you could get without going into a wilderness. "I imagined Mr. Blair would be closer to town, somehow," I observed.

"Tain't more'n a mile by water. You can see it right across from you at the end of River Street."

"What is the place," I asked, "a farm?"

"Used to be." His tone was uninflected, but I got the impression that he thought it ought to be one still.

"Mr. Blair isn't a farmer, exactly."

"No?" He drove on for some time without adding to his question. The car, I noticed, was going slower and, even though the road was rough, I had an idea he wanted an opportunity to talk further. "Folks around here don't exactly know what he is, anyhow," he said finally.

"He's an electrophysicist," I remarked, hoping he wouldn't know what the term meant.

"Do tell." His tone gave me no indication whether he did or did not know what an electrophysicist was. "Reckon you're right at that. Last summer, when he come here, he had the house wired fer e-lectricity. Edison people had to run poles in the better part of two miles."

"Is that so?" I responded, but the information made me feel lighter at heart. Perhaps Julian was really working at something important, then. Anyhow, the fact that he had brought current in to this remote house of his was a hopeful sign.

The driver apparently thought the whole thing was a piece of folly. "Ayuh," he went on, and there was satisfaction in his voice, "he did, and it cost him suthin' I reckon."

"It must have."

There was another pause while we jolted along a road that became progressively worse. Then he cleared his throat again. "Who's she? His wife?"

"No," I said. "I expect you mean his sister-in-law." Some impulse made me add, "His wife's dead."

"Hunh." The sound might have meant anything. Then he declared, "I thought that was the girl."

"Yes," I said. "She must be about twenty by this time."

He shook his head. "I don't mean her. The other one."

"What other one?"

"That woman." His tone implied that he had said all he intended to.

"I didn't know there was anyone else living with him." For a time I said nothing, and then my curiosity got the better of me. "What does she look like?"

"She ain't so much," he declared dispassionately. "Mebbe she's another of them electros."

I started to grin at that, but something stopped me. My eye caught the rearview mirror immediately over the driver's head. In it I could see his pale eyes, watching me intently; the glass was set at the exact angle to reveal everything in the back seat. The sight of those two cold eyes turned back upon me, appraising my least gesture, suddenly gave me pause. What business of his was it how I looked or what went on in this back seat? Did he retail the things he saw in that mirror to the whole town? Probably. This was not the city, I reminded myself.

In the next breath it occurred to me that this man was more than a simple countryman. He had a quality that made me realize suddenly how much of my life had been passed in universities, where people deal with each other according to special standards and codes, and where they conduct their lives with reference to reason and logic. Those eyes were not logical or reasonable. There was intelligence behind them—plenty of it, perhaps—but not the kind of intelligence to which I was accustomed. They had, too, their own kind of curiosity, a private brand which searched for the weakness in you and found satisfaction in it.

When my glance caught his eyes in the mirror I stared steadily into them until he dropped them again to the road. I had a feeling that the man was smiling faintly. At least, the skin at the outer corners of his eyelids had been creased into wrinkles that suggested amusement. Evidently he was not abashed at being detected in his scrutiny of myself.

Our road was running almost due south still, and somewhat to the right of the middle of the promontory between the bay and the river. Toward the bay side the land was low, but on our left it pitched up toward the river so that the actual surface of the water on that side was out of sight. The fields we passed were mostly overgrown with harsh clumps of goldenrod, patches of scrub cedar, and the spindling stems of young tamaracks.

There was something forlorn about the Point even in the brilliance of early morning. The occasional patches of potatoes, squash, or pumpkins only emphasized the idleness of most of the fields. These scrub trees and bushes were the outposts of the wilderness, and I had the sharp feeling that winter and the wilderness were the true season and mode of this land, that man was already in retreat before them. The road, too, was viciously potholed. Whenever a wheel dropped into one of those pits that pocked its surface the whole frame of the car was wrenched.

The only other thing worth remarking was a row of raw, yellow poles running along beside us with a single strand of wire looping between them. The power line to Julian's house, I thought. The cable looked thick.

We passed at least one farm shortly before we came to the end of that road. Perhaps there were more. Some things about the geography of Setauket Point will never leave my mind, but there are others about which I am not so clear. But however many places there were, Julian's was the last, clear at the end of the Point. I was so busy looking out at the unfamiliar landscape that we had jolted to a halt before I saw the place, dead ahead of us.

"Here y'are," the driver said. And then, "Fifty cents additional. Fer the wait."

I paid him because it was simpler than to haggle, though I suspected he was secretly despising me for not protesting. He took the money with a yellow grin and put it in his pocket.

"Oh, say," he added. "I got a telegram fer Blair. Come in yestiddy evenin', but my cousin, he just couldn't git round to deliverin' it. Asked me to take it out this mornin'." He handed me the envelope, watching me intently as I took it.

"So," I said. "I know what this is. It's my wire telling them I was coming. No wonder you were at the station. And maybe, no wonder the wire didn't get delivered."

"Asa's been porely this week. He couldn't make it. You didn't git stuck at the station now, did you?" His tone was amused.

I put the envelope in my pocket. "I believe I'll report this," I said, and dragged my suitcase out of the back of the car.

"Folks round here are satisfied with Asa," he observed, still grinning. "I reckon he won't lose his job, exactly, mister."

I said nothing for a minute, though there were plenty of words on the lips of my mind. Then I gave him a steady smile. "That'll be all. You can go back now and tell them how I looked and what I said and how you and Asa worked it so you got a call clear out here."

He met my smile with one of his own; it was plain that he was enjoying this situation. "We ain't so int'rested as all that in city people," he observed. "I wouldn't mind a particle if I never seen another."

"That mirror of yours tells a different story."

The shot told. He pulled the car into gear. "Just got shooken out of true on these roads," he said, but he did not look at me. "Wal, if you need a cab any time, the number's 517-J. Marcys have a 'phone down the road a piece. First place on yer right." He cut the wheel hard over, released the clutch so that the car spurted suddenly away from me, and was gone down the road.

The house which I found myself confronting was old and of a sort with which I was not familiar. I was surprised to see how large and high it stood. What appeared to be the main portion was a square, two-story clapboard building facing south. From the north wall a single-story ell extended perhaps thirty feet and linked the house proper to a barn considerably larger even than the residence part. The whole was made out of wood which the years had turned to a silver gray. The color would have delighted the eye of an artist; it was almost like that of old silver. The house was—had been—handsome, but to me it looked shabby and forsaken. Smoke was coming out of the chimney, but otherwise it looked abandoned; I could not even see curtains behind any of the windows.

In the corner of the ell, where it joined the house, was a door, but that was shut. I wondered whether I should go in there. It looked so unlike a front door that finally I carried my bag around to the south side. There was a fanlighted door there, in the middle of the wall, but it too was shut, and nothing ran to it except a beaten track through the tall weeds which skirted the baseboards of the house. Impatient with my own indecision, I finally walked along this path, my bag bumping my leg at every step, and went up three moldering wooden steps. There was no doorbell. I knocked once or twice. No answer, but when I put my hand on the knob it turned stiffly, and I walked in.

4.

INSIDE the door I found myself in a rather large hall and confronting a staircase which ran steeply up through a low ceiling. The light in the hall was dim, but I could see that the woodwork had once been very fine, the balusters beautifully turned, and the ceiling molding ornamented with dentils that looked hand cut. I put my bag down and said, "Hello, Julian," into the shadows, aware as I spoke that my voice was almost too low to hear. There was no answer to it, anyhow, and rather than call again I tried a door to my left. This room was even dimmer than the hall; the shutters were closed and at first glance I thought the place was furnished. Then I realized that here was nothing but a sort of lumber room, stocked with a broken chair, heaps of excelsior, several packing cases with their sides or tops wrenched open, and a miscellaneous litter of trash.

This, I thought with some surprise, must be one of the best rooms in the house, and yet here it was full of old junk that belonged in the barn. Julian had never cared much for the niceties of housekeeping, and I would not have been surprised by mere untidiness, but it was somehow disturbing to find a room that must have been intended as a sitting room or parlor full of nothing but discarded boxes and packing materials. I went back to the hall with a feeling of discomfort in my mind.

The door to the right of the stairs opened on a room equally dim, but I saw at once that it must be where Julian lived when he was not working. In the mood that had begun to come over me, it was actually pleasant to discover that the house was really inhabited; there had been an uncomfortable emptiness in the hall. I looked round with interest. It was a long room but wide enough to seem well-proportioned except for the ceiling, which was only some seven feet high, or perhaps a few inches more. There were three windows in the wall facing me, and two more in the wall on my right, but all of them were shuttered. Suddenly I found myself oppressed by the dimnesses of this house, the way it was closed in upon itself, and I did something which under more conventional circumstances I should not have dreamed of. I went over to the nearest window, opened it, and threw back the shutters.

Light streamed in with the intensity of a magnesium flare. The river was acting like a great reflecting mirror; it hurled the morning sun through the breach I had made in the house's defenses. The room leaped into view with a sudden sharpness that was cruel. The shabby furniture, the faded pattern of the wallpaper, the threadbare patches in the dull rug were exposed with bitter emphasis.

My first impression was that the place was dowdy beyond belief, and ill-cared for. Not that I have the tender sensibilities of an interior decorator, but I don't like living in disorder, and this room was untidy in an unpleasant way. The fireplace at the far end was empty but it was littered with odds and ends of refuse. There was a vase of flowers on the mantel, still fresh and glowing with color, but they served only to underline the drab dullness of walls, chairs, and woodwork. Three or four books were lying on the floor in front of the sofa, one of them open and face down on the faded rug. Magazines and periodicals were heaped in unstable piles on the table. What few pieces of furniture there were looked as if they had been stationed around the room without regard to proportion or comfort. I noticed that the lamp on a table between two of the windows was greasy with kerosene and had a sooted chimney.

Then I saw beneath the superficial appearances of the room. Whoever had built the place—presumably the Talcotts—had known how to take advantage of a lordly site. As I went from window to window, throwing open the shutters, the whole sweep of the river came before my eyes. This was the tip of the promontory and the room seemed built almost over the water itself. The two south windows looked downstream and revealed the great sweep of the Kennebec's course for miles. It almost seemed that in the clear sharpness of this morning I ought to make out the blue shimmer of the distant sea. The three windows along the eastern wall looked across water also—the width of the Kennebec itself. The river came down out of the northwest in a broad arc and leaned against the peninsula before it swung off toward Merrymeeting Bay and the ocean. Looking out of those windows, I half wondered why the pressure of that running water did not sweep the house away, but I was to learn that the eastern edge of Setauket Point was a natural dike of rock that was a match even for the river, and which lifted the house above spring floods and the winter ice.

Decidedly it was a seaman's location. I felt as though I were in the charthouse of a vessel, and if the first Talcott had not been a sea captain I missed my guess. The very loneliness of the spot where he had chosen to put up his mansion must have reminded him of the space and desert of the sea. I stood in that faded, splendid room, looking out across water and half hypnotized by the dazzle of the sun, and thought that this was no less surprising, in its way, than the idea of Julian's coming to Barsham Harbor. That he should have settled in such a house was beyond me then. In a way, it still is. And yet, there was a certain rightness about it, as I was to learn.

"Well?"

The voice came from behind me. It was sharply interrogatory, hard, but with something musical in it all the same. I whirled around, feeling like a child detected in naughtiness.

A woman was standing in the doorway, looking at me without moving. Seeing the bulk of her I wondered how she had managed to come within ten feet of me without making enough sound to attract my attention. She must have weighed all of a hundred and eighty pounds, and her big, loose-coupled body did not look as if it were easy to control.

I knew at once that this must be the woman about whom the taxi driver had been talking when he asked who "she" was. It was easy to see why she puzzled him and the rest of Barsham Harbor. My first flashing impression was that she looked as if she had once been a queen, and then I recognized that there was something less imperious, perhaps more assertive about her. The two impressions sound mutually exclusive and yet, there was truth in both of them.

For a moment I stared at her, too surprised to speak. Her obvious force and quality were so startlingly offset by the body that housed them. Apparently she had run to flesh as she grew older—there were heavy slabs of it on her arms, which were bare and soft but not mottled, as the skin of older women who put on weight so often is. Under the lusterless black of her dress her thighs looked tremendous, but her ankles were as thin as a girl's. Her feet looked almost tiny; I wondered how they managed to carry her bulk. She had the bosom of a retired opera diva. But for all her grossness, she carried herself with strength and purpose; there was no degeneration in that body of hers.

There was too much powder and rouge on her face. The accented red of her lips, the artificial shadowing under her eyes, the white dusting on nose and chin might not have been so conspicuous in the evening, but in the harsh brightness of this Maine morning streaming through the windows she looked raddled. Like her body, her chin and cheeks had gone to flesh, but under it was the architecture of what must once have been striking beauty, with wide, sharply planed cheekbones and a broad forehead. Her eyes were what remained of that magnificence, dark, so that I could see no bottom to them, and full of splendor. More than anything else about her they accounted for the effect of something regal in her appearance. She was looking at me out of them with the unconscious authority of a woman who does not have to ask for anything, but merely demands or takes it.

"Well?" she inquired again. The way she said that one word made me eager to explain myself.

"I beg your pardon," I began inanely. "I was just opening the shutters to get a little light in here."

"I can see what you were doing."

"My name is Richard Sayles." There was no sign that it meant anything to her, so I added, "Julian's friend."

"I have never heard of you."

Something about the way she said that made me think twice and decide not to retort in kind. Instead I bowed and pulled Julian's letter out of my pocket. "He wrote asking me to come at once," I said firmly.

She held out her hand for the letter. "He said nothing to me."

I did not hand her the letter. "Really," I told her, "this seems like an unfortunate way for us to meet. I have taken a liberty in walking in on you this way, but I have known Julian a long time." She said nothing, so I underlined it for her. "I'm afraid I don't even know who you are."

"Mrs. Walters." Her tone was impatient.

I bowed again.

"See here," she began, "Julian doesn't want to see anyone. I think you must be mistaken."

"Not at all," I replied, putting the letter back in my pocket. "If you'll just tell him I'm here, I think he will confirm what I've said."

Evidently she recognized an impasse when she came to one. "He's asleep. He was working late last night. I don't want to wake him."

"Please don't," I begged her. "There's no hurry and I'm painfully early, I know."

She shook her head. "I suppose that's your suitcase in the hall?"

"Yes."

"You can't stay, Mr. Sayles. We don't entertain visitors here. I'm sorry that you've had your trip for nothing."

I lifted my eyebrows. "Mrs. Walters, I assure you I am not a peddler or a salesman. I'm an old friend of Julian's and he has asked me to come up here as quickly as I could. I gave up a number of things in New York to get here. I'm afraid I must insist upon seeing him. After that, if he wants me to go back, I shall be only too glad to leave."

She shrugged. "You are a foolish young man. You will interrupt his work."

"In the letter he sent me he speaks of that. He apparently wants to ask my advice about something connected with it."

The effect of this retort of mine was surprising. The assurance faded from her stare and she put one hand against the door jamb as if to steady herself. "Your advice?" she asked incredulously. "What sort of advice?"

"I don't know."

"But how can you advise him?" She managed to put an unpleasant emphasis on the first pronoun.

"He didn't tell me that."

"Did he tell you what he was doing?" Her tone was only superficially casual; underneath its surface was a wariness, as if my answer to her question was the crux of something in her mind.

"No."

She drew a long breath and said, "If you are an old friend of Julian's you probably knew him when he was at the university?" When I nodded she went on, "That was when his wife died?"

"Yes," I admitted.

"You are much younger than Julian," she remarked. "Maybe you were one of his pupils?"

"Well, yes, once," I admitted. "I've been on the faculty for almost ten years."

"Oh," she said. Then, as if she were still puzzled by something, she inquired, "Did you know Helen well?"

Echoes went reverberating back and back in my mind, and I felt a natural resentment at the question. "Yes, quite well." That would do for her, even if it didn't begin to express the truth. This cross-questioning began to puzzle me. What made her so assured of her right to talk to a friend of Julian's in this fashion? The calm, impersonal way she kept looking at me while she asked me things that were none of her business was of a piece with her words. "Can I supply you with any further information?" I asked her.

She went on looking at me for a few seconds and then held out her hand. "I'm afraid I have seemed very rude, Professor Sayles. Please excuse it."

Her fingers were soft and unexpectedly cold, but there was strength in them. "Of course," I said. "After all, I did rather barge in and make myself at home."

She glanced over the room with a faint smile. "Not much of a home at that," she observed. "I'm afraid we've been too busy to pay much attention to the house. Julian and I are indifferent to such things."

I put out a cautious feeler. "We're all glad he's working again, Mrs. Walters. That is, I was glad to hear it and Julian's other friends will be, when they learn about it. He's too good a man, too important, to..." I could not think of a diplomatic way to end the sentence.

"These tragedies, Mr. Sayles, come to all of us. You cannot imagine what it means to lose touch with one you have loved."

"Perhaps not." I was content to let her statement ride along unchallenged. That was the easier way and, besides, some instinct warned me against letting this woman know anything too personal. Whatever she might be to Julian, I wanted nothing to do with her.

My lack of responsiveness did not seem to affect her one way or the other. She moved down the room and now, from a position at the farthest window, inquired, "Have you had your breakfast?"

"In the village on the way out."

"That horrible little town!" She was not even turning her head as she spoke.

"It's a lovely place to look at."

"Yes," she said in the most matter-of-fact voice, "it's lovely enough. The people who live in it are the worst feature of Barsham Harbor." I thought of the taxi driver and of his acquaintance who had moved away when I came out of the Elite Lunch, and had some inkling of what she meant. But it hardly seemed probable that the rest of the village would be just like them. I made no comment on what she had said and after a time she went on, still without bothering to look at me as she spoke. "We have a woman, a Mrs. Marcy, who comes over at eight to cook for us and do some of the housework. We generally have our morning meal at nine or even later. Julian is up so much of the night." She sighed. "He works too hard, but I cannot persuade him to slow down. He refuses to pay any attention to his health."

I wondered if what she was driving at was that she felt herself a martyr to Julian's habits. Perhaps she hoped I would intercede with him about staying up too late. But that was wide of the mark—she was getting at something else entirely, though I did not at first see what. "He always used to keep at it night and day when he thought he was on the track of something. In the old days, at least."

"The old days—" she began, and then stopped herself. "You will find him changed," she remarked, still without a glance in my direction. "I hope you won't blame me for that. I have done what I could to help him, but of course I have no right to manage his life."

Again I had the feeling that behind the screen of her words she was trying to pass along some sort of impression to me. What it was supposed to be I could not make out, and felt the discomfort of a man who can't quite hear a whisper addressed to him. Perhaps she wanted me to understand something about her relation to Julian, but I realized that it wasn't as simple a matter as that. I decided she was trying to tell me she was not the sort of woman she imagined I must be thinking she was, that she had not simply happened upon an older man broken and at loose ends because he had lost his wife, seen her opportunity and stepped into the gap. There was no possessiveness in the way she spoke of Julian Blair.

"It's his life," I agreed. "Don't worry about it too much; we all know that Julian won't listen to anyone. Helen was the only person who ever managed to make him take care of himself."

She nodded, and then she said a thing that left me staring at her. "In a way," she remarked judiciously, as if she were weighing one thing against another, "It's a pity that his wife died."

"Good God," I said, "how can you talk like that!"

She looked at me then, and when she spoke she sounded almost as if she were sorry, not for what she had said, but for me. "That must have sounded cold and unfeeling to you. I have a bad habit sometimes of thinking aloud. Don't misunderstand me—I was speaking purely in terms of Julian's work. Like you, Mr. Sayles, I believe in Julian—probably a great deal more so than you, as a matter of fact. I have made every sacrifice, contributed everything I could toward his work." My expression must have showed her what I thought of that high-flown speech, but she went on patiently. "You and I have different ideas about death, too, I don't doubt. To you it is always a tragedy. To me, seldom. Often death shows us which things are of greatest importance. That was certainly true in Julian's case."

I felt out of my depth and beginning to dislike this woman more with every passing minute. All the time she was talking in this bombastic fashion she had been standing by the window, looking out at the glittering water. I saw as I watched her that the pose was theatrical, that she was looking at the river with the eyes of a gaslight tragedy queen. And yet, there was something about her that was close to magnificence. I told myself that all she amounted to was a fat hulk of a woman, no longer young, in a shapeless sack of a dress and with a ruin of a face. And yet, the trouble was that here was something not quite normal—a woman with an old, sagging, lined face who deliberately let the hard harshness of morning daylight play on her face. "Look," she seemed to be saying indirectly to me, "see what a mountain of a woman I am! If I was ever beautiful you can see that there is nothing of it left."

The nub of the matter was that she ought to have been ridiculous and she wasn't. I could not feel like smiling at her, even inwardly. I tried to tell myself that this was a silly, vain old woman, but what I actually felt about her was less definable than contempt. It was a good deal closer to uneasiness; whatever was underneath that flesh of hers and that dramatized manner, it was not weak or negligible. Julian's life must have settled into a strange pattern indeed if it included this woman.

Finally she turned away from the window, knowing that she had got her effect, and moved heavily down the room once more. There was resilience in the way she walked, for all her weight, and the boards of the old floor did not creak under her tread as you would have expected. She went past me and I could feel the vitality in her. When she got to the doorway she paused and said, "I'll step into the kitchen for a moment before Mrs. Marcy comes. Just to make sure we have enough to eat. You may care for a second cup of coffee, even if you've already had your breakfast."

"Thank you," I said.

"If you don't mind, we'll wait till later to find a room for you. The bedrooms are all upstairs and I try to keep it quiet up there while he's asleep."

"That's all right," I reassured her. "Any time will do. This is an ungodly hour at which to arrive anyhow. If there had been any other train . . ."

"Of course. This . . . this wilderness is something that we have to adjust ourselves to." Her eyes avoided mine. "Sometimes I wish Julian hadn't felt it necessary to come here at all. But he is right, of course. The more remote we are, the better." She gave me a last quick look and went away down the hall.

I settled myself on the sofa and filled my pipe. The room was more comfortable now that she had left it, but I was far from feeling at ease. This was a curious situation into which I had strayed and, thinking back over the preceding minutes, it seemed to me that I had told Mrs. Walters a great deal about myself in return for almost nothing in the way of information about Julian or herself. What she was doing here with him was as beyond my power to imagine as why he was here himself.

Something about the woman stuck uncomfortably in my mind, something less tangible than her appearance or even the things she had said. I could not put my finger on it, but in some way it was connected with her attitude toward Julian. What was there about that which was peculiar? Well, the way she had said "we" in speaking about the two of them. That suggested intimacy, of course, but not the obvious kind of thing at all. There was none of that spurious tenderness that she would have employed if she'd had what used to be called "designs" on him. No, it was something less analyzable than that. There was a tie between them, at least in her mind, but it was not, at any remove whatever, a sexual one. She spoke almost as if she and Julian were partners in some sort of enterprise. Having thought that, I dismissed it because it seemed to me impossible that I could be right. Julian was a great scientist in his way, narrow and limited though he might be outside the field of his own work. This woman was unthinkable in the role of his assistant or collaborator. I let the thought slip away from me.

That curious theatricality of hers. She had acted at moments like a woman dedicated to something—to the return of the Hapsburgs to the throne or some other noble and semi-public conspiracy. It was something that she believed in herself—that much was plain. And in some way I suspected that it was bound up with her self-assurance.

After a time I gave up the puzzle and simply sat, smoking and looking out at the river. To eyes accustomed to the Hudson, it was amazingly empty. Not one boat, large or small, appeared on the whole expanse of water visible from the windows. And except for distant rectangles of ploughed fields and the roofs of a few diminutive houses on the opposite shore, it might have been a wilderness river, more primeval than it had been a century before. Staring at the long blue sweep of it and the unchanging outline of the hills beyond, the utter absence of humanity from the scene began to depress me. This was a lonely house and a lonely valley; it was not part of the modern world to which I belonged. That was a peopled world, full of human beings and their artifacts, full of movement and activity. This landscape into which I was looking was older and more primitive, unchanging except as the weather and the seasons altered it.

5.

FEET WERE coming down the stairs in the hall. The sound of them exorcised the vapors in my mind, and I was surprised at the way my pulse quickened. There was the rapid lightness of youth in the way the footfalls clattered on the stair treads and I knew by their very sound who it was that was coming. Anne, it had to be Anne. What would she be like? Five years would make a lot of difference ... I remembered the child, but it suddenly occurred to me that, much as we had been together in the old days, I had never noticed the woman that she was going to be. Naturally not, with Helen there and my whole eyes and heart centered on her. Anne had been—almost—my daughter, just as she had always seemed more like Helen's child than her sister.

In the instant before she appeared I found I could recall surprisingly little of what she had really been, as a person in her own right and not merely Helen's much younger sister. All I was sure about was that when I had taken her to the circus or on a picnic, and later to plays and concerts, it had been fun. She had been quiet, with serious eyes, but when she laughed I remembered that I had laughed too, irresistibly.

Of course she must have changed. But I wished that she could be the same.

When she came through the door I had a momentary shock. She looked like Helen all over again—the same straight carriage, the same eyes set deep and wide apart, the round, strong throat. Then I noticed the differences. Helen had been white and gold, and this girl was brown—her hair, and the even tan of her skin. Helen had walked gravely, and there was always a reservation in her beauty. Anne, I saw, was not so stately. Her mouth was larger, even making allowances for the grin on it now, and her eyes were a darker blue. She was less conscious of herself, I felt, and most amazingly alive, though it may have been that the house and my own mood contributed to that impression.

"Anne!" I said and felt like laughing at something pleasant when I said it.

"Uncle Dick!" She checked her rush forward and stood looking at me. "Good heavens!"

"What's the matter?"

She grinned again. "Why, just that…well, I guess I didn't remember you very well." She came over and shook me by the hand. "Welcome to Setauket Point."

"What's the matter with me?" I demanded. "Have I changed?"

"No. I thought you were an old man. I mean, not exactly old, but a lot older than you are."

"You don't seem to like my…" I couldn't think of a word that wouldn't sound worse than inane. "After all, you can't expect me to grow gray hair at thirty-three."

She sat down on the sofa beside me and went on looking at me in silence. The expression on her face delighted me—it was so obviously surprised and amused. After a time she remarked, "Well, I'm used to it now. But I'm not going to call you 'uncle' any more."

"That's all right with me." I didn't want to be called anything of the kind after that first look at her. "You startled me when you came in, yourself. For a second it was like seeing Helen again."

She looked away quickly. "Don't say that."

It had been a stupid remark and I was sorry the moment I'd said it. "Anyway," I went on, "I'm glad to see you here, Anne." Even that was awkward.

"You'll never know how glad I am to see you. I've been pestering Uncle Julian to write to you, but I never dreamed he really would. Why didn't you let us know you were coming?"

I told her about the telegram and the taxi driver.

"That's the way they are around here," she observed. "They don't like strangers. At least, they don't like us."

"It's just the old New England reticence."

She looked doubtful. "Probably. Only . . . well, let's not talk about that now."

"How is Julian?"

There was distress on her face. "He's changed. You'll be shocked when you see him. I was."

"Mrs. Walters told me the same thing."

"So you've seen her—" she said, and then stopped abruptly. I thought she was listening. "Where is she, do you know?"

"She said she was going out in the kitchen to get breakfast."

Anne glanced back at the door quickly and then began to speak in a low voice. "Look Unc—I mean Dick, I've got to talk to you, but not here. Later. Just follow any lead I give you, will you?"

"All right. But—"

She interrupted me by standing up. "Let's go see if breakfast is ready. You must be ravenous."

"I had something at what my driver called the Elite."

She grinned again. "All you need is a couple of soda mints and another breakfast and you'll get over that," she said, and led the way out of the room. "That is, if Elora Marcy's already here."

I followed her. Her yellow sweater made the dark hall seem bright, and I noticed that she could wear slacks and not make the toe of my foot itch. This, I felt, was not going to be such an uncomfortable visit, nor so dreary as its opening had made me fear. I was still not adjusted to the idea of Anne's being grown-up. After all, the first time I had seen her was when Helen left her in my charge for an afternoon and, not knowing what you did with girls of eleven, I'd taken her out to a drugstore and given her two chocolate malteds in succession. From then on she had been just Helen's small sister as far as I was concerned, a youngster that I liked, but a little girl for all that.

"Remember the chocolate malteds?" I said to her back as we went down the hall.

"Yes." Her laugh sounded good. "They make a pretty smooth malted in the Rexall store in town, the only good thing in Barsham Harbor as far as I'm concerned."

"We'll go sample them," I said.

"It's a date." At the door to the kitchen she paused. "Remember what I said," she whispered and pushed the door open.

To my surprise the kitchen was an agreeable room. It was in the northeast corner of the house, behind the room where I had been sitting and, though it was as dingy as the rest of the house, it looked a good deal more lived in. The sun was coming through the windows on our right and making the place bright; I noticed immediately that there was no dust and that both the old stone sink and the kerosene stove were clean and as shining as their age and wear permitted. One thing that pleased me out of all proportion to its actual importance was a geranium growing in a chipped pot on the window sill. It struck me as almost the first evidence I had seen that anyone thought of this house as a place in which to live.

Mrs. Walters and Anne exchanged good mornings in an insincere fashion. I noticed that neither of them looked at the other.

"I laid a place for you, Mr. Sayles. I'm sure you'll want something more besides coffee."

"Thank you," I said.

We all sat down at the table. The toast was just like the Elite's, but the coffee was not so bitter. On the other hand, it was considerably weaker. I ate as much as I could in order to seem like the untroublesome guest, but I saw Anne watching me in amusement.

"Where's Mrs. Marcy?" she asked after she had sampled her own helping of egg—which looked not so much scrambled as smeared.

"Late," said Mrs. Walters in a tone that implied she didn't care what Anne thought of the eggs. Then she smiled and remarked, "You two young people must have some good times together."

"Unaccustomed as I am to entertaining college professors..." Anne remarked in a thoughtful tone, "I shall do my small best." She turned to Mrs. Walters with what looked to me like a sweet smile— too sweet. "We already have a date."

"Oh?"

"Yes. For the cocktail hour and in the local drugstore."

This fencing between the two of them seemed likely to make an awkward moment even more so. I cut in quickly, "That is, unless Julian and I are busy then. After all, he's got first call on my time."

Anne's eyebrows went up but she said nothing. Mrs. Walters began to stack the dishes in the sink, her own plate scarcely touched. I wondered how she had managed to grow so heavy if that was all she ate. She looked from me to Anne thoughtfully and finally remarked, "I'll leave the dishes to you, Anne."

"Let me dry," I said. "I'm a great drier—All-American my sophomore year."

"Very good." Mrs. Walters sounded indifferent to the problem of the dishes. "If Mrs. Marcy doesn't come soon, we'll have to find out what's delaying her." She turned in the doorway. "I'll let you know, Mr. Sayles, when Julian is awake."

"Thank you."

"Do you want me to fix a room for him?" asked Anne.

"Later. After Julian is awake. I'll attend to that," she replied and disappeared.

Anne chucked a dish towel in my direction. "I didn't know you were planning to do any work with Uncle Julian," she observed.

"He asked me to give him some advice."

Anne said nothing for an interval of two plates and a coffee cup. Then she looked up. "What did she say when you told her that?"

"She didn't believe it at first. She acted odd about it."

"She would."

"Look here," I said. "What is going on in this house? Who is this Mrs. Walters? What is she doing with Julian?"

Anne turned from the sink and looked at me steadily. She was not smiling any more. "I don't know."

The answer floored me. "But surely you must have some idea?"

She shook her head. "I landed the first of August and I've been up here ever since, but I tell you, Dick, I haven't. I can't find out."

"But hasn't Julian told you?"

"No. I hardly see him anyway, except at meals, and she's always there. I haven't been alone with him four times since I came." She stopped abruptly and looked toward the door. It was still open but there was no one there. "Anyhow, we'll take a walk later and a swim. I'd rather say nothing till then. She has ears like a cat."

We went on with the dishes. Just as we finished, the back door opened and a woman came in quickly. She was out of breath and there was a comical look of apology on her thin face.

"Morning, Miss Conner," she said quickly. "I'm sorry I'm late, but I had to help Seth in the barn this morning. He's not so good again."

By the way Anne smiled at her I could see instantly that she liked this little woman. "That's all right, Mrs. Marcy. We're making out."

Mrs. Marcy looked at the sink and gave a horrified gasp. "You're doin' dishes! You ain't had breakfast already, surely?"

"Not really," Anne replied. "Just something that Mrs. Walters prepared with her own fair hands. But that's not your fault. Professor Sayles, here, arrived on the 6:20 and so we were roused out early. Dick, this is Mrs. Marcy, the only sane member of our happy household."

"How do you do," she said with a smile twitching the corners of her mouth. I could see that Anne delighted her.

"Look out for him," that young lady went on. "He's a college professor and you know you just can't trust them. Absentminded. Lots of mornings he forgets to put on his trousers, even."

Mrs. Marcy giggled. "Looks like you both remembered this morning," she observed with an eye on Anne's slacks.

I laughed. "Good for you, Mrs. Marcy," I said and we shook hands. "I see you know how to handle the younger generation here."

She laughed. "It's not so easy, but I do my best, Professor. Now you give me that," and she removed the dish towel with one dexterous swipe. "I don't allow any men to dry dishes in my kitchen. They ain't trustworthy."

Anne observed, "He's not so bad."

"Maybe not. But as time goes on they get less and less help, more and more of a nuisance. Take my advice and start keepin' him out of the kitchen right now."

Anne avoided my eye. "The voice of experience," she said lamely.

"Yes, child. I'll have to hump myself now, so you two run along. Oh, Miss Conner..."

"What?"

"Is she mad on account of my bein' so late?"

"Good heavens, Elora! You're only a few minutes late. Don't worry about it."

"I don't want no ruckus with her." She looked as if she meant it. And yet, it was hard to imagine that even Mrs. Walters could be severe with this person. She had the bright eyes and quick movements of a bird, and there was something ingratiating about the way she talked and smiled. Neither Anne nor I made a move to leave the kitchen in spite of her edict.

Probably I wouldn't have believed, at that moment, that she was only thirty-two. She looked ten years older and her hair was already fading into gray. Fourteen years of farm housework and the bearing of four children had faded her hair and skin, if not her eyes. She looked as if she didn't weigh more than a hundred pounds. Later, after she was dead, I learned something of her story. Married the year she got out of high school, and plunged at once into the grim business of making a living on a Maine farm, she hadn't really had more than half her youth. The children had come along at intervals of a year or so, and after the fourth she was middle-aged; when she smiled you could see what having them had done to her teeth, for one thing.

Prematurely aged she may have been, but she was not old in her heart or her courage. She must have had to get up at four to do the housework at her own place before she came down the road to Julian's, but she was as lively that morning as if the day were just beginning for her, instead of half over by any ordinary standards. Nothing daunted her, and the last thing she must have thought about was sparing herself. As I remember her again, I feel the sadness that comes when one thinks of a lost opportunity. I should like to have been able to do something for Mrs. Marcy.

Anne was putting dishes away in the cupboard. "Never worry about Mrs. Walters," she advised. "If she doesn't like your being late, walk out and let her see how she enjoys running one place, let alone two."

Mrs. Marcy shook her head. "We need the money. Seth's sciatica's back on him again. I don't know what we'll do if it gets any worse."

"That's a shame. I wish you'd let me help you."

"That's sweet, child, but I'll make out." She poured a cup of water into the geranium pot and I understood then where the plant had come from. "You folks goin' to be staying on much longer? They was here till November, last year."

Anne shook her head. "I'm going away the fifteenth. But of course I don't know about Uncle Julian. I don't suppose he'll stay here all winter, but he might. And she'll stay as long as he does."

"Oh, yes," agreed Mrs. Marcy. "Well, the longer the better for us."

Anne said, "You need a vacation," in a tone that expressed how impossible she knew that idea was.

"Not me," said the little woman brusquely. "But it would be right nice for Seth if he could go south this winter. The cold doesn't do him any good. And now, if you'll excuse me, I'll just put the mop to this floor."

We went out the back door into the yard and stood there in the sun for a while. I filled my pipe and Anne lit a cigarette. She must have seen some sort of look on my face, because she remarked "I've acquired a few bad habits, Dick," and laughed. I apologized and told her not to mind me. The more I looked at her, with the sun putting red-gold lights into her hair, the more I felt that it was going to be difficult to find a new basis for our relationship. If she had been a pupil in one of my classes, it would have been easy. I had long ago developed an immunity to all of them, no matter how charming. But Anne was a different problem. I felt responsible for her in a way, and there was the past in which she had loved me as her "favorite uncle" and I had played with her, helped her when her homework was puzzling, given her elaborate toys at Christmas, and done all the other pleasant things which had seemed to stem naturally out of being Julian and Helen's closest friend. When they had married, I had been glad of Anne. She gave me an outlet for the frustration I had felt...

Five years had changed everything. That much I perceived. But what to do about bridging the gap I could not wholly see. It was a problem that solved itself quickly, but at the time, it perplexed me. I did not want to go back into the past, and the present was decidedly odd. So I said nothing, but stood there smoking and looking at the sky and the bay, and every once in a while at Anne.

Finally she threw the end of her cigarette into the road. "Well, this is nice, but I want to talk to you, Dick. And we're too close to the house."

"You know more about this neck of the woods than I do. Anywhere you say."

"Did you bring a bathing suit?"

When I told her that I had, she suggested that I get it, and I returned to the hall and my bag. Mrs. Marcy was dusting in the living room. I waved to her but said nothing. In three minutes I was back on the road.

"Good," said Anne when I rejoined her. "There's not much to do hereabouts, but the swimming makes up for it."

We wandered along together and it was pleasant. The air was beginning to feel warm and you could smell the grass and the rich scent of the earth itself. My pipe tasted good and the sun was warm on my back. Our shadows went across the field ahead of us, and by their lengths I judged that it was about nine or perhaps later. I felt too content to bother with a watch.

After ten minutes or so we came to the edge of the bay. Here, almost at the Point's end, the shore line was not marshy; we were actually standing several feet above the water and on the edge of a cut bank. Below us was a twenty-foot crescent of brownish sand which was still in shadow and looked damp. Across the bay and at least a mile to the southwest the town lay white and green along the farther shore.

"This is where I swim," Anne said, breaking a long silence. We sat down and hung our legs over the edge of the bank. "I come here twice a day sometimes," she went on. "It's almost as private as if you were on an island. You need a place like this to come to, away from that house."

"I see what you mean."

She turned her face to me and there was a look of quiet contentment on it that I had not seen before. "I came up here just to be with Uncle Julian a while and because I thought I ought to come. It hasn't been much fun so far, but it was almost worth it just on account of lying in the sun here and watching the water. Sometimes it seems to me the river is alive."

"Yes," I said. "Yes."

She kept on looking at it for a time without speaking and, as I watched her, I thought that it had been a long while since I had felt so baselessly happy and relaxed. The whole world was fresh and shining, the water was one shade of blue, the sky another, the meadow grass along the bank was stirring in a faint breeze, the air was sweet, and the sun was making Anne's hair gleam. Her face was half in shadow, but as I studied it, I could see that it was a woman's face and not that of a child or a young girl. There was character in it, strength in the spring of her jaw and the line of the cheekbone but not obstinacy, humor in the corners of her lips. The young fellow that got her, I reflected, would have something worth holding on to. That thought ended by annoying me.

"I'd never believe Julian would pick out a place like this," I said.

"That's the way I felt, at first," she answered slowly. "But I think he likes it. Not the way I do, but because it's so far away from everything. He doesn't want people."

"For that matter, he never has."

"I know." She pulled a long stem of grass and put it between white teeth. "But he's more of a hermit than ever. Dick, he's changed. I said that before, didn't I? Well, I don't want to prejudice you, but I'm ... worried about him. He's so thin, too. He's not well at all."

"Of course Helen's death was an enormous shock to him. It was to all of us."

She nodded and without looking at me asked, "You were in love with her too, weren't you?"

"Yes."

"Are you still?"

It was a question I had not put to myself for a long time, and I was not sure of the answer. Helen's image was fresh in a part of my mind, but it did not hurt to think about her any more. A lot of water had flowed under the bridge since the time when I used to dream about her. "No," I told her finally, "I don't think I am."

"I should have thought Helen ..." she began and then hesitated. "Why did she marry Uncle Julian instead of you?"

"Because she'd been married once before, I think."

She looked puzzled. "I don't quite see that."

"Well, Ed Norton was a louse. He treated your sister like the dirt under his feet, once he had got her. And she married him when she was too young. So he took all the youth out of her, made her afraid of passion and of the future. The divorce hurt her a lot, too. Helen wasn't the kind that could take a thing like that in her stride. What she wanted after that was something gentle and settled, and someone whom she could cherish, if you'll forgive the old-fashioned word, without having to love the way I wanted to be loved. Julian was peace and security to her, and he needed her. Besides, she had you on her hands." I grinned at her. "You were a handful, too."

Anne nodded. "She was practically like a mother to me." She nibbled the stem of grass. "To Uncle Julian, too, in a way."

"In another way," I agreed. "He was forty-five when he married her, and he'd never had anything like Helen in his whole life before. Everything he'd been suppressing up to then was fastened on her. He didn't love her, he adored her." God knows I had had ample opportunity to watch Julian's happiness. I knew more about it than anyone else possibly could. "She gave Julian everything he'd never had—a whole new life beyond his work. She brought him out into the sun. She was beautiful and she was kind, and she made him happier than he'd ever been."

"No wonder," she said slowly, "that he's so queer now. I never thought about it in quite the way you describe, but I can see you're right."

One word struck me sharply. "Queer?" I said. "What do you mean by queer?"

For a time she did not answer and there was hesitation in her silence. Finally she turned to me. "He's obsessed in some way, Dick. Some way that isn't natural. And it's connected with Helen in his mind. The only times we've really talked since I came up here were all about her. It made me feel creepy. He never mentioned her as if she were dead. You know, he'd say 'is' instead of 'was' and so forth."

I digested that for a time and the more I thought about it the more my heart sank. This visit was going to be a difficult one. The time before I had had no luck trying to argue Julian out of a preoccupation, and it sounded as if...well, as if he hadn't forgotten anything. Still, I could not see just how a lot of the present facts were compatible with the unwelcome hypothesis that was forming in my mind. "What about this Mrs. Walters?" I inquired. "I don't see what she's doing here."

Anne lay back on propped elbows and looked up at me with eyes squinted from the sun. "You don't seem swept off your feet by the lady," she observed.

"I'm not. And I don't see what she's doing here."

"When I first came I simply thought she was after Uncle Julian," she remarked. "But I'm not so sure now. She's been with him more than a year—or so I gather from things they've said—and she's with him all day. Anything that woman couldn't get in six months wouldn't be worth going after with a vacuum cleaner. So it can't be matrimony."

"Money, perhaps?"

She shook her head. "I don't think so. Uncle Julian isn't exactly rich and he's been spending huge sums on all sorts of things for his laboratory, or whatever is in that room of his. I worry sometimes for fear he hasn't any left."

"How about yours?" I knew that Julian had been the trustee for Anne's inheritance. She and Helen had divided the Conner estate equally, and Helen had left her half to Julian. It must have amounted to somewhere around seventy thousand dollars. Anne was to get her share outright when she came of age, and the idea that Julian could in any way have been false to that trust was too sickening to entertain. Still, I was relieved when she answered.

"Mine is all right. He turned it all over to me on my eighteenth birthday. Government bonds, it was in. I put them in a bank in New York." She frowned and said, "He wanted to borrow some the other day."

"Good God!" I said with a sick feeling in the pit of my stomach. "How much?"

"Five thousand dollars."

"I suppose you gave it to him?"

"Not exactly. I told him he could have it if he'd tell me what was going on and why he needed so much."

"You shouldn't have promised even that. What did he say?"

She sat up again and kicked the bank hard with her heels. "He said he couldn't tell me, but that he needed some more equipment, and that once his work was finished he thought he would be able to repay me. She heard about it and told me I was a fool—that I'd lost a chance at a fortune, and that he'd borrow it elsewhere. That was meant to make me feel bad," she observed, "but I didn't. I don't care about the money. Uncle Julian could have it all as far as I'm concerned. But I tell you, Dick, I don't want him to go on the way he's going. He's so sick and old! I don't want her to have it, either, but I'm sure he didn't want it for that. It really was for things he uses. Twice since I've been here a truck's arrived with cases and cases of things. I don't know what they were, but I think that he and she spend all their time up there working on something or other. In fact, I'm sure that's all they do together. I don't think Uncle Julian cares about her and I know she doesn't even like him. They watch each other sometimes. You'll see."

"I should think you'd be relieved that there's nothing more to it than that. You sound bothered."

She shook her head. "After you've been here a day you'll be bothered, too. I hate that house. I loathe the people in the town, and the way they look at us. You'd think we were gangsters in a hide-out." There was defiance in her voice.

"Well," I told her, "it isn't for long. Summer's almost over."

"Yes," she replied, but not as if the thought made her particularly happy.

We sat there in the grass for a long time, talking about ourselves. She told me about the years since I had last seen her, most of them spent abroad. Behind her words it was easy to see that she had been lonely but unwilling to come home to Julian, whom she had never understood or loved without reservation. The fact that she called him "Uncle Julian" and always had since Helen married him was an indication of the way she felt toward him. And he, I suppose, was glad enough to have her take over the responsibility of her own life, leaving him free.

She seemed to have done a good job of it, and a notably mature one. The allowance from her money had enabled her to travel modestly and study what she felt like, so she had gone first to London and then to Paris, looking into the things that interested her and doing a good deal of hard work, too. She told me she'd had a job in the export office of a French textile company, for one thing, and another as assistant to a woman in charge of the entertainments on a Mediterranean cruise ship. Then she had studied drawing and fashions, working bitterly long hours for almost nothing in a Paris couturier's shop until she thought she had something to offer in the way of experience. A buyer from one of the New York department stores had been impressed with her when she decided to look for an American job, and the upshot was that she was back in her own country with a position waiting for her on the first of October.

She told her story with no sense of bravado and I could see that what she had done suited her perfectly, however unlike the conventional thing it had been. It gave me a sense of satisfaction to know she was going to be in New York.

When she asked me what I had been doing, I could not find anything to match her own account. A certain quantity of work performed, two promotions in academic rank, a few published articles, a couple of camping trips. That about summed up the five years. But it seemed to interest her; when I admitted that I was now an associate professor and in line to become a department head in a few years, she nodded as if she were satisfied.

"You always did work hard," she observed. "I can remember that." She looked at me and grinned again. "But really you aren't much the way I remembered after all. I expected to find you wearing a beard by now."

I rubbed my chin. "If I don't manage to get a shave pretty soon, I'll be wearing one all right."

She stood up. "Well, you'll find the house pretty primitive, but I guess the shaving can be managed. We don't have a tub though, and if you want a bath you'll have to take it in the river. I'm going in now." She made a grimace. "Swimming is absolutely the only entertainment we have to offer, and I've been doing a lot of it; twice a day, when it doesn't rain. Even Mrs. Walters swims." After a pause she added, "She swims well, too. You'd be surprised."

"I don't like to think of her in a bathing suit."

Anne laughed. "It's quite a sight." She pulled the yellow sweater up over her head, which disconcerted me until I saw that she had a bathing suit on underneath her clothes. "There's a clump of willows over there where you can undress," she observed when her head emerged from the seawater. "But look out for bees. I got stung once."

I went over to the willows and got into my trunks, thinking about how warm and brown her shoulders had looked, and how fantastic it would have seemed to me yesterday to be told that at ten the following morning I should be thinking about a girl's skin and the sun on her hair.

When I returned to the crescent of sand, Anne was already out in the water, swimming with an easy steadiness. I went in after her; the first shock of the plunge was breath-taking because the water was frost-cold, but after that it felt fine. The blood began to race under my skin and I could feel the grubbiness of the train disappear in the swift rush of water along my body.

I caught up with Anne a couple of hundred yards off-shore, and we stopped to tread water and look around us. It was amazing how low the shores looked from where we were, and how distant. We were in a level world of blue which sparkled as we turned to face the sun. Anne shook the water swiftly out of her eyes and said, "Don't you like it?"

"It's superb."

Anne turned on her back and began to kick gently with her feet. "Nothing matters when you're out here," she said. "Everything's clean and . . ." she paused slightly, "real." Then she said, "I'm glad you're here," turned over and began to swim toward the middle of the bay.

I followed her, wondering why she had paused before she said "real." Then I stopped thinking at all and we raced until we were winded. By that time the shore was perceptibly remote and I began to notice the chill in the water. Anne had stopped too, and I looked at her, panting and laughing, with her head mounted on the flat water like John the Baptist's on a plate. "This water is pretty cold," I observed.

"I'm used to it now," she answered, "but I'll have had enough in a few minutes. Let's swim back slowly."

So we did. I watched the flash and lift of her arm as it came out of the water, and the arc of ripples that pushed along in front of her bathing cap. The sun caught the wet rubber and made a point of fire on it. I found myself matching my strokes to hers, so that we were swimming beside each other in the same rhythm, sliding through the water like parts of a single entity. The patch of fire on her cap held my eyes until I was half hypnotized without knowing it, and only the grating of my fingers on the beach sand snapped the spell.

We stood up then and looked at each other. Drops of water fell from her body like fragments of light, and for an instant it seemed to me that there had been nothing whatever prior to this moment, that we had swum up out of some infinite reservoir of being until we stranded on the shore of the world. It is impossible to describe such an experience in the vocabulary of psychology, or any other, for that matter. It simply was. We stood there looking at each other, half smiling, not conscious of things but of everything fused into one universal sensation which vibrated in me to the tune of our swimming. I saw that Anne was lovely, smoothly and strongly made, but it was inevitable that she should be so. A sense of enormous contentment and satisfaction flooded through me.

The enchantment began to dissolve. She gave a laugh and splashed through the shallow water to the beach. I followed, and we sat on a log together in the sun, without speaking. The heat began to take the water chill out of our bodies and we relaxed. Anne stretched her legs ahead of her and dug her toes into the sand. "You see why I like to come here," she said.

"Yes."

"This was special, though," she said, half to herself, and I was glad because I didn't want it to have been that fine every time before.

After a while we got cigarettes and smoked until we were dry and warm. The sun was high and I began to remember why I had come to Barsham Harbor. "Julian must be up by now," I said. "Probably I ought to be getting back to the house."

"All right," Anne replied and there was regret in her tone.

We pulled on our clothes and I had to be diplomatic about that because she was right about the bees. There were a dozen of them buzzing in the willow alcove where I dressed. Afterwards we walked back across the meadow, not saying much. Halfway to the house I said, "I'll let you know what Julian has to say and then we can have another talk."

"Yes." Then she added earnestly, "Try to see him alone. Don't let her be there when you talk to him or you'll never learn anything."

"All right. But don't take her too much to heart. She's not the companion for a summer vacation, I admit, but there's no point in resenting her."

She looked at me steadily. "I don't resent her," she answered. "I'm afraid of her."

"Nonsense."

She said nothing to that and we walked on to the house. The magic had gone and we were just two people again, each wrapped in our own thoughts. We walked slowly.

6.

FIVE YEARS can change a man considerably, and Anne had warned me that I should find Julian unlike my memory of him. Even so, it hurt when I walked into the living room and saw what he had become. He was sitting in a sagging armchair with his back to the windows and the light, but even at first glance I saw that he was old. His narrow, angular face had never had much color in it, but now the skin was parchment tight and stiff over his cheekbones and his lips were bleached to a thick gray, as if there was almost no blood left in him. My second glance showed me he had lost something else, too—the sense of discipline which had always been characteristic of him. I remembered him as a neat man, controlled in his movements and meticulous about his clothes. This haggard figure in the shabby living room of the old house was another man, some sort of senile changeling. His clothes were not only rumpled but dirty. There was a triangular tear in the knee of one trouser leg. His shirt looked as if he had slept in it, and he was not wearing a tie.

For a moment he sat there motionless, looking at me, and then he pushed himself up by the arms of the chair and rose to meet me. As he stood there I saw that he was trembling almost imperceptibly. A sudden feeling of pity rose in my throat, and I went across the room quickly and took his hand. "Julian! It's grand to see you!" I said and hoped my voice did not betray what I was thinking and feeling.

Seen at close range, his face was not as lifeless as it had appeared at first. The eyes were alive and burning with the same eagerness that they had when he was working in the second-floor lab of McCann Hall in the old days. Only there was another quality there now, an intensity which was more than eagerness. Their brightness struck me as more than normal and I looked away from them after a second.

His hand when it took mine was dry and cold, but the pressure of his fingers was strong. "Richard," he said, "it is generous of you to have come so promptly." He looked at me appraisingly. "You seem to be keeping fit and you don't look a day older."

"I'm fine, Julian. What about you?"

He smiled then, a curious smile which did not match his words. "As you see. I have only a little time left, but enough . . . enough." He gestured to a chair. "Sit down. Good. We can talk, in comfort. I suppose you've seen Anne already?"

"Yes," I told him.

"She reminds me of her sister," he said and gave me the same quick, inappropriate smile. "Don't you think so?"

"In some ways."

"Well, I hope she will help to entertain you in the intervals when I am working."

I filled a pipe, not because I wanted to smoke but to give an air of casualness to what I was saying. "It's fine to hear you're working again, Julian. We've all missed you. I suppose you know that you can have your chair back any time you want it. Arthur Wallace has arranged for that."

"A good man. And thank you. I expect you had something to do with that, Richard, as well as he. But my work is here. And it is almost done. Afterwards I shall . . . retire." He paused before he used that last word and I did not like that hesitation. He must have seen me look at him sharply, because he went on in a stronger voice. "As a matter of fact, Richard, my strength is failing me rather alarmingly. That is why I sent for you in such a hurry. I must finish my work quickly or not at all."

"You've got plenty of years left, Julian. What you need is a rest. You've been at it too hard."

He shook his head. "It's the other way round, my boy. The work keeps me alive. Without it I should have died long ago." He smiled again and this time it was all right. "But this is morbid and unimportant. I must tell you wherein I think you can help me." His eyes fastened on me and he spoke more rapidly. "I venture to think that this errand on which I have called you is important. Even, perhaps, the most important thing in the whole world, not only for me but for every living person. I'm on the threshold of an enormous advance in human knowledge—the most enormous advance you can conceive of."

Sometimes a man's craft obtrudes itself upon him without warning or welcome. It was so with me at that moment. Hearing Julian speak, watching the tense way he was leaning forward in his chair, noticing the way the tendons ridged his throat I caught the outlines of what was not less than hysteria and more likely a deranging obsession of the mind. The thought made me miserable. I looked away from him so as not to see any more of it, but he did not notice. His voice, dry, strained, hurrying with an unnecessary urgency, went on.

"Yes," he was saying, "I'm on to something, my boy. I'm on to something that nobody since time began has found the real key to. Oh, a lot of them have worked on it, one way and another. Even inventors like Edison, I understand. But he didn't have the . . ." for the first time the spate of his words slowed and he hesitated. Some of the unnatural brightness in his eyes faded. He licked his lips and found a word that I felt was not the whole of his meaning. "The incentive that I have. I've *got* to succeed. Everything depends on it, everything. One more step, one small step, and I'll have it. You can help me make that step."

"I hope so," I said. "What is it you're working on, Julian?"

He leaned back in his chair and looked away from me. There was stubbornness in the set of his jaw. "That I can't tell you. It isn't wholly my secret, for one thing. For another, I'd rather not discuss it. I want only the answers to a few questions."

Here, I decided, was the place to call a halt to the vaguenesses and ambiguities in which we had been dealing. "Julian," I said firmly, "you know very well that I'll do almost anything for you. I'd be an ungrateful so-and-so if I didn't. But you've been talking in large terms. I think I ought to know what you're after before I give you any dope I may have, for your own sake as well as mine."

"Nonsense," he retorted. "You ought to be willing to trust me."

I decided to let him have it straight. "I would, under ordinary circumstances. But these aren't ordinary circumstances. You must see that. What sort of thing is it that you have to come to this God-forsaken place to work on? None of us has heard from you in years. This whole business is strange, Julian. Knowing you, I assume that everything is all right, but I've got to assure myself of that fact."

"Is that all?" he asked quietly when I had finished.

"Not quite," I answered. "I think you've been working too hard, Julian. I honestly believe you ought to take a rest. Anne thinks so, too. I'd much sooner persuade you to relax for a while than I would help you go on killing yourself by overwork."

He waved my words away with a gesture of one hand. "Come out with it, boy. What you really mean is that you think I am unbalanced and you don't want to encourage me in my insanity. That's in your mind, isn't it?"

"Well, you used some extreme words a minute ago, Julian. This thing of yours must be important, but you make it sound earth-shaking. Maybe you've brooded on it till you've lost some perspective."

His face was set and white when he turned it on me. "You're wrong, Richard. You're entirely wrong. As for my taking a rest, there will be time enough for that when my work is finished, and finished it is going to be, perhaps in a week, certainly in a month. I'm not crazy, my boy, but even if I were it wouldn't matter because the thing is done, anyhow. It works!" His voice, which had reached a crescendo, faltered. "That is, it works in a way, but not as I want it to do, and that is where I know you can help me. I've got to get the rest of it. Otherwise it means making my results public without the final step. Someone else will make that." The tension went out of his voice and he began to sound old and weak. "I don't want to wait any longer, my boy. I'm tired."

"Julian . . ." The distress in my heart was clouding my judgment and I knew that I ought to be on my guard, "I'll help you, of course. I don't want to know anything about the details of what you're doing. Just the general idea, that's all I ask." Doubtless this project of his was a legitimate, valid enterprise. In five years he must have found out the impossibility of what he had been planning when he left the university. But if he were still obsessed with it, I was not going to help him further into madness. "I don't think I'm asking anything unreasonable," I told him.

He shook his head. "Perhaps not. But if I tell you what it is, you will want to argue about it and I haven't strength nor time for argument now." He hesitated and drummed his long fingers uncertainly on the arm of the chair. Finally he said, "I'll strike a bargain with you. If you answer my questions—give me the data and references I need if you haven't the material yourself—then I'll tell you what I'm doing. But only afterward, and only if you promise me you will tell no one and do nothing. That's fair enough, isn't it?"

Without being able to see clearly why I thought so, I knew this was a moment of danger. His unwillingness to confide in me could mean only one thing—that he was still determined to reach Helen, assure himself that somewhere she still existed. If I refused to help him find her—or pretend to help him because, of course, no one could do more than that—would it not be more dangerous to his sanity than if I answered his questions and let him do what he liked afterward? My loyalty was to Julian, but which course would help, and which injure, him I could not tell.

The room seemed to close in on me. Between pity and doubt I could not decide what to do, and in that moment of indecisiveness I lost my last chance to checkmate Julian. Like a fool, I attributed the apprehension I felt to a mere personal concern over my friend, over his health and happiness. I should have known better. There was more in the warning my mind was giving me than could be accounted for in any such personal way. Behind the screen of my concern for Julian lurked thoughts that I did not dare allow to come forward, for fear of their implications. There was, for instance, the vague perception that Julian talked like a nervous man, obsessed by a tragic delusion, but still able to perceive reality from shadow; and the positive knowledge that he was a great man, too brilliant not to be able to complete almost any enterprise to which he had set that terrific mind of his. His own confidence in what he had accomplished so far should have impressed me more than it did.

For all that, I think anyone in my position would have done what I did. I decided that the only thing I could do was to humor Julian, be sympathetic, and do what he asked until the situation was plainer to me.

"All right, Julian. I'll help you any way I can. Though what *I* know that will be of any use to you…"

He smiled again, momentarily, and leaned forward in his chair. "Good," he said, "good." His face was terrifyingly intent. "What I am after is this…you have been doing certain work in your field that has interested me very much. I want to ask you some things about it."

Although I had expected something of the sort, I was surprised all the same. "I've done very little research these last years, Julian."

"That piece of yours in the *Journal* suggests otherwise, my boy. Now about these brain currents that you've been measuring…"

In the last few years a handful of doctors and experimental psychologists have been measuring the minute electric impulses which the living brain gives out. We have developed a machine which records these pulsations on a ribbon of paper that resembles a ticker tape. Each brain seems to produce a certain distinctive pattern of its own, and there are rhythms characteristic of sleep, concentration, or various kinds of emotions. Furthermore it appears that fatigue, various drugs, and many other things may influence those patterns.

Bill Rogers and I had got interested in the subject as a sort of hobby. At first we'd done little more than talk the subject over from the medical and psychological approaches. Then Bill had suggested that his hospital work gave him some unique opportunities for experimentation, and we had taken all sorts of brain records in the various wards there. One thing that excited Bill was the idea that pain might someday be "damped out" electrically in cases where drugs were dangerous. I was more interested in the phenomena as a whole, and particularly as they appeared in infants and in moribund cases. Some of my dope had been published later in the *Journal,* but of course I am a teacher and not a research man except incidentally. Still it's a new field and something may come of it in time and when we've accumulated a lot more data. Already we have got something, particularly in the case of measurements taken of schizophrenics and epileptic cases.

It was not altogether surprising that Julian should be interested in the thing, though it had all come up since he had withdrawn from active work. These minute, rhythmic impulses are electrical, as I've said, and Julian was an electrophysicist. His radio tube improvements, the Blair Wave Trap, and a lot of other things he worked out are still in use. But as he went on questioning me, I began to feel that his interest was not as abstract and coldly scientific as I should have liked.

All the while I was answering Julian's questions I had an inkling of that. I felt progressively more and more uncomfortable as his delight at my answers mounted. He kept nodding his head and jotting down notes in the shabby memorandum book he always carried. When I opened my suitcase and found an envelope of the encephalograms—the ribbons of paper tape marked with the trembling, jagged lines which depicted the electric pulses of the brain—about which I had been speaking, his excitement was close to frightening. He pored over those things, holding them close to his eyes and moving his lips soundlessly as he looked. Now and again a question came from him abruptly, and it is a measure of Julian's genius that whatever he asked went straight to the heart of some difficulty or other which Bill Rogers and I had debated fruitlessly. In half an hour, or perhaps a few minutes more, he had sucked me dry, of what I knew.

7.

THAT CONVERSATION with Julian has a fantastic quality as I look back on it. There in that faded magnificence of a room, with the running sweep of the river beyond its windows, we talked in the dry phrases and formulations of science. But all the time we were, between us and without knowing what we did, creating a horror. The sequence of our words was like an irrevocable syllogism, building step by step to a conclusion which was neither rational nor, in the abstract, credible. It was deadly just the same.

Something was born in that hour, something that Julian's mind had conceived years before and which was now in the very moment of parturition. He must have known, partly at least, what was happening, for the gathering triumph in his face and words gradually conveyed itself to me. At first I felt excited by his excitement, swept along by his enthusiasm. Then misgiving began to creep again into my mind and it seemed not so much strange as alarming that I should be telling this man things which appeared to possess some significance to him which they lacked for me. Finally he closed his notebook with a snap and put the encephalograms into the envelope again.

"I want to look these over with more care," he said. "I'll return them to you in a day or so. Perhaps I shall need to ask you something on one or two more points. But I think not." He spoke with a confidence which I found disquieting.

For a moment I was tempted to demand the graphs from him at once. The abnormal brightness of his eyes, the way his hand trembled when he put the envelope in his pocket, the feverish intensity of his examination of me had showed that far from pacifying the demon which was driving him, I had merely goaded it on. "I'm damned if I see what all this proves, Julian," I told him. "If you can make something out of that stuff I've told you, you're way ahead of the rest of us."

"Perhaps," he said slowly, "I am not looking for quite the same thing."

"You haven't told me yet what you *are* after," I reminded him. "Don't forget your promise."

"I haven't," he said absently and then was silent for a time. His eyes wandered to the door and I knew that having got what he wanted from me, he was impatient to be out of the room and away, working on it. "Richaid, I am afraid I should not have made that promise."

This was certainly not the old Julian, who would as soon have falsified an experiment as gone back on a promise. It gave me an unpleasant jolt. "Don't back down," I said. "You don't get out of this room until you tell me what you're after." My tone didn't sound as jocular as I'd intended.

His eyes swung back from the door and rested on me thoughtfully. "Very well," he said finally and with regret in his voice. "A promise is a promise, I suppose." He licked his lips and went on in a matter-of-fact tone which made what he said all the more insane. "I am working on the problem of immortality."

I cursed myself for every kind of fool in the calendar. "I see," I said, trying to sound noncommittal. "How are you tackling it, exactly?"

He shook his head. "I can't tell you that, my boy. Scientifically, of course. The way that men of reason and intelligence should have approached it centuries ago. I have constructed an apparatus which I shall give to the world when it is completed."

"Then it isn't finished?"

He looked uncomfortable for the first time. "Not wholly. I find that I have omitted an important element, a factor of control. Your answers to my questions, though, ought to give me what I need there."

"But you believe this thing of yours is going to work?" I could not keep the incredulity out of my voice. It was difficult to remember that he was not, could not be, rational. Since he was not a sane human being, of course he felt sure his device, whatever it was, would work.

To my surprise he hesitated. Finally he looked away from me and said, "In a way, Richard, it is already successful. But as I say, the element of control is lacking. Your data should—must—supply that. I think I shall be able to report success in a week or so. Perhaps even sooner." I saw the hands, linked in his lap, tremble as he spoke.

The monstrousness of what he was claiming swept over me and I forgot all discretion. "God in heaven, Julian!" I burst out. "You mustn't do that...you mustn't talk this way. Listen to me. You've got to listen to me. This is a mad project. It's blasphemous. It's impossible." As I spoke I wished that I were absolutely sure that it was impossible, but though every atom of sense and reasonableness in me affirmed that Julian was simply crazy, a cold dread that he wasn't fastened on me. "Even if it isn't impossible," I went on as earnestly as I knew how, "have you stopped to think what such a thing as you are trying to do would mean, Julian? What its effect would be?"

His thoughts seemed miles removed from my outburst. When he answered, his tone was quiet and gentle—I felt ashamed and confused by it because it made me wonder which of us was outside the normal pale. "I was afraid you would take it that way, Richard," he told me. "It is not my business to speculate what the effect of a discovery will be. Every new instrumentality of the human search for truth can be used or abused. You know that."

"But this is different. This is dynamite." A thought struck me. "I'm assuming that you think you can prove immortality?"

"Yes." That single syllable fell into the room with unarguable finality. In spite of myself I was impressed with the way he said it, momentarily completely convinced. Julian Blair was a great man and he made no positive affirmations unless he was sure. Time after time he had done impossible things. His theories, when he enunciated them, might sound radical and extreme to his contemporaries, but the event had invariably justified him and them. All that prestige was behind his single word of affirmation. Now of course he was old—senile. Something had slipped in that delicate and brilliant mind of his. But I could not be *sure*.

It never occurred to me that Julian could be both right and wrong.

After a long pause I said something that was foolish because I knew the answer to it already. I asked the question only because I wanted to put some words into the pit of silence that lay between us. What I said was, "But Julian, why? Why should you want to ... to do this thing?"

He brought his eyes back to me with an expression of faint surprise around them. "Surely I don't have to tell you that?" he said. And then I knew that what I feared was true: this work of his was not a labor of research, of pure science applied to an enigma presented by the physical universe. It was, instead, something intensely personal and urged upon him by emotion. I remembered the day when he had begun on it. For five years it had been in his mind, growing, spreading, burgeoning, until finally it had crowded out everything else. It was, if you like, a cancer of the mind.

8.

NOT MANY of us had come to the cemetery that day, partly because of the weather. But Helen and Julian had always preferred few
friends and close ones, so that her funeral would not have been large
under any circumstances. Julian, Anne, and I had driven out together, after the church service, and watched in numb silence the
end of that torturing ritual with which we dispose of the bodies of
our dead. I remember that the rain made a drumming noise on the
roofs of our umbrellas and that the grave was a brown scar on the
green of the cemetery lawn. Looking into it, I had seen the standing
water at its bottom. It seemed to me a sacrilege to put any part of
Helen into such a pit.... Anne's hand was cold and hard in mine as
we stood there, and I doubt if she, or I, or Julian even heard the minister's well-thumbed phrases.

Helen Blair, who had been Helen Conner, was the only woman I
had ever loved. I went right on loving her after Julian and she were
married; I was too fond of him, and she was too necessary to me, for
any complete severance of our relationships. Anyhow, I had been in
love with her before Julian had even met her and she had refused me
twice before he had proposed to her. That she had preferred a man
twenty years older than herself was natural enough under the circumstances, but the wonder was that Julian, with his enormous indifference to the ordinary human experiences and his relentless urge
toward work and discovery, should ever have fallen in love.

Not that any man could have overlooked Helen once he had seen
her. She had a still, sharp beauty that made you notice and respect it,

and a poise that had matured in her struggle to rise above the experience of her first marriage. When she was finally free of Ed Norton she arrived at a kind of compromise with herself and life that gave her tremendous control over herself, and deep simplicity of thought and feeling.

The statement that it was natural she should have preferred Julian to me needs amplifying. What made it so was her determination to found her life on something other than the heat and the insecure glory of young love. Julian needed her and, as she saw it, I did not. She could give him a life that would be richer than anything he had ever known and, if not the kind of love I wanted from her, at least a deep and sincere affection. Julian represented peace, security, and a tranquil future, and in those days he was far from the sort of person I have pictured, feeble and old, sitting in a broken-down armchair in the house on Setauket Point. He was a vigorous and distinguished-looking man of middle age then, the kind of man that exactly suited her need.

In the three years they were married, Helen made Julian's narrow life over into something rich and warm. To watch him come out of his dry reserve, crack the brittle shell of his past routines, until he actually learned how to laugh and mix a cocktail was a delight to his friends. For me it was, I'll admit, a painful pleasure. But for all my feeling that I had lost something which I should never find again, I was glad for both of them. It was a measure of her quality—and his, too, now that I think of it—that I never resented Julian.

In only one way Julian did not do better than I could have done myself. That was Anne. She had taken to me from the start and Helen was glad, I think, to have me around to make up for some of Julian's deficiencies as a foster father. That was what it came to, for she had been almost a mother to her younger sister, and the idea of Julian as Anne's brother-in-law was somehow ridiculous. She refused to call him anything more intimate than "Uncle Julian," and though she was fond of him, it was I who played with her and bought her chocolate malteds.

Helen died, very suddenly, of pneumonia. Her death was merciful in its speed, but the very abruptness of it was too much for Julian. One week he was this new, richly happy person that Helen had made him. The next he was a widower overwhelmed with the despair that comes to a man who has loved late in his life and lost his happiness before he has grown accustomed to having it.

After the funeral service Mrs. Wallace had taken Anne home with her, but Julian wanted to walk and I was the logical person to go with him. He said nothing for a long time. Our feet splashed in the puddles of the curving walk and the rain slithered down the polished surfaces of the headstones on either side of us. There was nothing I could think of to say to him; we simply walked on together slowly and heavily.

When we turned down Jefferson Street he lifted his head and looked at me like a man returning to consciousness after an operation. "I do not see how I am going to live without her, Dick," he said. His voice was steady and quite dead.

"She wouldn't want you to feel that way," I answered him gently "She wanted to make your life rich and happy. She did that. You mustn't throw away what she gave you."

He shook his head. "That part of it's over now," he remarked as if he were making an incontrovertible statement.

"You mustn't let it be over. She wouldn't like that. The way to feel about this is the way she'd want, I know. And that is to hang on to the things she gave you and make her memory something for joy, not sorrow." It sounded pretty evangelical in my own ears, but it was the best I could do.

Julian hardly seemed to have heard me. He said, "No," in a dull voice, but the word was addressed to something in his own mind, not to me. After that there was silence between us for several blocks, until he murmured something in a key too low for me to catch.

"What's that?" I asked him.

"'Stupid,' I said. It is stupid that we should know so little about what happens when…when a person dies. I have never thought about that before. All this agony…"

"Yes." The sorrow inside me made it difficult to follow what he was saying. I wanted to be alone, to remember Helen to myself, to get used to the fact that she was gone.

"If I knew I was going to see her again."

"You will, Julian. Of course you will."

He looked at me curiously. "Do you believe what you say, or are you just saying it?"

"People have always believed that," I said.

"Do you?"

Miserably I had to tell him that I didn't.

"You're a psychologist," he said finally. "Your science is supposed to deal with the human personality. And you understand no more than I about this thing."

"I know."

"You haven't even any definite evidence that death is the end of everything?

"No."

He struck his fist against the palm of the opposite hand. "Then I don't see how you can believe anything about it, one way or the other. Belief must be founded on some sort of knowledge or else it's superstition. Either you believe a thing because the evidence supports your position, or you are simply ignorant. In the dark."

"I'm not so sure of that, Julian. There's more than one way to know a thing."

"There is only one way to know anything. Experiment, test, check. Collect data and verify them. If the data affirm your belief, then you know."

"You can't do that with things like death and the soul."

"Have you tried?" He shook his head and walked on with lowered head. He was not looking at me or at anything else; his eyes were so wholly turned inward that I had to lead him down the sidewalk and across the streets. He was walking like a man asleep and I was hardly more aware of the physical world than he was. Each of us walled up in a private cell of grief and pain.

I left him at the door of his house. "Good-bye, Julian. I'll be over this evening." Then I remembered something. "Don't forget that Edith is going to bring Anne over some time this afternoon, after lunch," I said. "The kid will need a lot of comforting, Julian."

"Of course. Of course. I won't forget." But his attention was not on what I had said. "Good-bye, boy. Don't come this evening unless you want to. I shall be busy. I've got to think about this thing."

"No, Julian. Don't go over it in your mind any more. It won't do any good. She wouldn't want you to do that."

There was impatience in his tone. "I shall not be brooding. I must plan what I am going to do. There is no time to lose. I can't tell how long…" He went up the front steps of his house, stumbling once, and let himself in. I turned away with a sense of foreboding added to the misery in my heart.

Of course I had gone to the house that evening. I was so desperately lonely myself that I might well have gone simply because misery seeks company, but all through the afternoon I had found myself thinking about Julian and concerned over him. What I found when Anne let me in was unexpected. Julian was working. He was sitting at the long table which he used for a desk with a litter of papers around him and a stack of books beside his chair. It looked as if he had been there for hours.

"Hello, Julian," I said. "Don't let me interrupt you."

"That's all right," he replied without even raising his head.

I looked at Anne. Her white face with the dark circles under her eyes was puzzled. "He's been doing that all afternoon," she said, with a despairing break in her voice. "He wouldn't even eat any supper."

"How about you?" I asked. "Are you all right?"

"Yes," she said in a small voice. "I'm all right. I'm fine." Then she broke away from me and went out of the room, almost running. There was desperation in the pound of her feet on the stairs.

Perhaps it would be best to let her cry it out by herself, but Julian's absorption in what he was doing while a youngster like Anne was in need of comfort and love made me angry. He hadn't even looked up when she ran out of the room.

"I must say, Julian, that this is a curious time to be doing whatever it is you're working at. Don't you think Anne needs us more than—"

"No!" he interrupted in a harsh voice, turning in his chair to look at me with eyes that were too bright. "The child's grief will have to run its course. We can do nothing for her. Nothing immediate, that is." He struck his hand down on the table top. "Year after year, century after century, people have been feeling as she does—as we all do—this evening. Bitter and aching with grief. They comfort each other with empty, meaningless words, with prayers, with all the rigmarole of religion. It seems to me stupid and cowardly. If they had more courage and vision, more confidence in themselves, they would not take this fact of death so supinely. Long before this they would have done something about it."

"There isn't anything they can do."

He gave me a look of contempt. "How do you know that? Have you ever tried to find out, one way or the other? You, a psychologist, who ought to be more concerned with it than any other scientist? No, of course you haven't. You leave the whole question to mediums, quacks, crystal gazers." He looked at his papers. "My own colleagues are no better. Sir Oliver Lodge!" The scorn in his voice was acid. "And a man like Arthur Conan Doyle with his pictures of fairies! It's disgusting, almost the whole lot of it." His voice dropped to a more normal level. "Let me tell you something, Richard. I am a man of science. And science doesn't let things go by default. It investigates. That's what I'm going to do."

"Investigate what? God, Julian, you sit there and talk like this the very day that..." The sentence was better left unfinished.

He stood up and began to pace back and forth across the rug. I remembered thinking for the first time that he was looking his age. "I'm going to find out. This day of all days is the one to begin. This morning you said that people have always believed that we saw again those whom we have...lost. Presumably, you meant by that, after we ourselves have died?"

"Yes. Something like that."

"Well, I'm not going to wait for death." His voice was calm, but there was purposefulness behind it. "It will take time, but I think I shall succeed."

His attitude troubled me. The bitterness that was driving him into this project was all too apparent. "Listen, Julian," I began quietly, "I admit what you say as to the desirability of this thing you have in mind. But as a psychologist, even if I can't tell you anything about what you want to know, I can say positively that you are starting on it at the wrong time, when your emotion is obsessing your mind. Wait a while before you begin. Rest for a month. Perhaps take a trip somewhere with Anne. Then come back to it if you want to, with a reasonable amount of detachment."

He shook his head. "Waste a month? Every day will be a month in itself, without her." He sat down at the table again and picked up his pencil. "I have been making a survey to see how much reputable scientific work has been done. Apparently even less than I had supposed and none of it leading to any useful conclusions. I don't expect I shall find much of value in the whole background of the subject . . ." His voice trailed off in the intensity of his concentration.

Obviously there was no more use talking to him. After waiting a few minutes to see if he would remember that I was still there, I went upstairs to find Anne. She was in her room, face down on the bed, not even sobbing. When I touched her, I discovered that she was rigid all over, so tight with grief and loneliness that she hardly knew for a while that I was there. I shan't describe what happened between us in that dim room, but when I left she had cried herself out and was almost asleep. All the while I was comforting her, I felt a bitterness against Julian for letting the girl suffer alone as he had. I promised her everything I could think of to make her feel less lonely, and she clung to me desperately. It was horrible, and I don't remember it in any detail.

The clearest picture in my memory of that night is the one of Julian, gray-faced and oblivious of his surroundings, still working at his desk when I came down and let myself out of the house. I did not speak to him. I could not trust myself to suppress the anger I was feeling.

In the months that followed, Julian and I did not see each other a great deal. That was largely my own fault and choosing; I did not want to be reminded by seeing him of the fact that she was lost to both of us. I thought about Helen a good deal in those days, and much of it was stuff of a self-conscious morbidity which shames me when I remember it. Once or twice I even went so far as to blame Julian, in my thoughts, for her death. That was wildly irrational, I knew, and stupid. All the same, the sight of him woke something in me that I did not want to feel. So I stayed away from the house except when I called to take Anne out. Even then, as far as possible, I put Julian out of my thoughts.

That accounts, I suppose, for the fact that I did not pay much attention to the idea that he was still interested in the problem of immortality. I was too busy licking my own wounds to wonder much about his. When he resigned at the end of the year, it did occur to me to wonder whether he had got over that tragic notion, but I did not ask him about it. That would have made an awkward moment intolerable. Julian was set-faced, quiet, almost indifferent at that last meeting of ours. He spoke to me absently, as if he didn't care whether I had come or not.

The house was sold that summer. Anne, as I have said, had gone abroad. Julian began to fade into the background of his friends' thoughts, even those of us who had been closest to him. We wondered why he did not answer our letters. We learned, at last, that he had moved from the house in Scarsdale to which we had been writing, and we could not discover where he had gone.

Until that letter of his had arrived to stir the memory, I don't suppose I had thought seriously about that *ignis fatuus* of a project of his more than once or twice. He had become a figure which existed wholly in my past; I felt about him as much a sense of a final separation as I had about Helen. More and more, too, I had come to recall Julian as the man with whom I had once worked; the genius who stood for something superb in science. Perhaps that was because Arthur Wallace and some of the others felt that his leaving the university was an irreparable loss. Julian's work, his achievements as a research scientist and discoverer, were the things we talked about at the Faculty Club on the rare occasions when we did discuss him.

9.

ALL THE time that I was answering Julian Blair's questions there in the house at Barsham Harbor, I was struggling to realize that the greatest man in his field had devoted five long years to this madness; that the words he had spoken that night long ago had not been simply the expression of a distracted sorrow. It was bitterly sad to think of this man, my friend—and more than that a great and important person in his own way—mired in such a swamp of emotion and misdirected aspiration. That affirmation of his about having proved immortality stuck in my consciousness. It was the pathetic index of how far his mind had wandered from reality.

"Julian," I said, "if you have really proved immortality—"

He interrupted me. "I must have spoken somewhat imprecisely on that point, Richard. The truth is that with the data you have given me, I shall be able to prove it."

"Then you haven't...?" I let the question taper off in midair because I couldn't bring myself to end it. To go on, to say, "spoken with Helen?" was so fantastic that it gave me a feeling of revulsion. Even as it was I found myself looking away from him and embarrassed.

He seemed to understand what I was getting at. "It takes time to get accustomed to the idea, my boy. I know that. No, I have not talked to her, but I know that she is there, waiting. Yesterday, while I was experimenting, I thought for a minute...but it was not so. Merely certain epiphenomena which I find slightly puzzling." His voice lost some of its confidence; there was a note of indecision in it which came close to uneasiness.

Listening to him had given me a sense of despair. The very

directness of his emotion, the intensity of the excitement behind his eyes frightened me. He must be lost beyond recovery; the certainty of it settled in me like a lump of cold iron. To hear the Julian Blair whose lecture on "The Scientific Nature of Proof" was one of the events of the university year talking like a faith healer or a swami was a nightmare. I told myself that of course he was deranged, that his mind was sick and that he was not to be judged, but that didn't exorcise the feeling of miserable finality with which I looked at him. He had wandered far down this private road of his, and I wondered whether I or anyone else could turn him back.

Finally I said, "Julian, I don't know what to tell you about this. I'd rather think it over before I say anything more. Only, take it easy." I forced myself to go over to his chair and pat him on the shoulder. There was still enough loyalty and affection left in me for that.

He stood up and smiled at me as if I were his son. "Richard, you are a good friend and a kind one. By all means take time to think this over. But you cannot seriously expect me to 'take it easy,' as you put it. When a month's work—perhaps less, much less—will put the whole thing right in my hand?" His tone was amused and yet remote. We walked together to the hall and he turned and patted my arm. "Don't worry about me, Dick. I know what I'm doing." He did not look back as he went up the stairs, taking them a step at a time and with his long-fingered hand, serpented with blue veins, sliding up the banister beside him. Slowly as he went, with his physical weakness obvious in every step, there was something triumphant in that ascent of his.

For a minute or two after he had left me I did nothing, simply staring after him up the stairs with my thoughts in chaos. I could hear his footsteps overhead, going along what must have been an upper hall, and then the sound of a door closing. It was not a loud noise, and yet the house quivered slightly as if from the moving of a heavy weight, and I wondered briefly about that. Afterward, nothing but silence.

There seemed to be nothing more sensible to do, so I went back to the living room and sat down to put my thoughts into some kind of order. I tried to imagine what I ought to do next. Julian had pumped out of me everything he wanted to know and I did not believe that he would have any further interest in me. Probably Mrs. Walters would not be distressed, either, if I were to catch the evening train for New York. It was clearly the sensible thing to do.

On the other hand there was Anne. To leave her alone in this house seemed like an act of desertion, illogical as that feeling was on close examination. I told myself that Helen would have wanted me to stay and keep an eye on her, but that was an evasion. Whatever I did or did not do about Anne would not be for the sake of a woman five years dead whose image in my mind was now as evanescent as the smell of lavender in an old drawer. It would be for myself. I admitted that to myself, but left its implications alone.

The notion of two nights in a row on the train was repellent. I might as well stay, now that I was here, at least for another day. It was a part of the world new to me, and I ought to see something of it. Swimming with Anne had been fun and I wanted to do it again. Maybe some sensible way in which I could deal with Julian would present itself. There were still ten clear days before I had to be back at the university and I saw no reason to put too abrupt a termination to this visit.

While I was still engaged in this childish form of self-deception Mrs. Marcy came into the room, complete with broom, dustpan, and cloth. She seemed surprised and put out to find me.

"Oh, Professor Sayles! I didn't know you were in here."

"I'm just going. I won't be in your way."

"Lands! It wouldn't be a disturbance. It's nice to see a new face in the house." She leaned her broom against the end of the sofa. "Seems like a crime, this big house and only two people in it till Miss Conner came. I like folks, Professor Sayles, and there's plenty of room. I hope you're goin' to stay a while."

Her hospitable offer amused me, particularly since it was not her house, but it warmed me, too. It was pleasant to find that I was wanted, at least by one person—two, I corrected myself. "Thank you," I answered. "I am not sure how long I can stay, but overnight, at least. I've never been in Maine before and I want to see something of it. I never dreamed there were places like this up here."

She grinned. "We say 'down'," she corrected me. "Yes, it's a beautiful house. My own folks built it."

I was surprised. "I didn't know that."

"Yep. The Talcotts. We lived here more'n a hundred years, I reckon. My great-great-uncle Amos, he bought this land and put the place up. Used to be a sea captain." She looked out the window thoughtfully. "They say the river was full of ships in them days. Uncle Amos went to India and China and South America and I don't know where-all." Her face lost its brightness. "I'm the last of 'em. And times ain't what they was, around here at least."

"It's still a beautiful old house."

"It is, isn't it? Wherever you look, practically, your eye finds water. Feels almost like you're in a boat right on the river. That's why Uncle Amos got it, I reckon. He called it 'The Anchorage,' but it's been the Talcott place so long people don't call it anythin' else." She paused. There was something old and proud in her thin face and I knew that no matter what happened to her, she had this memory of her ancestors to make her seem important to herself. "Uncle Amos died right in that room above here." She gestured toward the ceiling. "He used to lie in his bed by the window with a spyglass, they say, lookin' down the river fer the ships comin' in."

"It must have hurt to see the place go out of the family."

She shrugged. "You got to take things as they come. Seth was put out more'n I was, I expect. I kinda wish we could have got *somethin'* out of it, but the bank had the mortgage and they sold it fer that. That and the back taxes... Seth claims it's a mortal shame to see farm land like this goin' back to goldenrod and scrub pine, but I tell him he ought to be thankful these folks have money to pay fer cleanin' and cookin'. I don't know where we'd be without it, the way times have been this year." She took up the broom and began to sweep. "I expect it's a blessing in disguise, Professor Sayles. And I aim to do what I can. *She* don't know nothin' about keeping a house, that's sure."

I sat there for a while watching her tidying the room and wondering how she could be so cheerful. It must have been a bitter experience to come back as hired girl to the house that her own family had built and inhabited, but she gave no sign of it. She was humming as she worked, and the tune was "Someday My Prince Will Come," from *Snow White*. Listening to her, a lump came into my throat.

"Can't give this room more'n a lick and a promise today," she remarked finally. "It's a right big house and today I'm supposed to clean out that room of his after lunch."

"Mr. Blair's room you mean?" I asked in surprise.

"Yes. Uncle Amos's room."

"I didn't suppose he'd allow anyone in there."

She stooped and began collecting the cigarette stubs from the empty fireplace. "You're right about that, mostly. But once a week they let me in to sweep the floor."

As casually as I could I put the question that was engrossing me. "What's he got in there?"

She turned round to face me and leaned back against the channeled pilaster which supported the mantel. "That's the question folks around here keep askin' me over and over. Seth fair devils me to find out an' that cousin of his, Harry, that drove you out here. All I know fer sure is that there's somethin' in the middle of that room as big as a grand piano, only more square-like. Before they let me in she always covers it with a lot of blankets an' sheets, so I can't tell you just what it's like under 'em. An' I don't get much chance to look. I can tell you that . . . All the time I'm sweepin' an' dustin' the window sills that woman stands right in the door, watchin' me, an' I have to keep humpin'." She shook her head. "But I don't reely care if I don't find out. There's a slew of wires snakin' in an' around that thing, whatever it is, an' I don't aim to get mixed up in them."

"Naturally not."

She turned back to her cleaning, crouched beside the fireplace like a sparrow, with her voice half muffled in it. "He does make a mess in there, though. The floor's a sight. Little pieces of wire and a lot of stuff that looks like gray sawdust, an' bits of copper an' hunks of glass, an' papers all over the place. You never saw such a mess of torn-up paper. In little tiny pieces, too, like he didn't want anybody to read what was written on 'em. *She* makes me burn it—all the stuff that will burn—once a week. Stands right over me while I put it in the stove. They ain't lettin' a soul in on that thing of theirs, Professor Sayles, I tell you."

"Inventors are likely to be that way."

She straightened up with the dustpan in her hand. "I guess you're right, though he's the only one I've ever seen." She collected her broom and dustcloth. "I'll tell you something, Professor Sayles. The folks around here don't understand a man like Mr. Blair."

"I suppose they don't."

"It's a fact. Even with us needin' the money like we do, I have to argue it all over again with Seth every week. You know," she laughed apologetically, "some of them thinks he's makin' one of these death rays like you read about in the papers. It was Cy Williams at the express office put that idea into their empty heads, if you ask me. Spreadin' all them stories about Mr. Blair getting this shipment from one electric company an' that from another. I didn't hardly know how to answer 'em till I got some idea what Mr. Blair reely was doing."

Momentarily her final sentence slipped past me as if it were nothing more important than the rest of what she had been saying. Then it struck home so abruptly that I came close to gasping. She was so calm about it that I looked at her incredulously. There was no sign in her expression that she considered Julian's invention anything but the most natural in the world.

"Oh," I said lamely. "I didn't know you knew what it was."

She smiled pleasantly. "I didn't have an idea, first off. But I kinda put two an' two together. Not that I'm one for poking my nose into other people's business."

"Of course not. I didn't mean that."

"No offense taken. You see, with them tubes an' things he ordered, an' with all the wire on the floor, an' all that, I just had a feeling what it was. Mr. Blair's shy an' quiet—he don't look well at all to me—an' I figured he wasn't the sort to be makin' a death ray. Though if he was to do it, I could suggest a few folks he could try it on." She compressed her lips and nodded defiantly. "Then one time I heard the noise of the thing an' I said to myself, 'Well, if it ain't some new kind of a radio he's got in there.'" She stopped and looked at me to see how I was reacting, and there was the look of a child that thinks it has been clever on her face.

"Noise?" I was trying to keep something horrible from coming into my mind. "What kind of noise?"

"You know. First that kind of humming, like when the set's first warming up. An' then a lot of sounds. Mostly static, it seemed like to me."

A curious wave of coldness was sliding down my spine. She wouldn't be so calm if she knew where that noise came from. I checked myself at that point. Where Julian would claim it came from, I made a mental correction. There was something I had to know immediately. "Tell me," I said and the words almost stuck in my throat, "does his radio ever get any voices? Talking or singing?"

She hesitated. "I expect it ain't that far along. It doesn't reely work right yet, but it's only the last week or so I've heard it at all. I guess he'll have it goin' better directly; about all you can tell now is it's goin' to be some special kind of radio. I haven't heard any voices, exactly. All I could tell was that it was one of them shortwave things."

"How did you know that?"

"Well, they say those things will get broadcasts from all over the world, though most of the time they don't sound so good to me. But this one of his has got the same kind of faraway note to it."

The breath seemed to be coming into my lungs with less effort. "But you never heard anything you could recognize?"

She reflected a minute, leaning on her broom and staring at the ceiling. "Well," this came slowly, "'bout a week ago he had it turned on one evening when I was washin' the supper dishes. I could hear it plain enough, even clear down in the kitchen. An' it sounded then like it *might* have been voices. Only there was too many of them at once to make out anything separate. If you've heard the people cheerin' at a football broadcast, you'll get the general idea of what I mean."

"I see." It was absurd how hard my heart was still hammering. For a moment I had been imagining something ridiculous and outside the bounds of sense. I felt ashamed of having given credence, even for an instant, to the thought that Julian might, indeed, have done what he claimed to be on the point of accomplishing. Even that instant's belief had showed me how frightening it would be to believe that he was not deluded. To let the world of the dead back in upon the living was a conception so horrible that I was shaken—a blasphemy more frightening than anything the theologians had ever conceived . . . And then I was smiling to myself as I understood what it was she had really heard.

That humming, that confused murmur—it was obviously nothing but tubes heterodyning in some way. Perhaps there had been an aurora borealis that night—it seemed to me that I'd heard it did funny things to all sorts of electric apparatus. If the thing made a noise, as Mrs. Marcy said, it was a noise which it induced itself. Yes, I told myself, there was no doubt that was what she had heard.

I felt weak and happy with relief.

When I could trust my voice again, I said, "Well, Mrs. Marcy, it's too fine a day to waste indoors. I'm going out and enjoy some of your famous Maine air and scenery."

She nodded with the birdlike jerk of her head that I already thought of as characteristic. "It's a beautiful state, the state of Maine. In summer, that is. Winter is something else again."

We left the living room together and, as we turned down the hall toward the kitchen, a thought occurred to me. "By the way, Mrs. Marcy, I wouldn't say anything about hearing the set working to anybody. Especially to Mrs. Walters and Mr. Blair."

She gave me a dry grin. "Don't worry. We scarcely so much as pass the time of day. She ain't exactly sociable."

I grinned back at her. "Poison ivy?"

She shrugged. "If you stay away from it, you never need worry," she remarked.

I thought of that afterward. It was the soundest sort of common sense and yet, it failed her. It wasn't a weed that she needed to beware, but an avalanche.

10.

MRS. WALTERS was sitting on the edge of the back steps when I came out the kitchen door, in the shadow made by the wall of the ell that ran out toward the barn. To my momentary astonishment, she was stringing beans. Little as I had seen of her, it startled me to find her at a natural household task; I had the instantaneous feeling she had been expecting me and that the beans had been pressed into service to complete a picture of herself which she was trying to draw for my benefit. Nothing in her face betrayed any surprise when I came in sight; she barely glanced up and promptly returned her gaze to the level meadow and the bay beyond it. The slow, even movements of her fingers were uninterrupted: pick up a bean with the left hand, snip off the tips with the knife in her right, two precise motions to strip off the strings, and a third to deposit the finished bean in the enameled cook pot in her broad lap... She was the quintessence of naturalness.

In saying that she was expecting me, I am merely guessing. Mrs. Walters was too clever a woman to make even the smallest slip; I never found out just how her intelligence worked. Even Julian, I think, never understood all that was in her mind, though he must have had one appalling glimpse, at least, of what she was capable of doing if she had to.

Anyhow, she was waiting for me on those steps and my instinct told me so at once. I debated going past her and on up the road with merely a casual word. If she wanted anything of me, that would force her hand, make her at least call after me. But I dismissed the idea instantly. She might see just why I had done so; the less she realized her effect on me the easier things were going to be—and the more likely I was to be of help to Julian. I sauntered calmly down the steps and sat on the bottom one.

"Gorgeous day."

"Yes." I thought again that there was some kind of music in her voice. "Those clouds mean rain, though. Perhaps this afternoon or tonight."

They were piling up over the far shore of the bay, only a low line of them, but they had not been there at all a few hours before.

"This is beautiful country," I said. "It's the first time I've been in Maine."

"Really. I suppose it is handsome. I never notice the places where I find myself."

"Oh, come now. Don't tell me you'd as soon be in Boston or New York as here?"

That experimental cast failed to produce a rise. If she had lived in either place, her reply gave no inkling of it. "There is no difference of importance," she declared. "My life is turned inward, Professor Sayles. I live in my mind and the surroundings of my body don't make a bit of difference."

This curious speech was delivered with a calmness that left me no loophole for further attack. Whether she actually meant what she said or not, the subject was closed. But I did not have quite wit enough to understand that; after I had seen more of her I should not have mistaken the note of finality in her voice. I tried again and, because I was challenged by her attitude, led a stronger card than I should have. "All that surprises me, then," I said, "is that Julian should come to a place like this. He's as indifferent to his environment as you are to yours. I suppose you were the one who had an enthusiasm for Maine."

I could not see her face without craning around, but I knew there was a smile on it. "Oh, no," she said. "Julian came here, I guess, to find privacy and freedom from interruption."

"He seems to have found the ideal place for that."

Her silence was so negative that it made me uncomfortable. I turned round and saw that she had withdrawn her scrutiny from the meadow and the clouds and was watching me, not narrowly or critically, but with an incurious steadiness that made me feel awkward and out of place. "You have talked to Julian already," she said, and it was a statement, not a question. She was perfectly well aware that I had done so, and there was a suspicion in my mind that she had also managed to overhear most of what we had said.

"Yes," I admitted. "We had a talk. I'm afraid I was not able to help him much."

Even through the back of my head I could feel her eyes continuing to regard me with the same persistence. "What do you think of what he is doing?" she inquired as if it were the most ordinary question imaginable.

"What can I think?" I retorted. She had taken me off my guard. "I'm not competent to judge, of course. But I think the same thing that every sane person would. I think it's mad." Then I began to regret the impetuosity of my reply. "Of course, it means only that Julian has never got over the shock of losing his wife. He loved her with his whole heart and her loss was a disaster for him. This idea of his is a compensation mechanism. He is not necessarily mad, but the idea is. That's what I think."

She smiled slightly. "I can see you're pretty strong-minded about it. What makes you believe that on the subject of this...what did you call it—'compensation mechanism'—he is insane? If that's what you meant." Her tone was not at all combative; it was neutral and reserved.

"His morbid obsession with death. His fantastic notion that he can prove immortality by making an instrument to talk to the souls of the dead. His conviction of the importance of his work, his absorption in it to the exclusion of everything else. His coming here, burying himself from his friends and his proper world."

She nodded. "I see. On your own premise, you are quite correct, Mr. Sayles."

"My premise?"

"That Julian's project is impossible."

"No normal person would consider that it was possible."

Speaking in a soft voice, but with the most complete conviction she answered me. "Julian's mind transcends the normal. And the thing he is trying to do is possible."

I tried to put the contempt I felt into my look. "See here," I turned and told her, "I'm not nervous, overwrought, broken, like Julian. You don't need to give me any of that."

She flushed and the darkness behind her eyes seemed momentarily to dilate. The blade of the kitchen knife in her hands trembled slightly, and for a second I was afraid of her and alert. Then her face changed to amusement and she looked at me as if I were a refractory child. "Professor Sayles, you are an ignorant man, but you seem to be intelligent, so perhaps I can say this without hurting your feelings. When you come to appraise Julian Blair and what he is doing, don't forget that you are doing so wholly from your own point of view. You are still a young man, in some ways I think a very young man, and there are a good many experiences still ahead of you."

Her manner and what she said were difficult to tolerate. "Thank you," I told her. "I shall remember what you say."

"That's wise of you," she said as if she had not heard the sharpness in my tone. "There are a good many things you and your science have left out of account, Mr. Sayles. Julian is tackling one of them now. If he succeeds, you admit he will be the greatest man in all human history."

"*If,*" I said and then changed my mind. "Will he? I wonder."

She turned away and began to watch the white ridges of cloud piled along the southwestern horizon. "All of us are too much concerned with this life," she remarked; she spoke as if what she were saying was an obvious fact instead of a philosophic platitude. "It is time that a man like Julian turned to the truly important problems." After that she was silent for a while, but I knew she had not finished and decided not to interrupt. When she went on again, her tone was more personal and definite. "I have devoted my whole life to the thing to which Julian is now devoting his, Mr. Sayles. You cannot ask me to consider him insane."

That turned me round again in my seat and I stared at her to see if her look gave any clue to the meaning of that cryptic statement. But her large, heavy face was without any expression and she was watching the horizon again. "You...what?" I said at last.

"I thought you knew that," she answered and there was something like regret in her voice, as if she were sorry she had told me anything that I had not heard before. "I was certain Julian would tell you. I am what you would call a medium."

That was it, of course! That explained everything...Why she was with Julian, and what there was about her that made me uncomfortable. A sense of relief went through me with the insight. It seemed to me that now it would be easier to help Julian. I had only to deal with a woman who was, after all, simply a member of a group of fakers. Every sensible person knew that mediums were cheats and frauds. I told myself triumphantly that however skillful and deep-seated her influence with Julian might be, it was still vulnerable.

"Yes," she went on quietly, "I am what we sometimes think of as a station. A person who lives mostly in this world but occasionally, in a limited way, and very partially, in the other." She smiled again, almost maternally. "I suppose you are one of the skeptics who does not believe there is another world."

"I am a real skeptic and I don't know whether there is another world—or not," I corrected her. "If there is, it must be one which is fundamentally unknowable in terms of human cognition."

"Cognition!" There was an edge of mockery in her voice. "You have a fine set of words to express your own prejudices." Then she sighed. "Well, I won't argue with you, Professor. Perhaps I'll have an opportunity some time to show you how limited your knowledge is."

"My vocabulary is probably no better than it should be," I said. "And I agree that there is no point in argument. But I want to tell you that I think you are doing a very dangerous thing, Mrs. Walters, one that you should stop at once."

"What do you mean?" Her voice was harder.

"I mean leading Julian deeper into this morass of his obsession with the loss of his wife," I said. "You are giving him hope and encouragement. Did you ever stop to think that he is, fundamentally, a scientist? That this pseudo truth you are giving him will be at war with the whole pattern of his mind, even if he seems consciously to welcome it? That you will ultimately produce a breakdown there—if it hasn't happened already?"

She stood up abruptly. "You are insulting," she said scornfully. "Insulting and ignorant. Julian would have had a breakdown, as you put it, if he had not found me. I gave him the hope he needed to go on living. Which is more than your wonderful science did for him. It was his science that almost destroyed him, not me."

She had her hand on the knob of the kitchen door. The blazing anger that looked out of her eyes made me afraid. But we had gone too far to withhold any trust. "Very altruistic of you," I remarked, looking her full in the face. "All of Julian's friends ought to be deeply grateful to you, Mrs. Walters. I wonder how you have been able to afford this generosity of yours?"

My meaning did not escape her. I watched the barb sink in and saw that she smarted under it, but I had expected it to produce an instantaneous retort that would show her in the true colors of the game she was playing. Instead, she was silent. She gave me a slow glance of smoldering anger and contempt, turned on her heel, and went through the door without a backward glance. She did not even slam it behind her, but closed it quietly and firmly. I was left to stand there and inspect its panels, bleached by the sun and weathered to a neutral silver-gray.

When I turned and began to walk along the road away from the house, it came over me that I had played my cards foolishly and that she had trumped every trick but one. She had given one point away—that she was a medium—but only because she was certain that I would find it out anyhow. For some obscure reason I felt ashamed. I had been rude, even if calculatingly and for good reason. But the anger with which she had met my final sneer was not, I felt convinced, a theatrical performance. She meant it. Whatever she was, she was not a pure and simple cheat. Much as I wanted to discount her, I had to admit to myself that when she spoke of her calling she had sounded genuine, in spite of her magniloquent words. And though I was convinced that mediums were never genuine, the deception in this case plainly included herself as well. She believed in her own power.

That fact made me pause in my thinking. I wondered whether I was competent to form such a judgment. Everything I had ever heard about mediums had convinced me that nine out of ten of them were charlatans. The tenth was a victim of self delusion; if you were willing to admit that clairvoyance and telepathy were possible, the results which that tenth psychic could sometimes obtain were explicable in terms of those powers. And impressive though it might be to admit that one person could read another's mind or perceive objects with an inner eye which could penetrate walls and mock at distance, it was still as far as ever from accepting the notion that anything human survived the phenomenon of death. Or, if survival were a fact, that anyone could communicate with the other side of the barrier.

Despite Mrs. Walters' faith in herself that she could actually bridge that gap—if it was a gap and not the ultimate abyss—I never for a moment believed it. I do not believe it now, though it is less easy to dismiss the hypothesis. But what was fatally wrong in my thinking, there on that empty road, was that since she was not what she claimed to be, she was not, therefore dangerous . . .

It should have occurred to me that, even in despair, Julian would be a hard man to fool and that Mrs. Walters must have shown him evidence of something more important than occasional flashes of telepathy. If I had thought about that for a while, tried to imagine what she had been able to do which would interest him, I might have caught a glimpse of what was likely to happen. Instead, the problem presented itself to me in a completely irrelevant light—the question of what I ought to do about Julian.

The answer was certainly not obvious. I mulled it over in my mind for a good while, but in the end came back to the only real idea I had, which was to wait a while, see more plainly what was going on, and try to persuade Julian to let me examine his work. Once I reached that point I counted on being able to see the flaw in it—the reason why it wouldn't do what he claimed. I never doubted that such a flaw existed. Perhaps I might be able to break him of this delusion at once, but if not, the entering wedge would have been driven. He had suggested that he'd achieved some partial success. (How partial they both were, I thought—Julian with his invention, Mrs. Walters with her contact in the "other" world.) Very well, then. I would persuade Julian to demonstrate to me how far he had got. He would have to talk to me as one scientist to another. That in itself would help. He would be reminded of his own innate standards and see that he was being false to them.

The plan was naïve, of course. I see that now. But it might have worked. Even now I can't say positively that it wouldn't have done what I hoped. But there was never an opportunity to test it. And when Julian unwittingly gave us a demonstration what he had accomplished, I did not know it for what it was.

11.

THAT PROOF did not come till later in an endless day. Meanwhile, the hours dragged along one after the other. By noon the weather had grown sultry and the bank of clouds across the bay was higher and darker. The air was without motion and full of an impending violence that made the hairs at the back of my neck prickle. There was certainly going to be a thunderstorm later.

By the time I had finished thinking out what I was going to do it was almost noon and I turned my steps back along the road to the house. As I walked toward it, the sun-heated air from the road made its image waver and tremble before me. It stood up at the end of the Point almost as naked as a lighthouse; there were no trees around it, and the three cubes in its composition—barn, ell, and house—were related to each other as arbitrarily as boulders on a beach.

Lunch, like breakfast, was in the kitchen; apparently it had "not seemed worthwhile to Julian and Mrs. Walters to clean out the junk in the other front room and eat there. It was typical of the whole ascetic and yet slovenly way in which they seemed to be living. The meal was desultory. Mrs. Marcy cooked well, but the dishes she set before us were all hot and there was too much of them. We were not harvest hands. Julian barely picked at his food, swallowing a mouthful now and then more out of deference to Anne's insistence that he eat something than out of any appetite. She hardly ate more herself and spoke scarcely at all. I felt that she did not know just what the *status quo* was and thought it better to take no chances. She kept one eye on Mrs. Walters most of the time, with now and then a grin in my direction. It was pleasant to see her across the table from me.

The only one who enjoyed that meal was Mrs. Walters, who sat on my left. She was as silent as the rest of us, but this time she ate steadily and with a heartiness that was faintly revolting to me.

None of our few and unimportant remarks is worth reporting. Twenty minutes after we sat down we had all left the table and gone our separate ways. Julian retired upstairs, presumably to continue his work though Mrs. Walters reminded him that he would have only an hour or two before it was time to clean what she called "our room," which I understood to mean the laboratory. He nodded and said that he would be through in plenty of time. Mrs. Walters stayed in the kitchen talking to Mrs. Marcy about supper and instructing her to fix a bed for me somewhere upstairs. I didn't pay any attention to what it was all about, but I am positive that it was mere household routine.

Anne and I wandered outdoors. Somehow I was beginning to feel that the less time I spent inside the walls of that house the better. Each time I stepped out one of its doors I felt indefinably relieved, freer. We wandered across the meadow again and lay down in the grass under the big maple tree near the edge of the river bay. It was peaceful there and I felt relaxed. My pipe, when I got together the energy to light it, tasted good. Anne lay beside me looking comfortable and intermittently braiding grass stems into some sort of bracelet. I knew she wanted to talk to me after a while, but that she was waiting, as I was, for the heavy mood of lunch to lift.

"Well," she said finally, "what do you think of our happy home, God bless it?"

"I don't like it."

"Were you shocked by Uncle Julian? He looks so old and sick to me."

"Yes," I said, "and I've been wondering whether to tell you what he had to say. Maybe I'm doing you a rotten trick, Anne, but I think you'd better know about it." And I told her what he was doing. She listened to me without interrupting once; the only way I could judge the effect of what I was saying lay in observing the steady drain of the color out of her face.

"He's really sick, then," she said when I finished speaking, "in his mind, too."

"I'm afraid so."

"And where does she come into all this? Or didn't he tell you that?"

"No, but she did. We sat on the back steps and had a chat." I told her about that, too.

"So that's it," she said, still weaving the stems of grass together. "What do you think we ought to do?"

"In a minute," I said. "Meantime, there's one more thing. Mrs. Marcy came in after I'd talked to Julian. She chattered away for twenty minutes or so. And she told me something odd..." I was conscious that my voice gave away some of the disquietude which the remembrance of that bustling little woman brought me.

"Don't tell me," Anne said, rolling over and sitting up in the grass, "that there's something queer about Elora, too? Elora—isn't that a sweet name? She must have been adorable ten or twelve years ago." Her voice sounded as if that was almost before the dawn of recorded time.

"Ages ago," I agreed drily. "The point that seems odd to me is that Julian and Mrs. Walters keep the thing covered when Mrs. Marcy's in the room. Or so she says."

Anne frowned thoughtfully and thrust a stem of grass between teeth that were white in her brown face. She sat so long without answering that I almost forgot what I had said in watching the leaf shadows brush to and fro across her forehead. Then she shook her head. "They're both taking no chances on letting the great secret escape them, Dick. But I don't see anything curious about covering the thing up. If only to keep the dust of sweeping off whatever it is."

"Well," I said slowly, "maybe there isn't. Probably it's just my imagination working overtime. There's something about this place that makes you do more wondering than thinking, anyhow. But if I were making a complicated piece of electrical machinery, I don't think I'd bother to shroud it over so even a Maine farmer's wife couldn't look at it. It's a stupid sort of precaution. A bit of dust wouldn't matter enough to go to all that trouble, and Mrs. Marcy couldn't grasp the least thing about it by looking at it. And Mrs. Walters is right there, she says, all the time she's sweeping."

"Yes..." Anne agreed without conviction. "Maybe they're afraid it would scare her."

If there were any truth at all in the superstition that coming events are foreshadowed, then was the moment for it to have been revealed. But I heard those casual words of Anne's with no reaction, no feeling of prescience. I laughed—and I should like to be able to call back that laughter now—without bothering to retort. The idea was so simple that it could not be true. Only later, when I saw the figures which are now nothing but puddled lumps of melted wire, did I think of Anne's remark again. A great many more important things than the first sight of those seven...things...happened to me before I saw the last of the house on Setauket Point, but none that come up more easily against the dark side of my lids when my eyes are closed.

Anne herself attached no importance to her suggestion. She grinned at my laughter and went on, "Anyhow, it doesn't seem to me to matter. The problem is what we're going to do."

"What I thought of this morning was trying to get into Julian's confidence to the point where he'd let me see this mechanical marvel of his. Perhaps he'd be willing to let me work with him and help him on it. I once had a laboratory job under him, you know. Little by little I might be able to prove to him that the thing won't and can't work, all the time pretending to believe in it myself."

It was Anne's turn to laugh. "Boring from within. You talk like the new Communist party line. But it might work, at that." Something must have occurred to her, because after a moment her voice took on assurance and lost most of its underlying amusement. "You've got something there, I think. It's the best suggestion I can think of. Provided you have the time?"

"I've got ten free days."

"That ought to be enough," she said, and though her face and tone were both sober, I had an idea she was smiling to herself about something. "Only look out for that woman. If she gets an idea what you're trying to do, or if you get her jealous of her standing with Julian..." She bit through the grass stem with an audible crunch.

That consideration gave me no pleasure. "She's going to be awkward," I admitted.

We had been talking earnestly but not, I think, with particularly heavy hearts. There was something exciting in the situation for both of us. I knew that no matter what happened I should enjoy the next few days because I could spend part of them with Anne. She must have been glad of any company in that lonely house and relieved because I had showed up. But simultaneously we realized what a tragic and pathetic sort of conspiracy we were cooking up. We each loved Julian, in my case remotely but genuinely for all that, and we had been forgetting him.

"Listen, Dick," Anne said, turning toward me and putting her hand on mine, "we've got to pull this thing off. We can't fail. It's sure to be the end of Uncle Julian if we do. I'll try to keep her out of the way as much as I can. But don't fail."

"I'll try not to."

"Do you think he believes the thing is nearly finished?" she said, to break the awkward pause that followed.

"I think so. I told you what he said about it, and Mrs. Marcy seems to have heard it humming, so he must have put the current through it, at least." I told her about the noises that Mrs. Marcy had described.

Anne looked at me steadily while I spoke, and there were amazement and something else in her face. "So that's what that noise is!" she exclaimed when I had finished.

"You've heard it too?"

"Yes. The humming. And the other thing too."

The same cold thrill that had gone through me once before that day, when I had been talking to Mrs. Marcy, swept into me again. I told myself I was a fool to be so affected by hearing that Julian's machine made noises. But if it made a certain kind of noise... I put that thought out of my head. The thing could not work and that was that. Still, I wanted to be reassured. "You didn't hear any voices, I trust?" I made my voice sound light and casual.

"No." The look was still on her face. "I never even thought of voices, though what Mrs. Marcy said about the cheering is close to it, in some ways. It wasn't such a loud noise. Maybe I mean that it sounded as if it were coming from a long way off. A roaring noise, like a waterfall, only coming to you down wind from very far away."

"Far away." It was strange that Anne and Mrs. Marcy should have chosen the same phrase to describe what they had heard. It was not a particularly helpful description and somehow I didn't like it. I turned the words over in my mind, trying to form an audible picture from them, but it was no use. It was just a phrase that I didn't like.

"Any sort of electric circuit with tubes and a speaker in it can be made to give off a noise. As Mrs. Marcy said, like a shortwave radio that's not tuned to any particular station. There's a phenomenon called heterodyning that might produce such an effect."

Anne looked unconvinced. "Uncle Julian ought to know that, I should think. I hope you're right and that's all it was." She looked away and said, very quietly, "All I can tell you is that it wasn't a pleasant sound."

"Not a bit like a lot of happy angels making music before the Lord?"

"Don't!" she said sharply and lay down again in the grass without letting me see her face.

The sultriness of the afternoon began to make us both drowsy. The smell of hot meadow grass and earth was heavy in the air, which was suddenly very quiet. I lay beside her and my eyes began to close. I didn't want to think; it had already been a fairly long day as far as I was concerned. I relaxed, maybe I dozed. At any rate, the next thing I noticed was that Anne was shaking my shoulder.

"The sun'll be under those thunderheads in a few minutes," she was saying. "Let's have another swim first."

Apparently she had gone back to the house while I lay there, because she had our suits under her arm. I stood up, groggy with sleep, and we went down to the small cove. Anne was right about the approaching storm; the clouds were towering high over the far shore of the bay and looked swollen and black. I left my clothes rolled up in a tight bundle and stuffed under the thickest willow I could find.

Anne was waiting for me on the sand; she looked minutely small under the great loom of the clouds beyond her. We waded out together. After the moist heat of the meadow the river felt sharply cold and clean—I was wide-awake at once with that heightened perception of everything round me which lets me know how seldom it is that I am altogether alive. The water, I noticed, was the color of amber and Anne's long legs below its surface were turned to gold. After a time I stopped swimming and dived to find out if I could reach the bottom. I went down a long way, with the water getting darker and colder and heavier around me as I pulled myself down, but I didn't touch anything. Evidently the bay was deeper than the configuration of the shore suggested.

"Deep out here," I said when I got back to the surface.

"Yes. Isn't it a wonderful color? Mrs. Marcy says the sawmills up the river dump sawdust into it, and that's what makes it look like liquid amber."

We swam on toward the approaching storm. Lifting my head to look at the far shore, I saw the edge of the cloud shadow racing across the river to meet us. There was something tremendous in its coming, soundless and swift as an avalanche and, for a moment, I had an impulse to flail my way back to shore before it could sweep over me. But it was moving with the speed of an express train; by mutual consent we stopped swimming and watched the edge of darkness bear down on us.

"Oh, here it comes!" Anne exclaimed like a little girl and plunged under the surface as if to escape its impact. When she came up the shadow was far over us and striding across the quarter mile of water to the Point. We turned and followed it. Now, with the sun covered, the water felt colder. Once in a while we stopped to look up at the towering blackness of the clouds over us. Thunder was muttering along the ridge across the river and there was an occasional pale flash of lightning under the fringes of the clouds. At last we saw the rain, silver-gray and opaque as a wall, sweep down the shoulder of the valley, obliterate the roofs and streets of Barsham Harbor, and charge out across the river. Puffs of wind struck the water ahead and around us and suddenly we were swimming through a crepe of ripples.

"We're going to get caught in the rain!" Anne shouted to me. Laughter and excitement were in her face.

"We better hurry if we don't want to get soaked," I answered and she grinned again.

In two minutes the edge of the squall was hissing in the water round us, slashing the surface of the river with an intensity that made it hard to see the shore toward which we were heading. We swam on, and I heard Anne suddenly singing in exultation:

"His chariots of wrath,
The deep thunderclouds form,
And dark is His path
On the wings of the storm."

I hadn't thought of that hymn for years, but it seemed to belong with the moment...

It may seem that I am including a great deal in this narrative which has no real bearing on the story of Julian Blair and the thing that happened in the house on Setauket Point. Perhaps, but I believe that even in a laboratory it is difficult to separate the experiment from the whole nexus in which it is performed, and in life impossible. My evidence will be more valuable for being presented in its setting, and every detail seems to me important. For instance, as a psychologist I should have to admit that by the time we reached the shore, I was sufficiently out of breath so the blood was pounding in my ears, and any statement of what we heard at such a moment should be discounted because of that simple physiological phenomenon.

This time there was no question of drying ourselves on the beach. We put on our shoes and rolled our clothes into tighter bundles. Then we struck off across the meadow toward the house, running not fast but steadily. Anne, I saw, was no more winded than I was—and I keep myself in good physical condition—and she ran with an effortless reach and drive of the legs that was pleasant to watch. The first frenzy of the rain had abated and the wind, at our backs, was less fitful as it slanted the rain over and past us in long streaks. There were still random bursts of thunder, but the heavy artillery of it had subsided. Our shoes made squelching sounds in the soggy grass.

It happened as we passed the maple tree under which we had been lying earlier in the afternoon. Between one step and the next I found myself stopped, as if I had run into a wall, or come to the edge of an unexpected cliff and halted instinctively. For a second I did not understand why I had brought up short, and then I knew. It was the thing Anne and Mrs. Marcy had tried to describe to me. By the time I was fully aware of it, the noise had stopped, but the echo of it was still in my ears.... From ahead of us somewhere—I felt certain that it was from the house itself—had come such a sound as I have never heard in any other place. It was a deep and indescribable thing, as single and yet as multiple as the noise of a tempest or the roar of a rock slide. An instant after it had reached us there was a sharp rush of wind and a stinging splatter of rain across my naked back, so that I checked my stride only momentarily and was running again toward the blurred loom of the house ahead in the same second, perhaps, that I had paused.

In saying that the noise came from the house, I must add that there was, then, no evidence to support that statement. Nothing more than intuition. No light flared behind the windows—there was nothing visibly altered in the aspect of the house which was turned toward us. But I knew the sound had come from it and the echo was in my ears as I ran.

So strong was that echo that it made me doubt the evidence of my eyes. That sound had had the timbre of catastrophe in it and yet, my eyes assured me that everything was as it should be. But no thing-as-it-should-be had produced that noise. There had been a tremendous quality about it, muted by distance and softened by the hiss of falling rain, but still terrifying. I thought of the echo that reached the people of Japan when the island of Krakatoa exploded two thousand miles and more away from them, in Sunda Strait. Listening to the percussion of that enormous event they must have felt the same vague terror and confusion that were in my own mind.

Anne, still running easily and lightly, turned her streaming face toward me and, in the twilight of the storm, I saw that her eyes were wide—with excitement or something less definable. "That's it!" she cried, "that's the noise."

"Good God," I said.

"The loudest it's ever been," she told me between the deep draughts of her breathing.

After that we wasted no more words. Together we pounded across the meadow and, long before we reached the house, the breath was whistling in my throat. Ahead of us, through the rain, the house began to loom larger and more distinct. When we were within two hundred yards of it I looked up once and saw something that puzzled me. There was a patch of white behind the blank darkness of one of the second-story windows, a vague glimmer of something that was the size and outline of a human face, though I could make out no features at all except, I thought, the eyes. I wondered who was watching us come pelting home. Julian? Mrs. Marcy?...It didn't matter. In two strides more of our running, that face was gone.

Maybe there had been nothing there except my imagination. I forgot about it immediately and it did not come back to my mind until events had forced me to review every least detail of this afternoon.

Panting and blown we flung through the kitchen door. There was no one in the room and it looked utterly normal. A pot of something was cooking on the stove and there was a good smell of steam and condiments in the air. We did not stop even to put on our clothes, but tossed the bundles onto the table almost without pausing and went on through the door into the hall.

That was where it was. I heard Anne give a gasp as she reached the foot of the stairs, and then I was looking over her shoulder and feeling suddenly numb. They were all three there—Julian, Mrs. Walters, and Mrs. Marcy. Two of them had whirled as they heard our feet on the boards behind them. The two were Julian and Mrs. Walters.

12.

MRS. MARCY was lying at the foot of the stairs, on her back, with her arms flung out. Her face was a flat gray-white and her eyes were closed. It was dim in that hall, and we were both winded and trembling with the aftermath of our sprint across the fields, but Anne and I had the same impression when we saw the woman lying there. In her limpness, in the sprawl of her arms, there was something not quite natural, a distortion that was almost imperceptible and which made me think of a doll flung into a corner by a child bored with playing.

In the next second, Mrs. Walters was kneeling beside that motionless figure. "She's had a fall." Her voice was decisive, almost unperturbed. "Did you see it happen, Julian?"

I was shocked at the way he looked—like a man who has received a sudden knife in his back. His eyes were staring and black, and he wavered as he stood there, three or four steps from the bottom of the stairs, with one hand on the balustrade to steady himself. "I...I don't know," he answered finally in a thin, groping voice.

"Of course you do," said the woman, without looking at him. "She must have slipped coming down the stairs. Or perhaps she fainted right on the stairs and fell. Didn't you hear it happen?"

Julian's eyes were still unfocussed on anything. "I don't know," he said. "I don't know."

I shook the inaction of surprise from me and started forward.

"Wait a minute, Mr. Sayles," the woman was saying, and her voice was so calm and steady that it was soothing, "let's get her on the sofa." She picked Mrs. Marcy up as if the burden was no more than a child and strode into the living room. As I followed, I noticed that one thin, freckled arm hung down, the palm of the dangling hand turned oddly outward from the limp body. I saw that, but I didn't think about it.

As a matter of fact, I did not behave with dispatch or assurance in those first few minutes. It was a shock, of course, to come on that scene at the foot of the stairs, and somehow a surprise, too. The note of disaster in that noise we had heard in the meadow had not prepared me for this ugly yet comprehensible accident. Mrs. Walters' calmness, the certainty with which she acted, kept me from anything except an incredulous contemplation of the whole scene. Probably fate was wise in making me into a college professor. I do not seem cut out to be a man of action.

Mrs. Walters put her burden down on the sofa and bent over it. Without turning round she said, coolly and rapidly, "Anne, there's a bottle of aromatic spirits in my room. Get it at once, please. Bring a glass and a spoon, too. Water in the glass. Mr. Sayles, will you give Julian a hand? This has been a shock to him."

Hypnotized by her assurance and uncertain of myself I went back into the hall. Julian was still standing on the same step, staring down at the boards where Mrs. Marcy had been lying a minute before. He was swaying on his feet, the look of blank surprise and horror still on his face. When I put my hand on his shoulder I felt his whole body trembling. "Julian," I said, "are you all right?"

"I'm all right." His voice was so low that I could scarcely hear it. Then he added something to himself, words that were hardly more than the sound of breath. I could not make them out.

The next few minutes are a kaleidoscope in my memory. Some way or other I got Julian down the steps and into the living room. I made him sit down in a chair. The only part of that which sticks in my mind is wholly irrelevant—the patch of wetness on his shirt where I made him lean against me. Then Anne's feet came hurrying down the stairs and the next thing I noticed was the white look of strain and alarm on her face as she brought the things Mrs. Walters had requisitioned. The big woman was the only one of us who seemed to be in perfect command of herself. She put a spoonful of the aromatic spirits between Mrs. Marcy's gray lips as calmly as if she were oiling a sewing machine. Anne and I stood behind her helplessly, looking down at the unmoving body huddled on the sofa. We could not see much of it over the immense black curve of Mrs. Walters' shoulders and back.

Suddenly she straightened and confronted us. "Put some clothes on, you ninnies," she said harshly. "Anne, as soon as you're dressed, get the car out of the barn and go to town. Get a doctor. Don't waste time stopping at the Marcy house, either. Their phone will be out—it always is after a thunderstorm. And hurry."

She was right, of course, and we retreated to the kitchen and found our clothes, still bundled. They were not really very damp—at least, mine weren't. Anne disappeared upstairs. I changed right there in the kitchen and I changed fast. These events which I am describing here in all the detail that I was subsequently forced to remember were actually happening to us with great speed. It was natural, I think, that we did not see what was going on.

By the time I had pulled on the most essential items of clothing, Anne was running downstairs. She scarcely paused on her way through the kitchen. "I'll get the car out and warm it up a minute," she said. "You can finish tying your shoelaces while I'm doing that." The kitchen door slammed behind her.

As I lifted my head from the second shoe I saw that Mrs. Walters was standing in the door to the hall, looking at me. She was, indeed, leaning calmly against the doorframe and I noticed with reluctant admiration that there was no confusion or uncertainty on her face. It was as placid as if this emergency were a matter of routine. "Mr. Sayles," she said in a level voice, "I'm assuming that you will go with Anne. I think an older head will be a good idea."

"Of course I'll go," I said. "Unless you need me here, or something."

"No, there's nothing more to do here. She's come to, now—the aromatic spirits I suppose—and she's not in any pain yet. But if she's seriously hurt, naturally she will be as soon as the shock wears off.

You and Anne will have to hurry. Look out for the road, though. It will be like grease after this rain."

"Certainly," I said, irked by the didactic tone of her speech.

She must have caught the irritation in my voice. "Excuse me if I sound bossy, but I'm in a rush. I don't want to leave her alone too long, even if she does seem to be all right, really. Anyhow, Mr. Sayles, I meant that about not stopping at Seth Marcy's house, partly for the reason I gave you and partly because I don't want that fool of a man over here till we're sure his wife's all right. He'll make a scene and a whole mountain out of a molehill, and not do her any good."

Much as I did not like that woman, I had to admire the sure, executive way she was handling the whole miserable business. I told her that I was not cross, and to get on back to Mrs. Marcy, and promised that we'd return with a doctor in an hour or less, and that we wouldn't stop at Marcy's—though I had some mental reservations about that last. Then a horn honked outside the door and I went out into the yard.

The rain was still falling, but not in gusts and torrents. It looked as though it might stop in half an hour or so, but it was still coming down fast enough to make me sprint for the battered Ford sedan in which Anne was sitting. Maine mud and dust were plastered all over it, but the motor sounded smooth under the hood. Even before my door was closed Anne was wrenching the car around and stepping it up from gear to gear. As we straightened out into the road the machine slewed sickeningly and I perceived that this was going to be quite a ride. The storm had soaked the loose top dirt of the track and turned it into a slimy lubricant between our wheels and the underlying hardpan. We skidded at every rut.

"How about chains?"

Anne didn't take her eyes off the road, but she grinned. "Haven't any, Dick. Don't worry." We struck a pothole. When the car was back on an even keel she said, "Do you think we ought to stop off at Marcy's anyhow? It'll be a mile, and ten minutes out of our way if the phone isn't working."

"No," I answered. "I guess Mrs. Walters is right about that. We won't save much time even if the phone is working and it seems to me like a poor gamble."

"Probably." She avoided a crater full of brown water and wrestled the car back across the slimy surface of the road. "Seth Marcy's nobody's pet, anyhow. I've only seen him a couple or times, but he's the kind of man who doesn't open his mouth unless he has something unpleasant to say. I feel sorry for Elora."

"We'll forget him, then, till we get a doctor. After that we can go to his house and tell him."

We went on, not exactly racing but making incredible speed for the condition of the road. Anne handled the car with a magnificent blend of daring and judgment; I thought we weren't going to make the bridge at the turn by the creek, but we got across it by a hair, and when we hit the road along the far bank of the bay the going was better. Even with the chances Anne took, I did not feel nervous about her driving. There was competence in the way her hands were resting on the wheel, in the way she sat behind it, alert but not tense. It was, indeed, strangely pleasant, that ride. We were in a private world of our own, with rain on our roof and streaking down the windows, shutting us in together. I liked it. For a mile or so I forgot our errand, forgot the bleak house behind us, and thought of nothing except that this fortuitous intimacy was different from anything that had ever happened to me before.

After twenty minutes or perhaps a little longer, the unlovely center of Barsham Harbor was flashing past our windows. I have often wished since that I had looked at my watch more frequently that day, but it was still in the side pocket of my coat, where I had put it when we went swimming, and I remembered it only as we pulled into town. It was ten minutes after four then and the light was already beginning to fade, thanks to the clouds and the rain.

Our luck seemed to be out from the moment we hit the town. There were, it appeared, three doctors in Barsham Harbor. Dr. Peters was out on a call. Dr. Solomon, whom we tried next, had gone to Bath and was not expected back for several hours. The third and last was Dr. Rambouillet. His house was beyond the Catholic church on the other side of the railroad tracks and his small shingle looked inauspiciously new. But he was at home.

"Dr. Peters is the Marcy family doctor," he said to us when we told him our errand. "I think you'd better get him. The people here..." he shrugged with the Latinity of the French Canadian.

"He's out on a call," I said. "This is an emergency."

With no more demur he picked up his bag and got into the car. "All right, but don't say I didn't warn you." The teeth under his narrow black mustache were startling when he smiled. He couldn't have been over twenty-eight. "I'll do what I can," he declared, "and then turn the case over to Dr. Peters. You see," and he smiled again disarmingly, "the people of Barsham Harbor either do want a French Canadian doctor or they don't. We keep to our own sides of the fence. Or perhaps I ought to say, of the tracks. You understand?"

"Yes," I said, "and sympathize...What was your school, Doctor?"

"McGill. And the ink is quite dry on the diploma."

I laughed. Anne was too busy driving to pay much attention to what we were saying. The day was drawing in and she switched on the lights when we turned right at the bridge. I watched the road slither and dance under our wheels. The thought went through my head that it was impossible I had got off the State of Maine express only that morning. This day had been going on for half a lifetime already. I was tired and sleepy. The thing to do would be to get to bed as soon after supper as was decently possible.

The sight of the house ahead of us, black and solid in the twilight, reminded me that there was plenty still to be done before any of us could think of supper or sleep. Anne slid the car to a stop right at the kitchen steps, and we piled out and through the door in a hurry. The situation on the other side of the threshold made me, for one, feel stupefiedly foolish.

13.

WHY I SHOULD have been so taken aback by the sight of Mrs. Walters setting the table I don't quite know, except that we had come racing home to the house to cope with an emergency, and Mrs. Walters at a household task was nothing like what I had expected. Perhaps it was her calmness that stopped me in my tracks, the very domesticity of her appearance in a big, blue-figured dress and an apron, leisurely laying out knives and forks. When she turned to face us, there was a look of embarrassment on her face.

"Oh, dear!" she said in the warmest tones I had yet heard from her. "What a pity you've had all the hurry and trouble for nothing."

"For nothing!" Anne's voice was incredulous.

"I'm afraid so. Mrs. Marcy is perfectly all right again. I suppose I took it too seriously when I saw her lying there at the foot of the stairs. She frightened me and I jumped to the conclusion that she was badly hurt. But she got up not five minutes after you'd started. I made her wait round for a while, but she was so obviously recovered that I finally sent her home. She insisted she was entirely over it, but I felt it would be better if she did not work any more today. She kept trying to help me and finally I sent her home, as I said. You were gone a long time."

Dr. Rambouillet put his black satchel down on the floor and sighed, but it seemed to me that there was an expression of relief on his face. "You are sure she was all right?" he inquired. "No sign of sleepiness? No thickness of the tongue? No difficulty in speaking?"

"Not that I could see." Mrs. Walters had returned to her table setting and I noticed that the hand with which she put out the water glasses was entirely steady.

That woman was, I think, a great actress, the greatest I have ever seen. Nothing in the way she looked, spoke, or acted, was other than natural, ordinary, even casual. After a silence that was long enough to show how calm she was, she turned to us and went on, "I wasn't sure I should let her start home so soon, frankly. I loaned her my umbrella and I went part way down the road with her to make sure. She was all right. I'm positive of it. She didn't seem to have even a sprain. Her only complaint was that she had a headache."

"Well..." the doctor said uncertainly, "from what you say, there should be no danger of a concussion. And evidently there were no broken bones."

Mrs. Walters bridled at the reluctance in his voice. "I would not have let her take a step out of this house if I hadn't been sure she was all right. Of course, you can stop by at Marcy's and see her, if you want, Dr...?"

"Rambouillet," said that young man politely.

"Oh. Are you the Marcys' usual doctor?"

"No," he answered shortly. "Dr. Peters was out on a call."

The minute he said that she had him right where she wanted him. But the way she managed it was masterful and, even now, in remembering it, I am moved to a grudging admiration of the way she carried it all off. "I see," she remarked so casually that I barely caught the note of triumph in her voice. "Well, then, I suppose they'll have called him by this time if there's any need."

Rambouillet nodded. "Undoubtedly." He turned to Anne and me. "I'm sorry, but there's apparently nothing here for me to do. And since I didn't come out in my own car, I'm afraid I'll have to trouble you to run me back into town."

We said we would and Anne went upstairs to get a coat. I offered the doctor a drink, which he declined, and forced him to accept three dollars, which he felt he hadn't earned. A call was a call, I pointed out, and he was entitled to a fee even if there had been no patient. He put the money in his pocket finally, with a wry smile. "A young doctor in this town," he remarked, "has no right to refuse anything that comes his way." We chatted quietly in that warm, agreeable kitchen, hardly aware of Mrs. Walters as she went about the room. And yet, it crossed my mind once or twice that she looked more attractive than she had in the morning. The lamplight was kind to her face and there was a touch of femininity about her dress that was welcome. I wondered idly why she had changed. Probably she'd got wet walking back in the rain after giving Mrs. Marcy her umbrella.

Later I came to have a different opinion about that, but at the time I hardly thought about it at all—what dress Mrs. Walters wore was a matter of no interest or importance to me. Or so I would have considered if I had thought about it at all, which I didn't.

Anne came back in five minutes and the three of us went out to the car. The rain had slacked to a drizzle and night was at hand. A heavy gray twilight shut the house in upon itself and the heat of the day had gone; the air was cold and raw. Mrs. Walters stood in the door and watched us as we drove off; the lamplight came out from behind her and threw a blotched, half-formed shadow of her big body across the yard.

As we drove in silence back toward Barsham Harbor I thought how puppetlike we had all been, moving around at the ends of our strings while Mrs. Walters pulled them. Able and competent she certainly was, but it was impossible to like her. Since Mrs. Marcy was all right, the episode had turned out to be a trivial one and yet, it seemed to me that Mrs. Walters had acted throughout it with a firmness and decision that were somehow unnecessary.

The truth was that I was full of that petty resentment which a man feels when he thinks a woman has acted with more authority and energy in an emergency than he himself has done.

On the trip home I drove the car and Anne sat beside me. In the glow of the dash light her face was tired and thoughtful. I thought how very young and sweet and defenseless she looked, and wanted to put my arm around her. But that would have been ridiculous. After all, a practically middle-aged college professor has no business making passes at girls. Besides, I was afraid of doing anything to mar the feeling between us. After a while she stirred in her seat and looked at me. "I'm glad Mrs. Marcy is all right," she said slowly. "I like that little person, Dick. She's had so much hard luck in her life."

"I know."

"If that woman let her walk home and she wasn't perfectly all right, I'm going to make trouble about it."

"She was all right. I doubt if Mrs. Walters makes many mistakes in the course of a year."

That brought a smile. "I suppose you're right. It's nice not having to confront her alone, Dick. I'm glad you're here."

"It sounds contrary to common sense," I said, "but I'm glad I am too."

We said no more on the ride. As the Marcy house dropped past us on the left I had a momentary impulse to turn in. But I didn't yield to it. There seemed no real necessity. When the car finally slithered to a stop in the yard, Mrs. Walters opened the kitchen door and called to us. "Hurry up, you two. Supper in five minutes."

I put the car in the barn and went back to the house. For the first time that day I went to my room to get ready for the meal. It was a square, small cubicle with two windows looking northward and also down onto the yard and the roof of the ell. There was nothing in it but a cot, a battered washstand, and one chair. The single candle they had given me burned small and cold on the stand; its light wavered and leaped in the raw air so that the place was full of sudden, shape-less shadows. As I changed my shirt and combed my hair I felt an uneasiness which I recognized coming back into my consciousness. It was a kind of mental discomfort, rather than anything stronger, and it had been in my mind more than once in the course of this day.

By a sort of casual introspection I tried to find out what, specifi-cally, it was that bothered me. The house, for one thing, I decided—if you are not used to dark, cold rooms with a single candle for light the experience is a strange one, belonging to our ancestors' ordinary routine of life, perhaps, but not to that of a modern city dweller. And Mrs. Walters. I did not like her, or the dark that had settled over the house—Julian ought not to have such a woman around and why hadn't he put electric lights into the rooms since he had wired in the power? The lamp in the kitchen and the candle in this room were separate islands of light and there were too many shadows between them. I thought of the hall outside my door and it seemed to me that there might be someone in it, but when I looked out it was empty and silent. I thought of the shadowy living room, of the river water noiselessly running and running, almost under the sills of its windows. A hundred years and more this house had stood here, alone on the Point. A hundred years of sun and storm, of winters and summers, of dark and light. It was old, but it was not its age that gave me the tight feeling I had in the pit of my stomach.

In the end I had to give up the effort to discover what I thought was wrong. There were too many possibilities and nothing probable. The accident, when I thought about it, did not seem to explain the feeling wholly, though I admitted to myself that when I had seen Mrs. Marcy lying in that unnatural way at the foot of the stairs I had thought for one instant, "Now it's happened." But that was obviously meaningless. As it turned out, nothing had happened. And equally, if the accident had been important in some way, I could not see why or to whom—except Mrs. Marcy—it was important. What the "it" was that had happened I did not understand, though I assigned it to the feeling of imminence which had come over me earlier in the afternoon. That, in turn, was unquestionably caused by the approach of the thunderstorm. Still, the lightning and thunder, and most of the rain, had long ago swept away to the northeast and it seemed to me that the air was as charged with suspense as ever. Suspense, I reminded myself, is a purely subjective matter. There was no way of telling whether the way I felt had any external foundation or not.

Difficult to believe though it may seem, I paid little attention to the notion that Julian and his invention might account for my disquietude. I felt pity and sorrow for him, but they were ordinary, normal emotions. As for the thing he had made, it was only too apparent that it was harmless—like those perpetual motion machines that unbalanced inventors are forever producing. No machine could approach the complex sensitivity of the human mind itself and, if our brains had not, after centuries, given us any sure proof that the individuality survives the fact of death, then it was certain that Julian's machine wouldn't either. Perhaps, if I had been superstitious, I would have been inclined to give more weight to that project of his. The house would have been "haunted" by its presence and the potential presence of the myriads of voices that were supposed to speak through it. But they weren't there. Of that I felt sure. Just as it was self-evident that a physical machine could not be expected to produce a nonphysical result.

The very impossibility of the machine's working brought home to me the difficulty of doing anything to help Julian. His frailty told me how little time there was left in which to save him, if he could be saved, and the driving eagerness I had heard in his voice when he talked showed how strong was the obsession I should have to break through. The impression which he gave of being cut off from all reality distressed me when I thought about it. I had promised Anne not to fail, and promised myself, too. I owed something to Julian and, as I thought about him, I was ashamed of myself for bothering with the vague fancies and premonitions that had been running through my head. Why had I puzzled so much over them and so little over how I was to save my friend?

As I stood in that dim, cold room, trying to straighten my tie in the shadowy disk of my shaving mirror, no answer came back to that question; only a vague feeling and intuition that the question itself was not the crux of the situation. It is hard to convey intangible suggestions in the rigid forms and patterns of words, but what I felt then was a kind of fear. The trouble was that it was a fear without an object. All I was sure of was that I was not afraid of Julian and not even for him, except in a general sort of way. Neither was it Mrs. Walters. Thinking about her intensified the sensation slightly, but she was not the source of it, and the fact that it apparently had no focal point began to annoy me. I was like a man walking down an unfamiliar street in a strange city, late at night, with a vague substratum of uneasiness in his mind. He does not say to himself, "Maybe I am going to get held up and beaten in this place." He simply feels uneasy. But if he sees the shadow of a man shouldered back in a doorway his fear rushes together like wind to the heart of a cyclone. It fastens itself on that figure and embodies itself with its image. My fear seemed to have no such focal point; it colored the rest of my thoughts but it had no shape of its own.

That, I was forced to tell myself finally, was evasion. In the back of my mind I did know of what I was afraid, but it was senseless to allow it to color my consciousness so poisonously. It was nothing more specific than the noise that we had heard, Anne and I, as we ran toward the house in the rain. But why was I afraid of that sound, or rather, of hearing it again? I finished my dressing quickly, not liking to think about it. For from the moment I had remembered that noise I found myself listening for it again.

Mrs. Walters was still alone in the kitchen when I got downstairs. In spite of all my thinking, not more than ten minutes had passed since I had gone upstairs. The table, I saw, was completely set and there was a comfortable smell of food in the air. I said "Hello," and she answered with a smile that would have been all right if we had been the best of friends.

"Supper's almost ready," she observed.

I brushed that aside. "Mrs. Walters, there's something I want to talk to you about."

She smiled again, more thinly. "Very well, Professor Sayles. Only let's be quiet. I have given Julian a sleeping tablet after the shock of this afternoon. It ought to make him sleep clear through tonight, but I don't want to take a chance on waking him. He needs all the rest he can get."

"Certainly." I kept my voice low. "This is it. When Anne and I were running back to the house just before we found you and Julian and Mrs. Marcy, we heard a noise."

"Did you?" Her voice was without intonation.

"Yes." She was looking at me steadily. I returned her stare and went on, "It was an odd sort of noise. We thought it came from this house."

She dropped her glance. "Perhaps it did. You haven't told me what it was like." Her tone was wholly indifferent, and while she spoke she carried a plate of soup from the stove and set it at one of the places.

"A sort of roaring, pulsing, crashing sound," I said and the words sounded silly in my own ears.

She did not permit herself a smile. "Goodness. It sounds complicated. No, I didn't happen to hear it, but of course I know what it was. So do you."

"Maybe I'm obtuse, but I don't think I do."

She went back for another plate. "Nonsense, Mr. Sayles. Thunder, of course. Sometimes here in the valley the claps echo back and forth. I've heard something like what you mention once or twice myself."

"The thing sounded as if it came from this house."

She shrugged. "From somewhere over the roof, perhaps. I may have heard it and forgotten it because of everything that happened right afterward. I don't know. What difference does it make?"

"It wasn't thunder," I said quietly. "Mrs. Marcy told me she'd heard it once or twice before. And she must know the sound of thunder in her own country. And Anne described it to me before it happened."

That seemed to have an effect upon her. She put the second plate down with a clatter and looked at me coldly. "You seem to have lost no time around here, Mr. Sayles. Talking to Mrs. Marcy and Miss Conner as if you were some kind of private detective. What's on your mind?"

"Julian's my friend, Mrs. Walters. I find him in a strange sort of ménage and obviously a sick man."

She gave me a look of contempt. "You're worried about Julian, so you talk to Mrs. Marcy about him!"

"No. I didn't talk to her about him. She told me about the noise amongst a lot of other things, all volunteered on her part." I despised myself for bothering to justify my actions to this woman.

For a time she paid no further attention to what I had said. Then she stopped doing things around the stove and turned to confront me. "I told you what the noise was, Mr. Sayles. If you don't believe me, there's no sense our wasting time about it. You can talk it over some more with Miss Conner—and Mrs. Marcy—if you're still determined to make a mystery out of a simple, natural thing. The three of you seem to have found something in common. Thunder."

The scorn with which she delivered this retort did not affect me, but clearly there was no point in going on with the subject. I sat down in a chair and kept my mouth shut. She looked at me once or twice as if she hoped I'd give her another opening and then went on with her work. At the end of an uncomfortable silence she remarked, "I shouldn't wonder if it was that very clap of thunder that frightened Mrs. Marcy. Something must have made her slip on those stairs."

I agreed to that hypothesis indifferently and went on watching the purple light outside the east window fade to blackness across the inky water of the river. The rain had stopped but the night was sullen and lowering.

Mrs. Walters did not seem anxious for another long silence between us. "You know," she said, "I should have asked if you knew first aid, Professor. It never occurred to me. You might have been the very man we needed." She smiled at me and I still did not like it. "I'm rather accustomed to taking care of sick people, so I just jumped right in. I'm afraid I was rather bossy."

"No," I answered, wondering idly what she was getting at. "I'm no expert on what to do till the doctor comes. I was glad you took charge." I turned to look at her. "You must have done a good job. I thought the woman was badly hurt."

But that was not what I had really thought. The moment I had caught sight of that fragile, tumbled body at the foot the stairs I had thought I was looking at death.

The big woman was watching me carefully. There was an alertness that amounted to tension under the make-up on her broad face. "She gave me a turn, too. She looked almost as if she was dead, didn't she?"

I nodded.

"I was never so relieved in my life as when the aromatic spirits brought her round. It's wonderful what that stuff will do." She gave a little laugh. "But up to then I was really frightened about her."

"You picked her up and carried her to that sofa as if you were used to that sort of thing all your life," I said, trying to make my tone sound admiring. It was a stupid little speech, as awkward as most efforts to give the devil his due, but I was surprised at its effect upon her. She bit her lip and turned away. After a while, with her back still turned toward me, she said, "Oh, that was nothing." And then, after a pause, "She wasn't heavy."

14.

ANNE CAME into the kitchen a few minutes later. She had on a dull-green dress that brought out the lights in her hair and the warmth of her skin and, for a second, as I looked at her, some of the depression went out of my mind and I forgot how tired I was beginning to feel. Supper was a silent meal because none of us seemed to be able to conjure up a topic of conversation that wouldn't leave one member of the trio out of it. After we'd eaten as much as we wanted—which in my case was no great amount—we washed dishes together by a sort of common consent. Personally, I don't like cleaning up after a meal—I did too much of it when I was a boy—but anything was better than leaving the warmth and company of the kitchen to adventure into the silence of the rest of the house. Anne, I think, felt the same way. After we had finished, Mrs. Walters laid a tray for Julian, "... in case he wakes up, though I hope he won't," as she put it, and then there was nothing more to do in the kitchen.

A trivial thing happened as we started to leave the place. "Well we can sit in the living room for a few minutes," Anne had just said, with no cheer in her tone, and picked up the lamp on the table when Mrs. Walters went over to her with sudden swiftness and took the thing out of her hand.

"You can't have that," she declared sharply. "I don't want to have to stumble around here in the dark if Julian should happen to need anything." And she put the lamp firmly back on the table.

Anne looked startled and indignant for a moment and then turned away. "I'm sorry. I didn't know you wanted it there." She looked at Mrs. Walters speculatively. "You take wonderful care of Uncle Julian," she observed.

"I try to," Mrs. Walters replied in a level voice.

We groped our way through the black hall and into the living room. Anne lit the lamp in there, but the pool of yellow light it spilled brightened only a fraction of the place; the shadows in the corners were thick and smooth as velvet. I put a match to my pipe and Anne smoked a cigarette. We sat together on the sofa, not too close together, and watched Mrs. Walters in the chair by the lamp. She had a basket of mending.

"What holes Julian does make in his socks," she observed at last. "He's got to get some new ones. Remind me, Anne, the next time we go to town."

Anne grunted. "You don't need to do all that," she said in a voice that was perceptibly too considerate. "Mrs. Marcy does the darning."

"I know," Mrs. Walters answered shortly, but I noticed that she went on with what she was doing.

For a while Anne and I talked in low tones about the past, about the university and things we had done together when she was a kid. "The girls used to tease me about you," she said once. "But they were only jealous." I grinned at that, but it was not an altogether happy feeling. After a while our small talk ran down and the silence took complete possession of the room. Fatigue was heavy in my body, but I was scarcely sleepy. Instead, it seemed to me that I was noticing things with more than normal distinctness. It was preternaturally quiet. I began to wish that the river outside would make more noise instead of slipping to the sea without a sound. My ears felt empty and, literally, I could hear the sound of my own heart and of Anne's breathing beside me. All the while I was listening, waiting to hear something and it did not come. After a time I transferred my attention to Mrs. Walters and wondered what was going on behind those eyes of hers. Nothing, to judge from the placidity of her expression and yet, I was sure that she was alert and aware of Anne and myself, perhaps even of what we were thinking. Was she listening, too?

Then I yawned and that seemed to break the shell of quiet in which we had been enclosed. "You must be dead for sleep," Anne exclaimed suddenly in a contrite voice. "It's practically bedtime, anyhow. Let's all go up."

My legs were heavy when I hoisted myself back on them.

"To tell the truth, it has been a long day. And your fresh country air has a numbing effect on a pair of city-poisoned lungs like mine."

Mrs. Walters nodded. "It has been a long day," she agreed. "Not the happiest possible one for your visit, Professor Sayles. But there's always tomorrow."

"Absolutely," I agreed. "Well, if you'll excuse me..."

She did not rise from her chair. "Certainly. Anne, you go along up, too. I'll follow you in a minute. I see there's still one more sock to finish. But don't wait for me; I'll be all right alone."

A flash of irritation went through me then, as it did so often after the things she said, because there was something obscurely contradictory between her words and the tone in which she uttered them. The way she spoke managed to imply that she wished one or both of us would stay there with her till she was ready to go. I could not see a reason in the world for obliging her. Companionship, at least of the negative sort that Anne and I had provided, could not be what she wanted from us. Neither could it be worry. Confused and unpleasant as the events of the day had been, they were over now. Or so I thought.

Anne went over to the mantel and lighted a candle. "Time to retire," she said and made a child's face. As I followed her, I turned once and looked back into the living room. Mrs. Walters was still sitting there quietly, drawing the thread steadily back and forth. The needle gleamed in the lamplight, but her face was turned half away and shadowed. "Good night," I said softly, so as not to wake Julian. "Pleasant dreams," she returned negligently, without lifting her head.

My room was colder and darker than before. Anne came into it for a moment and lit the candle on my washstand. "All the discomforts of a fine old colonial home," she said, smiling, and then her face was suddenly grave. "Oh, Dick, I can't tell you..."

"What, Anne?"

"How glad I am you're here. For Uncle Julian's sake and mine. I haven't known what to do..." Her voice sounded near tears.

I patted her shoulder. "It's going to be all right."

"If you say so," she replied. But there was doubt in her voice. "My room's next to yours, by the way, and hers is right across the hall. If you need anything, pound on the wall and I'll get it for you."

"Thanks. I won't. Unless it's waking up in the morning. You can pound on the wall when it's time to get up."

Then we said good night and I thought of all the other times we had done that in the old days... It wasn't the same at all, of course, and yet, I was reminded of the past in spite of myself. This time it was she who shut the door on me. I was left in the bleakness of my room, shivering; I undressed in silence, without bothering to unpack anything except my pajamas, and got into the cot before the candlewick had stopped glowing.

When I surrendered my weight to the bed, I expected that sleep would wash over me in a minute or two, if not immediately. For some reason it didn't. Even my eyes remained open for a long time, though there was nothing to see except the faintly lighter oblongs of the windows, unbroken by a single star. I deliberately made every muscle in my body relax, but still sleep didn't come, though in those days I never had any trouble about losing myself in unconsciousness the moment I went to bed. But this time my senses were still on the alert even after my body was utterly limp and, when I finally closed my eyes, oblivion was not complete.

Going to sleep is a mysterious process anyhow. The senses don't blur and fade simultaneously and merge into nothingness. The first one to go, of course, is sight, the minute the eyelids are lowered, and then I suppose the next to vanish are taste and smell, though it was a long time before I stopped being aware of the reek of the candle smoke in the air. For an even longer time I was conscious of the rough feeling of the blanket under my chin and, as for hearing, I don't believe I ever did wholly stop listening.

There was nothing to hear, nothing important. For a time there were the sounds Anne made in the next room, but they were soon over. And then the occasional crack and creak of an old house settling itself for the night. Outside the windows was the faintest possible rustle of air and every once in a while the minute plop of a drip from the eaves. These were trivial sounds and yet I kept hearing them in spite of myself. My mind stubbornly refused to relinquish its last sentry and I went on listening. Perhaps it was for the sound of Mrs. Walters coming upstairs, which I did hear after a while. She made very little disturbance about it, but I heard her come up the stairs, and it sounded as if she hesitated once or twice on the way up. Then she came down the hall; I could follow that cautious progress of hers there, too, and when she stopped for a long time outside my door I was not surprised. She was wondering, I knew, if I was asleep. I gave her no clue, though I had an irresistible impulse to utter one loud mock snore to startle her.

Even after the door of her room had closed behind her, I could not abandon myself wholly.... I was still listening and I faced the fact that what I expected, or dreaded, to hear was a recurrence of that sound of the afternoon. Whenever I thought squarely about it, the echo of that damnable noise went booming in my inner ear and, as I lay there, I could feel the prickle of sweat breaking out on the palms of my hands. What could have made such a noise?

The conviction was borne in upon me that Julian had progressed very far indeed with that thing of his. It, and it only, could account for the sound. Anne had even recognized it....We should have talked more about it, especially on the second ride back from town, when we were alone and safe from being overheard. But I knew why we had not. There was nothing we could have said about that noise because there was nothing familiar in it. And there was the possibility that Julian might be right, and that the reason the sound we had heard was so strange and terrifying was because it came—I put the thought out of my mind.

Lying in the dark with nothing by which to measure time except the beating of my heart, minutes or hours may have passed before I fell asleep. I have no precise idea how long I lay there listening, or even if I ever was wholly asleep. Probably I was, because the next thing I knew was that something was happening outside the house. The thing that woke me was surprising. My room, as I have said, looked down on the court between the shoulder of the house and the narrower strip of the ell back to the barn. Its windows faced almost north and hence along the road that led up the Point and ultimately to Barsham Harbor. The corner of the barn was between me and most of that road, which was perhaps why the sound of feet on it had not waked me sooner. Anyhow, there was the squelch and thud of feet outside. Someone was approaching the house, and the tempo of the steps was hurried. Whoever it was had a long stride and was hurrying, though not running.

The moment I opened my eyes I could see a faint line of yellow light along the underside of the top window casement on the left, a gleam that alternately dimmed and increased, but which was growing progressively brighter. Although I had never in my life seen that sort of thing before, I knew at once what it was—the light from a lantern carried by a walking man. I got out of bed with anxiety of a nameless sort plucking at my thoughts and went to the window. I was right. It was a lantern, swinging along the road, but I could see little of whoever was carrying it.

Even before the sound of knuckles on the back door I was into my trousers and shoes and was pulling on my old varsity sweater over my head. Quick as I was, Anne was ahead of me; I bumped into her in the hall outside.

"Dick," she said in a whisper. "What is it? Who's there?"

"Dunno. A man. That's all I could tell."

The knuckles were more urgent against the door and we stumbled down the stairs. Hot paraffin spilled on my hand from the candle I was carrying. Anne was right on my heels as I blundered through the hall and into the kitchen. The knocking sounded much louder in there, of course, and there was an urgency in it that suggested anxiety. And then, in that second as we were coming through the kitchen doorway the last vestige of comfort or security was stripped from us by a single word. It was spoken from the other side of the door, in a low voice, by the man outside.

"Elora!" he said and his tone was half-angry, half-anxious.

Mrs. Marcy's name, of course. I heard Anne give a gasp as she heard it. We both knew then who was on the other side of that door and the knowledge was appalling. It could only be her husband. And that meant—

The lamp in the kitchen was still burning and everything was completely ordinary. I blew out my candle and put it on the table as I went across the room. The bolt stuck in the door and I had to tug to get it open. All the while his knuckles were rapping against the panels. "Just a second," I said urgently, and then the bar slid back and I turned the door handle.

He was standing on the top step, a tall, slightly stooped farmer with a dark face and sullen mouth. In the air that blew past him into the room there was the ammoniacal pungency of the cow stable. He stared at me with momentary surprise and then pushed past me into the room. "Where's Elora?" he said harshly.

Anne was looking at him with recognition and a white face. "Why, Mr. Marcy," she told him in a thin voice, "did she come back here for something? She went home hours ago."

"Ain't been home yet," he replied, and stared round the room with anger and bewilderment. "Not since mornin'." He pointed to the lamp. "Her light's still goin', too."

"Her light?" I asked in confusion.

"Yeah. You can see that from our house. When it goes out I know she's started back. But it's past ten now. I come over to see what was keepin' her."

"Listen," I told him. "Your wife went home early. She had a minor accident. Nothing serious. But Mrs. Walters decided she oughtn't to work any more and sent her home in the afternoon. She even walked part way with her. She must be home."

"She ain't."

We stood there for a minute staring at him. I know that alarm was going through my mind siren-loud and sudden. Something was terribly wrong. "Sit down a minute," I said. "We'll tell you the whole thing."

He took a chair grudgingly. There was a truculence about him that made you dislike the man on sight, and yet he was Mrs. Marcy's husband and entitled to know what had happened. I gave it to him in as few words as I could.

He listened without interruption, though the rigidity of his big body in the chair suggested that he neither believed what I said nor cared much about it, one way or the other. He was not going to be easy to deal with. When I mentioned Dr. Rambouillet's name he snorted, but that was the only sound he made until I finished. "So," I concluded, "if she hasn't reached your house, we'd better go look along the road." Under the heavy impact of his silence I began to feel resentful and, when he made no move to get up, I added sharply, "If she's had a concussion, she may be lying unconscious. We've got to find her at once."

"She ain't on the road," he said heavily. "I come that way."

"Perhaps she wandered off it or you missed her."

He jerked a splayed thumb toward the lamp. "How come the light?"

We explained that Mrs. Walters had left it there in case Mr. Blair needed anything in the night. It sounded unlikely enough in my own ears as I told it, but he gave no indication of whether he accepted it or not. After a minute he grunted and got to his feet. "If anything's happened to her," he said, "you folks'll hev to answer fer it." In two strides he had picked up the lantern and was out the door.

Anne produced a flashlight from the hall and slipped it into my hand. We followed him without exchanging a word. Her face was still white and she was biting her lip. Outside, the night was raw and dark and a breeze had sprung up heavy with the smell of the sea. Anne and I let Seth Marcy go ahead of us and followed without exchanging a word. There was nothing I cared to say that I wanted him to overhear. So we went down the road in a triangle, Seth in front with his lantern, and the two of us, a few feet apart, with the flashlight trailing him. After some yards I went over to the side of the road and I confess that I was extremely frightened. If Mrs. Walters' story was a true one, I knew what we should find there, but if it wasn't . . . well, that didn't bear thinking about. The story she had told *had* to be true.

The prints were there, all right, and my heart gave a powerful thump of relief when I saw them. It was all right, then, and Mrs. Walters had not been lying. Though their edges had been softened by the tail end of the rain, which had fallen after they were made, the footsteps were distinct enough, punched heavily into the mud.

"Look!" I called, and Seth Marcy stopped and came back to me with his lantern.

"There are yours," I pointed out, "fresh and sharp. These others are blurred a bit but you can see them all right."

He stared down at them, his face heavy and uncompromising, but there was no misreading that track in the mud. Two sets of women's footmarks, with water shining in them blackly where the heels had sunk deep, headed in the direction we had been going. And a single set coming back toward the house. "You see," I said, "here's the two of them going toward your house, Mr. Marcy. And this other single set is Mrs. Walters coming back."

He nodded heavily. "Ayuh." I was rather ashamed of myself over the triumph that I was feeling. After all, these prints told us nothing about where Mrs. Marcy was now and it was selfish to be as relieved as I was. But we in the Talcott house were at least substantiated in our story. There had been no criminal negligence on our part.

Seth Marcy stood staring at the footprints for a full minute, and then grunted and turned on down the road, holding his lantern low and walking carefully to one side of the impressions. Every few steps he paused and re-examined the tracks. Thus we proceeded down the road, anxiously and wordlessly, for perhaps a quarter of a mile. Seth stopped then, so long that Anne and I had time to catch up with him. When we arrived, we saw what it was that had halted him.

There were a cluster of prints in the mud beside us, a number made by each woman. I could easily distinguish between Mrs. Walters' thinner, higher heels, and the wide, run-over ones of Mrs. Marcy, although without that difference it might not have been too easy. The shoes were within a half size of each other. From one cluster, a line ran back toward the house we had left. "This must be where they separated," I said.

"There's Mrs. Walters, going back to the house."

The farmer grunted. "Looks like it. Here's Elora, goin' on." He picked up the lantern and began to walk forward more slowly. The two of us stayed right behind him, now.

"The mud must have been awful," Anne remarked. "Look how deep she sunk in."

It was true that the prints were deep, but I remembered the greasy gruel of mud on the road that afternoon and was not surprised. We kept on. Mrs. Marcy's steps had evidently been steady enough at first; they were spaced evenly and in a straight line. But after a couple of hundred yards they began to waver and straggle uncertainly from side to side of the path. The picture was all too easy to reconstruct: these footprints had been made by a woman who was staggering. For a few yards they would run straight again, and then angle off in confused sorties, sometimes toward the center of the road and again toward the field grass along its edge. In the glow of the lantern Seth Marcy's face was set and the block of his jaw muscles stood out under the skin of his cheeks. He followed each of those pitiful divergencies in his wife's track patiently and without a word, but little by little his stride began to lengthen.

Abruptly he came to a second halt and when we reached him the reason was plain. In the mud was a rounded hollow, deeper at the end toward our line of direction, and beyond it the smudged outline of a hand which had slid through the mud. Either Mrs. Marcy had slipped or she had half fallen from weakness, catching herself on one knee and one outflung hand. None of us was an expert trail reader, but the meaning of those marks in the mud was primer plain. I thought of the two women, their backs toward each other, going their separate ways, and Mrs. Marcy faint and dizzy with weakness. Why hadn't she called out? Maybe Mrs. Walters had gone too far to hear her. It was a picture that I didn't want to reconstruct in my mind.

We pressed on more rapidly. There were other places where she had slipped and fallen—at one of them we could make out the mark of the curved umbrella handle and I told Seth Marcy what it was. He did not seem to hear me.

It was just after that when the anxiety in my mind turned to a sick anticipation of tragedy. The lights of the Marcy house were already in sight, ahead, and well to our right. The road in to it cannot have been more than a few rods beyond where we stopped, which was at the entrance to a rough sort of track which cut sharply off across the fields. It was nothing more than a haying road for farm wagons and machinery, but it was, even in the glow of one lantern, a perceptible turnoff, and it led to the right, just as the true entrance to the Marcy place did farther on. And the prints of Mrs. Marcy's shoes turned down that miserable byway.

When he saw that they did indeed leave the road, Seth Marcy gave a groan like a man in unbearable pain and began to run heavily down the false track into which, by some horrible error, his wife had turned. Anne and I pounded along after him and, as we ran, some change in the sky, or perhaps the sudden absence of tree masses against the night dark told us what must be in his mind. For this rough trace of a road ran straight toward the river.

We found the umbrella, its ribs broken and its handle coated with mud, caught against a scrub alder at the point where the field road turned again, to the left, and ran along between the edge of the field and the river. But it was a turn that Mrs. Marcy had never made. We stood for a long time beside the last print of her shoes, staring down at the crumbled lip of sod and below it, perhaps ten feet, the strong black swirl of the Kennebec where it cut in against the shore.

Seth Marcy stood there beside us like a man in a dream, looking down at the edge of the running water with dry, hot eyes. After a minute his lips moved. "God damn her," he said, "may her soul burn in hell for this."

Neither Anne nor I thought for an instant that he meant his wife.

15.

FROM THAT moment on, the night became a confusion and a madness of futile activities. I remember scrambling down that bank for one last, hopeless, stupid inspection of its slope, with Anne saying over and over, "Dick! Look out! Come back!..." and Seth Marcy running heavily up and down the edge of the bluff like a dog that has lost the scent of his quarry. There was no beach at the foot of that bluff, nothing but the deep swirl of the water against the same ledge of rock that lower down provided Julian's house with so firm a bulwark against the winter ice and spring floods. There wasn't even a tree against which she could have caught. For a minute I debated shedding my clothes and swimming down along the bank with the currents of the ebbing tide and the river boiling along together. But the enterprise, though it did look possible, was clearly both dangerous and foolish. Nothing would be gained by it.

When I scrambled up the bank, Seth Marcy was already plunging across the field toward his house. "He's going to telephone," Anne said, "and then go into town for boats."

"They won't find her," I said. "But I suppose I ought to go with him."

"No," she replied. "He said for us to keep out of it, that we'd done enough harm already. Oh, Dick!" Her voice broke and when I found her in the dark and put my arm round her shoulders, I felt that she was shaking. "It's so horrible!" she said in a small, broken voice. "She was sweet, Dick, and she never had any fun and now she's gone."

"Easy all," I told her. "Don't let go. Come on, now, we've got to get back to the house."

All the way home her hand was cold and tight inside mine and once I thought how glad I was to be there with her. But, most of the time my imagination was racing ahead, trying to foresee what this pitiful business was going to lead to in the next few days, and what I could do to protect Anne and Julian. And the more I considered it, the more it seemed to me that we were in for a very unpleasant time indeed.

Mrs. Walters was in the kitchen when we got back, tired, muddy, cold, and at least on my part, half stupefied with loss of sleep. I told her the story dully, not even bothering to watch her while I spoke. She said little, exclaimed with horror when I came to the part about the river bank, and finally declared in a low voice, "It's my fault, Professor Sayles. I accept the entire responsibility for what seems to have happened. I never, never would have let her start home unless I'd felt certain she was all right."

"I believe you," I said, "but I only hope to God the rest of them do. Particularly Seth Marcy."

She made no reply to that but poured out two cups of coffee, and Anne and I sat down to drink it. I discovered that my teeth were chattering and, when I picked up the cup, my hand trembled so that I hoped Anne wouldn't notice it. She kept looking at me most of the time and the sorrow and regret in her eyes made a lump come into my throat. "Elora was a darling," she said once. I nodded. There wasn't anything I could think of that would help.

When we finished the coffee, Anne and I went into the living room. Mrs. Walters said that she would make more of the stuff and that we could do what we wanted. "They'll be coming here later, of course," she added. "There's not much use in going back to bed." The living room was cold and, when we lighted the lamp, the shadows came back into the corners again. Through the south windows we could see that the black sweep of the river was sprinkled with distant lights, low against the water. I knew they were lanterns and flashlights in the bows of boats. They moved back and forth across the water, crawling from shore to shore with a grim persistence.

Anne saw them too. "They're looking now. I suppose there isn't a chance..."

"I shouldn't think so."

"She'd never be able to swim, of course...I hope it was quick for her."

"You mustn't think about it."

She lifted a white face to me. "I still can't quite believe it, Dick. How could she have taken that wrong turn? This is almost like her own back yard, this land around here."

I had been thinking about that and, even though it didn't wholly satisfy me, I said, "She must have had a bad concussion. They don't always show up right away."

"Oh. Yes, I suppose you're right."

"Now listen," I told her, "we've got to stop thinking about what's already happened and get ready for what's coming."

"Coming?"

"Yes. There'll be people here after a while and they're going to ask us a lot of questions. Even an accidental death..." That word was heavy in the air between us.

She nodded and the firelight was red gold in her hair. "I hadn't thought of that."

"Furthermore, they'll all blame us for what's happened. Seth Marcy isn't going to be easy to deal with, though I guess most of what he feels will be directed against Mrs. Walters."

She looked at me and her lips were thin and pale across her face. "It *was* her fault, Dick...if only we'd stopped at Marcy's on the way to town."

The same regret had been tormenting me. Being wise after the event is one of the things I do best and it occurred to me that if we— or even one of us—had gone over to the Marcy house after supper to ask about Elora it would have looked better. As it was, it seemed clear we had acted in a way that would look stupid and callous to any outsider. But there was nothing for it but to face the music, try to behave as decently and calmly as we could, and make any recompense we could find to Seth Marcy.

"Sure it was her fault, partly," I agreed. "But I'm to blame somewhat, too. We should have done it differently." I decided to talk it over with her. "I've been wondering if we ought to get a lawyer," I began, "but the objection to that is people will think we are protecting ourselves because we feel guilty."

She shivered. "The people here . . ." Her voice was low. "They're going to hate us anyway."

I began to pace back and forth across the room and, even in the absorption of what I was thinking, I noticed how my shadow swelled and shrank against the far wall of the room. "The only thing is to tell the truth and take the consequences." The prospect was a bitter one. "We'll have to hope they believe us."

Anne looked puzzled and it seemed to me that her face was paler than before. "What else can they think?" Her voice was low and there was a tremble in it.

"Nothing, of course," I said, damning myself for a fool. "We may have been stupid, but that's the worst anybody could say."

"What's the worst anybody can say?" Mrs. Walters had come into the room with the noiseless step that was one of the things about her I was beginning to hate.

"Anne and I were just talking about how all this was going to sound in Barsham Harbor," I said. "We both think they'll hate us."

She sat down on the sofa and looked at the pair of us in turn. "And what if they do?"

Anne stared back at her. "I should think you'd be a little worried about it," she said and her voice was bitter now, instead of afraid. "If you'd been listening to Seth Marcy and what he was saying, you wouldn't be so calm about it. He hates us. All of us. And you most especially." Her tone was clear and hard; it rang in the room.

Mrs. Walters folded her hands. "Don't shout at me," she said. "I want Julian to get all the rest he can." She studied the tips of her fingers and then flexed them slowly in a movement so feline and relaxed that it made me want to look away. "Seth Marcy is a lout. I know his kind. You leave Seth Marcy to me; if he tries to make any trouble I'll take care of it—and him."

Those words of hers may read like sheer bombast, but they did not sound so in that shadowy room. I was shocked by the cold determination in her voice, the flat indifference to a tragedy which had happened only hours before. "You know," I said as quietly as I could, "there's not a chance that Mrs. Marcy is still alive?"

She nodded without speaking.

"Well, we're all responsible for that simple, elemental, and horrible fact, Mrs. Walters. You more than the rest of us."

She gave me back as good as I gave her in the matter of glances; her eyes were perfectly steady and as deep as the shadows behind her. "Professor Sayles, I should expect more self-control and judgment in a man who's no longer a boy." Anne moved then as though she'd been flicked with a whip, but Mrs. Walters never so much as glanced at her, and for my part I hope I did not give any sign of what I was feeling. Her voice when she went on was controlled, but there was something cold and light in it that was close to contempt. "I'm as sorry as you both are for this accident. But Mrs. Marcy died quickly and with no pain. There was nothing here in this life for her anyway. I'm sure she is happier at this moment than she has ever been before." Something in my look must have warned her, for she added with what I still believe to have been sincere conviction, "Death isn't the terrible thing most people make it out to be."

"Of course not," I said and the pulse in my throat was so strong it partly choked me. "It's hardly more important than a dropped stitch when you're knitting, is it?"

At that she got up and went to the window. When she finally answered, with her back toward us, her voice was smooth and low, but I was sure that there was some reason why she wanted to keep us from watching her face while she spoke. "I forgot," she remarked, "that neither of you has faith or understanding. To you, what has happened to Mrs. Marcy must seem tragic and irrevocable. I am sorry for that." For a while after that there was silence in the room and, when she spoke again, her voice was wholly different, strained, taut, as if some control over herself were slipping. "We are all tired and frightened," she said. "It was my fault. I should not have let her go the rest of the way home alone. But when she was with me she seemed so perfectly natural..." She waited for one of us to make some comment, but Anne shook her head at me and we kept silent. "You must have seen how it was by our footprints... She was walking along like a person who was absolutely uninjured." The inflection in her voice at the end of that sentence was too faint to be definitely questioning, but I knew that she expected one of us to reply. And with that knowledge I suddenly became curious as to why, exactly, she wanted us to speak. Did she expect some approbation for her caution in going part way home with Mrs. Marcy? Or—and I could not see where this thought led—did she want us to admit that we had seen the footprints?

Anne had brightened at her words. "Yes," she said eagerly, "that's right. There are the footprints. Dick, that ought to help with... them—don't you think? And with Seth Marcy, too."

"They'll help," I said and then added reluctantly, "but they won't be enough to absolve us."

Mrs. Walters' tone was edged with scorn. "You talk as if we were going to be tried for something."

I shrugged. "Well, I don't know much about small towns, but I suspect we shall be tried and found guilty on every street corner."

"Nonsense. Guilty of what?"

"Criminal negligence."

She confronted me angrily. "Are we back on that same old track?"

"All right, Mrs. Walters," I said, "if you're tired of old subjects, here's a new one. There'll be a coroner's inquest when they find the body. We'll all be questioned then. And it's going to be hard to answer some of those questions. Notably, why you didn't go all the way home with Mrs. Marcy, and why one of us at least didn't bother to go over later to find out how she was and whether she was all right."

"Inquest!" Her tone was short, as though the thought had jolted her.

"But yes," I answered. "So Anne's thought about the footprints is a good one. It may help to clear your skirts."

Contempt and impatience were stamped on her face. "If both of you would stop talking as if I—as if we—were guilty of something, it would be at least sensible. I admit I hadn't thought about the inquest, but after all it's not going to do us any harm to be able to tell our story in public."

Anne and I let it go at that. I did not trust myself to say anything more to Mrs. Walters and she behaved as if the two of us were no longer in the room. She had turned back to her window. I wondered if the boat lights were still crawling back and forth across the invisible water. It was impossible to tell from her stance what she was seeing, if anything; her heavy body was simply at rest beside the window, bulking there without tension or an expressive line in it. After what seemed like—and may even have been—ten minutes, she turned away and passed us without a word. At the door to the room she paused and turned back toward us, the way actresses of the old school used to stop in their exits and turn back on the audience for one last line. "I'm going up again for a while," she said. "Call me if you need me. There's coffee on the stove if you want it or if anybody comes. I won't take my clothes off, so I can come right down." Neither of us answered, but I nodded. "And my advice to you both is not to sit round talking each other into a state of nerves. You both need sleep. They'll make enough noise when they come." Then she was gone. A stair tread creaked once when she put her weight on it and after that everything was silent.

We sat together on the sofa. This time I did put my arm around Anne and from the way her head went down against my shoulder I knew she wanted it that way. After a short time she said, "Do you mind sitting here a while? I'm tired, but I can't bear going into my room alone and I know I couldn't sleep."

She was soft against me and the smell of her hair reminded me of the grass and the morning sun by the beach. "I'll stick around as long as you want me to," I said.

"Thank you, Dick. It's been a long time since I've done this, hasn't it?"

"Yes."

"I'm glad you're back," she said and then looked up at me. There were circles under her eyes, I saw with a quick contraction of the heart, but she was laughing. "And I'm glad to be back."

"Don't do things like that to an old man," I said.

She stopped laughing and looked at me intently. "I suppose you *are* old, aren't you? Twelve years older than I am. Well...?" She dropped her head against my shoulder again and sighed.

We sat there together for a long time. After a while I got out my pipe and smoked it once, and then a second time. Anne used up several cigarettes, but most of the time she stayed with her head down, leaning against me while I thought about her, and about the mess we were in, and how much I wished things were different. I tried hard to be happy about one thing, which was that at least this business had brought Anne and me back together again in a single day. It might have taken weeks or months to recover our old intimacy without the pressure of disaster to bring us together. But the thought wouldn't work. It ought to have been a good thing to feel glad over, but it simply wasn't.

That in itself interested me as a psychologist. I knew that I was fond of Anne, just as I had been when Helen was alive, and that the events of this long, incredible day had wiped out the constraint that would normally lie between two people who have been separated for years. I even had enough sense to know there was a good chance that I would ultimately find myself in love with her as well. The very feeling of her weight against me, the sensation of her warmth, the scent of her hair—these things were keenly present in my thoughts. But not as I wished they were, clear down into the center of myself. There was something underneath my awareness of Anne, something cold and inhibiting.

They say that in Alaska the summer warms the surface of the land so that you can grow crops on it, but that underneath the ground is frozen even in August. That is something the way it was with me that evening in the living room of the house on Setauket Point. I think, if I had kissed her then and told her that I loved her, abrupt as it would have seemed under ordinary circumstances, she would have understood and responded to it. But I didn't because I couldn't. There was something in the way, the only thing, I suspect, that can come between a man and a woman when they love each other, and it was to lie between us not only then but later.

The sundering thing was fear. You can love when you are cold, hungry, sad, swiftly frightened, even when you are otherwise bored, as honeymoons go to show, but not when you are afraid. And I was afraid.

It was quiet in that room, unmovingly, oppressively, chillingly silent there and through the whole house. The faint hiss of the lamp-wick and the sounds of our breathing were the only ones in my ears. I knew that, because I was listening—nominally for the return of Seth Marcy and perhaps others with him. They would come here whether they found her or not; I was certain of that. But the noise of footsteps was not the only one in my imagination. There was that other sound, the thing we had heard as we ran across the meadow in the rain...

It must have happened the very instant that Mrs. Marcy had fallen on the stairs. I wondered if it had really been the reason why she had slipped. There might be nothing more in the two things than coincidence, but I am not a strong believer in that kind of coincidence. No, there was some kind of connection and I was far from feeling certain that it was the obvious one. If people fell down stairs often when there was a...well, a clap of thunder...But they didn't. And that hadn't been a clap of thunder.

My thoughts revolved around this point over and over again in futility. I would shut my eyes and try to think just what that sound might have been, and instead there against the lids I would see Julian and Mrs. Walters at the foot of the stairs, looking down at Mrs. Marcy. She had seemed small, lying there, like a bird that had run into a windowpane and stunned itself or broken its neck. Probably Mrs. Walters was right and she hadn't had much of a life. Whatever it had been, it was over now. Perhaps that was, as Mrs. Walters claimed, a merciful thing...

I jerked myself back from this kind of thinking with horror. Never before in my life had I entertained such a stupid and morbid notion as that death could be preferable to life—any kind of life, no matter how dismal. Although of course if Julian could actually prove that there was another life afterward... And that concept brought me up short. There must be something in the air of this house or in its silence to make me think in this maudlin fashion. Then I remembered how tired I was. That would account for everything—fatigue poisons in the blood.

16.

WE HAD a long wait that night, Anne and I, before anyone came to the house. Once I went to the back door and out along the road a short distance. But there were no headlights on it coming our way, though I could see that the Marcy house was still lighted. And straining my eyes in the blackness, I thought I could make out a cluster of yellow light flecks between me and it, far off to the right. That would be another party gone down to read the story in those footprints and look, as I had done earlier, at the cut bank and the black, silent sweep of the water against the shore. Remembering how it pressed in against the rock and ricocheted back and out again from the land, I felt a kind of horror. I am a good enough swimmer, but even fresh and uninjured, I should not have cared to go into the river where those footprints ended. I went back to Anne without a word and held her close again.

It must have been long past two in the morning when a car finally did drive up to the house. The two of us had heard it coming—in spite of fatigue our ears were preternaturally sharpened—and we were standing on the back steps when it swept around the end of the barn and the headlights flooded blindingly over us. I felt like an insect pinned to a board.

Whoever was driving brought the car to a sudden halt and switched the lights down to dim. There was the slam of a door and then, as the driver came between us and the headlamps, I saw to my surprise that it was a woman. All that I could tell about her at first was that she had thin legs and was wearing heavy, sensible oxfords.

It was not until she was almost up to the steps where we were standing that I could get any idea of her beyond that.

She was, I saw then, a woman of somewhere between forty and fifty, spare, erect, with the kind of long face and heavy nose that are supposed to be typical of the New England spinster. She had a bandanna of some sort tied over her hair and was wearing a tailored suit which was something short of fashionable. Her walk suggested that she used her legs for getting across country rather than fascination. And yet, there was nothing daunting or formidable about her. I liked the way she came over to us and did not begin speaking till she was on the steps.

"Hello," she said then, and her voice was open and quiet, grave but not somber.

"Good evening," I said.

"I'm Ellen Hoskins. Is my brother here yet?"

"Why, no. I'm afraid I don't know any Mr. Hoskins. Anne, do you?"

"No," said Anne, her voice sounding so cordial that I knew she liked this woman just as I had. "But that needn't matter... I'm sure I've seen you in town. Will you come in?"

The woman said "Thank you," and came into the kitchen. "My brother Dan," she told us, "is the sheriff."

Anne's "Oh!" was less cordial.

Miss Hoskins smiled. "But he's quite human. He asked me to bring the car out here and wait for him. He ought to be along any minute." She looked at us pityingly. "You must have had a horrible evening of it."

"Yes," I said and then, moistening my lips, "have they found her?" She nodded.

"Dead?" Anne's voice was steady but faint.

"Yes. I'm sorry."

The news was no more than what we had both known we should have to hear sooner or later, but for all that it settled into my mind cold and hard. A sudden wave of sadness went over me—sadness and fear, as I had to admit to myself. I wondered what was going to happen now.

Ellen Hoskins was looking round the kitchen. Her eye traveled to the lamp, still burning on the table, but it did not pause there. She surveyed the whole room quietly, as though it interested her. Its placid, shabby orderliness seemed to please her in some way and she nodded to herself. Anne and I looked at her with curiosity. It was hard to tell what she was, though if her brother were sheriff, presumably she belonged to Barsham Harbor. Still, I decided, not entirely. Her tweed suit, though old and unashamedly patched on one elbow, was well-tailored and I thought the brown sweater under it had probably come from England. There was something crisp and assured in her manner that was puzzling at first, until it occurred to me that it was business-like. Her hands, too, were not those of a housewife, country or town. Their fingernails were short and uncolored, but they were polished. And her shoes, though they were dark with age and wear and smeared here and there with mud, were definitely handmade.

She drew a deep breath. "It's good to get inside," she observed. "Summer's about over and the nights are cold."

Anne's response was quick. "Would you like a cup of hot coffee?"

"No, thank you. But Dan'll be glad of one when he arrives. It's been cold out on the water, I expect."

"Come on into the living room," I said. "The places to sit in there are somewhat softer."

She grinned at that. "I can see you're not from this part of the world," she said and then added, "either of you."

"No," I admitted and we went into the front of the house. Through the window at the end of the room I noticed that the night was now wholly black and empty. The lights had gone from the water.

Anne drew a deep breath and said, as if the words hurt her throat, "They... they found her quickly, didn't they? We thought it might take a long time."

Ellen Hoskins settled herself in the chair where Mrs. Walters had sat earlier that night and began to fish in a side pocket of her jacket. "There's an eddy below Barsham," she said matter-of-factly. "One of the men—Harry Miller his name is—happened to think that with the tide ebbing, if there was a body in the river, it ought to appear there. So he waited a while and finally found her."

"Oh." Anne's face was white and she sat down quickly on the sofa again.

The sheriff's sister watched her a moment and then produced a package of ten-cent cigarettes, extracted one, and lighted it. "It's a horrible thing," she said, and in spite of her casualness and unconcern her tone showed that she meant the adjective.

"But you mustn't think too much about it, Miss . . . ?"

"Conner," I said and added, "My name's Sayles. Richard Sayles."

She nodded as if our names interested her in some way. "Thank you. My point is that you ought to take this as quietly as you can. And don't worry about Dan's coming here to talk to you. It's his job, of course, even in cases of accidental deaths."

"We understand that," I said, with enough emphasis on the final word to make her smile.

"But not me? Well, Dan's a good sheriff but the sight of a pencil and a piece of paper is more than he can stand. He foists off the notes on me—when I'm home, that is."

"That must be interesting." Anne was smiling again.

"Sometimes." Ellen Hoskins was noncommittal. "But a lot of it's just hard work—or tragic."

"We'd all give a lot if this hadn't happened," I said into the pause that followed.

"Seth Marcy is taking it hard," she observed with what was too ladylike to be a sniff, "in spite of the fact that so far as I know he never did anything to make Elora's life pleasant, or even tolerable." Her manner changed. "But I should be careful if I were you, all of you. The people here are different from the ones you're probably accustomed to. They'll blame you for what's happened."

"It wasn't our fault."

"No, Miss Conner, but it is going to look that way to most of them. And then—" She broke off, abruptly, and put her head on one side. "I wonder what's keeping Dan?"

"Was he coming straight here?"

"No, he was going to see Seth Marcy home and come on to talk to all of you."

"It doesn't matter. We're not sleepy," I said.

"Maybe not, but you ought to be. You both look tired. And you, Professor Sayles, only arrived today. The train always tires me and probably it does you."

"So you know my title and when I arrived?" I was puzzled.

"Oh, yes. In Barsham Harbor we know everything half an hour after it's happened. Your arrival was all over town by the middle of the morning. And I deduced the 'Professor' part from the fact that you came from New York and have a more or less unusual name. Knowing that you are visiting Julian Blair, I conclude that you must be the Richard Sayles who wrote *The Elements of Experimental Psychology.* I'm a secretary at Cambridge in the winter, in the Department of Psychology." She gave a sort of dry smile. "You see how easy it was."

"I see why your brother is sheriff, Miss Hoskins."

She laughed at that. "Oh, I don't do any of the sheriffing. I take Dan's notes for him and type them, but he does all the hard work."

This was a clever woman. For all the pleasant homeliness of that long face of hers and the angular awkwardness of the way she sat in her chair, I was conscious of her shrewdness and mentally decided that it would be well to be cautious about what we said to her.

She took another pull on her cigarette and remarked, "I hope you're not offended by my knowing who you are."

"Not at all," I told her. "Flattered. But there does seem to have been a good deal of talk about Julian and the rest of us in the village."

"Inevitably. They haven't much else to do, so they talk about anybody and everybody. And when there's nothing else to say, they gossip. They've been gossiping about this house and the people in it, ever since Professor Blair came. Furiously. And, without anything really to go on. Which means that they've had to make up stories, for instance one about a death ray that a lot of them are convinced Mr. Blair is inventing."

She tapped the ash off her cigarette with an abrupt gesture. "Dan's going to have some trouble, I'm afraid."

I had a suspicion what that last remark meant. The good folk of Barsham Harbor, with this tragedy for a pretext, would expect the sheriff to take some kind of action—action against Julian, or Mrs. Walters, or all of us. Seth Marcy, of course, and that cousin of his who'd driven me out from the station. The thought of those two men made me uncomfortable. They wouldn't be easy to reason with.

Ellen Hoskins seemed unperturbed by the silence that followed, but after a time she looked from one of us to the other. "By the way," she said, "it's not my business, but where are the rest of you?"

"Upstairs. Julian—Mr. Blair—isn't strong, and after Mrs. Marcy's fall he took a sleeping tablet." Some unpremeditated impulse made me add, "At least, so Mrs. Walters told us. He doesn't even know what's happened yet."

It seemed to me that she sat up a trifle in her chair. "So. The fall was a great shock to him, then?"

"Yes. We all thought she was badly hurt for a minute." But even while I was making that reply it struck me as curious that Julian should have been so shaken by the accident. He must have changed a great deal, I reflected. In the old days he would never have been so disturbed by an event that affected him only at second hand. Impersonally kind and troubled he might have been, perhaps, but not reduced to the white and trembling figure I had taken in charge. All at once there was a thought in my mind which I had not summoned: that accident to Mrs. Marcy must have meant something to him, something important. But how could Elora Marcy have been anything important to Julian in any way at all? The idea was ridiculous.

"From what I hear," Ellen Hoskins was saying, "your Mrs. Walters is quite an unusual person."

"That depends on what you mean," I answered cautiously.

She had the grace to smile. "You don't need to worry. I'm not here in any official capacity. Maybe I just have the Barsham curiosity."

Anne broke in on that. "I can't understand why she hasn't come down. She's a very light sleeper. She hears the smallest noise."

"She must be worn out," Ellen Hoskins commented.

"Yes," I agreed, but the explanation was unsatisfactory to some watchful segment of my mind. I still believe that Mrs. Walters should have come downstairs when Ellen Hoskins arrived. I think she overplayed her hand, just that one time. She overplayed it because she should have realized that neither Anne nor I would be quite willing to believe that she was really asleep. And yet, it is actually possible she really was asleep. That day must have put an intolerable strain on her.

However it was, the three of us went on talking inconsequences for what seemed like an eternity, trying not to let the tide of silence dammed-up in that house flood over us. At least that was what Anne and I were talking for. Ellen Hoskins appeared to have no purpose but the social one. Once I thought to myself that this conversational night piece was fantastic beyond any credence. There we were, chit-chatting away as if it weren't three in the morning and as if this Ellen Hoskins' brother hadn't just been fishing a woman's body out of the river. A woman who had been alive, walking, talking, singing to herself in this very house a few hours before. And my friend, Julian Blair, lying asleep and drugged upstairs; this was going to be nasty for him in the next few days. And Anne . . . The pieces of it began to fall apart in my mind with fatigue. I could barely keep myself awake enough to make a decently conscious remark now and again. To this day I cannot remember what trivia we discussed in that half hour before the sheriff came.

17.

THE CLUMP of feet on the back steps brought my attention into focus again. I got heavily up from the sofa and went out to the door. As I stumbled through the dark hall I tried to remind myself of the need for caution, discretion, a tight rein of restraint on everything I said or did from this moment on.

The man outside was knocking before I got to the kitchen and he made a peremptory noise of it. You could have told by nothing more than the way he knocked that he was the law. When he came into the lamplight I saw that he was a big man, something like his sister in face, but heavier of nose and jaw. The humor that lay in the corners of her mouth was missing from his. He looked strong, solid, and not quite grim. Thoroughly determined would be closer to it. After my first glance at him I knew that nothing could be done to alter anything about this man's actions. He would do his duty as he saw it and the chips could fall anywhere they chose. We introduced ourselves and I took him into the living room. He didn't offer to shake hands, by the way.

"Hello, Ellen," he said. "Sorry I kept you waitin' so long. Took longer at Marcy's than I expected." He looked the room over once, without interest, and settled his gaze on Anne. "You're Miss Conner, I calculate."

"Yes, I am." Anne's voice was low but steady and calm; she was clearly in complete control of herself and I felt a rush of admiration for the way she sat there, her head high but not defiant, her eyes level.

Dan Hoskins wasted no more time on the civilities. "Well, it's kinda late and I'll try to get this over with fast as I kin."

He looked at us inquiringly. "You don't mind if Ellen, here, takes a few notes for me?"

"Not at all," I assured him.

"Good." He smiled faintly. "She likes to help me out—gives her something to do. Well, you two just tell her your addresses so we get *that* down all right and proper."

Ellen Hoskins had produced a notebook and several pencils, sharpened to needle points as I observed. I suspected that detail was typical of her. She was the kind of woman who never needed to ask for anything. We gave her the facts about ourselves while the sheriff watched the two of us without expression. Then he cleared his throat.

"This ain't anything reely official," he observed, "but I figger I better collect all the information I can as quick's possible. Folks in town is kinda wrought up about the whole thing and it'll be best for all concerned if we get it clear right away."

"Sit down," I suggested, "if it's just informal. All of us will be glad to tell you what we know. Shall I call Mrs. Walters?"

He shook his head. "Not yet. By the way, where-at is she and Mr. Blair?"

I told him about that and then suggested that if he wanted information I could tell him the story of the day as Anne and I knew it. Then, if he wanted to ask any questions, he could. Ellen Hoskins frowned when I advanced this proposal, but her brother seemed to approve.

"Might's well," he agreed. "Mebbe I ought to keep you two apart and see if you tell the same story, but God knows you've had a plenty time to go over it already. Shoot."

"Stop me if I go too fast for you, Miss Hoskins," I said.

She looked up from her notebook. "You've got only one mouth," she remarked drily, "I expect I'll be able to keep up with it."

"She's used to perfessors," her brother observed with satisfaction. "You don't need to worry about her."

I launched into the account of the day's events, summarizing them briefly up to the moment of our return to the house and the discovery of Mrs. Marcy lying at the foot of the stairs. When he heard that Anne and I were not actually in the house when the accident occurred, the big man frowned.

"So neither of you saw it happen, then?"

"No."

"D'you know if anybody did?"

Thinking back, I found that I was not wholly sure about that. "I don't believe so," I said. "Mrs. Walters did say something about Mrs. Marcy's having fallen, but I'm reasonably certain she used a word like 'must.' 'She must have fallen,' or something like that."

He turned to his sister. "Make a note to ask about that, Ellen."

"I've already got it." Her voice was wholly uninflected.

"How did she look when you saw her lying there?" He sounded as if he assigned a good deal of importance to my answer and I noticed that he was alert, for all the relaxation in his posture. Not in any tense or overt way, but with the patient expectation of a fisherman staring at the cork float on his line.

"Why... I don't know, exactly. Sprawled out and limp, I should say. She was right at the foot of the stairs, as I said, and lying perfectly still. Her face was grayish and her eyes were closed. At least I think they were."

"Yes," said Anne in a low voice.

The big man nodded. "Go ahead."

"Then Mrs. Walters picked her up—almost right away—and carried her in here to the sofa. I did notice then that the poor woman's arm hung down rather peculiarly. Her hand was turned out from her body, instead of in."

Dan Hoskins grunted at that and turned to Anne. "You see that, too?"

"No. I didn't notice."

He turned back to me and revolved one square, thick hand at the wrist. "Like that, hunh? Like her wrist—or her arm—was busted?" he suggested.

I nodded. "But of course it couldn't have been. The tracks along the road later pretty well disproved that idea."

"So? Well, anyhow, the reason I asked was that when we found her it seemed like both her arms was busted." He paused but I could think of nothing to reply. After a time he went on, dubiety in his tone. "Maybe not, of course. We'll know more about that when Doc Peters turns in his report. And then again, maybe it was the water did it."

"She couldn't have carried that umbrella if she'd had two broken arms." He looked puzzled at that, so I went on to finish my story— the whole miserable business, including our stupid failure to call at the Marcy house to find out about her. He listened with attention and never once interrupted, but I felt that my story was clashing with something else that was already in his mind. There was a stubborn set to his mouth.

"Sounds like you're right about the broken bones," he admitted when I finished. "But when we found her, seemed to me like she was all brukken. O' course that current sets in against the rock pretty hard when the tide's ebbin', but..."

I wondered what he was getting at. If Mrs. Marcy had any broken bones, it was clear enough that the current must have been responsible for them. Else how could she have walked as far as she did? Mrs. Walters was no fool, either. She would never have let the woman out of the house if she had thought Mrs. Marcy was seriously hurt. Her remarks about Seth Marcy proved that to my own satisfaction.

"But you saw those tracks in the mud, I suppose?" The question was put in as tactful a tone as I could muster, but I wanted to be sure that nothing which could exculpate us, wholly or in part, was omitted from those precise, rapid notes that Ellen Hoskins was taking.

He studied the palm of one big hand for a moment before he answered. "Yup. I saw them. I reckon there ain't much doubt about how it all happened." Somehow his tone contradicted his words, though he sounded not so much skeptical as dissatisfied. After a while he gave us the clue to what was in his mind. "It seems kinda queer to me, her fallin' in that way, even if she had hurt her head. This farm here and the next one were about second nature to her.

Must have been...." He closed his hand and looked up. "Wal, you can't help me there. I'll have to talk it over with Doc Peters."

The way in which this man asked his questions and thought aloud interested me. Generally, instead of looking at us he kept his eyes fixed on some corner of the room, or the line of the baseboard. Once, long ago, I had had a Latin teacher who did the same thing in class—never looked at you when he called for a recitation, but stared at an Alinari photograph of the Forum before Mussolini and said, "Mr. Sayles, can you give us the future perfect of *eo*?" He'd been the shrewdest teacher in school, for all that, and big Dan Hoskins made me remember him. In a moment he called on me to recite again:

"You and this young lady wasn't here, then, when Elora left the house?"

"No. She was gone when we got back to town."

"Uh huh. And you didn't worry about her special?"

"No." I went on to tell him briefly about my conversation with Mrs. Walters and suggested that he ought to question her about that part of it.

"I'll git to her," he remarked calmly and went on to make certain from me that the first indication we had of anything wrong was Seth Marcy's arrival at the back door. When I finished, he sighed, "'Bout what I expected, but thank you just the same, Perfessor. Now, just think back on the whole thing once more and see if there's anything you'd want to add to your statement."

That last word stuck in my mind. I didn't exactly like its implications. "Statement?" I said. "I don't see why I have to make a statement. There's no crime here."

"No," he admitted, and then paused. "Fact is, I'd like to make sure this thing ain't put in the wrong light around town, Perfessor." He cleared his throat. "Like I said, folks is some stirred up. Nacherally. Elora was well-liked and it'll be hard fer a lot of them to believe she'd make a mistake like walkin' off the medder road into the river, even considerin' she'd had a crack on the head. Fer Seth's sake, and yours, you understand, it would be a pity if anyone was to think she . . ." his voice stumbled, "say, jumped into it a-purpose."

I stared at him. The very notion was fantastic, but I began to see what he meant, or thought I did. "Oh. But they couldn't blame anyone round here for that, even so. I'm positive she didn't commit suicide, but even if she did, it wasn't because of anything connected with us here."

"No?" His voice was noncommittal. "I'm not sayin' it would be. Especially Miss Conner and you, Perfessor. But if you'll excuse my way of putting it, Mr. Blair and that Mrs . . . Mrs . . ."

"Walters."

"Walters, they seem like kinda queer people to us here in Barsham. We ain't accustomed to foreigners." There was a sudden half smile at the corners of Ellen Hoskins' mouth at that last word. "They bein' queer, let's say, and it bein' queer that Elora Marcy would walk into the river off her own field, there's some will make a connection." He looked directly at me and from his manner I guessed that what he was going to say was to be something he regarded as vitally important. "Just what is it that your Mr. Blair's workin' on here, Perfessor?"

The question took me by surprise and I knew the consternation it caused in my mind must be visible on my face. The control I had been able to keep in the course of the examination so far was instantly dissolved. It was impossible to foresee the results of any answer that I might make. I damned myself for not having prepared for this emergency. I should have had a good, workable half truth, or even a plausible lie, ready to meet that inevitable inquiry. For if I answered it truthfully Dan Hoskins and all Barsham Harbor would assume that Julian was mad (which I had to admit to myself he probably was) and immediately connect his insanity with Mrs. Marcy's death. Perhaps they would believe that Julian had driven her insane by the sheer madness of his project, or infected her with his own mental trouble, as if insanity were a contagious disease. Added to that, of course, they would be properly horrified and suspicious.

The problem we had to face was how to convince Dan Hoskins and, through him, the whole of Barsham Harbor, that there was no connection between the tragedy of the afternoon and anything which Julian was doing in that upstairs room of his. After all, that was no more than the simple truth—or so I assured myself. Yet the thrust of fear that had gone through me at the sheriff's question should have taught me better. There was a connection, more than one connection, between Mrs. Marcy and the invention of Julian Blair. Somewhere in my mind I was aware of that, but what the relationship between the two things was I did not know. Meantime, Dan Hoskins was waiting for his answer.

"Why, I don't know that I have the right to divulge anything about that," I began, sparring for time and an explanation of my hesitation in replying. "Julian's work is hard to describe to anybody who isn't an expert, anyway. He's an electrophysicist, and he's an expert on electric waves and circuits. He made most of the improvements on the modern radio tube, for instance. Right now he is studying some faint electrical phenomena that no one knows much about yet. Waves that are something like radio waves, if you want to put it that way."

"Hm..." The sheriff sounded mildly amused. "The talk is that he's buildin' a machine to make a death ray."

The unconscious irony of that struck me so swiftly that I wanted to burst into laughter. I managed to throttle the impulse into a smile. "No, Sheriff, nothing like that." Then I added, "Mrs. Marcy did tell me she'd heard the same story. But she knew better, too."

"I see," he said absently. Following the line of his eyes I saw that he was watching Anne. There was anxious apprehension on her face and in the way she was leaning forward to look at me. Her expression, every line in her body, revealed much more openly than anything I had said how deeply concerned we were with Julian's invention. If I had hoped the sheriff could be decoyed from that scent, I knew that after one look at Anne it was a forlorn expectation. Well, I reflected, she was young and tired, and she couldn't realize how much she was giving away to a shrewd man like Dan Hoskins. Probably it was a secret we shouldn't be able to keep indefinitely under any circumstances.

The sheriff watched Anne for a moment and then shifted his eyes to the baseboard. I had the uncomfortable certainty that he could observe all he wanted or needed out of their corners. "I see," he said again and went on, slowly and casually, "Mr. Blair wasn't usin' Elora in any way to help him with his work, was he?"

"What?" I was genuinely startled. "Good God, no!"

"All right, all right," he said soothingly. "I'm lookin' as much fer what didn't happen as fer what did." He scratched his head. "You're certain sure Elora wasn't mixed up in whatever it is the old man's makin'?"

It gave me a shock to hear him call Julian an old man, but of course that was true of him, physically at least. Only... it had been such a short time ago that Julian was far from old. I called my mind back with a jerk to the question. "I'm positive. All she ever did was to sweep out his work room once a week."

"Yestiddy?"

"I think yesterday was her day for that. I'm not sure. But honestly, Sheriff, I can't see any connection. Mrs. Marcy tried to find out from me in the morning what Mr. Blair was working on." That was stretching the truth a good deal, but this was no occasion for moral scrupling. "I didn't tell her much, so she finally informed me that she was certain Julian's work was on a radio of some sort. She poked fun at the people who talked about a death ray."

He nodded his head several times, heavily, and was silent. At length he sighed. "You can't think of anythin' more you'd like to tell me? I'm clean out of questions."

Fatigue was numbing my brain until I was almost unsure whether I was awake or asleep, but I went laboriously back over the story I had told. Most of it was the truth, if not the whole truth, but it finally occurred to me that I had made it unnecessarily meager. Mrs. Marcy's fall was a natural accident, but I could at least suggest a cause for it, and thereby make it somewhat more credible. "Yes," I told the sheriff, "there is one thing. It's possibly not important, or even relevant, but if I'm going to sign any statement I'd like to have it included. The point is just this: Coming back from the water toward the house there was an exceptionally loud and alarming clap of thunder."

Surprise was openly printed on Dan Hoskins' face. "Thunder?" he said as if he had not heard me rightly.

"Yes. The noise was so sudden and loud that it even frightened me in spite of myself. It must have been very near the house. ('another of my slippery half truths,' I thought. 'It was in the house or there's something the matter with my ears.') I'm inclined to believe that it must have startled Mrs. Marcy while she was coming downstairs. She slipped and fell."

Ellen Hoskins was watching me, I saw, with speculation in the set of her eyes, but she said nothing. Her brother nodded without much show of interest. "Put that down, Ellen," he said. "More'n likely the perfessor's got something there."

18.

Anne's story was substantially the same as my own of course. She told it in a low, steady voice that betrayed no emotion and in considerably fewer words than I had used. The sheriff listened to her with attention but no great show of interest. He did not interrupt at all and, even when Anne reiterated my statement about the noise we had heard, he asked no question, though there was a quirk in Anne's tone when she called it "thunder" that I thought would arouse his vigilance.

After she had finished, the big man sat silent for some time, slumped in his chair and staring at the rug. He lifted his eyes after a time and stared directly at Anne. "Miss Conner."

"Yes."

"When you came back from town with Dr. Rambouillet, was Mrs. Walters' dress wet?"

Anne knitted her forehead for a second. "No. She had on a different one. In the morning and early afternoon she was wearing a black crepe. When we came back she'd changed into a dark-blue wash-silk she has."

The sheriff grinned. "You got that, Ellen?"

"Naturally I've got it." Her fingers moved like a pianist's when she was taking notes. She was never a word behind. I began to envy the Cambridge professor who had her for a secretary.

Dan Hoskins seemed to have come to a dead end. He stretched his tree-trunk legs out in front of him and knocked the tips of his heavy shoes together slowly and rhythmically. It made a noise that was too loud for the hush of the room. The rest of us simply sat, waiting for his next move.

"I'm a nacheral-born fool, I guess," he said. "There ain't no real call I can see to keep you folks here any longer, or ask any more questions. O' course, I'll have to talk to Mrs ... Walters before I go. But somehow I got a feeling ..." His voice trailed off and he went back to knocking the toes of his shoes together. Then he cleared his throat. "Miss Conner," he began almost diffidently, "would you give me some kind of picture of how you folks are all connected?"

Anne was surprised. "You mean, what relation we all are to each other?"

He nodded. "Something like that. More, how you know each other, how it comes that you're all here at once in this house."

"Oh." She began to explain that Julian was her brother-in-law, mentioned Helen's death, floundered through an awkward explanation about me, flushing when her voice stumbled, and added that when she'd arrived she'd found Mrs. Walters with Julian, and what she'd been able to gather about that. "She's sort of an assistant of Uncle Julian's," was the way she summed it up, finally.

That, it seemed to me, was a dangerous simplification. If the woman herself did not subsequently admit what she was, Julian himself was likely to do so, and I didn't want the sheriff to begin wondering, later, if we'd been holding things back from him all along the line. Besides, it seemed to me that I saw a safe way of explaining Mrs. Walters. In thinking it would simplify things at all I was reasoning from an abysmal ignorance of Barsham Harbor and the way its people thought and felt. It would, perhaps, have been better if I'd kept my mouth shut then, but I wanted to forestall the obvious, scandalous implications in Mrs. Walters' presence in the house. "Wait a minute, Sheriff," I broke in. "There's more to it than just that."

He grunted. "There must be. They been here alone, or pretty much that way, most of the summer."

Ellen Hoskins frowned. "Really, Dan, I'm afraid you have an unpleasant imagination."

"Never mind about my imagination. Human beings're human." His tone was impatient but indulgent.

"What I was going to explain," I went on firmly, "is this. When Mr. Blair's wife died, it hit him very hard. He's never really got over losing her. So he did something that even the greatest scientists have done, more than once, in the same situation. He turned to spiritualism."

The big man snorted. In spite of my own convictions, which were all in agreement with him, the scorn and contempt he managed to make vocal in that short noise drove me to Julian's defense. "All right," I said sharply. "You've a right to despise the subject if you want, but there's nothing unusual or disgraceful in being a spiritualist. Lots of sane people are, I assure you. Even some scientists, as I said. And that's the explanation for Mrs. Walters. She's what is called a medium. Julian believes that he can communicate with Helen—with his dead wife, that is—through her. That's why she's here."

"Have it your own way, Perfessor."

"It's the truth," I said wearily.

"Of course it is, Dan." His sister's voice was quietly amused. "In Barsham, Professor Sayles, they relish their scandal and Dan's no better than the rest."

I thanked her with a smile, but what she said made me wonder whether I had been altogether wise. "By the way, Sheriff," I told him, "I don't know whether it will help particularly to have the fact of Mrs. Walters' being a medium known. Perhaps it would be better not to mention it."

He snorted again. "Don't worry. I ain't going to tell it. Folks would laugh at me fer listenin' to such trash. Some of 'em, that is . . ." His voice lost its certainty. "And the others might not take kindly to the idea of havin' one of those things in these parts, anyhow."

"Thank you." I tried to sound ironical.

He waved a large hand. "Don't mention it. Well, young lady, that's your story, eh?"

Anne nodded.

The sheriff pulled his watch out of his vest and looked at it. "Gettin' late. Or early, I should say. But I calculate we may as well hear the others right now, if there's no objection. It'll save me a trip back later."

"Certainly." I got to my feet. There was no sensation except that of leaden weight in my legs. "At least, I'll go call Mrs. Walters. I don't know about Julian. She may have given him a lot of opiate. The shock was severe, you know. He's still sleeping and I wish you'd take him last, if at all."

"O.K. Let's have the woman first. You two don't need to wait up. Just send her on down and get some sleep. From the looks of you, it'd be a good idea."

His thinly veiled command was not as welcome as it should have been. I was dead tired, fatigue had seeped into every cell of my nerves and muscles, and yet I did not want to leave that room. I wanted to watch the encounter between Dan Hoskins and Mrs. Walters. I wanted to be there in case she flared up and undid the job I had tried to do in presenting our story. I felt, without knowing quite why, that we were going to need the sheriff on our side and I dreaded the prospect that Mrs. Walters would estrange him. But Anne was already on her feet and walking slowly toward the door. Clearly, there was no pretext by which we might stay and perhaps it would be wiser to get some rest. We were likely to need it in the next few days.

"All right," I agreed. "We'll call her and send her down to you. There's coffee on the stove if you need it. And wake me if I can help."

"Sure, sure," he replied and we went out together. Going up the stairs, Anne and I exchanged no words. I put my arm around her and steadied her, but there was no emotion connected with that. The sense of unreality and dream was upon me strongly, then, and even Anne was a part of it. We were not real people, I thought, but only shadows on a screen or words on a page. We could not feel anything real. The sound of our feet on the treads seemed to come from a long way off.

We knocked on Mrs. Walters' door. Her voice, when she answered, was not sleepy. "Hello," she said. "Who's there?"

I told her and explained that she was wanted downstairs.

"Wait one second till I come out," she said urgently through the door. "I want to talk to you a minute."

When she opened the door and came into the circle of our candle's light, it was plain that sometime before she had been at least lying down in her blue dress. It was creased and wrinkled, and her hair straggled round her face. Most of the make-up was gone from her cheeks and lips, and she looked more than ever like a human ruin. But I swear there was no fear and no weakness in that face, or in the way she held her big, loose body. She stared at us each momentarily, as if trying to read from our faces what had been happening downstairs. It may even be possible that she was, but I think she had no occasion to wonder about that. I think she had been listening outside the door. She was too clever to leave anything to chance or guesswork. And she was in too tight a pinch to let even the smallest slip occur.

"I hope you told the truth," she said to us in a low voice.

"Of course." I could not resist adding, "And you'll be all right if you do the same thing."

She smiled at that and it was a thin, cold smile. "Thank you, Mr. Sayles. I was only hoping that you hadn't embroidered your story with—noises, let us say, or stupid conjectures about me."

"I mentioned the noise. As a clap of thunder, which I still don't believe it was. And we told Sheriff Hoskins that you were a medium. It seemed to me better to do that than to let him go on thinking what was actually in his mind."

"How chivalrous of you." Without another word she turned down the hall, moving in the dark like a cat, and went soundlessly down the stairs.

Anne and I stood there in the dark hall until we heard a murmur of voices begin in the living room. Then we separated without a word or a gesture, and went at once to bed. This time I did not lie awake, even to listen. No matter what lived in this house, or what danger might be in its air, I could not think longer about it. Sleep came up over me at once, with Lethean intensity.

19.

THE SUN was shining when I woke the next day. For a time I lay on my cot, simply observing the intense blue of the sky coming through the window and feeling the animal pleasure of a rested body. When I stretched, the blood in the muscles of my arms and legs felt like rich cream. I was content, and even more than that. I thought of Anne. I would see her again on this day; no wonder the sky was so bright. And then I remembered everything else, in a series of heavy resurgences of memory, and the good feeling went out of me.

It wasn't particularly cold when I got out of bed, so I knew the morning was probably well advanced. And when I went downstairs to forage for breakfast, I found it was close to eleven. To my surprise, Julian was sitting in the kitchen drinking a cup of coffee and picking at a piece of toast.

"Hello, Julian," I said. "I see you slept late, too."

He looked up at me, and I saw that his face was haggard and gray. "Yes. Later than I should have. I have no right to lose a morning in this fashion, but last night...yesterday, seems to have been a shock to me."

"Did the sheriff wake you?"

"Yes. Almost at dawn. I should have stayed up then and gone to work, I suppose. But I was tired..."

The coffee on the stove was still hot. I poured a cup for myself, found some bread and butter and an orange, and sat down opposite him. "What did Hoskins ask you?"

"Routine questions. I had not heard about the accident until Mrs. Walters told me when she summoned me. It was tragic." He massaged his face with his hand and took another sip of coffee. "I would give anything if it had not happened."

"We all would give that, I guess." When he made no further comment, I asked, "Did you see the woman actually fall on the stairs, Julian?"

His face was grayer than before, I thought, but his tone was steady. "I was in my own bedroom, Richard. I couldn't have seen her fall."

"My theory is that it was the noise that frightened her into falling."

He moistened his lips. "So you heard that?"

"Of course. Listen, Julian, what made that noise?"

As if he had been rehearsed in the answer, he said, "Thunder. It's often very loud and startling here in the valley."

I gave him a look which I hope expressed my skepticism and went on with my breakfast. "I suppose," I said at last, "you wouldn't be willing to use me as your assistant while I'm here, Julian? There's not much else to do and we used to work well together in the old days."

He smiled at that and there was human warmth in the look he gave me. "For an undergraduate, you were a remarkably capable laboratory man, Dick. But I don't need any help. It's best, I am coming to believe, if I work wholly alone. And besides, I'm relying on you to give Anne some fun."

"I'd have time to do both."

"No, Dick, no." He looked at me somberly. "What do you think of her?"

"She's a good kid."

He nodded. "And a lovely one, too. Dick, if I should ever have an accident—say like Mrs. Marcy and fall downstairs—I want to ask you to keep an eye on Anne. I've bequeathed what little property I have left to her, in my will. You're the executor."

"But Julian—"

He held up a thin hand. "Don't protest. There is no one else I could ask to do it."

"All right," I said. "I'll do my best."

"That's all I want," he said and finished his coffee. The piece of toast which he had been holding when I came in was almost untouched. I wanted to urge him to eat more, but from the way he shoved it back I was sure it would be useless. "Well, Dick, it's good to have you here. Perhaps I did not sound too cordial yesterday and I'm sorry. You're a comfort to us right now, though. I'm only sorry all this should have happened."

I told him not to worry and that it was nothing, and he moved out of the room. Even before I had finished speaking I could tell that his mind was abstracted, that he only half heard me, and as he went through the door his head was bent forward as I remembered it when he went into the lab in the old days. Without his telling me, I was sure he was going to that room of his where he worked and the thought gave me a twinge of uneasiness. Surely there were more important things to settle today? But I did not try to call him back. He had gone beyond me, beyond every other living person as well, I think. There was no way I could have held on to him. Even if I had known then what was to happen in the next forty-eight hours, I could not have held him back. Julian, in those last days, was scarcely a living person at all, as I have come to realize in thinking back over the whole terrible story. He was alive only because of the purpose that was in him, the determination to perfect that device of his before letting the death that was in every fiber of his body actually triumph.

After I had finished eating and washing my cup and saucer, I went outside. The sun was blazing down with a thin, sharp sort of autumn heat which felt good on my neck and shoulders. There was a chill in that house behind me that never wholly left it. Apparently the storm had blown itself out—there were a few clouds far to the east, but elsewhere the blue was unbroken. I let my eye range north to where the Marcy house stood, but there was no apparent movement around it. After a while a car came crawling down the road and turned into the drive, but that was all. That, and the fact that there was no one in the fields around the place, and no sound of any sort. It was a Sunday silence, but it wasn't Sunday.

I strolled aimlessly across the grass and down toward the bay. Looking at water is one of my favorite ways of doing nothing. Even if the thought of swimming was ridiculously inappropriate, and in spite of the fact that I should have loathed the sight of the river because it had just killed a woman the night before, it seemed better to stroll toward the bay than up the road past the ominous silence of the Marcy house. So I went toward the bay. The grass was quite dry again and the ground no longer muddy. Everything was so precisely the way it had been yesterday I could hardly believe that the things my memory told me had occurred were possible. Even when I remembered them most actively, they were not altogether real, as the sun, the grass, the blue sparkle of the water was real.

Anne was sitting on the bank over the swimming beach. She was wearing a tweed coat with a pattern that looked loud to my conservative masculine eyes and a plain dark-brown skirt. The sun was in her hair and lying gold on the skin of her neck and hands and bare legs. She was kicking against the cut bank with the heels of her sport shoes and staring out over the water. I dropped down beside her.

"Hello."

"Hi."

The ensuing silence lasted a long time. Finally she sighed and said, "It's hard to believe it all, isn't it?"

"Yes."

"Who'd you see this morning," she went on after a while. "Walters?"

"No. I had breakfast with Julian. Then I came on out here. I didn't want to hang round the house. I didn't see her at all."

"I did," said Anne. "Something's wrong there. She's desperately unhappy about . . . yesterday, I suppose. Or else something that happened this morning."

"What?" I couldn't feel much interested.

Anne shook her head. "I don't know. I just wondered if you'd noticed it . . . Did Uncle Julian tell you the inquest is this afternoon?

"No. Is it?"

She nodded. "We're all to go. At least, so Mrs. Walters says. I had breakfast with her. It wasn't cosy. She only spoke to me once and then it was to tell me that." She pulled a stem of grass and put it between her teeth. It was so much like yesterday that I felt confused for a moment, as though time had slipped, or I had become misplaced in it. Anne went on after a time. "She looked as if she had been crying. I think perhaps she and Uncle Julian had words this morning. Anyhow, she went into his room earlier to see if he was awake and she was gone quite a while. I could hear their voices through the door, but not what they were saying." She nipped the grass stem again. "It would be fine if they really quarreled and Uncle Julian sent her away."

Her mood struck me as odd, but my own was no more explicable. We both felt detached, passive, wholly centered in the moment. The past and the future were equally uncomfortable, and so we were just existing as nearly as possible in a pure present. There was nothing in our words or actions that morning to suggest that we were more than the most casual acquaintances and most of the time, I think, we were hardly aware of each other. Most of the time. But there were the moments when I would notice the light in her hair, or the faint fragrance of the perfume she was wearing, and I would be aware of her, all right. She hardly looked at me.

We stayed there by the water till one o'clock and by the time we returned to the house, lunch was on the table. A vile meal it was, too—canned peas, some warmed-over stew, and pale yellow, slippery canned peaches that reminded me of college commons. I looked curiously at Mrs. Walters while I was putting down as much of the food as I could manage. She was obviously outfitted for town, in a stiff blue dress. Her hair was more carefully arranged than I had yet seen it, and her make-up was straight again. But there was a sullenness in her manner, even toward Julian, and she obviously resented all of us. "You might have come in sooner," she said to Anne, "I had to get the lunch singlehanded." And to me, "I made your bed, Professor Sayles. But if you want any more tidying up than that, you'll have to do it yourself." As I recall, she did not address a single word to Julian.

There was something defiant about him. He ate more than he had at breakfast, rather as if to avoid the necessity for speaking than as if he were hungry. He must have been working hard. There was a black smudge on one cheek—the one he always rubbed when he was concentrating, I remembered—and his hands were grimy.

After the meal, Anne went over to him and gave him a kiss on the top of his head. "Now Uncle Julian," she said, "you go up and wash your hands, fix your hair, and put on a tie. Dick and I aren't going to take you to town looking like a mechanic."

"But that's what I am, my dear," he said absently. All the same he got up and went obediently out. Mrs. Walters followed him without a word to either of us, but the look she gave Anne was eloquent. Anne grinned sweetly back at her and went on collecting the plates. I felt the usual helpless embarrassment of the male caught in the cross fire of a woman's skirmish. When the door closed behind Mrs. Walters, Anne gave me a grimace that was funny enough to make me laugh. I hoped that Mrs. Walters didn't hear it, but I suspect she did.

The kitchen, though, was a cheerful place after Julian and Mrs. Walters had left. Anne and I washed the dishes slowly because it was something to do, and had a good time till the last one was racked away. Then there was nothing to think of but the trip into town.

We left the house about half past two and the ride was a stiffly silent one. Julian sat with Anne in front, and Mrs. Walters and I occupied opposite corners of the back seat. We neither looked nor spoke at each other in the course of the drive. All four of us were preoccupied with what was to come and yet, though we knew that we were going to face the hostility of all Barsham Harbor, we were not united by the opposition we were to confront. "This," I thought, "is no way to go into a thing of this sort," but I could not see what to do about it, so I kept silent.

As we passed the road into Seth Marcy's farm, a car swung out of it and followed after us. It came in so patly that I felt the driver had been waiting for our car to appear. Once Anne slowed down and pulled over to let it get ahead, but whoever was driving refused to go past. He kept his car an even distance behind us all the way into town.

20.

THE INQUEST was to be held in a courtroom on the second floor of the County Building. We had no trouble in finding a parking place and as we stepped out of our Ford the following car drove up behind us. It was the taxi in which I had ridden from the station the morning before. Seth Marcy got out of it and so did the driver, whom I recognized at once. They stared at us without any expression and waited till we entered the building and started up the stairs. Then they came after us, walking with the slow, loose-jointed stride of countrymen. I could feel their eyes on the back of my neck.

We found seats toward the front of the room and sat down. It was rather a dingy, large courtroom and there must have been well over a hundred people in it even before the presiding magistrate, whoever he was, arrived. I presume he was the coroner, but I don't know his name and never did. The irrelevant details of a situation like ours don't impinge much on your mind. Dan Hoskins was there, of course, and I saw Dr. Rambouillet sitting across the aisle from us. It was some time before I noticed Ellen Hoskins. She was sitting at a table with a man who looked like the court clerk, methodically sharpening a pencil with a pocket sharpener.

Most of the time before the hearing opened I spent looking at the people in the courtroom. They were a grim lot, on the whole. We New Yorkers become used to audiences which have a good deal of more or less ebullient blood in them—Italians, Spanish, all sorts of foreigners-that-were who have still not become "typical" Americans. Here it was different. These people were all of the same stock and startlingly alike underneath their superficial differences. They were, on the average, tall and inclined to thinness. Their faces were sharp and gray or weathered. Men and women, they had a look of being on the defensive toward life in some way that I could not define. They were inclined to shabbiness—again by New York standards—and there was a faint truculence about the way they sat and the looks they cast in our direction.

Good people they might be, but narrow and cold was the way they looked. I thought as I surveyed them that it was lucky we were innocent of any sort of wrongdoing. It would be hard to find an impartial jury among a people like this.

The jury was, actually, a cross section of the spectators. It was wholly composed of men, most of them apparently farmers, and all middle-aged or older. They were not in the least ill at ease in the jury box. Now and then a dry smile would cross the face of one of them, a long-boned fellow with a mackinaw jacket who sat on the end of the second row, when he caught sight of someone he knew in the audience. But it seemed to me, looking at them, that they were serious and dignified about what they had been called upon to do.

The formal proceedings began almost on time. The magistrate seemed to have no particular plan of inquiry. He took evidence first of all from the man who had found the body—Harry Miller. His testimony was nothing more than what Ellen Hoskins had told us the night before. Then Dr. Peters was called to testify, and here the examining officer showed a nice sense of economy by using the doctor first to identify the body, and then to describe the medical aspects of its condition.

Some of what he had to say belongs in this record, though it has already been suggested. Dr. Peters was a large, dignified medico with white hair and a weighty gold watch-chain. As the dean of the Barsham Harbor doctors and coroner's physician as well, he spoke with a good deal of dignity, and weighted his sentences with technical words and terms even when they were not necessary. He reported that when he first examined the body of Mrs. Marcy she was already dead. I felt an insane desire to smile at that.

"Can you give us the precise cause of death, Dr. Peters?" The coroner's tone was deferential.

Dr. Peters looked grave. "The cause of death might briefly be described as internal injuries," he declared, "that is, hemorrhage resulting from such injuries." He proceeded to launch into a Virgilian cascade of Latin terms, of which I recognized only a few, including the astounding fact that Mrs. Marcy had received an apparently terrible blow across the chest which had resulted in a fractured sternum, or breastbone, and a ruptured spleen. Further, both her arms had been broken.

A ripple went through the courtroom at his testimony. I know that it took me wholly by surprise, and even the coroner appeared incredulous. "Then you do not believe, Dr. Peters, that the deceased met her death by drowning?"

Dr. Peters looked pained. "I have testified as to the cause—or causes—of death. None of the symptoms of drowning were present. There was no froth in the deceased's mouth or nose, nor even in the trachea and bronchial tubes. Neither was there water in the stomach." He paused and cleared his throat. "The definitive test for drowning is the Gettler test. It depends upon a chemical analysis of blood taken from the pulmonary vein. If pulmonary blood contains a higher percentage of salt than the normal, the diagnosis is death from drowning in salt water. If the blood contains a lower salt content than the normal, the diagnosis is, of course drowning—more technically, asphyxiation—from submersion in fresh water. In the case of the deceased I did not apply the Gettler test."

He paused and the coroner supplied the cue for which he was palpably waiting. "Can you tell the court why you did not apply the Gettler test, Dr. Peters?"

"I can. There were two reasons. One, that the pulmonary vein had been ruptured as a result of the injuries which I have already described. The other, that the deceased—ah—entered the river at a time and point when the water was, in view of the condition of the tide, brackish." He brought the word out with a fine flourish of the tongue. "In my opinion the test would have been of no practical value."

That was Dr. Peters' testimony, though it took much longer to deliver than to summarize. I listened to it with amazement. It seemed to me entirely incredible that Mrs. Marcy should not have died as all of us had assumed she did. And yet, in spite of his bombast, Dr. Peters was clearly testifying with knowledge and authority. Pompous he might be, but I could not believe that he was ignorant of his facts. I stole a look at Dr. Rambouillet, but that young man's dark, handsome face was composed. Apparently he saw nothing in what his colleague was saying at which to cavil.

The coroner was as puzzled as the rest of us. He asked Dr. Peters if he had any idea what could have occasioned the numerous injuries he had described? Dr. Peters pointed out that his province was not speculation, but that the injuries were consonant with the deceased's having been struck violently across the thoracic—"or chest"—region by a bar or the edge of a plank. "Although," he concluded, "a fall against such an edge as I have mentioned might have produced the same result, provided the deceased had fallen from a sufficient height." He added that he had no reason to assume such a fall. In reply to a question from the coroner he admitted that he had been the deceased's personal physician "since the day she was born" and that he knew of no complaint which would have rendered her liable to sudden dizziness, or to fainting.

When he finally stepped down from the stand, my mind was in turmoil. If Mrs. Marcy was not alive when she went into the river, then how explain a thousand things? Her regaining consciousness, for instance? Her walk toward her home? When, and under what circumstances had she died? Obviously not in our house nor as a result of her fall on the stairs. Though I wondered numbly whether the edge of a stair tread could have inflicted the injuries which Dr. Peters had described. It seemed impossible and yet . . .

Seth Marcy was the next witness and he made a bitter one. He described his long wait for his wife's return, his eventual decision to come after her, and his summoning Anne and myself to the back door. "Her lamp was still burnin' in their kitchen," he said. "Tell me why that was. It was the only time she left it on. You can't get around that. They're hidin' somethin', and I look to this trial to git it outa them."

The coroner rapped with his gavel. "Now, Seth. This ain't a trial, and you've got to be careful about accusing people."

Seth's face flushed dark, but he said nothing more, returned a few sullen answers to minor questions and stepped down from the witness chair. As he strode along the aisle to his seat he almost brushed against Mrs. Walters and his thin, hooked mouth went down at one corner. "You dirty whore," he said out of the corner of it in a low voice, "you'll pay for this." Then he was past her and into his seat behind us.

Mrs. Walters said nothing, but her face went white and I saw that she was trembling. There was an anger in her eyes that was terrible. I would not have chosen to incur Seth Marcy's hatred, but I'd have taken it any day in preference to the ice-cold wrath that looked out of Mrs. Walters' eyes.

Our turns came next. Mine was first; I told the same story I had given Dan Hoskins, but I put as much emphasis as I could upon the thunderclap. The fact that I was a college professor and one from a New York university did not seem to please most of the courtroom; there were sneers on several faces confronting me. When I admitted that I had no idea how Mrs. Marcy had met so terrible and violent a death, the taxi driver laughed contemptuously and loud enough so that I heard him. It was possible, I suggested, that in falling from the bank she had struck against a ledge of rock, but I admitted I had not noticed such a rock at the place where Mrs. Marcy had fallen. I added that the evidence of the footprints, which I described in as much detail as I could remember, was plain and emphasized that Seth Marcy had been as convinced of their authenticity as I was. I pointed out that he had followed them in advance of Miss Conner and myself.

It was surprising how much latitude the coroner permitted. He interrupted seldom and allowed me to tell our side of the story without correction. "Thank you, Professor Sayles," he said when I had finished. "I reckon you've told us what we want to know."

"Or what he wants us to know," said a voice from one of the benches toward the rear of the room.

The coroner pounded with his gavel. "Silence. This is a court of law. If there ain't decent order here the room'll be cleared."

With that, I went back to my seat and it was Anne's turn next. She told the same story that I had and again there were no questions. I began to feel uneasy. There was a growing air of hostility in the room which was inescapable and I wondered why we were given so much latitude. It seemed to me that the coroner would naturally try to please the people to whom he owed his office, after all, by giving us an uncomfortable time of it. But on the contrary, he was quietly kind to Anne.

I looked at her on that raised chair and felt my heart contract within me. She didn't belong there. Her clothes, bright and smart by comparison with what any other woman in the room was wearing, were too gay for Barsham Harbor. Her hair was too gold, too much like sun in a room that was not meant to be other than shadowy. She was too lovely a contrast with the people who were here to look at us and judge by their own harsh standards. Beauty is a hateful thing if it is of a kind to shame you. And Anne seemed to me to shame these people. They stared at her with a sort of impudent curiosity, or at least the men did. That made me inwardly furious. The women stared coldly at her, but there was no mercy in their eyes.

Anne's voice was low and steady. She behaved as if she were accustomed to giving evidence, and her story was clear and direct. She told it her own way, too. I think no one would have been willing to believe that we had rehearsed our evidence beforehand. When she finished she turned to the coroner. "I don't know if what I'm going to say belongs in your records, but I do want to say that this thing that has happened is horrible and that I—that we all—feel terribly about it. Elora and I were friends, really. She was an adorable person . . . I wish it hadn't happened. That's all."

The coroner thanked her and she stepped down to a buzz of low-voiced comment in the room. I could not tell exactly what they thought of her, but I suspected it was the inevitable judgment—that is, the men were half won over by her sincerity but the women contemptuous. At least one thin, blowsy housewife a few seats away muttered something to the pallid man beside her which sounded like "baggage."

I find it hard to convey the inquest as it seemed to me while it was going on. My own emotions were too chaotic for exact definition—they were a blend of confusion underlaid by fear, of uncertainty, of surprise, of a gnawing anxiety as to what all this was going to mean for Anne, Julian, and myself, bitter regret that I had not secured a lawyer, and over them all a sort of numbness. The whole thing was too far outside anything that had happened to me before. I felt responsible for the group of us; it was up to me more than anyone else to see that we came out of this mess without tragedy and yet, I felt helpless to alter the course of events.

Never, in the most unfamiliar parts of Europe, had I felt so alien as I did there in that Maine courtroom. The lot of us were simply cut off from everyone else. When the coroner had reproved Seth Marcy for calling the inquest a "trial" he was only technically correct. For we were really on trial, in the eyes of Barsham Harbor. One of their own people had died a horrible and inexplicable death and we were somehow mixed up in it. We were outlanders. They meant to be sure that we did not get away with it. I squeezed Anne's hand when she sat down again beside me.

"Good work."

She did not reply. Her lips were pressed together hard and her fingers gripped mine. I knew that she wanted to cry and wouldn't permit herself to do so.

Then Mrs. Walters was called to the stand. Instantly the buzz of comment took on a new note, more sibilant, deeper in tone. They had been waiting for her.

21.

MRS. WALTERS took her place with an unruffled composure, gave her name and address without being asked for them, and settled herself in the witness chair. The coroner looked over at her above the rim of his glasses.

"What is your position in Mr. Blair's household?" he began at once.

"I am Mr. Blair's housekeeper and assistant."

"How long have you occupied that position, Mrs. Walters?"

"Over three years."

"I see. What do your duties as 'assistant' consist of?"

"I help Mr. Blair with his experiments."

The same voice in the rear of the room which had heckled me suggested, "Ask her what her duties are as housekeeper then."

The coroner's gavel was peremptory. "That's enough of that, Hank Mason. If you can't remain silent, you'll have to leave this hearing." But the muscles at the corners of his mouth were twitching.

Mrs. Walters said quietly, "I will answer any question which is put to me. But so far as I know, I am not on trial here. I do not see why I should tolerate insults."

"Now, now," said the coroner. "Please speak only in answer to my questions. Tell us what you personally saw of the accident to Mrs. Marcy."

Mrs. Walters' response was instantaneous. "Nothing directly. Mrs. Marcy had finished cleaning the room where Mr. Blair and I work. She was on her way back—I suppose to the kitchen. There was a sudden, very loud clap of thunder and it seemed to me I heard also a faint sort of cry. I left the room where I was and went to the head of the stairs. Apparently Mr. Blair heard the cry, too, because we met at the head of the stairs. When we looked down, there was Mrs. Marcy lying at the bottom. For a moment we were too surprised and alarmed to do anything. Then we went down the stairs. We stood there a moment, looking down at her, and Mr. Sayles and Miss Conner came in."

She told the rest of the story substantially as she had before, putting great emphasis upon the fact that she would not have let Mrs. Marcy leave if she had not been sure she was fully recovered and, even so, that she had gone part way with her. She admitted that she had been at fault in letting Mrs. Marcy go at all, but declared that the woman had insisted. "It's easy enough to see now what I should have done," she concluded. "But it wasn't so easy then. People fall more or less all the time and usually without any serious damage. I have had some nursing experience. I was satisfied that she was all right. But if there is any blame, I am willing to take it."

When she said that, it seemed to me that her eyes were fastened on Julian, but he did not acknowledge her glance in any way.

"When you carried Mrs. Marcy to the sofa," the coroner said, "did you examine her in any detail? Can you tell us, that is, if she had any of the injuries which Dr. Peters described and which I am sure you heard?"

Mrs. Walters shook her head contemptuously. "If she had, I would never have let her leave the house. And she could not have left it, either, because she would have been dead. Dr. Peters testified that she died of those injuries. But she did not get them from whatever accident she had in our house. She may have struck a rock in her fall into the river . . . I don't know how she got them."

Seth Marcy stood up in his seat. His face was livid and the finger he shook at her trembled. "You lie and you know it. Why was her light left burnin' in the kitchen, right where she always puts it? Answer me that if you can!" He sat down again, shaking with hate, and behind him a murmur of approval rose from the room.

Mrs. Walters was calm, while the coroner pounded for quiet.

"Let the court put the questions," he shouted as soon as he could make himself heard. "This here's a court of law." He turned to Mrs. Walters. "I was comin' to that question next. Seth Marcy testified his wife used to leave the lamp in your kitchen burnin' in the window until she started for home. Then she would put it out, and Seth knew she'd left your place. You knew of this arrangement?"

"Certainly."

"Then how do you explain the fact that you arranged the lamp so as to give Mrs. Marcy's signal to Seth?"

The look Mrs. Walters gave the coroner and the court was full of the most contemptuous scorn I have ever seen. "Why," she said as if speaking to a class of stupid children, "I thought of course that she was already home. I left the lamp lighted for my own convenience in case I had to get something later for Mr. Blair. Seth Marcy is making something up out of whole cloth. If he had the least intelligence he would see that there was no sense in what he's been saying."

"Please stick to the questions I ask you, Mrs. Walters. This court isn't to find out what you think of Seth Marcy—or any of the rest of us for that matter."

A murmur of satisfaction rose from the room and I damned Mrs. Walters under my breath. She was not doing us any good and I knew that the rest of us would be judged by her. These people would tolerate no arbitrary words from any of us, but least of all, from her. She was the focal point of their scorn and hate.

When the room had quieted once more the coroner went on with his examination, but it was plain that he was at a loss. He no longer knew what questions to ask; the evidence was at an impasse. Mrs. Marcy had not drowned, but had been killed by a blow or a fall. She had fallen in our house, but her injuries could not have been sustained there because she had been able to walk home. Mrs. Walters was stubborn in her testimony. After a time he gave it up and dismissed her from the stand.

The confusion in his mind was apparent in his next act, which was to call Dan Hoskins to the stand and question him about the footprints. The big sheriff was terse and direct in his evidence. He declared that although the rain had somewhat defaced the prints, he had tested them with Mrs. Marcy's shoes ("yes, the ones she had on when we found her") and a pair which Mrs. Walters had given him early that morning. He was in no doubt but that the prints had been made by the two women. The trail was an easy one to follow and its meaning inescapable.

"You believe then," the coroner demanded, "that the previous witness's story is correct?"

The sheriff nodded slowly. "I ain't got no choice but to believe it. The shoes fit the prints and you can see what was happenin' to her practically every foot of the way. Them prints are still there. I've looked at 'em twice. You can't git away from 'em."

The coroner went on to examine the big man about the way in which he had heard of the "accident," his connection with the search, his inspection of the ground, and his interrogation of us. As I listened to Dan Hoskins' replies I came to understand why Anne and I, at least, had been so gently handled in the examination. He was obviously concerned to make plain his conviction that we were not involved in anything criminal. "These folks gave me straight answers, so far as I'm a judge," he said once. And again, "There ain't any evidence I can see against anybody—at least so far." I knew that he was speaking not to the court but to the courtroom and the heavy silence with which his audience listened to him indicated how little they liked what he was saying.

"Maybe these folks were kinda careless," the sheriff declared at the end of his testimony, "but that's the wust I can say in the light of the evidence."

"Have you any theory as to how Mrs. Marcy came by the injuries Dr. Peters described?" The coroner's voice was openly puzzled.

Dan Hoskins shook his head. "I guess Perfessor Sayles is right. She musta hit a rock ledge. That current there could slam a body against the stone with turrible force, I calculate. If you ask me, she was unconscious but alive when she went into the water. Or maybe just conscious enough to fight a little against the water. Inside the first few seconds the river slammed her up against the rock."

The coroner thanked the sheriff and recalled Dr. Peters. He was questioned at some length as to whether the sheriff's explanation were a possible one. This time the doctor was not so positive. He admitted that with a chest injury of the extent he had found, there was no likelihood that Mrs. Marcy would have drowned, in the technical sense. He said he believed the injuries had been sustained before she went into the water at all, but declared that it would be impossible to testify certainly on this point. He could, however, say "with assurance" that Mrs. Marcy must have been struck immediately after she entered the river, for there was no water in her lungs, and undoubtedly instinctive breathing would have forced her to draw breath within a minute, thereby pumping water into the lungs and stomach. He gave it as his opinion that she would not have been capable of drawing a breath after the injury.

By this time even the slowest thinkers in the spectators had begun to see the intricacy of the problem. There were head scratchings on the part of the men and a steady hiss of whispers from the women. My own confusion had been supplanted by a deep feeling of alarm. Something had happened to Mrs. Marcy which was not yet explained. What it was I could not begin to imagine, but it must be connected either with Seth Marcy or with us. Seth was a brooding, angry man. Everything that I had seen of him made me positive that he was capable of violence, even to his wife. On the other hand, if his actions when he discovered what had happened to Elora were forced and nothing but pretense, then he was a superb actor. Beyond all that, there was the evidence of the footprints . . .

On the other hand, both Anne and myself were clearly not connected with whatever had actually happened. I, at least, could be wholly positive about that. Which left Julian and Mrs. Walters. Julian was, I considered, out of the question . . . My thoughts had reached this point when he was called to the stand.

Julian's testimony was curious. He gave it in a thin, uncertain voice which must have made a bad impression on the coroner. Certainly it did on his audience. He began by declaring that he had been in his room when the burst of thunder of which we had all spoken occurred. He had come out into the hall with a sense of vague alarm and found Mrs. Walters hurrying toward the stairs. He had seen Mrs. Marcy lying at their foot. "I was, of course, horrified." He said the words as if he did not entirely mean them. "I am afraid that I did not make any close examination of Mrs. Marcy or participate in what the others were doing to help her. It was a great shock." His voice quavered when he said that. He meant the last few words, at least, I decided.

"Mr. Blair," the coroner began after a pause, "you are a scientist?"

"I am."

"Would you tell us why you came to Barsham Harbor?"

Julian looked trapped. His eyes flickered round the room and he moved his hands nervously on the arms of the witness chair. "Why . . . for no special reason. That is, I wanted a place as isolated from large cities and power lines as possible. The location of my house is ideal for my purposes."

"In what way?" The coroner seemed determined to pursue the subject.

Julian drew a long breath, and said, "My work is concerned with delicate electrical impulses. If you like, they may be compared to very faint radio waves . . . I was anxious to carry on my researches as far as possible from heavy-duty electric machinery of all kinds and other disturbing influences. That is why I came to Maine. That, and its isolation from the more populous parts of the country. I am both a scientist and an inventor. Secrecy, in the early stages of a research, is important."

The coroner said "Thank you," in an unsatisfied tone. He looked hard at Julian. "Would you be willing to tell us the nature of the problem you're working on now, Mr. Blair?"

"I would prefer not to do so except to say that it involves research into very minute electric impulses."

"Was Mrs. Marcy aware of the nature of your work?"

Julian looked surprised. "It never occurred to me to wonder. I do not see how she could have been."

The coroner frowned. "When this work of yours is completed,

Mr. Blair, will it have any commercial application?" For the first time I noticed that the coroner was reading these questions from a slip of paper on the bench before him. I looked at Dan Hoskins. He was listening to Julian with complete concentration and I saw that Ellen Hoskins' pencil was racing across the paper in front of her. It had occurred to me for an instant that perhaps these questions had been supplied to the coroner by the sheriff. I discarded the thought. Their very phrasing was against such an assumption. But Ellen Hoskins might have written them.

Julian looked still more surprised. "I do not see what all this has to do with Mrs. Marcy," he declared in the firmest tones he had yet used. "But although I have not thought about the commercial applications of my research, I can say that I do not believe they will be very widespread. By that, I mean that my goal is not an ordinary commercial one. It is more…" he paused and groped for the next word, "humanitarian. And for me," he added with an undertone of defiance behind his words, "the problem does not arise in any case. I intend to make the discoveries which arise out of my work public property the moment I am convinced they are sufficiently advanced to do so."

Then I knew. In a single flash of intuition I saw one of the strains which was operating in that household of ours on the Point. The clue was the sudden stiffening of Mrs. Walters' back as Julian delivered his last sentence. Her eyes narrowed and she stared at him angrily. *She* did not want that mad invention of his made public. Furthermore, she believed it would work and she was angry at the thought of Julian's giving it to the world. For a moment I was incredulous. She couldn't really think that thing would do what Julian expected. She must have joined forces with him originally on a very different assumption—that he was an ideal client who would pay well and go on paying as long as she could consciously—or perhaps it was subconsciously—delude him. But now, she believed that he would succeed and she was determined that when he did he would not turn over his discoveries to the world.

It was a terrific commercial opportunity, of course. Julian was quite wrong on that point, at least. In one flash I saw the whole thing as it would be—the duplication in secrecy of Julian's machine, the advertising, the publicity, the carefully publicized proofs of the invention's actual validity. The long and pitiful queues of people who were bereaved, waiting to pay for the privilege of a few minutes' intercourse with those they had lost...A blackness came in front of my eyes. I felt suddenly dizzy and, more than that, afraid.

Odd that in all the talk with Julian, and all the high-flown things that Mrs. Walters had said to me, I had not once felt a real conviction of the possibility that Julian would succeed. But in that clash of anger and wills in the court I saw a stronger rebuttal to my skepticism than in anything which had gone before. Both Julian and Mrs. Walters were convinced, so convinced that they were already at odds over the future of the machine which Julian had fathered. He had actually done it, then...And even as I thought that, a revulsion occurred in my mind. "By God," I told myself, "you're crazy! He can't have. It's utterly and absolutely impossible!"

22.

THE CORONER was persistent. "What I am getting at, Mr. Blair, is the question of whether, if Mrs. Marcy had known of your work, she could have given away its secret or in any way affected the progress of your research?"

Julian frowned. "My working model," he declared, "is so complex that I doubt whether more than a few people in the entire country could grasp its nature, even after prolonged examination. I do not see how Mrs. Marcy could have understood it in the slightest."

(And yet, Julian, the most ignorant savage quickly finds out about a rifle, even if his most "prolonged examination" will not reveal the nature of that deadly tool. It was typical of you to assume that no one could know a thing unless he understood how and why it worked. But people do not think that way. They see only what it *does,* and understand the forces and instruments of their world by their effects, not the principles which lie behind them.)

Apparently the coroner had come to the end of his questions. He hesitated and I saw him glance down at Dan Hoskins, who gave an imperceptible shake of his head. Whereupon Julian was excused from the witness chair. Then followed one of the most curious speeches I have ever heard. The coroner addressed the jury as if they could help him resolve the problem which confronted him. He reminded them that they had seen the body and that it was their duty to decide how Mrs. Marcy had come to die. If they felt that she had met her death by misadventure—"or accident, that is"—they were to find a verdict to that effect. If, on the other hand—and here he shrugged—they had any idea that she had died as the result of negligence, or deliberate intention on the part of some person or persons, they would bring in a verdict to that effect. He himself could not comment on the evidence beyond remarking that it was contradictory and confusing. On the other hand, there appeared to be no ground for suspicion that anyone could have desired the death of Elora Marcy or stood to profit from it in any way. While the witnesses from the house where she worked had admitted to a certain lack of suitable caution in letting her leave their house, there was apparently some reason to suppose that almost anyone would have done the same thing in their place. The evidence which Dr. Peters had presented was one thing they had to bear in mind. And another was the evidence of the sheriff and the footprints...

It went on like that for some time and had I been on that jury I would have been puzzled to know what sort of verdict the coroner expected me to reach. He simply laid his own perplexity in their laps and said in effect: "I don't know what to make of this, but maybe you do. Anyhow, you've got to bring in a verdict."

The jury was out for a long time. At least it seemed so to all of us. When they filed back into the court there was a look of sheepishness on most of their faces. The foreman stood up with some embarrassment. "We've talked this thing over, Ben," he said to the coroner, "and we don't figger to know any more about it than you do. So we kinda reached a compromise. We find the deceased met her death as the result of internal injuries like Doc Peters said, but we don't know how she come by 'em." He sat down and wiped his forehead with a blue bandanna handkerchief.

A babel of talk burst out in the room behind us. Everyone stood up at once and began shuffling, not back, toward the door, but down forward, where we were sitting. The final words of the coroner were lost in the general noise. Almost at once Dan Hoskins was standing at the end of our bench, beckoning to us.

"This way. You better go out the side door."

We followed him without further urging. None of us wanted to stay behind in that crowd. The noise at our backs was louder and there were some shouts which I could not make out. We found ourselves almost at once passing through what must have been a judge's chambers and then down a private stair of some sort. Julian and Mrs. Walters were the first in the single file by which we descended, and I brought up the rear. Although no one came after us, the skin on my back crawled as we went.

The sheriff wiped his own forehead when we reached the sidewalk. "Git in your car right off," he said, "and go on home. I'll expect all of you to stay there till you hear from me. And listen. For God's sakes be careful what you say and do. I never seen folks so stirred up."

Our car was almost opposite the door by which we came out. I drove, with Anne beside me, and we went down to the highway by back streets. The impulse to stamp on the throttle was panic-strong in me, but I managed to resist it. We rolled out along the edge of the bay at forty-five and as Barsham Harbor dropped behind us I began to breathe without feeling as if a bar of iron were clamped around my chest. Anne's face beside me was white, but she lit a cigarette with steady fingers.

"Fools," said Mrs. Walters after a time. "Small-town ignorant fools, that's what they are."

None of us could think of a suitable comment to that, and we drove on in silence.

"That sheriff better keep them in order," she went on, after a silence.

23.

DUSK HAD drawn in by the time we reached the house and once more the chill of autumn was in the air. Anne and Mrs. Walters went about the preparation of supper in silence. After I had put the car in the barn, I foraged round until I had collected all the wood I could find. Then I went into the living room and built a roaring fire.

"Swell!" said Anne when she came in and saw it. "Now, if we just had some—"

"I have," I told her. "In my bag. You bring glasses."

What obscure impulse had led me, day before yesterday, to buy a bottle of Scotch and put it in my suitcase I cannot say, but I was never gladder of anything than of the first draught of that whiskey and well-water highball we drank in front of the fire. Just the two of us. Mrs. Walters stayed in the kitchen and impatiently refused an invitation to come and join us. Julian had gone upstairs the moment we had got back to the house and, though Anne knocked on the door of his room, he declined to come down. He told her that he would appear for supper, but that he did not want to be interrupted until then. So we drank alone and I was not sorry to have it so.

We did not talk about the afternoon, nor mention the disturbing inconclusiveness of the inquest. We did not even comment on the ways in which Julian and Mrs. Walters had behaved. Instead we talked about things we had seen and done on our respective travels in Europe, about the foods we'd eaten, the wines we had drunk. It was pleasant merely to listen to the way she spoke, softly and with humor. From time to time we clinked the rims of our glasses and took another sip. The firelight was comforting in that room of shadows. Anne felt the same relaxation, almost contentment. Once, after a silence, she said, "This is the first time things have felt right, isn't it?"

"Yes," I admitted.

"And that's funny, because things aren't at all right, really."

"We won't talk about them now. Later. But let's have this as long as we can."

We stayed there in front of the fire until Mrs. Walters came into the room and informed us tersely that dinner was ready. A minute later we could hear her knocking at Julian's door, but when she came into the kitchen where we were sitting down, she said shortly, "He won't come. Says he has to work. I'll take a tray up to him."

The meal, like all the others in that house, was a quick and silent one. At least until the very end. Then, to my surprise, Mrs. Walters looked at me and said, "What did you think of that farce this afternoon, Professor Sayles?"

"That we were lucky to come out of it comparatively scot-free."

"Nonsense."

"And that I still don't see what happened to Mrs. Marcy."

"You don't? Why, your own explanation is the only possible one."

"Is it?" I said softly. "Maybe. But it is so unlikely that I'm not satisfied with it. Don't forget, I looked at that bank where she went into the river. There's no ledge there sharp enough to do what Dr. Peters described in the way of injuries."

She leaned forward and looked heavily into my eyes, as if she wanted me to feel an additional weight behind what she was saying. "But there are *under*water ledges, Professor Sayles. It must have been one of those."

"No," I answered. "I don't think so. A body weighs much less in the water. Even the full sweep of that current wouldn't do to a person the things that happened to Mrs. Marcy. Waves—a heavy surf—might possibly. But not the steady thrust of that river, strong as it is."

She drew back and her voice was lower. "You are quite mistaken. You must be. There is no other way it could have happened."

"You're very positive," I told her.

"For Julian's sake, at least, I should think you'd be equally positive."

"Why?" I demanded. "I'm sure Julian had nothing to do with the whole thing. I'm not, to tell you the honest truth, so sure about you, Mrs. Walters." The moment I had said it my doubts rushed together and I knew that in some obscure way I had hit close to home.

She stood up and it seemed to me that she was making a tremendous effort to master herself. "Don't you see what you are doing when you make such statements, Professor Sayles? Can't you understand that if there is too much doubt about the way that poor woman came to die, the first thing that will happen is that we shall all be investigated?"

"Very likely," I told her. "'Let the galled jade wince, our withers are unwrung.' In other words, I have no objection to being investigated." I looked full at her. "Have you?"

"Good God!" she flung out at me, "must you go on thinking in this childish, superficial way? Can't you see that any investigation would result in the police coming here, in their going over the house? Have you no imagination whatever? Where do you think they'll look?"

"Everywhere, I suppose."

"Yes, everywhere. Including Julian's laboratory. And then what do you think would happen?"

The fury of her outburst, the way she flung words at my head as if they were scalding hot, both amused and irritated me. "I don't know what would happen, Mrs. Walters. Nothing very serious, I should think. Julian said that no one could understand his apparatus but a few experts anyhow."

She shook her head with a sort of wild impatience. "He's just a child, Julian is. He cannot imagine how things will look to an ordinary human being. He's right so far as the principles go. I don't even understand those myself. But I tell you that one look in that room of his and we should all be in a serious predicament, Professor Sayles. You haven't been there, so you don't know, but you've got to believe me when I say that. The police would never keep their mouths shut. They would tell what they saw. And that would be the end of our chance to finish the work here. Those horrible people in Barsham Harbor would never leave us alone, once they heard ..."

"Heard what?" I asked sharply. Her whole manner was so wild and excited that I was afraid she was going to have an attack of hysteria.

The sharpness of my tone apparently brought her to her senses. She made a visible effort to get control of herself. "I've said too much," she declared finally, in a milder voice. "I realize that you can't believe in what Julian is doing. But I do. And it will be the end of everything if that sheriff and his men come poking into this house. Even if you believe Julian is mad and that I'm—well, I can guess what you think of me and perhaps some of it is true—you might stop to consider that it will kill your friend Julian Blair if his work is destroyed now. So, Professor Sayles, the only course for all of us is to tell the same story that we've told already."

"It's too late," I told her. "After that verdict at the inquest, the sheriff will be bound to investigate the whole thing until he finds out the truth." I looked at her hard and long. "My story has been true. Anne's story is also true. If you and Julian have not told the truth, this is the time to come out with it."

She gave me a single sidelong look out of her dark eyes and moved toward the door. "What a fool you must think I am," she said and shut it behind her.

Anne stared at me speechlessly. "Well, well, well," she said. "You certainly struck oil."

"Yes." I picked up a dish towel. "Let's clear this mess up; we can talk while we work."

"Immediately, sire," she answered and began filling the dishpan. "I couldn't tell what that was all about. Could you?"

"No. But she told us one thing. If there was anything funny about what happened to Mrs. Marcy, the motive for whatever part Mrs. Walters had in it is plain enough. She wants to protect Julian until he finishes his work. She won't stick at anything to do it, either."

"What do we do now?" she asked after a while.

"Nothing," I said. "Nothing until I get a look at that device of Julian's and find out why it would be so fatal to have anyone see it."

"That won't be so easy, Dick. He keeps the door locked every second except when he's actually going in and out of the room."

"He must have a key," I said. "If we get hold of that the rest will be easy."

Her reply was a noise which, if it wasn't a snicker, was an exact replica of one. "Dick, this is too absurd. We're plotting together like a couple of characters in a B picture. It's all ridiculous, somehow."

"Maybe. It wasn't so funny earlier today."

"Or last night." Her tone was apologetic. "But let's not forget our original plan."

"What?"

"To do what we can for Uncle Julian."

"Yes," I said. "I'd rather lost sight of that. Well, let's think some more before we decide on anything."

"*You* think," she said. "You're the brains of the conspiracy... If only there were somebody around I could vamp for you."

"There is," I told her.

"Who?"

"Me."

"Good heavens," she said, "I've been working on you all along."

24.

THAT EVENING was a strangely happy one. For one thing, Anne and I had the living room to ourselves. Mrs. Walters was nowhere to be seen when we came out of the kitchen, nor did she put in an appearance thereafter. Julian was apparently up in his room; from time to time we could hear the sound of steps over our head and once a thump that suggested his having dropped a tool. But otherwise the house was silent and we were alone in it. Thinking back on that strange interlude, I believe that Mrs. Walters had decided she could no longer trust herself to talk with us and that she felt she had said too much already. So she went to her room. I imagine she even went to sleep. She had nerves of iron, that woman. Much as I hated her then, bitterly as I remember her now, I am compelled to admire her. More than once I have caught myself hoping that she is still alive somewhere. I cannot imagine what she would be doing, or how she was able to explain herself if she did make a new start—in another country, perhaps, or at least, another part of this one.

But Anne and I were not thinking too much of her. We were not really thinking much about anything. We sat on the floor in front of the fire and sipped whiskey and water at intervals that were not too long. I know that the strain of the afternoon had begun to tell on both of us. We were thoroughly relaxed, disinclined to anything important, though we both knew, I think, that we were living that evening not in peace but an armistice. The fire was warm on our faces and the liquor grateful in our stomachs. We smoked. We talked occasionally and lightly. The things we said have no place here because they had nothing whatever to do with the story of the house on Setauket Point. But they were pleasant and full of meaning when we said them.

Once, when the firelight fell on Anne's face at a certain angle, I remembered Helen. The recollection, I found, did not hurt. Instead, it was oddly embarrassing. All at once it seemed to me that I had let part of myself live too long in the past. I was not ashamed of having loved Helen, but rather of the fact that it had taken me so long to get over it. A love that is true to living persons and existing realities is steadfast and fine. But I saw then, for the first time, that a love which was fastened upon the dead and true to nothing but a past that was finished, is not a good nor true emotion. If it went on too long, it could become an incubus, throttling a man from the real life of the present, which is the life that we were fashioned to meet and experience.

After a long time I said something of that to Anne. I knew that it would have to be explained sometime and that it would be easier now than ever again. She listened to me quietly and said nothing after I had finished. I wanted not to stop then. I wanted to tell her something of what I felt about her, but I found that I could not. In that house I could confess to things that were over and dead. I did not seem able, somehow, to go on and talk of the future, of anything which looked beyond the instant in which we were.

The fire had died to coals when we finally left it to go upstairs. This night I did not put my arm around her, as I had the time before when we went up those stairs together. We said good night in the hall, whispering because we did not want to wake Julian if he had gone to sleep, and we said it almost as casually as if we had been strangers. That seems strange to me now, but it was inevitable then.

My room was cold and bleak. I undressed as quickly as I could and lay down in the thick dark. It was the proper time, I told myself, to think things over carefully, to sum up the inquest and that amazing scene in the kitchen with Mrs. Walters. But my mind refused to tether itself to any one subject. It ranged over an extraordinary melange of things. It tossed up at me the picture of Ellen Hoskins, sitting beside the court clerk and taking her own notes, presumably for her brother. She was a shrewd woman, that sheriff's sister. Much cleverer, perhaps, than her brother. No wonder he let her assist him . . . Then there was the recollection of Anne's brown legs swinging against the cut bank . . . The curious timidity of Julian's face at the inquest . . . and then there was nothing. I was asleep.

When I woke to a room that was still as black as blindness I thought at first that I had been having a nightmare. My skin was cold with perspiration and my heart was pounding with that terrible fear which half strangles you with its intensity. And there was a horror in my mind, unformed and unrecognizable, but washing up over my consciousness in great black waves. I wrestled with that fear as Jacob wrestled with the angel. I told myself that I was awake now and that there was no more cause to be afraid. But there was.

I heard the sound at first almost subconsciously, as I must have been hearing it in my sleep. It was not loud, but I knew it for what it was—the same sound that the two of us had heard in the meadow at the moment when the storm was over the house. But this time there was no storm. The night outside the window was still; I could see stars in the sky. And yet the noise was present in my ears and there could no longer be any doubt at all where it came from. It was in this house.

At first that one fact was all I was able to decide about it. The cold, heavy air of my room was threaded with sound which appeared to have no point of origin and which was as much a vibration I felt through my skin as a resonance in my ears themselves. If you have ever waked in a Western night to hear coyotes howling on a ridge, you will know something of the primitive, irrational fear that it induced in my mind, but nothing of its quality. Perhaps the slither of a snake's scales across a stone floor . . . I thought of those things and others as I lay there listening. I remembered a night I had once passed in an anchored boat. There had been a small leak in her hull, and all night long I had heard the gurgle and bubble of the sea, deep and very cold, coming in through her bottom. It had not been a dangerous leak and we pumped it out easily in the morning, but the chuckle of the water as it came up from that gulf under our keel and invaded our small floating world had remained in my mind as a symbol of dread.

Not that the thing in the air of that old house resembled in any physical way these sounds that I have described. It was rather a sort of cold, humming whisper which seemed as I lay listening to increase and increase by such imperceptible degrees that whole minutes must have passed before it was recognizably louder. At the beginning I had to strain my ears to catch it, but after a time it was inescapably easy to hear. Then it stopped abruptly and there was nothing but an occasional night noise in the timbers of the house. I began to relax. The air was easier to breathe without that undertone in it. When it began once more it was so low that I was unsure at first whether I was hearing it again or only remembering. After a while there was no possible doubt and I lay there, feeling fear collect in me more and more coldly and insistently, until the tension was almost unendurable. Any kind of action was preferable to this lying in the dark with terror for a bedfellow. I swung my legs over the edge of the bed and got up.

By the time I had groped for matches in the pocket of my coat and got the candle lit the noise had stopped. I stood there in the raw air of the room, holding the candle in a hand that shook in spite of all my will power, and staring stupidly toward the door. How long I waited like that I have no way of reporting. Long enough to be chilled to the core, at any rate. Gradually I was aware of another kind of noise, a faint rustle which came through the wall behind me. Anne was moving in there and the thought steadied me. No matter what was happening it was my job to keep unafraid and calm. She must be as terrified as I, and she would need whatever strength and poise there was in me. I started toward the door.

Before I had taken three steps I knew, rather than heard, that the noise had begun for the third time. It was in the air again, as intangible as the first smell of smoke and more frightening. The boards under my bare feet were like ice, and it took all my resolution to keep walking cautiously toward the door and the thing, whatever it was, that was making that sound. Julian's invention it must be, of course, but I wondered what his invention really was; what abominable sort of thing would make that noise . . .

It was louder when I opened the door into the hall and, for the first time, I was aware of the general direction from which it came. A hall ran past me to right and left, and the noise was stronger toward the left. As I stood indecisively looking along that dark passage, there was a click on my right. Anne's door was opening cautiously, the yellow shine of her candle came through it and in a second she was beside me. She could not have been as cold as I, for she'd had sense enough to put on a long red dressing robe and slippers, but she was shivering violently.

"What is it?" Her whisper was low.

"That thing of Julian's I suppose. Beat it back to your room, Anne. I'll look into it."

"No. I don't want to be alone."

"All right," I told her, "but stay behind me."

We went down the hall toward the crescendo of that sound and as we walked, I noticed a curious thing to which I paid only casual attention at the time. There was a draft along the floor of the hall, a trickling creep of air that froze my ankles and made the hem of Anne's robe flutter. It was a quiet night. I should have thought more about such a draft of air around our feet, about where it was going and what had set it in motion. But I was so deeply preoccupied with the business of forcing myself to approach the source of that rushing, humming whisper of fear that I could think of nothing else.

Our candles threw a good deal of light when we started, but by the time we had covered half of the eight full paces that lay between my door and the one to Julian's workroom, they had begun to flicker and burn blue. My shadow tumbled and darted ahead of me down the hall, cast by the light from Anne's candle. There was something horribly incongruous in the way it alternately shrank and grew on the boards before me.

No, I don't think I shall ever forget that short eternity of a walk from my door to Julian's.

His door, when we came to it, was tightly closed. To my surprise there was no knob on it, in fact, nothing at all except a new round brass lock that shone yellow in the light of our candles. The door, I saw, was not like any of the others in the house. They were old Maine pine, paneled in a graceful twofold cross. This door was perfectly flat and when I touched it I perceived that it was not even made of wood, but of metal. The cold of steel came through the paint to my fingers,

The noise was on the other side of that door. There could be no doubt of it. It was louder here than at any other point and I could discriminate a number of the elements that went to make it up. There was, below everything else, a humming, tonal constant, but besides that there was a faint, roaring sound which I find it hard to describe, but which was something like the noise of a firebox in a furnace that is running full blast. And then, mingling with those two elements, was a third which I could recognize—the hiss of moving air. The draft which had swirled round our feet was strong in front of that door. Air, it seemed to me, was being sucked into the room, forcing its way into it through the crevices where door and jamb met, brushing past Anne and me as if it were impatient to seek the heart of that sound.

I wondered at that motion of air, of course, but only with a small segment of my attention. The rest was engrossed in listening. In both Anne's mind and mine, I think, the irrational fear which that sibilant, roaring hum evoked was overlaid with another, horrible sort of dread. Suppose that noise should change, should alter, should begin to define itself? As we heard it then it was a sort of echo of chaos, but if it were to change and become coherent? If, indeed, there should be whispers that were not those of air in motion?

The anticipatory dread of voices was so tremendous that for a time I could only stand before that steel door, pressing the fingers of my free hand against it to steady myself. Half consciously I began to mutter to myself under my breath: "The dead do not come back. No matter where or what or if they exist at all, they will not speak through this thing of Julian's. He is mad, and it doesn't matter that he is a genius and that I know it. He is mad and there is no possibility there will be more than one voice on the other side of this door.

Julian's voice yes, but only his. Never that of Helen or Mrs. Marcy, or the old captain who used to lie in this room and look down the river. They are all gone."

The noise continued. It grew louder, until it seemed to me that the floor trembled with it. The air that went past us whittled the flames of our candles to bluepoints. I could not stand it a second longer. With my clenched fist I beat against the door. "Julian!" I shouted. "Julian! Stop it, I say! Turn that damned thing off!" My fist made a kind of metal thunder against the door and, though I was ashamed of the way my voice trembled when I shouted, I kept on yelling until the noise on the other side of that door stopped.

It ceased abruptly, with a roaring crash that was almost like an explosion. It was, on a lesser scale, the clap of thunder that Anne and I had heard in the meadow.

The sudden hush that followed that final crash rang in my ears almost as loud as the clamor of the minute before. Anne drew a deep uneven breath. "Thanks," she said, whether to me or to the silence I don't know. We stood there together, shivering and weak, and waited. I was determined to speak to Julian. He would have to leave that monstrous business of his alone, at least for the rest of this night. The kaleidoscope of all that had happened since I came to Barsham Harbor rushed over me; I felt tired, bewildered, afraid, and more than anything else, angry.

Two things happened at once. The door before our faces opened the fraction of an inch and Mrs. Walters came heavily down the hall at our backs. Julian's voice, hoarse with some emotion which I could not define, came through the crack of the door. "Get away," he said. "Get back down the hall and I'll talk to you. But get back from this door."

Mrs. Walters was saying, in a tone of sneering triumph, "So, Julian. You see I was right!" She looked at us with contempt. "Hasn't either of you enough sense to stay where you belong?" she demanded.

I put my hands against her shoulders and pushed her backward down the hall. "Later," I said. "We'll have all this out in the morning. But not now."

She retreated. From the expression on her face I think she was surprised that I had dared to touch her.

Julian came out of his room before we had time to become further embroiled. He opened the door, I noticed, just enough to slip out and then drew it shut and locked it before he turned toward us. His face was gray-white in the glow of our candles—burning steadily now that the draft was gone from the hall—and his eyes were rimmed with the black stain of fatigue. He came toward us down the hall as if his strength were almost gone. Apparently he had not yet been to bed. At any rate, he was fully dressed in the suit he had worn to the inquest.

"Never do that again," he said and his voice trembled with wrath. "Never!"

"See here, Julian," I said in as restrained a tone as I could bring myself to employ, "you simply cannot run that damn thing of yours in the house at night. Neither I nor Anne can bear the noise it makes. You ought to be in bed."

He looked at me dully. "What time is it?"

"I don't know. After midnight."

"Two in the morning," Anne's voice contributed.

"Trying to do it all yourself, Julian?" Mrs. Walters' tone was harsh and sarcastic, but her face was strained and there was pleading in it.

Julian made a motion toward me. "All right, Dick. No more tonight, I promise. In the morning I want to have a talk with you." He sounded merely tired. There was no more anger in his voice.

"Good," I told him. "Only get some sleep first. There's no need to work yourself to death you know. You mustn't drive yourself so hard."

He shook his head. "I'm not so sure, my boy. Not after today— and yesterday," he added as an afterthought.

Mrs. Walters was still staring at him. "Three years, Julian. Three years. And you lock me out at the end."

His voice was dull, everything but fatigue and despair was gone out of it. "You know why that is, Esther. I cannot trust you any more." With that he turned on his heel and opened a door across from the steel one which gave onto his workroom. "Good night," he said heavily. "Anne, my dear, I am sorry that you were frightened. It's all right now."

The three of us looked at each other after he went. Mrs. Walters was haggard, her face modeled by frustration and unhappiness. I felt an uncomprehending pity for her. "Well," I said with an unpleasant false brightness, "we may as well get some sleep now."

Anne's shoulders shook, and suddenly she was crying and clinging to me. Over her shoulder I said to Mrs. Walters, "All right. I'll take care of her."

She looked at us for a slow minute, almost as if she doubted our existence, turned, and went back to her room. We were left standing together in the hall, and I forgot about everything else while I used my arms and hands and lips to exorcise Anne's tears. I put our candles on the floor, and after that it was easier.

25.

BREAKFAST next morning was a strange meal. None of us had slept much, so that we all looked hollow-eyed and as if we hated each other. Certainly there was a coldness between Julian and Mrs. Walters, but it took no overt form because none of us said anything. I ate my food with determination and coaxed Anne to swallow a few mouthfuls of toast beside the coffee which we all gulped.

When we were clearing up the dishes, Mrs. Walters announced that we would have to drive into town to buy food. She volunteered for the trip, but I think she was relieved when I vetoed that idea at once, and declared that Anne and I would go. I had no intention of risking the effect of Mrs. Walters' appearance in the streets of Barsham Harbor.

It was odd how our spirits lifted when the two of us got past the Marcy house and onto the open road. The day was gloomy enough, with an overcast sky and a thin, cold wind that came down the river valley as though it were scouting the way for winter. But the car ran smoothly, we were warm in its cabin and, most of all, the house on Setauket Point was behind us.

"I was a dreadful baby last night," Anne said.

"I'm glad you were," I answered. "Knowing that you needed support was the only thing that kept me from losing my own grip."

The memory of that eternity in front of Julian's door made us both silent.

Long before I was ready for it, Barsham Harbor was on our either hand. Without discussion we selected the A & P store that stood at the far end of River Street. It was out toward the edge of town, for one thing, and, for another, it was a chain store and I felt that it would not be so likely to serve as a gathering place for...well, for people who might be talking about us.

All the same there were a good many people there when I went in with the grocery list. I wouldn't let Anne come in with me, and I'd made her promise to lock the doors of the car. She didn't argue about it. The moment I pulled open the screen door I knew that this was not going to be pleasant. There had been a hum of voices before I entered, but in almost no time the store was heavy with silence. They were all looking at me and they had all stopped buying—if that's what they had been doing. Clerks and customers alike, they stared at me.

The mass silence and hostility of a group of unfamiliar people can be a terrible thing. I felt my skin crawl when I went to the counter. The clerk who waited on me was a pallid youth with adenoids. He took my list, looked at it, and began taking things off the shelves without a word. It was a big order and by the time he'd finished collecting it, two cardboard cartons were pretty well full. I paid and the clerk shoved the two boxes toward me without a word. I had a struggle to get them both into my arms, but I knew better than to ask him to carry one of them out to the car for me.

As I went toward the door a voice behind me said, "Some people can eat, I guess, no matter if there's blood on their hands." It was a woman's voice, harsh and bitter with prejudice. I paid no attention. Another voice, this time a man's, observed, "If I was them, I wouldn't be buyin' all that food. I'd take the fust train," and a third added, "And they wouldn't need but a one-way ticket, at that." The rest I could not distinguish clearly; there was only a hissing gaggle of voices at my back.

As I was loading the boxes into the car, a man came out of the store after me. He was a heavy-faced fellow with huge shoulders and some kind of badge pinned to the inside of his coat. "Buddy," the man said.

"Yes."

"Don't take that talk about leavin' town too much to mind. Don't none of you go till Dan Hoskins gives the word."

"And who are you?"

"Pete Barnstable, Deppity." He touched the badge.

"Thank you," I told him. "And let me give you a word of advice, while we're both on that track. Don't take sides. All we ask is justice." It sounded fatuous when I said it, but it made me hot with anger to find one man who should have been open-minded so obviously join the rest in hating us.

He spat into the road, just past my foot. "You'll git justice," he remarked briefly and went back into the store.

We drove home without talking.

26.

JULIAN was waiting for me in the living room when we returned to the house. I looked at him with something close to dislike. Perhaps it was the aftermath of that five minutes in the store, but it occurred to me that I had had about enough of this house and the people in it. I wanted to leave it and them behind me forever. Anne I wanted to take with me when I went, but beyond that I did not care. I reminded myself that Julian was my friend, had given me the opportunity to go into my own chosen field of work, and that there were inescapable ties between us. But they meant nothing in my mind at that moment.

"Hello, Julian," I said dully.

"Richard. I have been waiting for you to come back..." he hesitated and then went on with a rush "to have that talk that I promised you last night."

"Anything you want to tell me, Julian, I'll be glad to hear. But I don't know that I can help you. I don't know that you ought to go on with this notion of yours. It's absurd to believe it will work."

He stood up and the corners of his mouth twitched with something that might have been a smile. "No," he said, "it's absurd, as you say. And yet, last night, you were hammering at my door and shouting—"

"I give you that. But the damn' noise gets on your nerves." That was the most complete understatement I think I have ever made.

He nodded vaguely. "I suppose it might, if you were not as familiar with it as I am. But come, my boy. We cannot talk here. I don't want anyone to overhear us. We can talk best in my room, I think."

419

I followed him up the stairs. He climbed them so slowly and with such difficulty that I had to wait on each step until he was above me once more. Watching that weak and uncertain ascent of his, I felt once more the pity and the desire to help him that had been so strong in me on the first morning of my visit. In all this confusion and tragedy Julian had behaved with more poise than the rest of us, an undeviating control over himself which contrasted with my own behavior of the night before. But then, he knew what it was all about. There was no reason for him to feel fear.

Julian's room was a good deal like mine in its bleakness, though it was smaller. There was something monastic about the meticulously neat bareness of that cubicle where he slept. It must have been a servant's room when the house was first built, but the fact that it was immediately opposite the door of his workroom was obviously the reason for his selecting it. We sat on the edge of his narrow cot, and I filled and lit my pipe. Julian watched me with impatience.

"Richard," he began, "before I show you my work in the next room, I want to explain it to you in some detail. Otherwise, you will not be able to appraise the nature of the difficulty that confronts me."

"I wish you would," I told him. A sense of sudden excitement came over me. This was the opportunity for which I had been waiting, the chance that Anne and I had tried to plan for. If I was ever to be able to save Julian, it would be now, in the next few minutes. I shook the lethargy and resentment out of my mind and leaned forward to listen.

"You probably know," Julian began, "that a good many men have tried to do what I am engaged in at the moment. That is, create a mechanism for communication with those who are no longer alive."

"I didn't know that."

"Oh yes. All kinds of machines have been built. Even Thomas Edison tried his hand at one. But of course he never completed it. He had not the background, for one thing... In any case, these machines have had one element in common. They have proceeded upon the principle of delicacy. The men who built them apparently believed that sensitivity of mechanism was the most important thing. So they used delicately balanced scales, or needles. Or they created, in a room where all other conditions were controlled, a diaphragmed pressure chamber, wired to reveal whether there was any sentient control able to alter pressures on either side of their instrument. And so on. Hundreds of such experiments must have been made. I surveyed them all years ago. All were failures. Inevitably, because they proceeded on the wrong basis. Radio itself, for example, would have failed as an important medium of communication had it been compelled to rely on nothing but the old-fashioned crystals. It was the vacuum tube, or valve, that opened the way..."

He stopped speaking for a moment and I noticed that he was kneading his fingers together as though this summary of his were causing him intense pain. Then he went on, his gaze fixed at the gray sky beyond the window. "When I had finished my survey of the preceding work in the field, I was discouraged. I realized that I should have to begin at the very beginning and I knew there might not be enough time in which to finish. So I did something that you will believe was weak and credulous, Richard. I went to seances." He looked sidewise at me to see how I took this statement; then apparently reassured by my lack of surprise, he continued: "I can only compare that experience to Benjamin Franklin's, in his investigation of electricity. He found it in the lightning, so to speak, but mostly there was nothing but darkness." He smiled at that, slowly and with relish. "Not a bad joke, my boy. 'Mostly there was darkness.' But once in a while there was a flash of revelation. I won't bore you with accounts of them. They convinced me, personally, that Helen was not...gone. That she was still alive, and waiting for me. It was in those days that I first met Esther Walters."

I knew that was the way it must have been, but I was not quite prepared for the sudden wave of sympathy that came up in me as I listened to Julian. Something about that desperate search for reassurance which had taken him so far afield, into places and groups of people that must have seemed fantastically unrelated to his academic life and his own rigid standards of work, made a lump come in my throat. He had always had courage ... I had to remind myself that I was there to cure Julian, not to abet him in his obsession.

"Of all the people to whom I went," he continued, "she most clearly demonstrated the power to transcend the immediate physical world. I say 'immediate' because, Richard, I am coming to believe that in the space-time continuum there is, perhaps, another world, and that what we call death is more like a ... removal ... from our world to that other one. I hope in a moment to give you some proof of that. Anyhow I began to think about my problem in a new way. It was, essentially, a question of bridging a gap. I looked into many things before I satisfied myself that the gap could be bridged." He looked at me gravely. "I am talking to you as if you were still an undergraduate, Dick. But I want to be clear and untechnical, at least at the start."

"Quite right," I assured him. "You understand that I know nothing about this problem of yours. We psychologists leave it alone."

The irony that I had intended missed its mark. "Yes," he remarked tolerantly, "I know you do. You put rats in mazes. One of your fellow scientists," and the way he pronounced that word made me squirm, "once went so far as to put a crab in a maze. The miserable creature darted into one blind alley after another. Then, when it could not solve the maze and reach the food, it huddled in a corner and pulled off its own legs, one after the other ... That crab was an experimental psychologist of the first water." He gave me a dry smile.

"What I did next," he said finally, "was to attempt to discover how, or in what way, the occasional seance, the rare medium of Mrs. Walters' type, was able to bridge that gap and why the process was so unreliable. My work on this point led me back into my own field of electrophysics. I came to the conclusion that the human nervous system is, in part, an electrophysical field, to put it crudely, and that the elaborate machinery of the seance was a rough and unreliable method of charging that field with a certain potential. In some way which I do not wholly understand, that potential is what bridges the gulf between ourselves and the others."

This was getting beyond me. It seemed the rankest form of wishful thinking on Julian's part, a hocus-pocus of hypotheses that no sane research man would bother with for a moment's time. But Julian was never wholly a sane man. His genius was too great for any such label. He was now, however, so fully launched into his explanation that I had no time for reflection. "Of course," he pointed out, "I knew that my time, like that of every living man, was limited. In my case only a few years remained to complete the work. So I was unable to make the exhaustive researches at every point in my progress which you and my own colleagues would no doubt regard as essential. I formed the conclusion that the uncertainty of the seance, or of the single medium, and the transitory manifestations of the true other world, were due to the difficulty of building up this potential and the relative speed with which it was discharged. It occurred to me that I might reasonably expect to achieve far better results if I could create that potential, independently of the seance room and even of a medium."

His eyes were now alive in his head. They no longer looked burnt-out and heavy with weakness and fatigue. His voice was louder, more sure of itself. He stood up and began to pace up and down the room before me. "So I studied the whole matter of the body's electrical fields. I measured them by certain criteria. I reduced my problem to a formula. And I began the construction of a machine which would make that formula a fact, which would build and maintain the potential of which I have spoken, not only at the level of the seance room or the mediumistic trance, but with infinitely greater power." He paused in his striding and for the first time his voice lost its assurance. "Possibly I have employed too much power."

"Is this machine of yours complete, Julian?"

He shook his head. "No, because it does not do all the work for which it was built. And yet, I have put into it everything I know. Everything I have been able to discover. There have been times when I was certain of success. But last night—and several times before as well—I have been genuinely distressed by the appearance of certain epiphenomena that I had not expected and which I should like to show you for the benefit of your opinion. Of course," he said, more to himself than me, "you will not be able to understand my invention. But you may be able to suggest something in connection with these epiphenomena . . . they worry me a good deal."

"Is that noise one of them?"

He looked away from me swiftly, as if to hide something which I might read on his face. "You can judge that better in a few moments. All that I want to add now is that Mrs. Walters is at the end of her usefulness to me. She does not understand that fact. Of course I am grateful to her. I shall see that she is rewarded for what she has contributed." He sighed. "But that does not appear to satisfy her. She wants control over what we have worked out together. We have quarreled about this and a day or two ago I discovered that, against my express instructions, she has been tampering with the machine itself." He hesitated for a second and I saw his tongue slide over his gray lips. "Tampering is not quite the right term. Experimenting with it. Naturally, in spite of all my warnings and in spite of my telling her that we must proceed with great caution, she has no real understanding of the enormous energies, the terrific potential which the apparatus creates . . ." Something passed across his face as he spoke that elaborate sentence. It was a shadow, whether of sorrow or horror I could not quite determine.

"I have forbidden her further entry to the room where the apparatus now is—across the hall, as you know. She believes that I am trying to exclude her from the final fruits of the research. She also is afraid that I mean what I said yesterday, in that dismal Barsham Harbor courtroom, about making my discovery public without commercializing it." His face darkened. "Mrs. Walters is a paradoxical person. I think she is as genuinely eager to . . . communicate . . . as I am, but she wants also to make a business of it when we have succeeded. That, of course, is impossible. This is my last piece of work, Dick. I want it to mean the most to the whole world. It should be— it must be—absolutely free to anyone who has need of the same kind of assurance as that for which I have been hungry these last years."

When he had his voice once more under control, he said, almost humbly, "Well, that's the story. I have told you because there is a chance that you will need to know it. And because, if you are to observe with intelligence what I want to show you you will have to understand at least as much as I have told you. I know that you will never repeat it, even to Anne."

"Of course not, Julian."

"If you have any questions, save them until later. I want to give you a demonstration now, before we are... interrupted."

I wondered how he expected us to be interrupted, but forbore putting the question. Instead, I followed him out of the room and across the hall. The steel door opened to his key and I stepped behind him over the threshold. I heard the door click shut behind my back.

27.

THREE people only had seen that room in which I found myself: Julian, Mrs. Walters, and Elora Marcy. I was the fourth. Whatever was in here, it would be strange. My heart was hammering at my ribs, and expectation had keyed my nerves high and tense. Julian's long speech had impressed me. It had left a thousand unanswered queries behind it, but it had convinced me that I was to see something of a sort which no one had beheld before.

My first sensation was one of disappointment. The four windows of the room were shuttered so tight that no light at all came into them except a gray crack or two that left the room almost black. Then there was a click and a sudden blaze of strong light. Julian had turned on a great reflecting lamp that was fastened to the ceiling. The very shock of electric light was a considerable one. The rest of the house, a century old, and the candles and lamps to which I had grown accustomed in the two days I had been in it, made the sudden flood of white light that struck my eyeballs seem unbelievable and out of place. I blinked and looked round me. And then, in one sudden instant, I knew why Julian had kept his apparatus covered when Mrs. Marcy came in to clean. The first sight of it nearly stopped the heart in my chest.

The thing was right in the middle of the room and there was almost nothing else in the place except a pair of wooden kitchen chairs and an old table littered with papers. The walls were bare and discolored with age, but I knew that, like the living room below it, this had once been a noble room. There were windows along the east and south walls and, in the sharp light of the ceiling reflector, I saw that they, too, were of steel like the door. The green paint on their inside surfaces glistened as if they had just been completed and I guessed that they had not been open, in all probability, since the day they were installed.

The apparatus itself was so much of a nightmare that my glance slid off it the first time without any precise attempt to understand what I saw. My impression was of seated figures, human and yet horribly not human, ranged round a black table with a sort of lectern at one end... On the second inspection I saw the thing more intelligently. There was, indeed, a table, its top made of ebonite, or some similar plastic, and rubbed to a polish, so that it caught the light from the ceiling in a sort of dark mirror and gave it back to the eye in flashes of negative light.

They were sitting around this table.

There were seven of them. One, with its back toward me, at the rear end of the table, and three along either side. The far end, where the lectern was, appeared to be empty. They were, I saw, all alike, all polished till the copper of their wires glowed, and they were holding hands. At least, their arms ended in five filaments of wire and these were, in each case, linked with the fingers of the figures on either side. From head to foot they were made of wire and there was something terrible in the fact that I could look clean through them. Ludicrously enough, though their posture was that of seated figures, there were no chairs. Instead, they seemed to be fastened to the table itself and supported by ebonite braces at regular intervals.

I looked for one freezing instant at the tableau and then, half-hysterically, I began to laugh. "Good God, Julian," I said, "when you duplicate a seance, you duplicate it. This looks like a Black Mass in a futurist play."

He smiled absently and went down the room. "Yes, I suppose it is a bit startling at first. I suspect, too, that a good deal of this is unnecessary. But as I told you, I had no time to experiment at every step of the way. Having discovered how to increase my bridging potential, I made my electronic fields from circuits as close to the ones which actually exist at a seance as I could."

He went down the row of those fantastic figures, touching one after another. "We have our silly moments, I suppose, Mrs. Walters and I. We've named them all."

"Have you really?" I said in a faint voice.

"This is Hugo," Julian remarked. "Mrs. Walters named him after a man that used to come to her seances. She told me once he used to try to pinch her in the dark. I've never known whether to believe her." He patted one of the figures on its insubstantial head. "The others are various people, of course. I call the one at the end of the table Arthur. You know, after Arthur Wallace. He loves to preside at any kind of meeting. Or used to."

"He hasn't changed," I replied. It was difficult for me to speak at all. Surprise, the kind of aberrant impulse of humor that makes you want to laugh in church, and a deep alarm and revolted incomprehension made my throat thick. Was it possible that this gleaming travesty of wires and plastics was the source of that sound that had gone whispering through the old, shadowy house and terrified me the night before past all endurance? Had it created that torrent of noise that rolled over Anne and me in the rain-lashed meadow?

Julian was matter-of-fact, of course. It was a familiar story to him and, in one unexpected way, I felt no unfamiliarity myself. Julian's handiwork was always distinctively his own. Even here I recognized the style of his work, once the first shock of my surprise had worn off. The apparatus shone just as all his equipment had gleamed in the big laboratory back at the university. The absence of every comfort and convenience except the essentials was typical of him. And the curious blend of literalness and imagination, that had made him one of the great creative minds of our time, was evident in this last project as in all the others. Only a literal mind would have been directly impelled to so tremendous a project in the first place. And that same literalness had made him recreate this optical travesty of a seance in the second.

"Come here, Dick," he said when I remained rooted by the door, staring at his handiwork, minute after minute. "I know this is a curious experience, but I have brought you here not to look at my apparatus, but to show you what it does." He was standing at the upper end of the table, behind the thing that looked like a reading desk. I went toward him, walking wide around the table, and looked over his shoulder.

It was not a lectern, but a control board. Its face slanted toward him and the dials that sprinkled its slope were, I saw, lighted dimly from below. In the middle of the thing was a single large handle which appeared designed to move in a slot in the face of the instrument itself. Below the table, I noticed, and across the floor, electric cables snaked to a number of outlets along the wall.

"Lord," I told Julian, "but you've polished everything off neatly. It looks completely finished."

He gave me a single abstracted glance. "Yes. I like things neat. But that is not the point, either. We must hurry; I want you to have plenty of time to observe the phenomena of which I spoke. Are you ready?"

I swallowed. "Yes," I answered.

He pressed a button and the ceiling light became dim. There remained plenty of light by which to see. I think I could well have read by the light which remained, and that is important in view of what I am about to describe. Julian was talking more to himself than to me, in a low, rapid voice. "I am not sure whether light has an inhibiting effect. It does, of course, in a seance, but that may be a human psychological factor unconnected with the bridging potential. Generally I reduce the amount of illumination and I believe, too, that the power should be applied slowly..."

His hand came to rest on the control lever. The fingers gripped it until their joints were yellow-white. He moved it perhaps an inch from left toward right and waited. Nothing happened at first and I began to breathe more comfortably. Then I was aware of a low hum, like that which an old-fashioned radio set makes when the tubes are warming. The skin at the base of my neck began to crawl, but I damned myself for a fool. This was all normal enough.

Julian listened to the hum for a time and then nodded his head and moved the lever again. The hum became deeper, but Julian paid no attention to it beyond a casual glance at the dials in front of him. Once more he moved the lever and this time I was aware that he expected something to happen. He looked up from the panel in front of him and stared down the table. The seven copper figures sat there immovably. I guessed that current was pulsing through them, but nothing was changed in their surrealist outward aspect.

In what way I first became aware that an alteration was taking place in that room, I find it hard now to say. The noise of the tubes continued, deeper than before, but it was so low a hum that I could not believe it would be audible outside the room. It was definitely not the sound I had heard the night before. I think that the first thing I noticed consciously was the air around me. It was moving, not in any one direction but in eddies and whorls, like water in a saucepan before it comes to a boil. I felt the twists and turns of draft touch my face and then my hands, and finally they were brushing against me from head to foot. Julian, I saw, paid no attention to this phenomenon, at least for a while. Then he turned to me.

"You feel that?" he asked.

"Of course; what is it?"

"Air," he answered, and then left the panel and went to the nearest window. "We had best open this somewhat," he remarked and tugged up the sash. Then he fumbled with the steel shutter behind it and swung it open. There must have been a wind on the river. At any rate, I saw his hair move and blow.

After a while it seemed to me that the air which was eddying in the room had settled to a steady single direction. At any rate, I was aware of a draft against the back of my neck, but no more of the tendrils of motion which had brushed my face. Julian was again at the control panel, his eyes once more fixed on a spot which was apparently somewhere over the middle of the table and above the heads of Hugo, Arthur, and their nightmare companions.

"What do you see?" His voice was hoarse and low.

I strained my eyes in the direction of his gaze. "Nothing." But I heard something, so faint that I could not certainly have identified it if I had not been expecting it. The sound of the night before was in that room with us. In spite of being prepared for it, I was once more, irrationally, afraid.

"Now watch!" Julian's voice was shaking. His hand moved the lever over to a point midway between the left and right ends of its slots with a motion so jerky that I knew the thing, whatever it was, that he wanted me to observe was going to happen. There was a sudden stir in the air at my back. I could feel it streaming past me now with renewed speed and the humming roar of the machine deepened. As I stood there, following with my own eyes the direction of Julian's stare and listening to that unimaginable sound roll through the room around us, I began to understand that the noise did not come from the machine, nor was the hurrying river of air that passed us both being drawn into any part of Julian's apparatus. Something was happening in the sheer empty space above the center of the table.

To this day I cannot be sure what the thing was that I saw happen there. It began as a point of blackness which I could see with great distinctness because it was between me and the far wall. "Point of blackness" is not a good description, and yet I hardly know what else to call it. There against the grayish-yellow of the room's faded wallpaper was a thing, suspended in the air as it seemed to me at first. It was in no way human. It hung there, pulsing faintly and unevenly, but always growing with each expansion slightly more than it shrank with the contractions. When I first noticed it, the thing was the size of a large pea. I have called it black and yet it was actually a colorlessness so intense (to define the thing in terms of its opposite), that it seemed to absorb the very glance with which I looked at it.

I can remember nothing further of the way that thing appeared to me, or of the emotions I experienced watching it. My memory presents every detail of what followed, but not as a part of my own experience. As I stood there, my eyes fixed on that black focal point, I lost awareness of myself in an emotion so appalling and overwhelming that there is no accurate term for it. Fear it was not, for I was past the point of being afraid. I think perhaps the word "awe" comes closer to it than anything else....

The blackness over the center of the black table grew. It expanded in the air with steadily increasing speed. The seven figures never moved, never looked at it, were deaf to the sound that filled my ears and hammered at the walls of the room till it was wonderful that they did not shatter. As the thing grew, it became more clearly three-dimensional, although that description is in itself meaningless. We know, in actual experience, nothing which is not three-dimensional. Dimension is a fact with three attributes, length, breadth, and thickness, but they are triune and inseparable aspects of material existence. Not so this heart of darkness that beat in and out, to and fro, larger and smaller, over the center of the table. It had no dimension at all. It consumed dimension, negated it, developed like a parasite on the shape and frame of the familiar world.

Julian was staring at it with the same fixed look. His hand still rested on the control lever, but the knuckles were no longer white with contraction; he was paying no attention to anything but what was in front of us. The wind which was streaming through the window had risen till it shrieked like a gale and his hair blew forward, thin and stringy, toward that center of nothingness in front of us. I saw him lean forward slowly, reluctantly, as if he were being pressed from behind. I saw my own hand, white and shaking, go down against the face of the control panel and stiffen into a brace, though I was not aware of moving it, nor even of the weight of driving air behind me that must have forced me into the action.

The edges of the blackness were not precise. They wavered and changed like the outer rim of a whirlpool and, as the thing got bigger, I noticed that it had a sort of penumbra, a rim of shadow through which I could make out the shapes of wall and floor and ceiling behind it.

Let me say at once that there was nothing about this presence which suggested life, either present or past, to me. It was no more alive than a tornado or a maelstrom. It was simply an existence of forces so enormous that I could not grasp what they meant, or what was actually taking place. But I did see the inexorable spread of that thing, saw it numbly until it bulked as large as the table and the room grew dim because it was between us and the light on the ceiling. In its larger diameter it must have been several feet through at that moment. Dust, bits of stuff, the papers on Julian's desk were being snatched up by the wind and carried into that blackness in front of us. None of them came out again. I am sure that the very air which rushed into that chasm is gone forever....

How long it took the thing to grow until it was almost at the edge of the lectern I could not say. Several minutes, certainly. Some blind instinct of self-preservation moved in me then, though it was nothing conscious. But somehow I managed to get my left hand over Julian's and grip the handle of the control. With every ounce of power I had, I slammed it back to the starting point.

Instantly, so sudden was the release of the pressure from behind, we both staggered backward, away from the table. The black gulf into which we had been staring vanished as though it were a light which had been turned off. The room sprang full into the glow of the lamp. Simultaneously, the air, meeting at the heart of the space where the thing had been, roared tumultuously in our ears.

And then the room was still, silent, unchanged.

We looked at each other without words. Both of us were panting; I felt spent, as if I had run for miles, and there was a thin ringing in my ears. Julian groped his way to the desk chair and sat down, trembling. He buried his face in his hands and did not look up for a long time. I stood staring down at him vacantly, my mind empty of anything except wonder that I was still alive and an incredulous surprise that nothing had altered. The thing had left no trace behind it.

He looked up at me after a time and licked his lips. "You see," he said.

"Yes."

After a second long silence he said, slowly, "I told you that I would show you the other world. Well?"

With some difficulty I remembered back to our talk in his room before this demonstration had begun. "Oh, yes. But Julian..." I could not think how to go on in any rational terms.

"What?"

"This...thing...you just showed me, that cannot be the other world you meant. That black thing was no world. It was opposite to any world at all."

He shook his head. "You're wrong about that, Richard. It is her world...Helen's...I know that. But I have not found the right door. Surely you see that this is at least the right track?"

I did not answer that question. Instead I demanded, "Why did all the air rush into that thing?"

He looked away and his voice was very low when he replied, "I don't know."

And yet, it seemed to me that perhaps he did, that the same theory that was formulating itself in my own mind must have been in his, and long before now. But believing as he did that he had discovered the formula for the one thing he wanted, he would never believe that he had actually found something else. He would even reject the single hypothesis that could explain what we had just seen. In that moment of insight I felt pity for him and yet, I was more afraid of him than anything else.

"What am I to do?" he asked me, his face still averted. "I tell you, Dick, I do not see where I have gone astray on this thing. I've checked and rechecked my figures. I've tried one set of adjustments after another. You heard me doing that last night...and still it is always the same. Sometimes it happens more quickly than others." He put his hand on a black notebook in front of him. "All the data are here. All my work, for six years. It must be right..."

"Let's get out of here," I told him. "I can't think in this place. I want to talk to you, Julian. But not now."

He stood up stiffly and walked down the room. I followed him. The table gleamed as before. The seven figures along its edges sat there on their nonexistent chairs, their faceless heads turned toward its center, their copper fingers still in contact. I wondered then how Julian could have named them. Still, Clotho, Lachesis, and Atropos were named, and if men had found words for those three fatal sisters, it was permissible, I suppose, to christen the things around the table.

Julian unlocked the door without a word and we went through it.

He was silent as we crossed the hall. In his room again I made him lie down. "We won't talk just yet," I told him. "Stretch out a while and rest. I want to think. This afternoon is time enough."

He looked up at me heavily. "Perhaps. All right."

"I take back everything, Julian. I thought you..."

"I know," he said wearily. "Thank you, Richard. I feel easier now that you have seen that black...node. We must work together on it, find out why it isn't what we want, and discover what we can about it."

The thought of creating that thing even once again made me deadly afraid. "I'll talk to you later about that, Julian. Promise me you'll rest a while now. And promise that you won't go back into that room again alone. It isn't safe. If I hadn't moved that lever for you..."

"Yes," he said again, "I know." He brushed his hand across his eyes. "Thank you for that."

"One more thing, Julian," I said. "I want you to give me the key to that room."

"Why?" He was instantly alert.

"Because I don't trust you. I think you're planning to go right back there when I leave this room."

"I'll rest. I promise."

"Give me the key and I'll believe you. I promise not to go in myself or to let anyone else in. But to tell you the truth, Julian, I'm afraid of that thing of yours. Unless I know that you won't be going back in there, I won't be able to think clearly about this whole problem."

"You'll return it when I ask?"

"Yes," I said. I could not persuade myself that I intended to keep my word, but Julian must have decided to trust me. His secret had become, I think, too much even for him to carry alone. He took the key out of his pocket and handed it to me. "Here."

I dropped it into my own pocket with a sense of triumph which I did not want to analyze too closely. Then I pulled a blanket up over him. "Get some rest now, for God's sake," I told him. "I'll call you in time for lunch. I may even lie down myself. I feel a bit rocky some-how."

"It's a relief to know that you understand about it now," he said. "I think I can rest to advantage. But we must have another talk this afternoon. There is something else I think I had best tell you."

"Sure," I answered and left him lying there. His eyes were closed, even before I got to the door. He looked old and weak.

I went down the stairs heavily and quickly. I wanted time to think, to arrange the chaos of impressions in my mind into some coherence. The cold air outside felt good on my face. I walked up and down in the grass in front of the house and tried to reason things out. The more I thought about the apparatus of Julian's, the more sure I was that it was beyond my understanding. But other things began to fall into a sort of pattern. After a time I went to look for Anne.

28.

I FOUND her in the barn, washing the car with a sort of desperate concentration. I knew what was wrong, of course, but there had been no way I could warn her about the sound. When it began she must have come out here to get away from it and, in desperation, begun to clean the automobile.

"It's all over," I said.

She straightened suddenly and looked at me with panic in her eyes. Then she caught her breath and smiled. "Dick!"

"All quiet along the Kennebec," I told her. "I've seen Julian's invention."

She said quietly, "You look as if you'd seen a ghost."

"No ghosts," I said. "But something. A nice little something."

"As bad as that?"

I sat down on the running board. "Worse."

"I suppose you don't want to tell me?"

"I can't," I said. "I promised him."

She nodded. "All right. But what I don't know won't hurt me and it's a relief to be sure that he hasn't succeeded."

"Yes...well, maybe I'm wrong in thinking I know what he's actually accomplished. But I don't think so and I think he knows it, too. Only he won't admit it to himself. And it's got to be stopped. If that thing ever got out of control..." I thought of that for a moment and then pulled myself together. There was something else I had to do before I could be sure that the peril in Julian's apparatus was ended forever. "I have to talk to Mrs. Walters."

Anne stared at me as if I were suddenly demented. "All right. She's in the kitchen, I think."

"Don't come with me," I said. "This isn't going to be nice."

I left her sitting on the running board; once I turned and looked back. She was still there. I saw her give a sort of mock salute with her hand and then reach for the chamois with which she'd been doing the car. It felt good to see her, just to know that she was there. Because what I had to do now was a thing which I could contemplate only with loathing.

On a sudden impulse I did not go in the kitchen door, but went round to the front and wrenched open the door into the hall. Then I went upstairs to my room and took the bottle of whiskey out of my bag. I poured about four stiff fingers of it down my throat and then sat down to think.

I would have to act quickly if I was to prevent Julian from going on with that thing of his. And yet, there was a pang of regret in my mind at the thought of what I had to do. For he had accomplished something that no man before him had ever achieved. He had gone out to the very edge of the physical world, and beyond it. In some way which I did not begin to understand, that black thing I had seen was an aperture. What it opened into, or upon, was no concern of mine; I did not want even to speculate about that. There was nothing on which to go. But my theory about its nature was the only possible one—of that I was sure.

I took another small and careful drink. The evidence for my conclusion was purely circumstantial. But that was plenty. The rush of air into the center of the thing, as if it were being drawn into a complete vacuum; the fact that neither the air nor the things it had carried with it returned; the very appearance of the blackness, like an extra-dimensional whirlpool; and, above everything else, the cold conviction that the thing which Julian Blair's potential created was beyond all the bounds of our universe. It seemed to me that something in my mind recognized it.

That was absurd, of course. And yet, how had Julian created this thing? By magnifying the radiations, the waves given off by the human brain and nervous system. Something like that, according to his own account. I snatched my thoughts back from the gulf toward which they were headed. If man were not altogether a physical being, if he possessed in himself a contact with an existence neither spatial nor of time, and if that contact were to be artificially produced, even by sheer imitation of the sort to which Julian had openly confessed, then...then what would be created would be no bridge, but a mechanical, arbitrary rent in the warp and woof of the fabric of the physical universe. A lesion, indeed, through which everything known streamed into the unknown. A hole in the dike. No, that wasn't quite accurate. A leak in the helmet of the diver would be closer.

I got up then and went down into the kitchen. Mrs. Walters was there, not working but simply sitting heavily in a chair looking out the window. Her face looked older than it had before, and there was something at once defiant and defeated about her. I sat down across the table and looked at her.

"Mrs. Walters, I want to talk to you for a few minutes."

She turned her head slowly away from the window. "About what? I should think you had accomplished everything you wanted now." There was bitterness in her final word. "He has showed you the communicator. You know as much as I do. More, perhaps, because you are a scientist and I am not. But remember that I contributed as much to that thing as Julian. I have given him everything I could. I have worked for years. I have protected him—and it—in ways that you and all your kind would never have the courage to do. Now I suppose he's through with me."

The whiskey was warm inside me. I felt a certain impersonal pity for her, a desire to make this easy. But I did not dare. "Listen," I said, "that thing of Julian's is dangerous. Maybe he knows how dangerous it is, but if he does he won't admit it. I doubt if you have any conception. I'm not even sure that I'm right. But I'm sure enough to act on what I believe. Have you got a key to that room?"

"No." Her voice was heavy and noncommittal.

"Have you ever had one?"

"No."

"I want you to promise me that you will never, even if you have the opportunity, touch that thing again. At least, until I am sure about it."

She smiled unpleasantly. "So it's got you, too," she observed. "You see now that your friend Julian is not mad, as you thought so charitably when you came here. And you want control of it for yourself."

"Have it any way you like," I said. "But I know one thing. Nobody must touch that machine of his again."

"I make no promises," she said.

"In that case I'll have to threaten you."

There was an abrupt stiffening to her bulky body, a sort of wary tension to the way she sat. "I have nothing of which to be afraid."

"Haven't you?" I said. "Well, perhaps not. But I think you do. Something recent, Mrs. Walters. Something connected with Elora Marcy."

The words fell into the silence between us. She made no answer to them. I went on. "I think I know one thing, now. That is, the way Mrs. Marcy was killed. I think, to go a step further, that the thing that made those injuries across her chest, that broke her arms, was not a rock ledge, nor even the edge of a stair. I think it was the edge of a table."

She stared at me. "You're crazy." Her voice was no more than a whisper.

"Am I? I hope so." I got up. "But unless you're quite sure that I am, I suggest that you do as I say. Remember, Mrs. Walters, how that air jams you forward toward the blackness? Suppose someone were in that room. Suppose that someone had separate access to that room only once a week—when she had temporary possession of the key to let the cleaning woman in. Suppose that person was afraid that the apparatus was almost finished and that the man who had built it proposed to throw it away by making it public. Suppose that he had been working alone on it a great deal. What do you think such a person might do?"

"This is all impossible."

"Certainly. But while Mrs. Marcy was sweeping the floor, this person—a woman—went to the apparatus. She lifted the covering from the control panel. There was the lever, convenient to her hand. There was the opportunity to find out, once for all, if the thing worked. In such a blinding instant of temptation, even a woman of your control might have weakened, might have lost all caution. Might have thrown that lever over toward the right, and thrown it too far. The blackness sprang into existence and with a strength of which you had never dreamed. Mrs. Marcy was, perhaps, between the window and the open edge of the table. The gust of air struck her back. She was a light woman, anyhow. She was hurled forward—and killed ... How did you manage to shut the machine off?"

I had her. She made no sign of defeat, but for the first time since I had known her, she was looking down, at the floor. Her voice was low. "The control panel saved me. My body must have knocked the lever back."

"Lucky," I commented. "But your moment of stupidity was over. You thought of everything. How you managed I don't know. Perhaps you'd got Mrs. Marcy's body to the foot of the stairs before he saw you. Perhaps he knows the whole thing. Anyhow, he was stunned—by your treachery and the accident itself. You persuaded him to let you handle it. You saw us coming across the meadow and persuaded us that Mrs. Marcy had had a fall. It was a wonderful job. Then you got us out of the way, Anne and me, and covered up what had happened." As I spoke, the details of what she must have done came crowding into my mind. "You have small feet. You went out in the rain twice. First with your own shoes. Then Mrs. Marcy's. That second time it was you, not she, who went into the river. That took courage. I admire you for it. Anne said you were a wonderful swimmer, but I forgot that until this moment. I suppose you landed down near the house here?"

She nodded. There were no words left in her.

"You put Mrs. Marcy's shoes back on her body. Then you carried it out of the house and put it in the river. I suppose the whole thing didn't take half an hour. You came back to the house, changed your dress, and were waiting for us when we got back with Dr. Rambouillet."

"What are you going to do about it?"

"I don't know yet. You haven't, at least in my eyes, committed any crime. I suppose that technically and legally you're guilty of several things. But the criminal thing you did was to turn on that apparatus of Julian's when he was not in the room . . ."

"I had to know," she said.

"What I don't yet understand—any more than you—is what that apparatus of his really does. All I know is that it's a horror, more dangerous than if this house was stored solid with nitroglycerin. That's why I want your promise that you will never touch that machine again." A thought occurred to me. "And that you will go away from here at the first opportunity. As soon as the sheriff gives any of us permission."

She stood up at that and the humility was gone out of her. She had heard the worst there was to say and she was fighting now, suddenly. "And leave you alone with Julian? I hope you don't think I swallow that sermon of yours about the danger of the communicator? Julian and I know that it is not yet perfect. But you've seen enough to know that it will work. You've seen the edge of the other world about which I think I know more than you." She sneered openly. "After all, Professor Sayles, you're only a two-bit professor in a college. You aren't the kind of man that Julian is. But you want the glory of being associated with him, now, at the end, when the years of work are over. Well, I won't do it. I want something to show for what *I've* done. I won't go away. I intend to stay right here. Get me out if you can."

I looked at her steadily. "I've warned you."

She gave no ground. "You can't do a thing to me without involving all of us. And Julian most of all. Put that in your pipe and smoke it."

"Mrs. Walters," I said, "I've told you everything that's on my mind. After this morning, I won't hesitate to involve all of us if I have to do it to get that damn' thing of Julian's stopped."

"Including Anne, I suppose."

"Including her if it's unavoidable."

"Thank you," she said, "for telling me so plainly what you intend to do." With that she walked past me and out the kitchen door. It slammed behind her.

I felt good about that interview. It seemed to me that I had been right, that I had taken the wisest course, and that the control of the situation in this terrible house was now in my hands. After a time I changed my mind. That was when I heard the roar of the car backing out of the garage. By the time I got outside, it was already diminishing up the road toward the village. I watched it go with complete incomprehension. It was only when I saw Anne standing beside the doorway, looking after the car with as much bewilderment as my own that I understood how far out of my control events actually were.

29.

"FOR HEAVEN'S sake!" Anne sounded half amused, half furious. "You said you were going to talk to her, but I never thought you were going to have that much effect. She's mad, Dick."

"Oh, yes," I admitted.

"She came stamping out the back door and just climbed into the car without a word. I was doing a front fender when she got in. She just backed the car right out from under my hand." She held up the chamois skin in proof. "What in the world did you say to her?"

"Amongst other things, I told her she was responsible for Mrs. Marcy's death and how she fooled all the rest of us. I threatened to tell somebody about it if she didn't do what I wanted, which was to go away at once."

"So she's running away?"

"No," I admitted slowly. "I don't think so. I think she's trying to steal a march on us. If she does..." My mind raced ahead, trying to estimate the probabilities and it seemed to me they were not promising. "If she does, it will almost have to be at Julian's expense."

Anne said, "I don't know what you're talking about. What did Mrs. Walters have to do with Elora's death? She didn't kill her, did she?"

"No, not that bad." I summarized most of it for her, being careful to say as little as I could about the nature of what I had seen in Julian's workroom. I said that there had been an "accident" in there, and then hurried on to the rest of the story. Anne listened without interrupting me. "Now," I said, "she's gone. But I have an idea she'll be back. And I don't know what to do in the meantime."

Anne remarked thoughtfully, "We better tell Uncle Julian. Then I think we might have lunch, cooked by my own fair hands." She was even smiling.

I liked the way she took it. Not a reproach to me for having bungled things nor a single word about the likelihood that we were in for an even more unpleasant time than anything that had happened so far. As we were walking back to the house, she remarked once, "Poor Uncle Julian," and that was all. In the kitchen she turned and confronted me quietly. "Before you talk to Uncle Julian," she said, "I just want you to know whatever happens, it'll be all right with me."

"Thanks." The word seemed inadequate, so I tried thanking her another way. That was better. Finally I said, "Darling, this is the craziest thing of all. I'm twelve years older than you."

"In that case," she said softly, "I think it's high time you stopped being a chivalrous idiot."

So I did my best.

30.

JULIAN was actually sleeping when I went up to his room. I woke him as gently as I could and told him that he had better come down right away and have a talk. He looked at me curiously. "What's happened, my boy?"

"I'll tell you later, Julian."

He got up and straightened his clothes. "Let me have my key again."

"No. You won't need it till after lunch, at least. You've been half starving yourself lately, Julian. You eat with us first and then we'll see."

He sluiced his face in the washbasin and combed his hair in the old, impatient way. "Richard, I just want to remind you that you are a college professor and not a male nurse."

"The rest did you good," I told him. "You sound pretty chipper."

"Yes. But this is all a waste of time. I must get back to work right away. Have you been thinking about our problem?"

"Yes."

"And what is your conclusion?"

"After lunch," I said inexorably. "Come along now."

Anne's idea of a meal was infinitely more edible than Mrs. Walters' had been. Julian ate a surprising amount, and though I wanted to burst right out with my story, and explain what had happened, I managed to restrain myself. Still, the tick of the kitchen clock seemed to me faster and faster.

As soon as the meal was over I told Julian directly that I had confronted Mrs. Walters with the facts about Mrs. Marcy's death. He listened without any comment.

"That is so, Richard," he admitted finally. "At least, it must be. I was not, as you surmised, in the room when the accident occurred, but I knew what must have happened. Somehow I was so startled and horrified that I did not think as clearly as I should have. I let her do what she wanted. It was all about as you described it. She came to me afterward, told me what she had done, and I agreed to back her up. I wish now—"

"Meantime," I interrupted, "She's gone to town. Or somewhere. And I'm afraid of what she may do."

"If she tells the true story, with variations," Anne inquired, "what do you think will happen?"

The same wonder had been in my own mind. "I suppose we'd have to submit to a second inquiry. Anyhow, I think, the thing to do as soon as we can is to get a lawyer."

Julian's expression had been slowly changing as he thought over what I had told him. A set look had come into his face. "Richard," he said finally, "I want that key. I want it right now."

"Listen, Julian. Don't go back to work yet awhile. Not till I've had a chance to talk to you about that other part of it."

"Are you trying to tell me that you won't give me the key?"

I began to be alarmed by what I saw in his face, but I held my ground. "Yes, Julian. That's what I mean. The key stays in my pocket until after this whole mess is over. That thing of yours is too dangerous. I don't think you understand quite how appalling it is, Julian."

He looked as if I had put a knife in his ribs. "But Dick, can't you see how little time . . ." His face was pitiful. I found myself suddenly hating the role I was playing. "You must realize, Dick, that if anything were to happen before . . . before I finish, everything will be lost. It will be failure. You're enough of a scientist to know that no one else could complete my work?"

I knew that. I know it still. I trust with all my heart that those words of Julian's were true, but there is just a chance that they were not. And I hope that if there is anyone, now or ever, who tries to follow in Julian's track, he will be fully aware, as Julian was not, of what his work will mean. That whirling gulf of blackness is not a mere danger, like an explosive. It is, in the end, a breach in the whole of life. How much it is capable of devouring once it is set loose I do not think any one can predict.

Julian's plea made me feel like a traitor, but it did not shake my determination. Even treachery to a friend can be the lesser of two evils. I turned through the door. "Let's go into the living room a minute," I said to him. "I want to try to explain, Julian, why I'm doing this to you."

I remember a few things after those words. I recollect opening the door into the hall. I have a vague image of a sudden burst of stars inside my skull and then a roaring blackness diminishing into oblivion…

The next thing I saw was Anne's face, bending over me, white and frightened. My head was a jumble of pain and confused thoughts; it appeared to be lying in her lap. After a while I made out the shape of the stairs and knew that I was still in the hall.

"Dick," she was saying, "Dick darling!"

"I'm all right." The pain in my head was so terrific that I could hardly think. But there was something more important than my head, something I had to remember. "Where's the key?" I said and began to fumble in my pocket. It was gone, of course.

"Lie still," she said. "You'll feel better in a minute."

"The key, Anne. He's got the key." I tried to sit up, but it was no go. "Listen, darling," I said. "Don't worry about me. Go upstairs right away and listen at his door. Find out where he is, somehow. And come back and tell me."

She lowered my head to the floor gently. "You be absolutely quiet, now."

"Sure," I said. "Only hurry."

I lay there through several eternities of time until I heard her feet on the stairs. "He's in his laboratory," she told me. "Working at something. He wouldn't let me in."

"Oh, God," I said and tried to sit up again. This time I succeeded after a fashion. When the walls, floor, and ceiling of the hall stopped going round I looked at her and tried to smile. "You'd never think he was strong enough to hit that hard. What did he do it with?"

She held out the heavy-duty flashlight that they kept in the hall. "This. It weighs pounds. How do you feel now?"

I examined the back of my head with cautious fingers. "There's going to be a lump there. But I'm better. I don't think he broke anything." I got a firm grip on the bottom of one of the balusters and hauled at it. After a while I was on my feet. Once again the room spun round me, but this time it came to rest sooner. Anne was watching me. "Give me a hand," I said. "I'll try that sofa in the living room for a while. And if there's any ice, you might bring me a chunk of it."

With my arm over her shoulders I managed to make the living room. Julian must have hit me a fearful crack; the whole back of my head was throbbing with every pulse beat. Anne told me to lie still while she got something and slipped quickly out of the room.

I tried to think what was to be done. There was no sense reproaching myself for a fool. I had simply underestimated the desperation that keeping the key from him would engender in Julian's tortured mind. The imperative thing was to stop him from trying that apparatus of his again. My head was throbbing like an anvil on which incandescent iron was being beaten into shape, but a single idea did come to me. If the power cable could be cut, the current would be shut off. That would stop him and it was the only thing that would. But I dared not send Anne out to climb a pole and cut it. If Mrs. Walters had not taken the car, she could have thrown a rope over the cable, fastened it to the bumper, and simply pulled till something tore loose. But any such expedient was out of the question now.

I tried standing up alone. That was no dice. The agony in my head and the weakness in every part of me made it impossible to take a step. I sat down on the sofa with a groan.

Anne heard it as she came in. "What are you trying to do?" she demanded. "Sit still."

She had brought some pieces of ice and a towel, and she put them immediately against the back of my head. It may not have been the medically orthodox thing to do, but it helped. The waves of fire inside my skull gradually went out. "Thanks," I said after a time. "That's the ticket, all right." She was looking at me with such anxiety and sympathy that I wanted simply to surrender to it. But the thought of Julian kept me from it. I wondered what to do. "So he's locked himself in up there..."

"Yes."

The house seemed utterly still. "I don't hear the noise."

"It isn't going."

"It will be," I said. A thought struck me. "Listen dearest. Do me a favor and don't argue at all about this. Get clean outside this building and just wait. I want to try to talk to him through the door. But if I'm right, this house is no place to be in right now. God knows what he will do. He knows that he hasn't got time for anything much. He may turn that thing on full. If he does, I don't want you to be around."

She kissed me. "You don't suppose I'm going to leave you, Dick?"

I wanted to argue with her, but there was no opportunity. We heard something that made me aware the time for talk was over. There was the noise of a car, two cars, three, roaring into the yard. People were arriving, and I thought I could guess who and why they had come.

"All right," I told her. "This is the pay off. Stick with me and don't say a word more than you have to."

31.

THEY CAME through the back door without knocking. We could hear their feet in the kitchen. In a minute the living room was full of them. Big Dan Hoskins was the first, moving with a deceptive calm. Behind him was the man who had spoken to me outside the store that morning, the deputy, Pete Barnstable. Seth Marcy, of course, and his taxi driver cousin, his narrow eyes sharp with excitement and a vicious sort of satisfaction. There were others, too, several of them. Last of all, two women.

One of them was Mrs. Walters. The other, inevitably, was Ellen Hoskins, looking quietly anxious. I wondered what Mrs. Walters had told them all, but there was no time for speculation.

"Where's Blair?" the sheriff demanded, looking down at me.

"Upstairs," I told him.

He whirled on his feet and started for the door.

"Wait a minute, Sheriff, and listen to me before you do anything. He's locked himself in up there, and he's desperate."

"Desperate or not, he's got somethin' to answer for."

"What?"

"Causin' a fatal accident. Failure to report the same. Connivin' to cover the hull thing up."

"The bastard," said Seth Marcy and his voice was heavy with satisfaction.

"Most of that," I pointed out, "was done by Mrs. Walters, here."

"You're all guilty, if it comes to that. But Blair's gonna be under arrest the minute I lay my hands on him. I done my best for you people, but I'm through." He went out the door. There was a general surge after him. "If I need the rest of you," his voice came back down the stairs, "I'll call you."

There was silence in the room for a minute after he left. They stared down at Anne and me on the sofa, their faces heavy with anger and a kind of fierce pleasure. I felt cornered, but I hope I didn't show it. Anne sat perfectly quiet beside me. After a minute she opened her compact and powdered her nose. It was the first time I had seen her do that and I knew it was a gesture of defiance. Ellen Hoskins chuckled, but Seth Marcy scowled. He shouldered his way past Pete Barnstable and halted in front of me.

"Git up," he said to me.

"Don't, Dick," Anne said and then to Seth Marcy, "He's hurt."

"Not as much as he's going to be." His heavy boot caught me square in the shin. For a moment I thought the bone would break. He drew his foot back again. "I aim," he said slowly, "to teach you something, you dirty woman-killing son of a bitch." That time the kick did not land. Ellen Hoskins caught his ankle on the backswing with the crook of her umbrella handle.

"Your language is nasty, Seth," she said calmly.

"Yeah," said Pete Barnstable. "That's enough rough stuff, Seth. We'll give these folks what's comin' to 'em, legal." He grinned.

"You see, Professor Sayles, I am not a good person to threaten." It was Mrs. Walters' voice.

"Shut up, you," said the deputy.

I looked at Ellen Hoskins. The pain in my leg and the heavy throbbing in my head made it hard to keep my voice under control. "What did she say to you?" I asked.

Ellen looked at me curiously, without pity but with no hate. "She simply told Dan how you had all arranged Mrs. Marcy's death to look like an accident. How Mr. Blair planned the thing, how she made the footprints, how you, Professor, put the body in the river before Miss Conner and you drove into town and got Dr. Rambouillet."

"You believe that?"

"I don't know."

Anne looked at Seth Marcy steadily until he dropped his eyes. "For the first time," she said pleasantly, "I see how lucky Elora really was. I used to wonder where she got those bruises on her arms. I see now, of course. You used to beat her."

Big Dan's feet were loud on the stairs before there was any answer to Anne's quiet speech. He came into the room and confronted me. "Well, you were right. He's locked in there, all right, and he won't come out. It's a steel door, and I don't reckon it'll break easy. We'll have to go in through the windows."

"There are steel shutters on those."

He glared at me. "Go outside, Pete, and take a look." The deputy reluctantly made his way through the crowd. After he had gone the sheriff demanded of me, "You been inside there?"

"Yes."

"What's he got in the place? Any weapons? Guns?"

"Nothing," I told him, "but a piece of scientific apparatus. But I wouldn't break in. If I were you, I'd get out of this house as fast as I could."

"Why?"

"Because that apparatus of his is the most dangerous thing I've ever seen in my life." The difficulty of explaining that seemed too much to me in the state I was in. "I have an idea you'll be finding that out before long. Did Mrs. Walters tell you about it?"

"She said it was some kind of a crazy machine for talkin' long distances."

"That's right," I told him, "very long distances. For talking with the dead." I let that sink into a silence that was suddenly so intense that I had an insane desire to laugh at the lot of them. "The reason Mrs. Walters didn't tell you the whole story, as well as the reason she wants to implicate us with herself, is because she believes in the thing. She thinks it will work and she wants to have it for herself."

The sheriff was nonplussed. He looked, I was interested to notice, first toward his sister. Seth Marcy said, "Let's cart the whole lot of them back to town, Dan. A coupla nights in the cooler and they won't talk brash like this rooster any more."

Ellen Hoskins' voice was cool. "You don't seem to believe in this invention of Mr. Blair's."

"Not in that way," I answered, "But I meant what I said about its being dangerous." I thought perhaps she might believe me so I went on. "I saw it work this morning. It builds up a potential somehow—creates a vortex in space—I don't know exactly what. But if he turns it full on, the lot of us may—or may not—be here after it's over."

She nodded. "Dan," she said, "why don't you let Professor Sayles talk with Mr. Blair? Maybe he can persuade him to come out."

"No," I said. "He won't come out for me. You'll have to get through that door somehow. Maybe a blowtorch will do it." Then I remembered my earlier idea. "Anyhow, Sheriff, don't think too much about getting him out right now. The most important thing of all is to cut off the electric power that runs that thing of his. Tell one of your men to do it right away, for the love of God."

He looked at me curiously. "Why?"

"So he can't work it," I answered impatiently. "Hurry up, I tell you."

The big man did not move. "That ain't in my province. Anything I do to get him out is one thing. Destroying property except in line of duty is another."

"He's just tryin' to distract you, Dan." It was the taxi driver again.

"You folks talk a lot out here," the sheriff said. "I can't tell the sense from the lies." He made no further move.

I opened my mouth to plead with him once more, but before I could say anything, Pete Barnstable came in, his jaw sagging. "That's right about the shutters, Dan. You can see it from the ground that they're made outa steel, like a safe. And they're all shet tight. Reckon we won't git in that way."

The sheriff nodded. He told off a man to drive to town and bring back a blowtorch at once. As an afterthought he ordered Ellen Hoskins to go along. But she shook her head. "I can look after myself, Dan. And you'll need a record of what happens. I'm needed here."

He shrugged his tremendous shoulders. "Have it your own way, Ellen," he said. Then he looked over the room. "I don't guess we'll be needin' the rest of you," he observed. "You better clear out. This here's the law, not a tar and featherin'. Or a wire pullin'," he added for my benefit.

They showed no disposition to leave at first, but he simply stood there and waited. After a while they began a sheepish sort of exodus. In five minutes the room was clear except for Seth Marcy and his cousin. Dan Hoskins looked at them. "I'll call you if I need you," he said.

Seth stood his ground. "I aim to stay right here till you get that crazy bugger out'n that room, Dan. It wuz my wife."

Ellen Hoskins sniffed audibly. For my part I did not care what happened. Things were beginning to seem shadowy to me. The pain in my head and my leg were almost unendurable. I simply sat still and waited. Most of my mind was not in the room, anyhow. With Julian locked in that place of his upstairs I felt it didn't matter much what happened down here. He knew—he must know—that this was his last opportunity with the thing on which he had labored so long and with such passionate hope and faith. What chance was there, I asked myself, that he would not try it once again? And having tried, and failed, would he not throw that fatal lever clear to the right? My imagination failed to picture what would happen then.

The sheriff cleared his throat indecisively. "All right, Seth," he said at last. "You can stay, if you behave yourself. But he'll have to go." The cousin shifted his narrow eyes from Seth to the sheriff and back again. Neither of them gave him a sign. In the end he muttered to Seth, "give him one for me," and went out. We could hear the sound of his car starting out back and then the rasp of gears. He was gone.

"Now, Perfessor, I want you to go upstairs with me and we'll try talkin' to him through the door once agin. Ellen, you and Miss Conner and Mrs. Walters stay down here with Seth and Pete."

I stood up on my good leg and set the other to the ground. It hurt like the devil, but I could stand on it. As I went past Seth Marcy I looked him in the eye. "Like to try it again?" I asked.

"Sure." He started a punch that might have killed me if it had landed. I caught him full in the throat with my fist and let him have the other under the ear as he went down. His breath came out of his windpipe with a heavy gurgle. "That's for the shin," I said, "and to help you keep a civil tongue."

"You shouldn't have done that, Perfessor," the sheriff said while I was pulling myself up the stairs.

"I know. You didn't see him kick me in the leg a minute ago, while I was sitting on the sofa, but your sister did. If she wants to press the charge, go ahead."

He grunted. "Seth's kinda mean sometimes."

The hall was dark. We stood at the head of the stairs and looked around us. "Listen," I said to the sheriff, "I want you to promise one thing. If you begin to hear something you've never heard before, don't stay with me. Go down those stairs like a bat out of hell and get everybody outside at once. That thing he's got in there is perfectly capable of destroying the house. Don't believe me if you don't want to. But your sister's down there."

He looked at me carefully, as if to find out whether I was telling the truth, then nodded, and we went slowly down the hall together. The window at the end was a dull gray; twilight was already gathering in the air outside. We stood a while outside the cold steel of the door, listening. Julian was moving around inside. There was the occasional clink of metal on metal and another sound that puzzled me at first. It was, I realized finally, Julian muttering to himself. The sound of his feet on the floor when he moved was hurried.

"Julian," I cried and pounded on the metal. "It's Dick. Open the door."

"Go away." His voice was urgent, defiant, curiously roughened, as if he were breathing hard and with difficulty.

"Julian, for the love of God! Leave that thing alone. The house is full of people. It isn't safe."

His steps came rapidly across the floor, louder as they drew nearer. "Richard," he said and I could even hear him panting. "I will never open this door. Get away from it. You're only making me lose time."

The sheriff stirred at my side. "We'll have to burn the door down if you don't come out, Mr. Blair. This is the law, Dan Hoskins, sheriff."

There was something hysterical in the laugh with which Julian answered him and then we could hear his footfalls receding. I had a sudden flash of understanding. He was laughing because a lummox of a country sheriff wanted to stand between him and the greatest enterprise—and the maddest—which a man ever undertook.

I tried once more. "Julian!" I shouted and hammered at the door till my fist ached. "Think what you're doing! Anne's here. If you start that thing again, you may be endangering her. Let me in, for God's sake!"

His voice was curiously thin and faraway as it came to me, through the steel of the door. "Too late," he said. "Too late, Dick. This time I'm going to find out..."

The rest of what he may have said was lost in the whispered hum that began to fill the air round us. The sheriff turned a white face in the gloom of the hall. "My God!" he said.

I gave him the hardest push I could from only one sound leg. "That's it, you fool!" I shouted. "Get them out of here. Then cut the wire if there's time. I'll keep on trying, but get downstairs and get them out."

"Jesus," he said wonderingly and then he was off down the hall. His feet lumbered loud and heavily on the stairs, but I did not listen to his going. The draft was beginning to suck round my ankles.

"Julian! Not all the way! Julian!" I could hear no answer. Very likely my voice never reached him at all. The roaring tumult of that thing inside was growing with every passing second. I could see it in the eye of my imagination, hovering now in the space between the ceiling and the black table, already ominously grown. If only the power had been cut off! But it was too late now. I turned to go down the hall. The farther away I was when it happened, the greater the chance that I might escape. But I had no real hope, only an instinct to try even the most forlorn chance.

The wind in the hall was so strong now that I could scarcely make progress against it. The noise was cataract loud, but even through it I could hear the timbers of the old house cracking. Dust began to fill the air so that I could scarcely see my way. It came swirling up from every crevice between the boards, sucked out by the air. I looked back. The steel door, it seemed to me, was coming loose on its hinges. I could see a thin line of yellow light along the top and bottom of its surface. The noise of the maelstrom inside was so terrific that I could no longer hear. It was like being in the heart of a cyclone.

Somewhere between Julian's door and the head of the stairs the thing happened. The old house had been strained even beyond the power of shipwright's timbering to resist. There was a crash, a series of crashes. Plaster fell from the ceiling somewhere; boards screamed as they were wrenched loose from their moorings of a hundred years. And then there was a clap of thunder so loud that nothing which had gone before it mattered.

I found myself lying on the floor of the hall. I was numb, almost without feeling of any sort. Plaster was scattered in fine lumps over my head and shoulders, and it gritted under my palms when I got myself heavily into a sitting position and leaned against the wall. But the thing was over. I drew a deep breath and coughed; dust and powdered plaster were in every cubic centimeter of the atmosphere. Gradually I pushed myself up against the wall. I wondered dully about Anne. The sheriff had had enough time to get her out. I prayed that he had. Then I began to grope my way back down the hall, littered as it was with wreckage. Why I went that way instead of toward the stairs I could not have said. But go I did, feeling my way along the wall. I made slow time of it, partly because I was dazed and more because the air was blindingly full of plaster dust.

Before I had gone ten feet a voice bellowed up the stairs behind me. I knew it must be Dan Hoskins, but I paid no attention. The dust was beginning to settle and I could make out the rectangle of the window. The whole of the sash had been torn away, but the frame was still there. I put each foot down cautiously, and tried to see whether the floor was complete under me. It seemed to be.

The door of Julian's room was gone from its hinges. I stumbled into the place, my eyes smarting. The place was so altered, even in the gray light of the three windows from which the shutters appeared to have been blown bodily inward, that I hardly knew it. Plaster, lathing, boards, bits of glass, fragments of ebonite, and pieces of wire were everywhere. The ceiling, I saw, had been forced inward and was wrecked over the whole of its middle. The floor bulged upward, except at the center, and there it gaped open in an irregular hole that must have been several feet across.

"Julian!" I shouted his name aloud, but I knew that he would never answer me. That he must, inevitably, be dead.

There was no reply. I moved cautiously into the room, looking in the litter at my feet for what I dreaded to find. Before I reached the center of the room the white, sharp glare of a flashlight cut through the murk behind me and I saw the bulk of the sheriff in the doorway.

"Perfessor," he shouted. "Are you here?"

"Yes, I'm here," I said.

He came cautiously up to me, walking close to the walls. The remnants of the floor creaked under his weight, but it held. "Where's Mr. Blair?"

"I haven't found him yet."

He ran the finger of his light over the floor. I have never seen anything so completely devastated as that room. It seemed to me, as he picked out one fragment of debris after another, that there was, on the whole, less volume of wreckage than I would have expected, but greater destruction. One steel shutter was lying near the edge of the hole in the floor. Another still hung, bent limply double from a single hinge, so that it lolloped into the room like one of Dali's deliquescent watches. Of the table there was no trace except the fragments I have mentioned.

"There he is," the sheriff exclaimed suddenly and began to circle the rim of the crater in the floor. I saw what he meant. A body was lying almost on the lip of the hole. The sheriff stopped opposite it and crawled toward the thing. Gingerly he reached out a hand and drew it toward him. It came with a sudden and horrible ease and, as it moved, it made a scratching noise on the floor. I knew then what he had found. Not Julian, but one of the seven who had sat around the table. His lamp played on it for a moment, and then I heard him scuttling abruptly backward.

"Jesus!" There was unadulterated horror in his voice. "That wasn't a man, Perfessor."

"I know. There were seven of them once. I can't see the others, but maybe these snarls of wire are what's left of them . . ."

The sheriff, back against the comparative safety of the wall, played his light over the room. His hand shook, but he did it methodically. The bar of light probed the place from corner to corner and from end to end. Twice he moved to scuff at a heap of rubble. When it was all over he came and stood beside me. "You try," he said.

"There's no use," I told him. "He's not here."

"You mean he got away? Damn it—"

"No, he didn't do that either."

"What are you givin' me, a Chinese puzzle?"

"Call it that if you want. But don't look at me, Sheriff. Try looking for that steel door. It must have weighed two hundred pounds, and where is it now? There's a shutter or two missing and a lot of other things that were in here. They're gone, too. Some of them," I said slowly, "were a lot heavier than a man." The numbness that had clotted my thoughts began to lift. "What about the others?" I demanded, and my voice sounded surprisingly loud and harsh in that room. "Are they all right?"

"Yep. I got 'em out, like you said to."

"Let's go, then," I said. "There's nothing here."

"We ain't found him yet."

I started for the door. "I'll look downstairs, under the hole in the floor. If I find him I'll holler."

"Do that." He sounded suddenly as if the whole thing were a nightmare past believing. I left him still pushing at heaps of rubbish with his foot. But I knew he wouldn't find Julian.

There was almost nothing in the living room under that hole up into Julian's laboratory. Even the plaster must have been sucked clean through, up and into that maw of darkness there at the last. I shouted through the hole: "Nothing at all down here. Not even plaster!"

The sheriff's voice boomed down at me. "Wait outside, Perfessor. I'll be down in a minute."

They were all standing in a huddled group on the edge and triangle of ground at the end of the Point, almost at the water's edge a hundred yards away from the house. The moment I started toward them there was a cry and a figure came flying across the grass toward me. Anne. Her arms were round me in one instant. That made up for the rest of it. We held each other for a while and laughed and babbled incoherencies, and she exclaimed at the plaster in my hair, and we kissed each other. Then I hobbled over to the rest of them with my arm around her. I looked at Mrs. Walters first.

"He's gone," I said.

She did not flinch. "And the communicator?"

"What's still there is wire and powder. I think the thing got most of it."

Ellen Hoskins' voice in the dusk was cold as steel. "It was all for nothing, then, Mrs. Walters."

The big woman turned and faced her. "So you believe that ninny of a girl."

Ellen's voice was still light, but its tone was unyielding. "You're a great actress, my dear. But you should never have asked him that question about the communicator. That gave you away. You must have wanted it very much."

Mrs. Walters said nothing. In the shadow it was impossible to make out her impression. Suddenly she spoke. "Look!" she said. "The lights on the road!"

We all turned our heads at her exclamation. Far up along the head of the bay and even closer, along the road down the Point, we could see the head lamps of cars. There seemed to be dozens of them, headed toward the house. It gave me a sensation of panic to see them coming on. I knew who was in those cars. The people of Barsham Harbor.

"Reckon they heard the explosion," said a voice that sounded like Pete Barnstable's.

They must have done so, of course. I wondered what would happen to us when they arrived. It was in my mind that we could expect short shrift from them, but I was too tired to care.

Mrs. Walters was no longer in front of me when I dragged my eyes away from the oncoming lights. None of the shadowy outlines I scanned seemed to be hers. "Where's Mrs. Walters?" I asked with a sudden feeling that something was happening of which I ought to be aware and wasn't.

For a second, no one answered. Then we saw her, on the very tip of the Point, standing alone. There was enough light left to turn the water of the river to a dull steel color, and show the line of ripples where the current sucked against the ultimate rock and swirled away toward the sea.

We all shouted. Pete Barnstable broke into a lumbering run, but he had no possible chance of catching her. She was into the river before he had gone three steps.

That was the last of it, the end of her ambition and her dream. The river took her out of our sight and world. Once I thought I saw the black outline of her head against the water and the flash of drops as she lifted her arm to swim. But I could not be sure.

32.

SOMETIMES Anne and I wonder whether she got clean away, swimming with the ebb of the tide till she came to land in some deserted place. If she did so, we have never heard of her since, and there is not much chance that it was so. The river had been kind to her once, there at the end of the haying road by Seth Marcy's farm, but I do not believe that it was again. That water was too cold, too deep, too implacably strong even for her indomitable will. We are both happier, I think, in believing that Mrs. Walters never left the river again and yet, when we speak of her, as we sometimes do, it is with a reluctant admiration.

As for the rest of it, we do not talk about that often. We were, I suppose, exceptionally lucky to come out of the whole thing with no more than several uncomfortable days of interrogation and examination in Barsham Harbor. The crowd of shouting, angry citizens, who arrived at the Point soon after Mrs. Walters escaped, meant business. What they might have done without the presence of Dan Hoskins I don't care to speculate. He took us through the seething crowd of them with a heavy-shouldered insistence, a glowering obstinacy about doing his duty. Even so, he might not have succeeded if he had not had the fire to attract their attention to something besides ourselves.

The house began to burn within a few minutes after Mrs. Walters had plunged into the river. The cataclysm that destroyed Julian's laboratory must have ripped the insulation from the power cable somewhere and, of course, the whole building was tinder dry after a century of existence. It burned high and yellow against the dark sky.

Perhaps she saw it from the water before the end, lifting her head to gaze back at the house for one final look. We watched it from the sheriff's car as we went toward the town along the far shore of the bay. The distance shrank it to a house in a microcosm, but it burned with a fierce, bright splendor.

Of Julian we speak scarcely at all these days, but neither of us believes, I think, that he was in the house when it burned. We know that he was neither there nor in any other part of this substantial earth. Where that black vortex may have taken him I do not even speculate. It may have snatched him to itself as it must have devoured everything that it could tear loose from that room. But the few times when I have tried to imagine what that final moment was like for him, my mind does not picture it quite that way. The funnel of blackness must have grown hideously large by then. Perhaps it filled most of the room, from ceiling to floor. I think Julian may have made no effort to resist it. At least, in the picture in my mind, he is simply walking into it, like a man going through a door....

OTHER NEW YORK REVIEW CLASSICS

For a complete list of titles, visit www.nyrb.com or write to:
Catalog Requests, NYRB, 435 Hudson Street, New York, NY 10014

* *Also available as an electronic book.*